J. R. **Ward** lives in the South with her incredibly supportive husband and her beloved golden retriever. After graduating from law school, she began working in health care in Boston and spent many years as chief of staff for one of the premier academic medical centres in the nation.

Visit her and the Black Dagger Brotherhood at www.jrward.com

DARK LOVER

J. R. WARD

piatkus

PIATKUS

First published in the United States in 2005 by New American Library,
A Division of Penguin group (USA) Inc, New York
First published in Great Britain in 2007 by Piatkus Books
This paperback edition published in 2011 by Piatkus

A CIP catalogue record for this book
is available from the British Library.

ISBN 978-0-7499-5522-9

Typeset in Garamond 3 by
Palimpsest Book Production Limited, Falkirk, Stirlingshire

Printed and bound in Great Britain by Clays Ltd, St Ives plc

Papers used by Piatkus are natural, renewable and recyclable
products sourced from well-managed forests and certified
in accordance with the rules of the Forest Stewardship Council.

Mixed Sources
Product group from well-managed
forests and other controlled sources
www.fsc.org Cert no. SGS-COC-004081
© 1996 Forest Stewardship Council
FSC

DEDICATED TO:

You, with awe and love.
Thank you for coming and finding me.
And for showing me the way.
It was the ride of a lifetime,
the best I've ever had.

ACKNOWLEDGMENTS

Thank you so very much: Karen Solem, Kara Cesare, Claire Zion, Kara Welsh, Rose Hilliard.

To my Executive Committee: Sue Grafton, Dr Jessica Andersen, Betsey Vaughan. Burning up the Internet, the phone lines, and the Hutchins and Seneca Park ring-arounds with you has kept me focused, sane, and smiling.

With love to my family.

GLOSSARY OF TERMS AND PROPER NOUNS

Black Dagger Brotherhood (pr. n.) Highly trained vampire warriors who protect their species against the Lessening Society. As a result of selective breeding within the race, brothers possess immense physical and mental strength as well as rapid healing capabilities. They are not siblings for the most part, and are inducted into the brotherhood upon nomination by the brothers. Aggressive, self-reliant, and secretive by nature, they exist apart from civilians, having little contact with members of the other classes except when they need to feed. They are the subjects of legend and the objects of reverence within the vampire world. They may be killed only by the most serious of wounds, e.g., a gunshot or stab to the heart, etc.

blood slave (n.) Male or female vampire who has been subjugated to serve the blood needs of another. The practice of keeping blood slaves has largely been discontinued, though it has not been outlawed.

the Chosen (n.) Female vampires who have been bred to serve the Scribe Virgin. They are considered members of the aristocracy, though they are spiritually rather than temporally focused. They have little or no interaction with males, but can be mated to warriors at the Scribe Virgin's direction to propagate their class. They have the ability to prognosticate. In the past, they were used to meet the blood needs of unmated members of the brotherhood, but that practice has been abandoned by the brothers.

doggen (n.) Member of the servant class within the vampire world. *Doggens* have old, conservative traditions about service to their superiors, following a formal code of dress and behavior. They are able to go out during the day, but they age relatively quickly. Life expectancy is approximately five hundred years.

the Fade (pr. n.) Nontemporal realm where the dead reunite with their loved ones and pass eternity.

First Family (pr. n.) The king and queen of the vampires, and any children they may have.

hellren (n.) Male vampire who has been mated to a female. Males may take more than one female as mate.

leelan (n.) A term of endearment loosely translated as "dearest one."

Lessening Society (pr. n.) Order of slayers convened by the Omega for the purpose of eradicating the vampire species.

lesser (n.) De-souled human who targets vampires for extermination as a member of the Lessening Society. *Lessers* must be stabbed through the chest in order to be killed; otherwise they are ageless. They do not eat or drink and are impotent. Over time, their hair, skin, and irises lose pigmentation until they are blond, blushless, and pale-eyed. They smell like baby powder. Inducted into the society by the Omega, they retain a ceramic jar thereafter into which their heart was placed after it was removed.

needing period (n.) Female vampire's time of fertility, generally lasting for two days and accompanied by intense sexual cravings. Occurs approximately five years after a female's transition and then once a decade thereafter. All males respond to some degree if they are around a female in her need. It can be a dangerous time, with conflicts and fights breaking out between competing males, particularly if the female is not mated.

the Omega (pr. n.) Malevolent, mystical figure who has targeted the vampires for extinction out of resentment directed toward the Scribe Virgin. Exists in a nontemporal realm and has extensive powers, though not the power of creation.

princeps (n.) Highest level of the vampire aristocracy, second only to members of the First Family or the Scribe Virgin's Chosen. Must be born to the title; it may not be conferred.

pyrocant (n.) Refers to a critical weakness in an individual. The weakness can be internal, such as an addiction, or external, such as a lover.

rythe (n.) Ritual manner of assuaging honor granted by one who has offended another. If accepted, the offended chooses a weapon and strikes the offender who presents him or herself without defenses.

the Scribe Virgin (pr. n.) Mystical force who is counselor to the king as well as the keeper of vampire archives and the dispenser of privileges. Exists in a nontemporal realm and has extensive powers. Capable of a single act of creation, which she expended to bring the vampires into existence.

shellan (n.) Female vampire who has been mated to a male. Females generally do not take more than one mate due to the highly territorial nature of bonded males.

the Tomb (pr. n.) Sacred vault of the Black Dagger Brotherhood. Used as a ceremonial site as well as a storage facility for the jars of *lessers*. Ceremonies performed there include inductions, funerals, and disciplinary actions against brothers. No one may enter except for members of the brotherhood, the Scribe Virgin, or candidates for induction.

transition (n.) Critical moment in a vampire's life when he or she transforms into an adult. Thereafter, they must drink the blood of the opposite sex to survive and are unable to withstand sunlight. Occurs generally in the mid-twenties. Some vampires do not survive their transitions, males in particular. Prior to their transitions, vampires are physically weak, sexually unaware and unresponsive, and unable to dematerialize.

vampire (n.) Member of a species separate from that of Homo sapiens. Vampires must drink the blood of the opposite sex to survive. Human blood will keep them alive, though the strength does not last long. Following their transitions, which occur in their mid-twenties, they are unable to go out into sunlight and must feed from the vein regularly. Vampires may not "convert" humans through a bite or transfer of blood, though they are in rare cases able to breed with the other species. Vampires can dematerialize at will, though they must be able to calm themselves and concentrate to do so and may not carry anything heavy with them. They are able to strip the memories of humans, provided such memories are short-term. Some vampires are able to read minds. Life expectancy is upwards of a thousand years, or in some cases, even longer.

ONE

Darius looked around the club, taking in the teeming, halfnaked bodies on the dance floor. Screamer's was packed tonight, full of women wearing leather and men who looked like they had advanced degrees in violent crime.

Darius and his companion fit right in.

Except they actually were killers.

"So you're really going to do this?" Tohrment asked him.

Darius glanced across the shallow table. The other vampire's eyes met his own. "Yeah. I am."

Tohrment nursed his Scotch and smiled grimly. Only the very tips of his fangs showed. "You're crazy, D."

"You should know."

Tohrment tilted his glass in deference. "But you're raising the bar. You want to take an innocent girl, who has no idea what the hell she's getting into, and put her transition in the hands of someone like Wrath. That's whacked."

"He isn't evil. In spite of the way he looks." Darius finished his beer. "And show a little respect."

"I respect the hell out of him. But it's a bad idea."

"I need him."

"You sure about that?"

A woman wearing a micromini, thigh-high boots, and a bustier made of chains trolled by their table. Her eyes glittered from behind two pounds of mascara, and she worked her walk as if her hips were double-jointed.

1

Darius gave her a pass. Sex was not on his mind tonight.

"She's my *daughter*, Tohr."

"She's a half-breed, *D*. And you know how he feels about humans." Tohrment shook his head. "My great-great-grandmother was one, and you don't see me yakking that up around him."

Darius lifted his hand to catch their waitress's eye and pointed at his empty bottle and Tohrment's nearly dry glass. "I'm not going to let another one of my children die. Not if there's a possibility I can save her. And anyway, there's no telling whether she'll even go through the change. She could end up living a happy life, never knowing about my side. It's happened before."

And he hoped his daughter would be spared. Because if she went through her transition, if she came out alive on the other side as a vampire, she was going to be hunted as they all were.

"Darius, if he does it at all, he'll do it because he owes you. Not because he wants to."

"I'll take him any way I can get him."

"But what are you giving her? He's about as nurturing as a sawed-off, and that first time can be rough, even if you've been prepared. Which she hasn't."

"I'm going to talk to her."

"And how's that going to go? You're just going to walk up to her and say, 'Hey, I know you've never seen me before, but I'm your dad. Oh, and guess what? You've won the evolutionary lottery: You're a vampire. Let's go to Disneyland!'"

"I hate you right now."

Tohrment leaned forward, his thick shoulders shifting under black leather. "You know I got your back. I'm just thinking you should reconsider." There was a heavy pause. "Maybe I could do it."

Darius shot him a dry look. "You want to try and get

back into your house after the fact? Wellsie will stake you through the heart and leave you for the sun, my friend."

Tohrment winced. "Good point."

"And then she'll come looking for me."

Both males shuddered.

"Besides . . ." Darius leaned back as the waitress put their drinks down. He waited until she left, even though hard-core rap was pumping all around them. "Besides, we're living in dangerous times. If something happens to me—"

"*I'll* take care of her."

Darius clapped his friend on the shoulder. "I know you will."

"But Wrath is better." There was no jealousy in the remark. It was a statement of fact.

"There's no one like him."

"And thank God for that," Tohrment said with a half smile.

Their band of brothers, a tight circle of strong-backed warriors who traded information and fought together, were of the same opinion. Wrath was off the chain when it came to the business of vengeance, and he hunted their enemies with a single-minded purpose that bordered on the insane. He was the last of his line, the only pure-bred vampire left on the planet, and though his race revered him as its king, he despised his status.

It was almost tragic that he was the best bet Darius's half-breed daughter had of surviving. Wrath's blood, so strong, so untainted, would increase the chances of her getting through the transition if it hit her. But Tohrment wasn't off the mark. It was like turning a virgin over to a thug.

With a sudden rush, the crowd shifted, people backing into each other. They were making way for someone. Or something.

3

"Shit. Here he comes," Tohrment muttered. He tossed back his Scotch, swallowing it whole. "No offense, but I'm outtie. This is not a conversation I need to be a part of."

Darius watched the sea of humans split as they steered clear of an imposing, dark shadow that towered over them. The flight response was a good survival reflex.

Wrath was six feet, six inches of pure terror dressed in leather. His hair was long and black, falling straight from a widow's peak. Wraparound sunglasses hid eyes that no one had ever seen revealed. Shoulders were twice the size of most males'. With a face that was both aristocratic and brutal, he looked like the king he was by birthright and the solider he'd become by destiny.

And that wave of menace rolling ahead of him was one hell of a calling card.

As the cool hatred hit Darius, he tilted his fresh beer back and drank deeply.

He hoped to God he was doing the right thing.

Beth Randall looked up as her editor leaned his hip on her desk. His eyes went straight to the vee of her shirt.

"Working late again," he murmured.

"Hey, Dick."

Shouldn't you be getting home to your wife and two kids? she mentally added.

"What are you doing?"

"Editing a piece for Tony."

"You know, there are other ways of impressing me."

Yeah, she could just imagine.

"Did you read my e-mail, Dick? I went down to the police station this afternoon and talked with José and Ricky. They swear a gun dealer's moved into town. They've found two modified Magnums on drug dealers."

Dick reached out to pat her shoulder, stroking it as he took his hand back. "You just keep working the blotter.

Let the big boys worry about the violent crimes. We wouldn't want anything to happen to that pretty face of yours."

He smiled, eyes growing hooded as his gaze lingered on her lips.

That stare routine had gotten old three years ago, she thought. Right after she'd started working for him.

A paper bag. What she needed was a paper bag to pull over her head whenever she talked with him. Maybe with a picture of Mrs. Dick taped to the front.

"Would you like me to give you a ride home?" he asked.

Only if it were raining thumbtacks and hairpins, you letch.

"No, thanks." Beth turned back to her computer screen and hoped he'd take the hint.

Eventually he wandered off, probably heading for the bar across the street that most of the reporters hit before going home. Caldwell, New York, wasn't exactly a hotbed of opportunity for any journalist, but Dick's big boys sure liked keeping up the appearance of carrying a heavy social burden. They relished cozying up to the bar at Charlie's and talking about the days when they'd worked at bigger, more important papers. For the most part they were just like Dick: middleaged, middle-of-the-road men who were competent, but not extraordinary at what they did. Caldwell was big enough and close enough to New York City to have the nasty business of violent crimes, drug busts, and prostitution, so they were kept busy. But the *Caldwell Courier Journal* was not the *Times*, and none of them was ever going to win a Pulitzer.

It was rather sad.

Yeah, well, look in the mirror, Beth thought. She was just a beat reporter. She'd never even worked at a national-level paper. So when she was in her fifties, unless things changed, she'd have to be at a free press polishing classifieds to have a shot at reflected glory from her *CCJ* days.

5

She reached for the bag of M&M's she'd been nursing. The damn thing was empty. Again.

She should probably just go home. And pick up some Chinese down the street.

On her way out of the newsroom, which was an open space cut up into cubicles by flimsy gray partitions, she hit her buddy Tony's stash of Twinkies. Tony ate all the time. For him, there was no breakfast, lunch, and dinner: Consumption was a binary proposition. If he was awake, something was going into his mouth, and to keep himself supplied, his desk was a treasure trove of caloric depravity.

She peeled off the cellophane and couldn't believe she was biting into the artificial swill as she hit the lights and walked down the stairwell to Trade Street. Outside, the heat of July was a physical barrier between her and her apartment. Twelve straight blocks of hot and humid. Fortunately, the Chinese restaurant was halfway home and heavily air-conditioned. With any luck they'd be busy tonight, so she'd get to wait a while in the coolness.

When she was finished with the Twinkie, she flipped open her phone, hit speed dial, and put in an order for beef with broccoli. As she walked along, she looked at the familiar, grim landmarks. Along this stretch of Trade Street, there were only bars, strip clubs, and the occasional tattoo parlor. The Chinese food place and the Tex-Mex buffet were the only two restaurants. The rest of the buildings, which had been used as offices in the twenties, when downtown had been thriving, were vacant. She knew every crack in the sidewalk; she could time the traffic lights. And the patois of sounds drifting out of open doors and windows offered no surprises either.

McGrider's Bar was playing blues; Zero Sum had bleating techno coming out of its glass entrance; and the karaoke machines were fired up at Ruben's. Most of the places were reputable enough, but there were a couple she stayed away from on principle. Screamer's in particular catered to a scary-ass clientele. That was one door she wouldn't go through without a police escort.

As she measured the distance to the Chinese restaurant, a wave of fatigue hit her. God, it was humid. The air was so heavy she felt as if she were breathing water.

She had a feeling the exhaustion wasn't just about the weather. She'd been pooped for weeks, and suspected she was dancing with depression. Her job was going nowhere. She was living in a place she didn't care about. She had few friends, no lover, and no romantic prospects. If she looked ahead ten years and pictured herself staying put in Caldwell with Dick and the big boys, she only saw more of the same routine: getting up, going to work, trying to make a difference, failing, going home alone.

Maybe she just needed out. Out of Caldwell. Out of the *CCJ*. Out of the electronic family of her alarm clock and the phone on her desk and the TV that kept her dreams away while she slept.

God knew there was nothing keeping her in town but habit. She hadn't spoken to any of her foster parents for years, so they wouldn't miss her. And the few friends she had were busy with their own families.

When she heard a leering whistle behind her, she rolled her eyes. That was the problem with working near the bars. On occasion you picked up gawkers.

The catcalls came next, and then, sure enough, two guys crossed the street at a jog and came after her. She looked around. She was heading away from the bars and into the long stretch of vacant buildings before the restaurants. The night was thick and dark, but at least there were streetlights and the occasional car passing.

"I like your black hair," the big one said as he fell into step beside her. "Mind if I touch it?"

Beth knew better than to stop. They looked like college frat boys out for the summer, which meant they were just going to be annoying, but she didn't want to take any chances. Besides, the Chinese place was only five blocks up.

She reached into her purse anyway, searching for her pepper spray.

"You need a ride somewhere?" the big guy asked. "My car's not far. Seriously, how 'bout you come with us? We could go for a little ride."

He grinned and winked at his buddy, as if the smooth rap was definitely going to get him laid. The crony laughed and circled her, his thin blond hair flopping as he skipped.

"Let's ride her!" the blond said.

Damn it, where was her spray?

The big one reached out, touching her hair, and she looked at him good and hard. With his polo shirt and his khaki shorts, he was BMOC handsome. Real all-American material.

When he smiled at her, she sped up, focusing on the dim neon glow of the Chinese place's sign. She was praying someone else would walk by, but heat had driven the pedestrian traffic indoors. There was no one around.

"You want to tell me your name?" all-American asked.

Her heart started banging in her chest. The spray was in her other bag.

Four more blocks.

"Maybe I'll just pick a name for you. Let me think . . . How's pussycat sound?"

The blond giggled.

She swallowed and took out her cell phone, just in case she needed to call 911.

Stay calm. Keep it together.

8

She pictured how good the rush of air-conditioning in the restaurant was going to feel as she went inside. Maybe she'd wait and call a cab, just to make sure she got home without being further harassed by them.

"Come on, pussycat," all-American cooed. "I know you're going to like me."

Only three more blocks . . .

Just as she stepped off the curb to cross Tenth Street, he grabbed her around the waist. Her feet popped off the ground, and as he dragged her backward, he covered her mouth with a heavy palm. She fought like a madwoman, kicking and punching, and when she reached behind and belted him in the eye, his grip slipped. She lunged away from him, legs driving her heels hard into the pavement, breath trapped in her throat. A car went by out on Trade Street, and she yelled as its headlights flared.

But then he got her again.

"You're going to beg for it, bitch," all-American said in her ear as he put her in a choke hold. He wrenched her neck around until she thought it was going to snap and pulled her deeper into the shadows. She could smell his sweat and the college-boy cologne he wore, could hear the high-pitched laughter of his friend.

An alley. They were taking her into an alley.

Her stomach heaved, bile stinging her throat, and she jerked her body around furiously, trying to get free. Panic made her strong. But he was stronger.

He pushed her behind a Dumpster and pressed his body into hers. She drove her elbow into his ribs and kicked some more.

"Goddamn it, get her arms!"

She got in one good heel punch to the blond's shins before he caught her wrists and held them over her head.

"Come on, bitch, you're going to like this," all-American growled, trying to get his knee between her legs.

He ground her back against the building's brick wall, holding her in place by the throat. He had to use his other hand to rip open her shirt, and as soon as her mouth was free, she screamed. He slapped her hard, and she felt her lip split open. Blood rushed onto her tongue, pain stunning her.

"You do that again and I'm cutting your tongue out." All-American's eyes boiled with hate and lust as he shoved up the white lace of her bra and exposed her breasts. "Hell, I think I'll do that anyway."

"Hey, are those real?" the blond asked, as if she would answer him.

His buddy grabbed one of her nipples and pulled. She winced, tears making her vision swim. Or maybe her eyesight was going because she was hyperventilating.

All-American laughed. "I think she's natural. But you can find out for yourself when I'm finished."

As the blond giggled, some deep part of her brain kicked into gear and refused to let this happen. She forced herself to stop fighting and reached back to her self-defense training. Except for her heavy breathing, her body went still, and it took all-American a minute to notice.

"You want to play nice?" he said, eyeing her with suspicion.

She nodded slowly.

"Good." He leaned in, his breath filling her nose. She fought not to cringe at the rank smell of stale cigarettes and beer. "But if you scream again, I'm going to stab you. Do you understand me?"

She nodded once more.

"Let her go."

The blond dropped her wrists and giggled, moving around them as if he were looking for the best angle.

All-American's hands were rough on her skin as he fondled her, and she held Tony's Twinkie down by force of will, her gag reflex pumping her throat. Even though she loathed the sensation of the palms pushing into her breasts, she reached for the fly of his pants. He was still holding her by the neck, and she was having trouble breathing, but the moment she touched his privates, he moaned and his grip loosened.

With a hard jam of her hand, she grabbed his balls, twisted as hard as she could, and kneed him in the nose as he crumbled. Adrenaline shot through her, and for a split second she wished his buddy would come at her instead of staring at her stupidly.

"Fuck you!" she screamed at them both.

Beth bolted out of the alley, holding her shirt together as she ran, and she didn't stop until she was at the door to her apartment building. Her hands were shaking so badly she could barely get her key in the locks. And it wasn't until she stood in front of her mirror in the bathroom that she realized tears were pouring down her face.

Butch O'Neal looked up when the police radio under the dash of his unmarked patrol car went off. There was a male victim, down but breathing, in an alley not so far away.

Butch checked his watch. A little after ten o'clock, which meant the fun was just getting started. It was a Friday night in the early part of July, so the college turks were still fresh out of school and aching to compete in the Stupid Olympics. He figured the guy had either been mugged or taught a lesson.

He hoped it was the latter.

Butch grabbed the handset and told Dispatch he'd head over even though he was a homicide detective, not a beat cop. He had two cases he was working right now, one floater in the Hudson River and a hit-and-run, but there was always room for something else. As far as he was concerned, the more time away from home, the better. The dirty dishes in his sink and the wrinkled sheets on his bed were not going to miss him.

He hit the siren and the gas and thought, *Let's hear it for the boys of summer*.

TWO

Walking through Screamer's, Wrath sneered as the crowd tripped over itself to get out of his way. Fear and a morbid, lusty curiosity wafted out of their pores. He breathed in the rank odor.

Cattle. All of them.

From behind his dark glasses, his eyes strained against the dim lights, and he shut his lids. His vision was so bad that he was just as comfortable with total blindness. Focusing on his hearing, he sorted through the beats of the music, isolating the shuffling of feet, the whisper of words, the sound of another glass hitting the floor. If he ran into something, he didn't care. Whether it was a chair, a table, a human, he'd just walk over the damn thing.

He sensed Darius clearly because his was the only body in the place that wasn't reeking of panic.

Although even the warrior was on edge tonight.

Wrath opened his eyes when he stood in front of the other vampire. Darius was a blurry shape, his dark coloring and black clothes the only information Wrath's vision gave him.

"Where'd Tohrment go?" he asked as he caught a whiff of Scotch.

"He's taking a breather. Thanks for coming."

Wrath lowered himself into a chair. He stared straight ahead and watched the crowd gradually swallow up the path he'd made.

He waited.

The pounding beat of Ludacris faded into old-school Cypress Hill.

This was going to be good. Darius was a real straight shooter who knew Wrath couldn't stand having his time wasted. If there was silence, something was up.

Darius tipped back his beer, then let out a deep breath. "My lord—"

"If you want something from me, don't lead with that," Wrath drawled, sensing a waitress approach them. He had the impression of big breasts and a strip of flesh between her tight shirt and her short skirt.

"You need a drink?" she asked slowly.

He was tempted to suggest she lay herself on the table and let him go to work on her carotid. Human blood wouldn't keep him alive for long, but it sure as hell tasted better than watered-down alcohol.

"Not right now," he said. His tight smile spiked her anxiety and gave her a shot of lust at the same time. He took her scent into his lungs.

Not interested, he thought.

The waitress nodded, but didn't move away. She kept staring at him, her short blond hair a halo in the darkness around her face. Spellbound, she seemed to have forgotten her own name, much less her job.

And how annoying was that.

Darius shifted impatiently.

"That's all," he muttered. "We're good."

As she backed up, getting lost in the crowd, Wrath heard Darius clear his throat. "Thanks for coming."

"You already said that."

"Yeah. Right. Ah, you and I go way back."

"We do."

"We've fought some damn good fights together. Cut down a lot of *lessers*."

Wrath nodded. The Black Dagger Brotherhood had been protecting the race against the Lessening Society for generations. There was Darius. Tohrment. The four others. The brothers were vastly outnumbered by *lessers*, de-souled humans who served a nasty-ass master, the Omega. But Wrath and his warriors managed to hold their own.

And then some.

Darius cleared his throat. "After all these years—"

"D, you've got to cut to the point. Marissa needs to do a little business tonight."

"Do you want to use your room at my place again? You know I don't let anyone else stay there." Darius let out an awkward laugh. "No doubt her brother would prefer you not show up at his house."

Wrath crossed his arms over his chest, pushing the table out with his boot to give himself a little more room.

He didn't give a crap that Marissa's brother had delicate sensibilities and was offended by the life Wrath lived. Havers was a snob and a dilettante who had his head up his ass. He was totally incapable of understanding the kind of enemies the race had and what it took to defend the population.

And just because the dear boy was offended, Wrath wasn't going to play dandy while civilians were getting slaughtered. He needed to be in the field with his warriors, not taking up space on some throne. So Havers could shove it.

Although Marissa shouldn't have to deal with her brother's attitude.

"I just might take you up on that offer."

"Good."

"Now talk."

"I have a daughter."

Wrath slowly turned his head. "Since when?"

"A while."

"Who's the mother?"

"You don't know her. And she . . . ah, she died."

Darius's sorrow rose up around him, the acrid smell

of old pain cutting through the stench of human sweat, alcohol, and sex in the club.

"How old is she?" Wrath demanded. He had a feeling where this might be headed.

"Twenty-five."

Wrath cursed under his breath. "Don't ask me, Darius. Don't ask me to do it."

"I have to. My lord, your blood is—"

"Call me that again and I'll close your mouth for you. Permanently."

"You don't understand. She's—"

Wrath started to get up. Darius's hand grasped his forearm and then was quickly removed.

"She's half-human."

"Jesus *Christ*—"

"So she might not survive the transition if she goes through it. Look, if you help her, at least she has a chance of living. Your blood is so strong, it would increase the likelihood of her making it through the change as a half-breed. I'm not asking you to take her on as a *shellan*. Or to protect her, because I can do that. I'm just trying to . . . *Please*. My other sons are dead. She's all that could be left of me. And I . . . Her mother is one I loved."

If it had been anyone else, Wrath would have used his favorite pair of words: *fuck* and *off*. As far as he was concerned, there were only two good positions for a human. A female on her back. And a male facedown and not breathing.

But Darius was almost a friend. Or would have been one, if Wrath had let him get close.

As Wrath stood up, he closed his eyes. Hatred washed through him, directed into the center of his own chest. He despised himself for walking away, but he just wasn't the kind of male who could help some poor half-breed through such a painful and dangerous time. Gentleness and mercy were not in his makeup.

"I can't do it. Not even for you."

Darius's agony hit him in a great swell, and Wrath actually swayed under the emotion's force. He squeezed the vampire's shoulder.

"If you really love her, do her a favor. Ask someone else."

Wrath turned and stalked out of the bar. On his way to the door he wiped the memory of himself from every human cerebral cortex in the place. The strong ones would think they had dreamed him. The weak ones wouldn't remember him at all.

Out on the street, he headed for a dark corner behind Screamer's so that he could dematerialize. He passed a woman deep throating some guy in the shadows, a bum who'd collapsed in a stupor, a drug dealer arguing on a cell phone about the going price for crack.

Wrath knew the moment he was followed. And who it was. The sweet smell of baby powder was a dead give-away.

He smiled widely, opened his leather jacket, and took out one of his *hira shuriken*. The stainless-steel throwing star felt comfortable in his palm. Three ounces of death ready to hit the airwaves.

With the weapon in his hand, Wrath didn't change his stride, even though he wanted to rush into the shadows. He was spoiling for a fight after shutting down Darius, and the Lessening Society member behind him had perfect fucking timing.

Killing the soulless human was just what he needed to take the edge off.

As he drew the *lesser* into the dense darkness, Wrath's body primed for the fight, his heart pumping steadily, the muscles in his arms and thighs twitching in antici-pation. His ears picked up the sound of a gun being cocked, and he triangulated the weapon's aim. It was pointed at the back of his head.

In a fluid motion, he wheeled around just as the bullet exploded out of the muzzle. He ducked and threw the star, which flashed silver and twirled in a deadly arc. It caught the *lesser* right in the neck, splitting his throat open before continuing on its path into the darkness. The gun dropped to the ground, clattering across the asphalt.

The *lesser* grabbed his neck with both hands and fell to his knees.

Wrath walked over and went through its pockets. He took the wallet and the cell phone he found and put them into his jacket.

And then he withdrew a long, black-bladed knife from his chest holster. He was disappointed the fight hadn't lasted longer, but going by the dark, curly hair and relatively inept attack, this was a new recruit. With a quick thrust, he pushed the *lesser* onto its back, flipped the weapon in the air, and caught the handle with a swipe of his palm. The blade plunged into flesh, cut through bone, reached the black void where the heart had been.

With a strangled sound, the *lesser* disintegrated in a flash of light.

Wrath wiped the blade off on his leather pants, slipped it back where it belonged, and stood up. He looked around. And then dematerialized himself.

Darius had a third beer. A couple of Goth lovelies dropped by, looking for a chance to help him forget his troubles. He passed on the invites.

He left the bar and walked over to his BMW 650i, which was parked illegally in the alley behind the club. Like any vampire worth his salt, he could dematerialize at will and travel over vast distances, but that was a hard trick to pull off if you had to carry anything heavy. And not something you wanted to do in public.

Besides, a fine car was a joy to behold.

Darius got into the Beemer and shut the door. From out of the sky rain started to fall, dappling the windshield with fat tears.

He wasn't out of options. The talk of Marissa's brother had gotten him thinking. Havers was a physician, a dedicated healer of the race. Maybe he could help. It was certainly worth a try.

Distracted with plans, Darius put the key in the ignition and twisted. The starter wheezed. He turned the key again and then had a terrible premonition as he heard a rhythmic clicking.

The bomb, which had been attached to the undercarriage of the car and hardwired into the electrical system, went off.

As his body was incinerated by a blast of white heat, his last thought was of the daughter who had yet to meet him. And now never would.

THREE

Beth took a forty-five-minute shower, used half a bottle of body wash, and nearly melted the cheap wallpaper off the bathroom walls because she kept the water so hot. She dried off, threw on her bathrobe, and tried not to catch another shot of her reflection in the mirror. Her lip was a mess.

She stepped out into her cramped studio apartment. The air conditioner had died a couple of weeks ago, so the room was nearly as smothering as the bathroom. She eyed her two windows and the sliding door that led out to a wilted courtyard. She wanted to open them all, but checked the locks instead.

Even though her nerves were shot, at least her body was rebounding fast. Her appetite had returned with a vengeance, as if it were pissed at the diversion of dinner, and she went around to her galley kitchen. The chicken leftovers from four nights ago even seemed inviting, but when she cracked the foil package, she caught a whiff of sweat socks. She pitched the load and tossed a Lean Cuisine into the microwave. She ate the macaroni and cheese standing up, holding the little plastic tray in her palm with a pot holder. It wasn't enough, didn't even make a dent in her hunger, so she had another one.

The idea of putting on twenty pounds in one night was damned appealing; it really was. She couldn't help the way her face looked, but she was willing to bet that Neanderthal misogynist attacker of hers preferred his victims with a tight ass.

She blinked her eyes, trying to get his face out of her

mind. God, she could still feel his hands, those awful, heavy palms bruising her breasts.

She needed to file a report. She should go down to the station.

Except she didn't want to leave her apartment. At least not until morning.

She went over to the futon she used as a couch and a bed and curled her legs in tight to her body. Her stomach was doing a slow churn job on the mac and cheese, waves of nausea followed by marching rows of shivers passing over her skin.

A soft meow brought her head up.

"Hey, Boo," she said, wiggling her fingers listlessly. The poor guy had run for cover when she'd come through the door tearing her clothes off and throwing them across the room.

Meowing again, the black cat padded over. His wide green eyes looked worried as he leaped into her lap with grace.

"Sorry about the drama," she murmured, making room for him.

He rubbed his head against her shoulder, purring. His body was warm, his weight grounding. She didn't know how long she sat there stroking his fine, soft fur, but when the phone rang, she jumped.

As she reached for the receiver, she managed to keep pace with the petting. Years of living with Boo had honed her cat/phone coordination skills to perfection.

"Hello?" she said, thinking it was past midnight, which ruled out telemarketers and suggested either work or some sicko crank-calling her.

"Yo, B-lady. Get your dancing shoes on. Some guy's car blew up outside of Screamer's. With him in it."

Beth closed her eyes and wanted to weep. José de la Cruz was one of the city's police detectives, but he was also a friend of sorts.

21

As were most of the men and women in blue, come to think of it. Because she spent so much time at the station, she'd gotten to know them all pretty well, although José was one of her favorites

"Hey, you there?"

Tell him. Tell him what happened. Just open your mouth.

Shame and remembered horror tightened her vocal cords.

"I'm here, José." She pushed her dark hair out of her face and cleared her throat. "I can't come tonight."

"Yeah, right. When you ever turn down a good tip?" He laughed easily. "Oh, but take it smooth. Hard-ass is on the case."

Hard-ass was Homicide Detective Brian O'Neal, better known as Butch. Or just plain *sir*.

"I really can't . . . make it tonight."

"You getting busy with someone?" Curiosity spiked his voice. José was married. Happily. But she knew down at the station that they all speculated about her. A woman who looked like her without a man? Something had to be up. "Well, are you?"

"God, no. No."

There was a stretch of silence as her friend's cop radar obviously kicked in. "What's up?"

"I'm fine. Just tired. I'll come to the station tomorrow."

She'd file the report then. Tomorrow she'd be strong enough to go through what had happened without breaking down.

"Do I need to do a drive-by?"

"No, but thanks. I'm okay."

She hung up.

Fifteen minutes later she was in a pair of freshly laundered jeans and a floppy shirt that covered her butt and then some. She called for a cab. Before she left she rummaged through her closet until she found her other purse. She grabbed the pepper spray and held it hard in her hand as she stepped out of her apartment.

In the two miles between her front door and the bomb scene, she was going to find her voice. And she was going to tell José everything.

As much as she hated the idea of reliving the attack, she wasn't going to let that asshole walk free and do the same thing to someone else. And even if he was never caught, at least she would have done her part to try to nail him.

Wrath materialized in the drawing room of Darius's house.

Damn, he'd forgotten how well the vampire lived.

Even though D was a warrior, he had the tastes of an aristocrat and it made sense. He'd started life as a high-born *princeps*, and fine living was still of value to him. His nineteenth-century mansion was well cared for, filled with antiques and works of art. It was also secure as a bank vault.

But the drawing room's soft yellow walls hurt Wrath's eyes.

"What a pleasant surprise, my lord."

Fritz, the butler, came in from the front hall and bowed deeply while shutting off the lights to ease Wrath's squint. As usual, the old male was dressed in black livery. He'd been with Darius for about a hundred or so years and was a *doggen*, which meant he could go out in the day but aged faster than vampires did. His subspecies had been serving aristocrats and warriors for millennia.

"Will you be with us for long, my lord?"

Wrath shook his head. Not if he could help it. "Hour, tops."

"Your room is ready. Should you need me, I am here." Fritz bent at the waist again and walked backward out of the room, closing the double doors behind him.

Wrath went over to a seven-foot-tall portrait of what he'd been told was a French king. He put his hand on the right side of the heavy gold frame, and the canvas pivoted to reveal a dark stone hall lit with gas lamps.

Stepping inside, he took a set of stairs deep into the earth. At the bottom landing there were two doors. One went to Darius's sumptuous quarters. The other opened to what Wrath supposed was a home away from home for him. Most days he slept in a warehouse in New York City, in an interior room made out of steel with a lock system along the lines of Fort Knox's.

But he would never invite Marissa there. Or even any of the brothers. His privacy was precious.

As he stepped inside, candles mounted into the walls flared around the room at his will. Their golden glow barely made headway against the darkness. In deference to Wrath's eyesight, Darius had painted the walls and twenty-foot-high ceiling black. In one corner there was a massive bed with black satin sheets and a thicket of pillows. Across the way was a leather couch, a wide-screen TV, and a door that opened into a black marble bathroom. There was also a closet full of weapons and clothes.

For some reason, Darius was always bugging him to stay at the mansion. It was a goddamned mystery. There wasn't a defense issue, because Darius could handle himself. And the idea that a vampire like D would be lonely was ludicrous.

Wrath sensed Marissa before she came into the room. The scent of the ocean, a clean breeze, preceded her.

Let's get this over with, he thought. He was itching to get back to the streets. He'd had only a taste of battle, and tonight he wanted to gorge himself.

He turned around.

24

As Marissa bowed her slight body to him, he sensed devotion and uneasiness weaving together in the air around her.

"My lord," she said.

From what little he could see, she was wearing some kind of flowing white chiffon thing, and her long blond hair cascaded over her shoulders and down her back. He knew she dressed to try to please him, and he wished like hell she wouldn't make the effort.

He took off his leather jacket and the chest holster he carried his daggers in.

Damn his parents. Why had they given him a female like her? So . . . fragile.

Then again, considering the shape he'd been in before his transition, maybe they'd worried anyone sturdier would have hurt him.

Wrath flexed his arms, his biceps curling up thick, one shoulder cracking from the force.

If they could only see him now. Their little boy had turned into a righteous, cold killer.

Probably better they were dead, he thought. They wouldn't have approved of what he'd become.

Then again, if they'd been allowed to live into old age, he would have been different.

Marissa shifted nervously. "I'm sorry to disturb you. But I cannot wait any longer."

Wrath headed for the bathroom. "You need me, I come."

He turned on the water and rolled up the sleeves of his black shirt. With steam rising from the rush of the faucet, he cleaned the grime, sweat, and death from his hands. Then he worked the bar of soap up his arms, covering with suds the ritualistic tattoos that ran down the insides of his forearms. He rinsed, dried himself, and walked over to the couch. He sat and waited, grinding his teeth.

They'd been doing this for how long? Centuries. But every time it took Marissa a while before she could approach him. If it had been anyone else, his patience would have snapped within moments, but he cut her some slack.

Truth was, he felt sorry for her because she'd been forced to become his *shellan*. He'd told her time and again that he'd release her of their covenant, free her to find a true mate, one who would not only kill anything that threatened her, but would love her, too.

Funny thing was, Marissa wouldn't give up on him, as fragile as she might be. He figured she probably feared no other female would have him, that none would feed the beast when he needed it and then their race would lose their strongest line. Their king. Their leader who wasn't willing to lead.

Yeah, he was one hell of a catch. He stayed away from her unless he had to drink, which wasn't often because of his lineage. She never knew where he was or what he was doing. She passed the long days alone in her brother's house, sacrificing her life to keep alive the last purebred vampire, the only one with not a single drop of human blood in him.

Frankly, he didn't know how she stood it—or him.

Abruptly, he felt like cursing. Tonight was stacking up to be a real party for his ego. Darius. Now her.

Wrath's eyes followed her as she moved around the room, circling him, getting closer. He forced his face to relax, kept his breathing even, made his body still. This was the hardest part of being with her. He panicked at not being free to move, and he knew when she started to feed, the choking sensation would get worse.

"You have been busy, my lord?" she said softly.

He nodded, thinking that if he was lucky, he was going to get even busier before dawn came.

Marissa finally stood before him, and he could feel her hunger cutting through her uneasiness. He sensed her desire, too. She wanted him, but he blocked out that particular emotion of hers.

There was no way he was going to have sex with her. He couldn't imagine putting Marissa through the things he'd done to other female bodies. And he'd never wanted her that way. Not even in the beginning.

"Come here," he said, gesturing with his hand. He dropped his forearm on his thigh, wrist up. "You're starving. You shouldn't wait so long to call on me."

Marissa lowered herself to the floor at his knees, her gown pooling around her body and his feet. Her fingers were warm on his skin as she softly ran her hand over his tattoos, stroking the black characters that detailed his lineage in the old language. She was close enough so he caught the movement of her mouth opening, her fangs flashing white before she sank them into his vein.

Wrath closed his eyes, laying his head back as she drank. The panic came on him fast and hard. He curled his free arm around the edge of the couch, his muscles straining as he gripped the corner to keep his body in place. Calm, he needed to stay calm. It was going to be over soon, and then he'd be free.

When Marissa lifted her head ten minutes later, he bolted upright and walked off the anxiety, feeling a sick relief that he could now move around. As soon as he had his shit together, he went over to her. She was replete, absorbing the strength that came to her as their blood mixed. He didn't like the look of her lying on the floor, so he picked her up and was thinking about calling Fritz to take her back to her brother's house when there was a rhythmic knock on the door.

Wrath glared across the room, carried her to the bed, and laid her down.

"Thank you, my lord," she murmured. "I will take myself home."

He paused. And then pulled a sheet over her legs before walking over and cracking open the door.

Fritz was all jazzed up about something.

Wrath slid outside, closing the door tight. He was about to ask what the hell would warrant the disruption when the butler's scent permeated his irritation.

He knew without asking that death had paid another visit.

And Darius was gone.

"Master—"

"How?" he growled. The pain he would deal with later. First he needed details.

"Ah, the car . . ." Clearly the butler was having trouble holding it together, his voice reedy and thin as his old body. "A bomb, my lord. The car. Outside of the club. Tohrment called. He saw it happen."

Wrath thought of the *lesser* he'd taken down. He wished he knew whether it had been the one who'd done the deed.

The bastards had no honor anymore. At least their precursors, going back for centuries, had fought like warriors. This new breed were cowards who hid behind technology.

"Call the brotherhood," he ground out. "Tell them to come now."

"Yes, of course. And master? Darius asked me to give this to you"—the butler held something out—"if you were not with him when he died."

Wrath took the envelope and went back into the chamber, having no compassion to offer Fritz or anyone else. Marissa was gone, which was good for her.

He tucked Darius's last missive into the waistband of his leather pants.

And let his rage out.

28

The candles exploded and fell to the floor as a whirl-wind of viciousness swirled around him, growing tighter, faster, darker until the furniture flipped off the floor and traveled in a circle around him. He leaned back his head and roared.

FOUR

By the time Beth's cab dropped her off outside of Screamer's, the crime scene was alive. Lights flashed blue and white from the squad cars that blocked off access to the alley. The bomb squad's boxy, armored vehicle had shown up. Cops milled around, both uniformed and plainclothed. And the requisite crowd of drunken kibitzers had set up shop at the action's periphery, smoking and talking.

In her time as a reporter, she'd found that murder was a community event in Caldwell. Well, certainly for everyone except the man or woman who'd actually done the dying. For the victim, she had to imagine death was an alone kind of thing, even if he or she were staring into the face of the killer. Some bridges you crossed on your own, no matter who drove you to the edge.

Beth brought her sleeve up to her mouth. The smell of burned metal, a tangy chemical sting, filled her nose.

"Hey, Beth!" One of the cops motioned her over. "If you want a closer look, go through Screamer's to the back. There's a corridor—"

"Actually, I'm here to see José. Is he around?"

The cop craned his neck, searching the crowd. "He was here a minute ago. Maybe he headed back to the station. Ricky! You see José?"

Butch O'Neal stepped in front of her, silencing the other cop with a dark look. "Isn't this a surprise."

Beth stepped back. Hard-ass was a lot of man. Big body, deep voice, attitude to spare. She supposed a lot of women must be attracted to him, because God knew he was a looker in that rough, tough kind of way. But Beth had never felt a spark.

Not that she ever did when it came to men.

"So, Randall, what's doing?" He popped a piece of gum in his mouth, wadding up the foil into a tight little ball. His jaw went to work like he was frustrated, not so much chewing as grinding.

"I'm here for José. Not for the scene."

"Sure you are." His gaze narrowed on her face. With his dark brows and deep-set eyes, he always looked a little angry, but abruptly his expression got worse. "Would you come with me for a sec?"

"I really want José—"

Her arm was taken in a tight grip.

"Just come over here." Butch backed her into a secluded corner of the alley, away from the commotion. "What the hell happened to your face?"

She put her hand up and covered her split lip. She must still be in shock, because she'd forgotten all about it.

"Let me repeat the question," he said. "What the *hell* happened to you?"

"I, ah . . ." Her throat closed up. "I was . . ."

She was *not* going to cry. Not in front of Hard-ass.

"I want José."

"He's not here, so you can't have him. Now talk." Butch braced his arms on either side of her body, as if he sensed she might run. He was only a couple of inches taller than she was, but he had at least seventy pounds of muscle on her.

Fear kicked in like an ice pick punching through her chest, but she'd had quite enough of being physically bullied tonight.

"Back off, O'Neal." She put her palms squarely on his chest and pushed. He moved. A little.

"Beth, tell—"

31

"If you don't let me go"—her eyes held his—"I'm going to do an exposé on your interrogation techniques. You know, the ones that require X rays and casts after you're through?"

His eyes narrowed again. And then he pulled his arms away from her body, holding his hands up as if he were surrendering.

"Fine." He left her and went back into the fray.

She collapsed against the building, feeling as if her legs were never going to work right again. She looked down, trying to gather her strength, and squinted at something metal. She bent her knees, getting down on her haunches. It was a martial-arts throwing star.

"Hey, Ricky!" she called out. The cop came loping over, and she pointed to the ground. "Evidence."

She left him to do his job and hurried out to Trade Street to catch a cab. She just couldn't keep it together any longer.

Tomorrow she would file an official report with José. First thing in the morning.

When Wrath reappeared in the drawing room, he was back in control. His weapons were strapped on, and his jacket was heavy in his hand, filled with the throwing stars and knives he liked to use.

Tohrment was the first of the brotherhood to arrive. His eyes were all fired up, pain and vengeance making the dark blue glow so vividly even Wrath caught the flash of color.

As Tohr settled back against one of Darius's yellow walls, Vishous came into the room. The goatee he'd recently grown made him seem even more sinister than usual, although the tattoo around his left eye was what really put him into ominous territory. Tonight his Red Sox hat was pulled down tight so the complex markings on his temple barely showed. As always, his black

32

driving glove, used to keep his left hand from inadvertently making contact with anyone, was in place.

Which was a good thing. A goddamned public service.

Rhage followed, his cocky attitude dialed down in deference to what had brought the brothers together. Rhage was a towering male, big, powerful, stronger than all the other warriors. He was also a sex legend in the vampire world, Hollywood beautiful with the drive to rival a barnful of stallions. Females, vampire and human alike, would trample their own young to get at him.

At least until they got a peek at his dark side. When Rhage's beast came out, everyone, the brothers included, looked for shelter and took up praying.

Phury was the last, walking through the front door with his limp barely noticeable. His prosthetic lower leg had recently been updated, and he was sporting a state-of-the-art titanium-and-carbon composite number now. The combination of rods, joints, and bolts was screwed into the base of his right shit-kicker.

With his fantastic mane of multicolored hair, Phury should have been in Hollywood's league with the ladies, but he'd stuck solid to his vow of celibacy. There was room for one and only one love in his life, and it had been slowly killing him for years.

"Where's your twin, man?" Wrath asked.

"Z's on his way."

That Zsadist was late was no big surprise. Z was one giant, violent fuck-you to the world. A walking, sometimes talking, usually cursing SOB who took hatred, especially toward females, to new levels. Fortunately, between his scarred face and his skull-trimmed hair, he looked as scary as he was, so folks tended to get out of his way.

Stolen from his family as an infant, he'd ended up a blood slave, and his abuse at the hands of his mistress had been brutal on every level. It had taken Phury almost a century to find his twin, and Z had been tortured to within an inch of death before the rescue.

A fall into the salty ocean had sealed Zsadist's wounds into his skin, and in addition to the maze of scars, he still bore the tattoos of a slave. As well as various piercings he'd added himself.

Just because he liked the feel of pain.

Hands down, Z was the most dangerous of the brothers. After what he'd been put through, he didn't give a shit about anything or anyone. Including his twin.

Even Wrath watched his back around that warrior.

Yeah, the Black Dagger Brotherhood was a hell of a group. All that stood between the civilian vampire population and the *lessers*.

Crossing his arms, Wrath looked around the room, taking each one of them in, seeing their strengths but mostly their curses.

With Darius's death, he was reminded that though his warriors were hitting the society's legions of slayers hard, there were so few of the brothers going against an inexhaustible, self-generating pool of *lessers*.

Because God knew there were plenty of humans with an interest and aptitude for murder.

The numbers were simply not in the race's favor. He couldn't escape the fact that vampires didn't live forever and that brothers could be killed and that the balance could be thrown off in an instant. In favor of the race's enemies.

Hell, the shift had happened already. Ever since the Omega had created the Lessening Society aeons ago, vampire numbers had shrunk until now there were only a few enclaves of population left. Their kind was flirting with extinction. Even though the brothers were deadly fine at what they did.

If Wrath had been a different kind of king, one like

his father, who wanted to be the adored, revered pater-familias to the species, maybe the future would have seemed more promising. But the son wasn't as the father had been. Wrath was a fighter, not a leader, better on his feet with a dagger in his hand than sitting around being adored.

He refocused on the brothers. As the warriors stared back at him, they were looking to him for direction. And their deference made him edgy.

"I'm taking Darius's death as a personal attack," he said.

There was a low grunt of approval from the brothers.

Wrath took out the wallet and cell phone he'd liberated from the Lessening Society member he'd killed. "I took these off a *lesser* earlier tonight behind Screamer's. Some of you mind doing the honors?"

He tossed them into the air. Phury caught both and passed the phone to Vishous.

Wrath started pacing. "We need to go raiding again."

"Damn straight," Rhage growled. There was a metallic shifting and then the sound of a knife being driven into a table. "We need to get them where they train. Where they *live*."

Which meant the brothers were going to have to do some recon. Members of the Lessening Society weren't stupid. They changed their centers of operation regularly, constantly moving their recruiting and training facilities from place to place. Because of this, the vampire warriors typically found it more efficient to make themselves targets and fight what came after them.

Occasionally the brotherhood had gone on raids before, killing dozens of *lessers* in one evening as a pack. That kind of offensive tactic was rare, however. Full-scale attacks were efficient, but they were also a tricky proposition. Big battles tended to attract the attention of human police, and keeping a low profile was in everyone's interest.

"There's a driver's license," Phury muttered. "I'll scope the address. It's local."

"What's the name?" Wrath demanded.

"Robert Strauss."

Vishous cursed as he examined the phone. "There's not much here. Some shit in the call log, some speed dials. I'll hit the computer and find out who's been calling and what's been dialed."

Wrath gritted his teeth. Impatience and rage were a hell of a cocktail to swallow. "I don't need to tell you to work fast. There's no way to know whether the *lesser* I picked off tonight was the one who did it, so I'm thinking we need to do a clean sweep of this whole area. Kill them all no matter how messy it gets."

The front door swung open, and Zsadist strode into the house.

Wrath glared. "Nice of you to show up, Z. Busy tonight with the females?"

"How about you get off my dick?" Zsadist went over to the corner, staying away from the rest.

"Where you going to be, my lord?" Tohrment asked smoothly.

Good old Tohr. Always trying to keep the peace, whether by distraction, intervention, or flat-out bullying.

"Here. I'm going to stay here. If the *lesser* who nailed Darius is alive and interested in playing some more, I want to be available and easy to find."

After the warriors left, Wrath pulled on his jacket. In the process Darius's envelope poked him in the side, and he took it from his waistband. There was a strip of ink on the front, which he assumed was his name. He cracked open the flap. As he drew out a creamy piece of paper, a photograph fluttered to the ground. He picked it up and had the vague impression of long dark hair. A female.

Wrath stared at the paper. The writing ran together,

a meaningless, blurry scrawl he had no hope of deciphering no matter how hard he squinted.

"Fritz!" he called out.

The butler came rushing in.

"Read this."

Fritz took the sheet and bent his head, falling into silence.

"Aloud," Wrath bit out.

"Oh. My apologies, master." Fritz cleared his throat. "'If I haven't spoken to you already, ask Tohrment for details. Eleven eighty-eight Redd Avenue, apartment one-B. Her name is Elizabeth Randall. P.S. The house and Fritz are yours if she doesn't survive to adulthood. Sorry it had to end so soon. D.'"

"Son of a bitch," Wrath muttered.

FIVE

Beth had changed into her nocturnal wardrobe of boxers and a T-shirt, and was pulling the futon out flat when Boo began to meow at the sliding glass door. The cat paced in a tight circle, eyes trained on something outside.

"Are you trying to get at Mrs. Di Gio's tabby again? We did that once and it didn't go well, remember?"

A pounding on her front door brought her head around and kick-started her heart.

She walked over and put her eye to the peephole. When she saw who it was, she rolled over and pressed her back against the cheap wood panels.

The pounding started again.

"I know you're in there," Hard-ass said. "And I'm going to keep this up."

She flipped the locks and threw open the door. Before she could tell him to go to hell, he barged past her.

Boo lifted his back and hissed.

"Pleased to meet you, too, Panther Boy." Butch's deep drawl seemed totally out of place in her apartment.

"How did you get into the lobby?" she said as she shut the door.

"I picked the lock."

"Was there any particular reason you chose this building to break into, Detective?"

He shrugged and sat down in her tattered wing chair. "Thought I'd visit a friend."

"So why are you bothering me?"

"Nice place you got," he said, looking at her stuff.

"You're such a liar."

"Hey, at least it's all clean. Which is more than I can say about my own hovel." His dark, hazel eyes went to her face and stayed there. "Now, let's talk about what happened when you left work tonight, shall we?"

She crossed her arms over her chest.

He chuckled softly. "Man, what's José got that I don't?"

"You want a pen and some paper? It's quite a list."

"Ouch. You're cold, you know that?" His tone was amused. "Tell me, do you only like the unavailable ones?"

"Look, I'm exhausted—"

"Yeah, you left work late. Nine forty-five-ish. I talked to your boss. Dick said you were still at your desk when he went to Charlie's. You walked home, didn't you? Down Trade Street. Just like I'll bet you do every night. And you were alone. For a while."

Beth swallowed as a soft sound brought her eyes to the sliding glass door. Boo was back to his pacing and meowing, his eyes reaching out into the darkness.

"Now, are you going to tell me what happened when you hit the intersection of Trade and Tenth?" His eyes softened.

"How do you know—"

"Just talk to me. And I promise, I'll make sure that mother-fucker gets it right good."

Wrath stood in the still night, staring at the shape of Darius's daughter. She was tall for a human female, and her hair was black, but that was all his eyes could tell him. He breathed in, but he couldn't catch her scent. Her doors and windows were shut, and the wind blowing from the west carried the fruity decay of trash.

He could hear the drone of her voice through the closed door, however. She was talking to someone. A man whom she apparently didn't trust or didn't like, because her words were clipped short.

"I'll make this as easy on you as I can," the guy was saying.

Wrath watched as she walked over and looked outside through the glass door. She was staring right at him, but he knew she couldn't see him. He was deep in the shadows.

She opened the door and put her head out, blocking a cat's exit with her foot.

Wrath felt his breath catch as her scent came to him. She smelled positively beautiful. Like a rich flower. Night-blooming roses, maybe. He dragged more air into his lungs and closed his eyes as his body reacted, his blood stirring. Darius had been right; she was nearing her transition. He could smell it on her. Half-breed or not, she was going to go through the change.

She slid the screen in place and turned back to the man. Her voice was much clearer with the door open, and Wrath liked the husky sound of it.

"They came at me from across the street. There were two of them. The taller one pulled me into the alley and . . ."

Wrath snapped to attention.

"I tried to fight him off. I really did. But he was bigger than me, and then his friend pinned my arms." Her breath hiccupped. "He told me he'd cut out my tongue if I screamed, and I thought he was going to kill me, I really did. Then he ripped open my shirt and pushed up my bra. I came so close to being . . . But I got free and ran. He had blue eyes, brown hair, and an earring, a square cut diamond, in his left ear. He was wearing a dark blue polo shirt and khaki shorts. I didn't get a good look at his shoes. His friend was blond, short hair, no earrings, dressed in a white T-shirt that had the name of that local band, Tomato Eater, on it."

The man got up and went to her. He put his arm

40

around her and tried to hug her against his chest, but she pulled away and put distance between them.

"Do you really think you'll be able to get him?" she said.

The man nodded. "Yeah. I do."

Butch left Beth Randall's apartment in a foul mood.

Seeing a woman who'd been clocked in the face was not a part of his job he liked. And in Beth's case he found it particularly disturbing, because he'd known her for a while and he was kind of attracted to her. The fact that she was an unusually beautiful woman didn't make it any more egregious. But her swollen lip and the bruises around her throat were glaring defects within the otherwise perfection of her features.

Beth Randall was flat-out, hands-down gorgeous. She had long, thick black hair, impossibly bright blue eyes, skin like pale cream, a mouth just made for a man's kiss. And she was built. Long legs, small waist, perfectly proportioned breasts.

The men at the station were all in love with her, and Butch had to give her props: She never used her attractiveness to get inside information from the boys. And she kept everything professional. She never dated any of them, even though most would have given their left nut just to hold her hand.

One thing was for sure: Her attacker had made a hell of a mistake when he'd picked her. The entire police force was going to be gunning for that fool when they found out who he was.

And Butch had a big mouth.

He got into his unmarked car and drove to the St. Francis Hospital complex across town. He parked at the curb in front of the emergency room and went inside.

The guard at the revolving door smiled at him. "You heading for the morgue, Detective?"

"Naw. Just visiting a friend."

The man nodded him through.

Butch walked past the ER's waiting room with its plastic plants, dog-eared magazines, and anxious people. Pushing open a set of double doors, he headed into the sterile, white, clinical environment. He nodded to the nurses and docs he knew as he went to the triage desk.

"Hey, Doug, you know that guy we brought in with the busted nose?"

The attending looked up from a chart he was reading. "Yeah, he's about to be released. He's in the back, room twenty-eight." The internist let out a little laugh. "I tell ya, that nose of his was the least of his problems. He's not going to be singing low notes for a while."

"Thanks, buddy. By the way, how's the wife?"

"Good. She's due in a week."

"Let me know how it goes."

Butch headed for the back. Before walking into room twenty-eight, he looked up and down the hall. It was quiet. There were no medical personnel around, no visitors, no patients.

He opened the door and put his head inside.

Billy Riddle looked up from the bed. There was a white bandage running under his nose like the thing was holding his brains in. "What's up, Officer? You find the guy who got me? I'm about to be released and I'd feel better knowing you had him in custody."

Butch shut the door and quietly flipped its lock.

He was smiling as he crossed the room eyeing the square cut sparkler in the guy's left lobe. "How's the nose, Billy boy?"

"Good. And the nurse was a piece of ass—"

Butch grabbed the front of the punk's blue polo shirt and yanked him to his feet. Then he slammed Beth's attacker against the wall so hard the machinery behind the bed wobbled.

42

Butch put his face so close they could have kissed. "Did you have fun tonight?"

Wide blue eyes met his. "What are you talking—"

Butch slammed him again. "I've got a positive ID on you. From the woman who you tried to rape."

"That wasn't me!"

"The hell it wasn't. And given your little threat about her tongue and your knife, I might even have enough to send you to Dannemora. You ever have a boyfriend before, Billy? I bet you're going to be popular. Nice white boy like you."

The guy went pale as the walls. "I didn't touch her!"

"Tell you what, Billy. If you're honest with me, and if you tell me where your buddy is, you might actually walk out of here. Otherwise I'm going to take you down to the station on a stretcher."

Billy seemed to consider the deal for a moment. And then the words came out of his mouth fast. "She wanted it! She was begging me—"

Butch brought up his knee and pressed it into Billy's crotch. A high-pitched yelp cut through the air. "Is that why you're going to have to piss sitting down for the next week?"

As the punk started babbling, Butch dropped him and watched him slide down onto the floor. When Billy saw the handcuffs come out, the whining got louder.

Butch flipped him over roughly and was none too gentle as he pulled the guy's wrists together. He clipped the cuffs in place. "You're under arrest. Anything you say can and will be used against you in a court of law. You have the right to an attorney—"

"Do you have any idea who my father is!" Billy yelled, as if he'd gotten a second wind. "He's going to have your badge!"

"If you can't afford one, one will be provided for you. Do you understand these rights as I've stated them?"

"Fuck you!"

Butch palmed the back of the guy's head and pressed that busted nose into the linoleum. "Do you understand these rights as I've stated them?"

Billy moaned and nodded, leaving a smear of fresh blood on the floor.

"Good. Now let's get your paperwork done. I'd hate not to follow proper police procedure."

SIX

"Boo! Would you cut that out?" Beth punched her pillow and rolled over so she faced the cat.

He looked at her and meowed. In the glow from the kitchen light she'd left on, she saw him paw at the glass door.

"Not likely, Boo-man. You're a house cat. House. Cat. Trust me, the big outdoors isn't as grand as it seems."

She closed her eyes, and when the next plaintive meow came, she cursed and threw off her sheet. She went to the door and stared outside.

That was when she saw the man. He was standing against the back wall of the courtyard, a dark shape much larger than the other, familiar shadows cast by the trash bins and the moss-covered picnic table.

With shaking hands she checked the lock on the door and then went to her windows. Both were locked as well. She pulled the shades down, grabbed her portable phone, and went back to stand over Boo.

The man had moved.

Shit!

He was coming toward her. She checked the lock on the door again and backed away, catching the edge of the futon with her foot. As she tumbled into space, the phone fell out of her hand and bounced away. She hit the mattress hard, head bobbing on her neck from the impact.

Impossibly, the door slid open as if the lock had never been turned, as if she'd never clicked it into place.

Still flat on her back, she pumped her legs wildly,

knotting the sheets as she pushed her body away from him. He was tremendous, his shoulders wide as I beams, his legs as thick as her torso. She couldn't see his face, but the menace coming off him was like a gun aimed at her chest.

She whimpered as she rolled over on to the floor and crawled away from him, her knees and palms squeaking against the hardwood. His footsteps behind her landed like thunder, getting louder. Cowering like an animal, blinded by fear, she knocked into her hall table and felt no pain at all.

Tears streamed down her cheeks as she begged for mercy and reached for the front door—

Beth woke up, mouth open, a terrible noise shattering the dawn's silence.

It was her. She was screaming at the top of her lungs.

She clamped her lips together, and sure enough her ears stopped hurting. Shuffling out of bed, she went to the sliding door and greeted the sun's first rays with a relief so sweet she got light-headed. As her heart slowed, she took a deep breath and checked the door.

The lock was in place. The courtyard was empty. Everything was normal.

She laughed tightly. Of course she'd have a bad dream after what had happened last night. She was probably going to have the heebie-jeebies for a while.

She turned and headed for the shower. She felt half-dead, but the last place she wanted to be was alone in her apartment. She craved the bustle of the newsroom, wanted to be around all of its people, and phones, and papers. She'd feel safer there.

She was about to step into the bathroom when a lick of pain shot through her foot. She cocked her knee and picked a piece of pottery out of the tough skin of her heel. Bending down, she found the bowl she kept on the hall table in pieces on the floor.

46

Frowning, she cleaned up the mess.

She must have knocked the thing off when she'd first come home after the attack.

As Wrath walked down into the earth under Darius's mansion, exhaustion followed. He closed and locked the door behind him, disarmed, and drew out a battered trunk from the closet. Flipping the lid back, he grunted as he lifted up a slab of black marble. It was four feet square and four inches thick, and he put it down in the middle of the room. He went back to the trunk, picked up a velvet bag, and tossed it on the bed.

Stripping down, he showered and shaved, then walked back into the room naked. He grabbed the bag, untied the satin ribbon at its neck, and poured out the rough-cut, pebble-sized diamonds onto the slab. The empty satchel fell from his hand and floated down to the floor.

Wrath bowed his head and spoke the words of his mother tongue, the syllables rising and falling with his breath as he paid tribute to his dead. When he finished speaking, he knelt down onto the slab, feeling the stones cut into his flesh. He settled his weight back on his heels, placed his palms on his thighs, and closed his eyes.

The death ritual required him to pass the day without moving, to bear the pain, to bleed in memory of his friend.

In his mind he saw Darius's daughter.

He shouldn't have gone inside of her home like that. He'd scared her half to death, when all he'd wanted to do was introduce himself and explain why she was going to need him soon. He'd also planned to tell her he was going after that human male who'd fucked with her.

Yeah, he'd handled it beautifully. Smooth as gravel.

The moment he'd come inside, she'd bolted in terror and he'd had to strip her memories and put her in a light trance to calm her down. After he'd laid her out on her bed, he'd meant to leave right away, but he hadn't been able to. He'd stood over her, measuring the blurry contrast between her black hair and her white pillow-case, breathing in her scent.

Feeling a sexual stirring in his gut.

Before he'd left, he'd made sure her doors and windows were locked. And then he'd looked back at her one more time. He'd thought of her father.

Wrath focused on the ache that was already setting up shop in his thighs.

As his blood turned the marble red, he saw his dead warrior's face and felt the tie they'd shared in life.

He had to honor his brother's last request. He owed the male at least that for all the years they'd served the race together.

Half-human or not, Darius's daughter was never going to walk the night unprotected again. And she wasn't going to go through her transition alone.

God help her.

Butch finished processing Billy Riddle around six A.M. The guy was offended by the class of drug dealers and thugs he'd been put into the holding cell with, so Butch was careful to make as many typographical errors as possible on his reports. And what would you know, Central Processing kept getting confused about exactly which forms needed to be filled out.

And then the printers had gone on the fritz. All twenty-three of them.

Still, Riddle wasn't long for the station house. His father was indeed a powerful man, a U.S. senator. So some fancy lawyer was going to get Billy sprung quicker than shit through a goose. Probably in the next hour.

'Cause that was the criminal justice system for you. Money talked, and creeps walked.

Not that Butch was bitter or anything.

As he walked out to the lobby, he ran into one of their regular overnight guests. Cherry Pie had evidently just been released from the women's side. Her real name was Mary Mulcahy, and from what Butch had heard, she'd been working the streets for about two years.

"Hey, there, Detective," she purred. Her red lipstick had pooled into the corners of her mouth, and her black eyeliner was smudged. She would have been pretty, he thought, if she put the crack pipe down and slept for about a month straight. "You going home alone?"

"As always." He held the door open for her as they went outside.

"Don't your left hand get tired after a while?"

Butch laughed as they both paused and looked up at the sky.

"So how you been, Cherry?"

"I'm always good."

She put a cigarette between her teeth and lit it while eyeing him.

"You know, your palms ever get too hairy, you could call me. I'd do you for free, 'cause you sure are a handsome SOB. But don't tell Big Daddy I said so."

She blew out a cloud of smoke and absently fingered her ragged left ear. The top half was missing.

Man, that pimp of hers was a rabid dog.

They started down the concrete steps.

"You check out that program I told you about?" Butch asked as they reached the sidewalk. He was helping a friend start up a prostitute support group that would encourage women to get free of the pimps and out of the life.

"Oh, yeah, sure. Good stuff." She flashed him a smile. "I'll see you later."

"Take care of yourself."

49

She turned away and slapped her right butt cheek with her palm. "Just think, this could be yours."

Butch watched her sashay down the street for a little while. And then he got into an unmarked car and, on impulse, drove across town, back to the Screamer's neighborhood. He pulled up in front of McGrider's. About fifteen minutes later a woman in a tight pair of blue jeans and a black belly shirt came out of the joint. She blinked myopically at the brightening light.

When she caught sight of his car, she fluffed her auburn hair and walked over to him. He put the window down and she leaned in, kissing him on the lips.

"I haven't seen you for a while. You lonely, Butch?" she said against his mouth.

She smelled like dried beer and maraschino cherries, every bartender's perfume at the end of a long night.

"Get in," he said.

She went around the front of the car and slid beside him. They talked about how her night had been as he drove out to the river. She was disappointed that the tips had been light again. And her feet were killing her from running back and forth behind the bar.

He parked under the span bridge that crossed the Hudson River and linked Caldwell's two halves. He made sure they were far enough away from the homeless men lying in beds of rags. There was no reason to have an audience.

And he had to give Abby credit: She was fast. She had his pants undone and was working his erection with a good stroke before he even had the engine off. As he pushed the seat back, she straddled him and nuzzled his neck. He looked past her kinky, permed hair and out to the water.

The sunlight was so beautiful, he thought, as it dappled over the surface of the river.

"Do you love me, baby?" she whispered in his ear.

"Yeah, sure." He smoothed her hair back and looked into her eyes. They were vacant. He could have been any man, and that was why their relationship worked.

His heart was as empty as her stare.

SEVEN

As Mr. X crossed the parking lot and headed for the Caldwell Martial Arts Academy, he caught a whiff of the Dunkin' Donuts across the street. That smell, that gorgeous, thick smell of flour and sugar and hot oil, was heavy in the morning air. He looked over his shoulder, watching as a man emerged with two white-and-pink boxes under his arm and a huge travel mug of coffee in his other hand.

That would be a nice way to start the morning, Mr. X thought.

Mr. X stepped up onto the sidewalk that ran beneath the academy's red-and-gold awning. He paused, reaching down and picking up a stray plastic cup. Its previous owner had been careful to keep an inch of soda in the bottom so his or her cigarette butts could enjoy floating around while they waited for someone else to throw them away. He pitched the nasty swill in the trash and unlocked the doors to the academy.

The Lessening Society had turned a corner in the war last night, and he was the one who had done the deed. Darius had been a powerhouse of a vampire, a member of the Black Dagger Brotherhood. One hell of a trophy.

It was a damn shame there was nothing left of the corpse to mount on a wall, but Mr. X's bomb had performed adequately and then some. He'd been at home, listening to his police scanner, when the report had come in. The op was everything he had planned it to be, perfectly executed, perfectly anonymous.

Perfectly deadly.

He tried to recall the last time a member of the brotherhood had been taken out. Well before he'd joined the society decades ago, certainly. And he'd expected to get a few pats on the back, not that such accolades motivated him. He'd figured he might even get a bonus out of it, maybe an expansion of his sphere of influence, maybe a greater geographic radius in which to work.

But the reward . . . the reward was more than he'd expected.

The Omega had paid him a visit an hour before dawn. And conferred upon him all the rights and privileges of *Forelesser*.

Leader of the Lessening Society.

It was an awesome responsibility. And exactly what Mr. X had been angling for.

Power granted was the only form of praise he was interested in.

Walking with long strides, he headed for his office. The first classes would start at nine, and there was plenty of time for him to lay down some of the new rules for his subordinates in the society.

His first instinct after the Omega had left was to send an announcement out, but that would have been unwise. A leader gathered his thoughts before he spoke; he did not rush to the podium to be adored. Ego, after all, was the root of evil.

So instead of crowing like a fool, he'd gone outside and sat down in a lawn chair, looking over the meadow behind his house. In the dawn's nascent glow, he'd reviewed the strengths and weaknesses of his organization and allowed his instincts to show him the way to manage both. From the tangle of images and thoughts, patterns had emerged, the future becoming clear.

Sitting behind his desk now, he signed on to the society's secured Web site and made it clear that a change in leadership had occurred. He ordered all *lessers* to come to the academy at four P.M. that afternoon, knowing that some would have to travel, but none was farther away than an eight-hour car ride. Anyone who did not show up would be excised from the society and hunted down like a dog.

Gathering the *lessers* together in one place was rare. At this time their numbers hovered in the fifty to sixty range, depending on the number of kills the brotherhood got in on any given night and the number of new recruits that were brought into service. The society's members were all in and around New England. This concentration in the northeastern United States was dicatated by the prevalence of vampires in the area. If that population moved, so would the society.

As had been the way throughout the generations of the war.

Mr. X was aware that getting the *lessers* to Caldwell for an audience was critical. Although he knew most of them, and some of them rather well, he needed for them to see him and hear him and measure him. Especially as he redirected their focus.

Calling the meeting in the daylight was also important, as it would ensure they weren't ambushed by the brotherhood. And he could easily pass it off to the academy's human employees as a seminar on martial-arts technique. They would hold the gathering in the large conference room in the basement and lock the doors so they wouldn't be intruded upon.

Before he signed off, he posted an account of his elimination of Darius, because he wanted the slayers to have it in writing. He detailed the kind of bomb he'd used, the way to manufacture one from scratch, and the method for hardwiring the detonator into a car's ignition system. It was so easy once the thing was set. All you needed to do was arm it, and then the next time the engine was started, anyone in the car was turned to ash.

For that split second of payoff, he'd tracked the warrior Darius for a year, watching him, learning the rhythms of his life. And then two days ago, Mr. X had broken into the Greene Brothers BMW dealership when the vampire had sent his 6-series in for service. The bomb had been set, and then last night Mr. X had walked by the car and activated the detonator with a radio transmitter without missing a step.

The long, concentrated effort to set up the elimination was not something he shared. He wanted his *lessers* to believe he was able to execute such a flawless move on a whim. Image and perception played important roles in the creation of a power base, and he wanted to start building his command credibility right away.

After signing off, he leaned back in his chair, steepling his fingers. Ever since he'd joined the society, the focus had been on reducing the vampire population through civilian eliminations. This would remain his overall goal, of course, but his first decree would be a change in strategy. The key to winning the war was taking out the brotherhood. Without those six warriors, the civilians would be naked against the *lessers*, undefended.

The tactic was not a new one. It had been attempted in generations past and discarded numerous times when the brothers had proven either too aggressive or too elusive to be taken out. But with Darius's death, the society had momentum.

And they had to do something differently. As it stood now, the brotherhood was cutting down hundreds of *lessers* every year, requiring the ranks to be fed with new, inexperienced slayers. Recruits were trouble. They were hard to find, hard to induct into the society, and not as effective as seasoned members of the society.

This constant need to bring in new men led to a critical weakness for the society. Training centers like the Caldwell Martial Arts Academy served an important purpose in identifying and enlisting humans to join the ranks, but they were also points of exposure. Avoiding interference by the human police—and protecting against a siege by the brotherhood—required constant vigilance and frequent relocation. The moving around from place to place was disruptive, but how else could the society stay stocked and yet the centers of operation not be ambushed?

Mr. X shook his head. At some point he was going to need a second in command, though he wouldn't bring one on for a while.

Fortunately, nothing he was going to do was particularly complex. It was all basic military strategy. Marshal your forces. Coordinate them. Acquire information on the enemy. Advance in a logical, disciplined manner.

He was marshaling his forces this afternoon.

As for coordination, he was going to arrange them into squadrons. And he was going to insist the slayers start meeting with him regularly in small groups.

As for information? If they were going to take out the brotherhood, they needed to know where to find the brothers. This would be difficult, though not impossible. Those warriors were a cagey, suspicious lot who kept to themselves, but the civilian vampire population did have some contact with them. After all, the brothers had to feed, and it couldn't be off one another. They required female blood.

And females, even if most of them were sheltered like precious art, had brothers and fathers who could be persuaded to talk. With the proper incentive, the males would reveal where their womenfolk went and who they saw. And then the brotherhood would be revealed.

This was the key to his overall strategy: A coordinated program of capture and motivation, focused on civilian males and the rare female who was out and about, would eventually lead to the brothers. It had to. Either because the brothers became incensed that the civilians were being used so roughly and came out with all daggers flashing. Or because someone talked and their locations were divulged.

The best outcome would be to find out where the warriors spent their days. Taking them down while the sun was shining, when they were at their most vulnerable, was the course of action with the highest probability of success and the lowest likelihood of society fatalities.

All things considered, killing civilian vampires was only slightly more difficult than knocking out your average human. They bled if you cut them, and their hearts stopped beating if you shot them, and if you got them into the sunlight they burned up.

Killing a member of the brotherhood was a very different proposition. They were monstrously strong, highly trained, and they healed up fast, a subspecies all their own. You had one shot with a warrior. If you didn't make it mortal, you were not making it home.

Mr. X stood up from the desk, taking a moment to study his reflection in the office's window. Pale hair, pale skin, pale eyes. Before he'd joined the society he'd been a redhead. Now he couldn't remember what he'd looked like anymore.

But he was very clear about his future. And the society's.

He locked the door behind him and went down the tiled hall to the main arena, waiting by the entrance, nodding at the students as they came inside for their jujitsu lesson. This was his favorite class, a group of young men, ages eighteen to twenty-four, who showed a lot of promise. As the fleet of guys in white, belted jujitsu *gis* bowed their heads to him and addressed him as sensei, Mr. X measured each one, noticing the way their eyes moved, the way they carried their bodies, how their moods seemed.

With his students lined up and prepared to spar, he continued to look them over, always keeping an eye out for potential recruits to the society. He was searching for just the right combination of physical strength, mental acuity, and unchanneled hatred.

When he'd been approached to join the Lessening Society in the 1950s, he'd been a seventeen-year-old greaser in a juvenile delinquent program. The year before he'd stabbed his father in the chest after the bastard had knocked him one too many times in the head with a beer bottle. He'd hoped to kill the man, but unfortunately his father had survived and lived long enough to go home and kill Mr. X's mother.

But at least dear old Dad had had the sense to blow his own head all over the wall with a shotgun afterward. Mr. X had found the body on a visit home, right before he'd been caught and thrown into the system.

On that day, as he'd stood over his father's corpse, Mr. X had learned that screaming at the dead wasn't even remotely satisfying. There was, after all, nothing to be taken from someone who was already gone.

Considering who'd sired him, it was no accident that violence and hatred were thick in Mr. X's blood. And killing vampires was one of the few socially acceptable outlets for a murder streak like his. The military was a bore. Too many rules, and you had to wait until an enemy was declared before you could get to work. And serial killing was too small-scale.

The society was different. He had everything he'd ever wanted. Unlimited funds. The chance to kill every time the sun went down. And, of course, there was that all-important opportunity to mold the next generation.

So he'd had to sell his soul to get in. That was not a problem. After what his father had done to him, there hadn't been much of it left anyway.

In his mind, he'd definitely come out on the money

side of the trade. He was guaranteed to be young and in perfect health until the day he died. And his death would be predicated not on some biological failure, like cancer or heart disease, but on his own ability to keep himself in one piece.

Thanks to the Omega, he was physically superior to humans, his eyesight was perfect, and he got to do what he liked best. The impotence had bothered him a little at the beginning, but he'd gotten used to that. And the not eating or drinking . . . well, it wasn't as if he'd been a gourmand anyway.

Besides, making blood run was better than food or sex any day.

When the door to the arena opened abruptly, he shot a glare over his shoulder. It was Billy Riddle, and the guy had two black eyes and a bandaged nose.

Mr. X cocked an eyebrow. "You sitting out today, Riddle?"

"Yes, sensei." Billy bowed his head. "But I wanted to come anyway."

"Good man." Mr. X put his arm around Riddle's shoulders. "I like your commitment. Tell you what—you want to put them through their paces during the warm-up?"

Billy bowed deeply, his broad back going nearly parallel to the floor. "Sensei."

"Go to it." He clapped the guy on the shoulder. "And don't take it easy on them."

Billy looked up, his eyes flashing.

Mr. X nodded. "Glad to see you get the point, son."

When Beth walked out of her building, she frowned at the unmarked police car parked across the street. José got out and jogged over to her.

"I heard what happened." His eyes lingered on her mouth. "How you feelin'?"

"Better."

"Come on, I'm giving you a ride to work."

"Thanks, but I want to walk." José's jaw set like he wanted to argue, so she reached out and touched his forearm. "I won't let this scare me so badly that I can't live my life. I've got to walk by that alley at some point, and I'd rather do it for the first time in the morning, when there's plenty of light."

He nodded. "Fine. But you're going to call a cab at night or you're going to get one of us to pick you up."

"José—"

"Glad you see it our way." He walked back across the street. "Oh, and I don't suppose you've heard what Butch O'Neal did last night?"

She almost didn't want to ask. "What?"

"He paid a little visit to that punk. I understand the guy had to get his nose set again after our good detective was finished with him." José opened the car door and dropped down into the seat. "Now, are we gonna be seeing you today?"

"Yeah, I want to know more about that car bomb."

"Thought so. See you in a few." He waved and peeled away from the curb.

But by three in the afternoon, she still hadn't made it to the police station. Everyone in the office had wanted to hear about her ordeal, and then Tony had insisted they go out for a big lunch. After rolling herself back into her cubicle, she'd spent the afternoon chewing on Tums and dallying with her e-mail.

She knew she had work she needed to be doing, but finishing up the article she was drafting on those handguns the cops had found was just not happening. Not that she was under any kind of deadline. It wasn't as if Dick was in a big hurry to give her front-page space in the Metro section.

No, what he gave her was editorial work. The two

latest pieces he'd dropped on her desk had both been drafted by the big boys, and Dick wanted her to fact-check them. Adhering to the standards he'd gotten familiar with at the *New York Times* by being a stickler for accuracy was actually one of his strengths. But it was a shame he didn't care about sweat equity. No matter how many red marks she made, she had yet to get a shared byline on a big boy article.

It was nearly six when she finished editing the articles, and as she dropped them in Dick's in box, she thought about skipping the trip to the police station altogether. Butch had taken her statement last night, and there was nothing more she needed to do about her case. More to the point, she was uncomfortable with the idea of being under the same roof with her attacker, even if he was in a holding cell.

Plus she was exhausted.

"Beth!"

She winced at the sound of Dick's voice.

"Can't talk, I'm going to the station," she called out over her shoulder, thinking the avoidance strategy wouldn't put him off for long, but at least she wouldn't have to deal with the guy tonight.

And she did want to know more about that bomb.

She bolted from the office and walked six blocks to the east. The station house was typical of 1960s-era muni-architecture. Two stories, rambling, modern for its time, with plenty of pale gray cement and lots of narrow windows. It was aging with no grace whatsoever. Black streaks ran down its flanks as if it were bleeding from a wound in the roof, and the inside looked terminal as well. Nothing but nasty, chalky green linoleum, fake-wood-paneled walls, and chipped brown trim. After forty years of cleaning, the heartiest of dirt had moved into every crack and fissure, and the grime wasn't coming out without a spray gun or some toothbrush action.

And maybe a vacate order from the court.

The cops were really good to her when she arrived. As soon as she set foot in the building, they started fussing over her. After talking them down off the walls while trying not to get teary eyed, she went to dispatch and chatted with a couple of the boys behind the counter. They'd had a few folks brought in for soliciting or dealing, but otherwise it had been a quiet day. She was about to leave when Butch came through the back door.

He was dressed in a pair of jeans and a button-down and had a red windbreaker in his hand. Her eyes lingered on the way his holster crossed over his wide shoulders, the black butt of his gun flashing as his arms swung with his gait. His dark hair was damp, as if he were just starting his day.

Which, considering how busy he'd been the night before, was probably the truth.

He came right up to her. "You got time to talk?"

She nodded. "Yeah, I do."

They walked into one of the interrogation rooms.

"Just so you know, the cameras and the mikes are off," he said.

"Isn't that how you usually work?"

He smiled and sat down at the table. Linked his hands together. "Thought you should know that Billy Riddle is out on bail. He was sprung early this morning."

She took a seat. "His name's Billy Riddle? You're kidding me."

Butch shook his head. "He's eighteen. No priors as an adult, but I hacked into his juvie file and he's been a busy boy. Sexual assault, stalking, some petty theft. His dad's a big shot, so the guy's got one hell of a lawyer, but I talked to the DA. She's going to try to plea him hard so you won't have to testify."

"I'll take the stand if I have to."

"Good girl." Butch cleared his throat. "So how you doing?"

"I'm fine." She wasn't about to have Hard-ass play Dr. Phil on her. There was something about the radiant toughness of Butch O'Neal that made her want to appear strong. "Now, about that car bomb. I hear it was probably plastics, and the detonating mechanism was blown sky-high. Sounds like a professional hit."

"You eat yet tonight?"

She frowned. "No."

And considering what she'd pulled down at lunch, she should be skipping breakfast tomorrow morning, too.

Butch got to his feet. "Good. I was just going to hit Tullah's."

He walked over to the door and held it open for her. She stayed put. "I'm not having dinner with you."

"Suit yourself. Guess you don't want to hear about what we found across the alley from that car, then."

The door slowly eased shut behind him.

She was not going to fall for this. She was not going to—

Beth leaped out of the chair and went after him.

EIGHT

Standing in her pristine cream-and-white bedroom, Marissa was unsure of herself.

As Wrath's *shellan*, she could feel his pain and knew by its strength that he must have lost another of his warrior brothers.

If they'd had a normal relationship, there would be no question. She would go to him and try to ease his suffering. She would talk with him or hold him or cry with him. Warm him with her body.

Because that was what *shellans* did for their mates. What they got in return, too.

She glanced at the Tiffany clock on her bedside table.

He'd be heading off into the night soon. If she wanted to catch him she'd better do it now.

Marissa hesitated, not willing to fool herself. She wasn't going to be welcome.

She wished it were easier to support him, wished she knew what he needed from her. Once, a long time ago, she'd spoken with his brother Tohrment's *shellan*, hoping Wellsie could offer some hint as to what to do. How to behave. How to make Wrath see her as worthy of him.

After all, Wellsie had what Marissa wanted. A true mate. A male who came home to her. Who laughed and cried and shared his life with her. Who held her.

A male who stayed with her during those torturous, mercifully rare times when she was fertile. Who eased her terrible cravings with his body for as long as the needing period lasted.

Wrath did none of that for or with her. Especially not

the last part. As it was, Marissa had to go to her brother for relief of her needing. Havers would put her out cold, tranquilizing her until the urges passed. The practice embarrassed them both.

She'd so hoped that Wellsie could help, but the conversation had been a disaster. The other female's pained looks and carefully couched replies had burned them both, pointing out everything Marissa didn't have.

God, she was so alone.

She closed her eyes, feeling Wrath's pain again.

She had to try to reach him. Because he was hurting. And because what else was there to her life other than him?

She sensed that he was in Darius's mansion. Taking a deep breath, she dematerialized.

Wrath slowly eased off his knees and stood up, hearing his vertebrae crack back into place. He brushed the diamonds off his shins.

There was a knock on the door, and he allowed it to open, thinking it was Fritz.

When he smelled the ocean, he tightened his lips.

"What brings you here, Marissa?" he said without turning to her. He went to the bathroom and covered himself with a towel.

"Let me wash you, my lord," she murmured. "I'll take care of your skin. I can—"

"I'm fine."

He was a fast healer. By the end of the night the cuts would barely be discernible.

Wrath walked over to the closet and looked through the clothes. He took out a black long-sleeved shirt, a pair of leather pants, and—jeez, what was this? Oh, not fucking likely. He was not going to fight in BVDs. He'd go commando before he got caught dead in those things.

The first thing he had to do was make contact with

Darius's daughter. He knew he was almost out of time, because her transition was coming quick. And then he had to link up with Vishous and Phury to find out what was up with that dead *lesser*'s leftovers.

He was about to drop the towel to get ready to roll, when it occurred to him Marissa was still in the room.

He looked over at her.

"Go home, Marissa," he said.

Her head dropped. "My lord, I can feel your p—"

"I'm perfectly fine."

She hesitated a moment. And then quietly disappeared.

Ten minutes later he came up to the drawing room.

"Fritz?" he called out.

"Yes, master?" The butler seemed pleased to have been summoned.

"Do you have some red smokes on hand?"

"Of course."

Fritz went across to an antique mahogany box. He brought the thing over, opening the lid and angling the contents outward.

Wrath took a couple of the hand-rolled cigarillos.

"If you have a taste for them, I'll get more."

"Don't bother. This is enough." Wrath wasn't into drugging, but he was willing to put the smokes to good use tonight.

"Will you be needing something to eat before you go out?"

Wrath shook his head.

"Perhaps when you return?" Fritz's voice grew small as he closed the lid.

Wrath was about to shut the old male down when he thought of Darius. D would have treated Fritz better. "Okay. Yeah. Thanks."

The butler's shoulders squared off with purpose.

Good God, he seemed to be smiling, Wrath thought.

"I shall make you lamb, master. How do you like your meat cooked?"

"Rare."

"And I'll wash your other clothes. Shall I also order you a new set of leathers?"

"Don't—" Wrath shut his mouth. "Sure. That'd be great. And, ah, could you get me some boxers? Black? XXL?"

"With pleasure."

Wrath turned away and headed for the door.

How the hell had he found himself with a servant?

"Master?"

"Yeah?" he growled.

"Take care of yourself out there."

Wrath paused and looked over his shoulder. Fritz seemed to be cradling the box against his chest.

It was goddamned weird having someone waiting for him to come home, Wrath thought.

He left the mansion and walked down the long drive to the tree-lined street. Lightning streaked across the sky, a promise of the storm that he could smell brewing to the south.

Where the hell was Darius's daughter right now?

He'd try her apartment first.

After Wrath materialized in the courtyard behind her place, he looked into her windows and returned her cat's purr of welcome with one of his own. She wasn't inside, so Wrath took a seat on the picnic table. He'd give her an hour or so, and then he was going to have to find the brothers. He could always come back at the end of the night, although given how things had gone the first time he'd come into her place, he figured waking her up at four A.M. wasn't the smartest move.

He took off his sunglasses and rubbed the bridge of his nose.

How was he going to explain what was about to

happen to her? And what she'd have to do to live through the change?

He had a feeling she wasn't going to be too happy about the news flashes.

Wrath thought back to his own transition. What a goddamned mess that had been. He hadn't been prepared either, because his parents had always wanted to shelter him, and they'd died before they'd told him what to expect.

His memories came back with a terrible clarity.

London in the late seventeenth century had been a brutal place, especially for someone who was all alone in the world. His parents had been slaughtered in front of him two years before, and he'd run from his species, thinking his cowardice on that awful night was a shame only he should bear.

Whereas in vampire society he'd been nurtured and protected as the future king, he'd found the world of humans to be based largely on a physical meritocracy. For someone built as he'd been before he went through his change, that had meant he'd been on the bottom of the social rung. He'd been whip-thin then, scrawny and weak, and easy prey for human boys looking for fun. Over the course of his time in London's slums, he'd been beaten so many times he'd grown used to parts of him not working right. It was nothing new to have a leg that wouldn't bend because the kneecap had been stoned. Or to have an arm that was useless because it'd been popped out of his shoulder as he'd been dragged behind a horse.

He'd been living off garbage, squeaking by on the edge of starvation, when he'd finally found work as a servant in a merchant's stable. Wrath had cleaned shoes and saddles and bridles until the skin on his hands had cracked, but at least he'd been fed. His pallet had been in the stables, on the second-floor hayloft. It was softer than the ground he'd grown used to, but he'd never known when he'd be woken up with a kick to the ribs because some stable boy wanted to bed down a maid or two.

Back then he'd still been able to be out in the sunshine, and the dawn was the only thing in his pitiful existence that he looked forward to. To feel the warmth on his face, to draw the sweet mist into his lungs, to relish the light—these pleasures were the only ones he had, and they were dear to him. His eyesight, impaired from birth, had been poor back then but far, far better than it was now. He could still remember with aching clarity what the sun had looked like.

He'd been at the merchant's for nearly a year when everything had been turned upside down.

The night the change had come upon him, he'd fallen into his nest of hay, utterly exhausted. He'd been feeling sickly lately, struggling through his work, but that was nothing new.

The pain, when it hit, had racked his weak body, starting in his abdomen and radiating outward until the tips of his fingers, his toes, the ends of every piece of hair on his head had screamed. No broken bone, no concussion, no fever or beating had even come close. He'd curled into a ball, eyes straining against the agony, breath coming in bursts. He'd been convinced he was going to die, and he'd prayed for the darkness. He'd only wanted some peace, an end to the suffering.

And then a beautiful blond waif had appeared before him.

She was an angel sent to carry him to the other side. He'd been convinced of it.

Like the pathetic wretch he was, he'd begged her for mercy. He'd reached out to the apparition, and when he'd felt her touch, he knew the end was near. As she'd called him by name, he'd tried to smile at her in gratitude, but his lips hadn't been working. She'd told him she was the one who had been promised to him, who had taken a sip of his blood when he was a small boy so she would always know where to find him when the transition hit. She'd said she was there to save him.

And then Marissa had scored her wrist with her own fangs and held the wound to his mouth.

He'd drunk desperately, but the pain hadn't stopped. It only changed. He'd felt his joints popping out of shape, his bones shifting in horrible waves of snapping. His muscles had strained and then split open, and his skull had felt as if it were going to burst. As his eyes had bulged, his sight had receded, and then all he'd had was his hearing.

His rasping, guttural breath had hurt his throat as he'd tried to hang on. He'd blacked out at some point, finally, only to wake up to a fresh agony. The sunlight he'd loved so much was streaming through the gaps in the barn's clapboards, pale shafts of gold. A strip had landed on his arm, and the smell of burning flesh was terrifying. He'd snapped his arm back and looked around himself in a panic. He hadn't been able to see anything but vague shapes. Blinded in the light, he'd lurched to his feet, only to find himself falling facedown in the hay. His body hadn't acted at all like his own, and it had taken him two tries before he could stand, wobbling on his legs like a foal.

He'd known that he needed to find shelter from the daylight, and he'd dragged himself to where the loft's ladder should have been. He'd miscalculated, however, and had plunged down the hay shaft. Lying in a daze, he'd figured he might be able to make it to the grain cellar. If he went down there, he'd be in darkness.

He'd flailed around the barn, banging into stalls and tripping over tack, trying to stay out of the sunlight while controlling his unruly arms and legs. As he'd headed for the back of the barn, his head had struck a beam he'd always easily walked under. Blood had run into his eyes.

Right after that, one of the stable hands had come in, demanding to know who Wrath was. Wrath had turned to the familiar voice, thinking maybe he could get help. He'd reached out and started to speak, but his voice hadn't sounded like his own.

And then he'd heard a pitchfork coming through the air at him in a vicious stab. He'd meant only to deflect the blow, but when he'd grabbed the handle and pushed at it, he'd sent the stable hand smashing into a stall door. The man had let out a screech of fear and run off, no doubt looking for reinforcements.

Wrath had finally found the cellar. He'd taken out two huge bags of oats and put them next to the door so no one would have to come in during the day. Exhausted, hurting, blood dripping off his chin, he'd crawled inside and settled his bare back against the earthen wall. He'd drawn his knees up to his chest, aware that his thighs were four times the size they'd been the day before. Closing his eyes, he'd rested his cheek on his forearms and shivered, fighting not to disgrace himself by crying. He'd stayed awake all day long, listening to the foot-steps above him, the stamping of the horses, the patter of talk. He'd been terrified someone would open the double doors and expose him. And glad that Marissa had gone so she wasn't exposed to the threat from humans.

Coming back to the present, Wrath heard Darius's daughter walk into her apartment. A light came on.

Beth tossed her keys down on the hall table. The quick meal with Hard-ass had been surprisingly easy. And he'd given her some other details about the bombing. They'd found one of those modified Magnums in the alley. And Butch had mentioned the martial-arts throwing star she'd pointed out to Ricky. The CSI folks were working on the weapons, trying to get any prints or fibers or other evidence off them. The gun didn't appear to offer much, but the star, not surprisingly, had blood on it, which they were putting through DNA analysis. As for the bomb, the police were thinking it was a drug-related hit. The BMW had been sighted before, parked in the same spot behind the club. And Screamer's was a hotbed for dealers who were very particular about their territories.

She stretched and changed into a pair of boxers. It was another hot night, and as she pulled out the futon, she really wished the air conditioner were still working. She turned the box fan on and fed Boo, who, as soon as he'd polished off his Fancy Feast, took up pacing in front of the sliding door.

"We're not going to be doing this again, are we?"

Lightning flashed, and she went over and slid back the glass door, moving the screen into place and locking it. She'd leave the thing open for only a little bit—the night air smelled good for once. Not a whiff of garbage.

But man, it was hot.

She ducked into the bathroom. After taking out her contacts, brushing her teeth, and scrubbing her face, she ran a washcloth under some cold water and rubbed the back of her neck. Cool rivulets ran down her skin, and she welcomed the shivers as she walked back out.

She frowned. There was the strangest scent in the air. Something rich and spicy . . .

She went over to the screen and sniffed a couple of times. As she breathed in, she felt the tension in her shoulders ease.

And then she saw that Boo had sat down on his haunches and was purring as if he were welcoming someone he knew.

What the . . .

The man from her dream was on the other side of the screen.

Beth leaped back and dropped the washcloth, dimly hearing the fleshy flop when it hit the floor.

The screen slid open. In spite of the fact that she'd locked it.

And that wonderful smell got thicker as he stepped into her home.

She panicked, but found she couldn't move.

Oh, man, he was colossal. If her apartment was small to begin with, he turned it into a shoe box. And all that black leather just seemed to make him bigger. He had to be six-feet-six, two seventy-five at least.

Wait a minute.

What was she doing, measuring him for a suit? Running, she should be running. She should be making a break for the other door, running like hell.

But all she could do was stare at him.

He was wearing a biker jacket in spite of the heat, and his long legs were covered in leather as well. He had steel-toed shitkicker boots on, and he moved like a predator.

Beth craned her neck to look up at his face.

God, he was *gorgeous.*

His jaw was a straight shot of bone, his lips full, the hollows under his cheeks casting heavy shadows. His hair was straight and black, falling to his shoulders from a widow's peak, and he had the shadow of a dark beard. The black sunglasses he wore, wraparounds that fit his carved face perfectly, made him look like a hit man.

As if all that menace wouldn't have given him away as a killer.

He was smoking some kind of thin, reddish cigar, and he took a long drag, the end flaring bright orange. He blew out a cloud of that fragrant smoke, and as it hit her nostrils, her body loosened even further.

73

He must be coming to kill her, she thought. She didn't know what she'd done to deserve a hit, but as he breathed out another drag of whatever he was smoking, she could barely remember where she was.

Her body swayed as he closed the distance between them. She was terrified of what was going to happen when he reached her, but noticed, absurdly, that Boo was purring and wrapping himself in and around the man's ankles.

That cat was a traitor. And if by some miracle she lived through the night, he was getting downgraded to Tender Vittles.

Beth's neck jacked back up as she met the man's steady, feral gaze. She couldn't see the color of his eyes through the glasses, but his stare burned.

And then the extraordinary happened. As he stopped in front of her, she felt a blast of pure, unadulterated lust. For the first time in her life her body got wickedly hot. Hot and wet.

Her core bloomed for him.

It was chemistry, she thought numbly. Pure, raw, animal chemistry.

Whatever he had, she wanted.

"I thought we'd try this again," he said.

His voice was low, a deep rumble in his solid chest. He had the sliver of an accent, but she couldn't place it.

"Who are you?" she breathed in a whisper.

"I'm here for you."

Dizziness made her reach out for the wall.

"For me? Where—" Confusion closed her mouth. "Where are you going to take me?"

To the bridge? Where he'd toss her body into the river?

His hand crossed the distance between their bodies, and he took her chin between his forefinger and thumb. He tilted her face to one side.

74

"Are you going to kill me fast?" she mumbled. "Or slow?"

"No killing. Protection."

As his head bent down, she told herself she should fight him off in spite of his words. She needed to get those arms of hers working, her legs, too. Trouble was, she didn't really want to push him away. She took a deep breath.

Good heavens, he smelled fantastic. Fresh, clean sweat. A dark, masculine musk. That smoke.

His lips touched her neck, and she heard him inhale. The leather of his jacket creaked as his lungs were filled and his chest expanded.

"You're almost ready," he said softly. "And it's coming fast."

If the *it* he was referring to had anything to do with their getting naked, she was totally on board with the plan. My God, this had to be what people talked about when they waxed poetic about sex. She didn't question the need to have him inside of her. She only knew that she was going to die if he didn't take his pants off. Now.

Beth reached out, curious to touch him, but when she let go of the wall she started to fall. In what seemed like one motion, he put the cigarillo between those cruel lips of his and caught her easily. As he swept her off the floor, she leaned into him, not even bothering to put up a pretense of fighting. He handled her as if she were weightless, crossing the room in two strides.

When he laid her down on the futon his hair fell forward, and she lifted her hand, touching the black waves. They were thick, soft. She put her palm on his face, and though he seemed surprised, he didn't pull back.

God, everything about him radiated sex, from the strength in his body to the way he moved to the smell of his skin. He was like no man she'd ever come across before. And her body knew it just as clearly as her mind did.

"Kiss me," she said.

He hovered above her, a silent menace.

On impulse her hands went to the lapels of his jacket, and she tried to pull him down to her mouth.

He captured both her wrists in one of his hands. "Easy."

Easy? She didn't want easy. Easy was *not* part of the plan.

She struggled against his hold, and when she couldn't get free she arched her back. Her breasts strained against her T-shirt, and she rubbed her thighs together, anticipating what it would feel like to have him between them.

If he'd only put his hands—

"Sweet Jesus," he muttered.

She smiled up at him, relishing the sudden hunger in his face. "Touch me."

The stranger started shaking his head. As if he were trying to clear it.

She opened her lips and moaned in frustration.

"Pull up my shirt." She arched again, offering her body to him, dying to know if there was something even hotter inside of her, something he could bring out with his hands. "Do it."

He took the cigarillo from his mouth. His eyebrows were drawn tight, and she had some vague thought that she should be terrified. Instead, she brought her knees up and lifted her hips off the futon. She imagined him kissing the insides of her thighs, finding her sex with his mouth. Licking her.

Another moan boiled out of her mouth.

Wrath was dumbfounded.

And he wasn't a vampire who got struck stupid very often.

76

Holy shit.

This half-human was the hottest thing he'd ever gotten anywhere near. And he'd cozied up to a lightning strike once or twice before.

It was the red smoke. That had to be it. And the stuff must be getting to him, too, because he was more than ready to take her.

He eyed the cigarillo.

Well, that's some damn good rationalizing, he thought. Too bad the shit was a relaxant, not an aphrodisiac.

She groaned again, her body undulating in a sexy wave, her legs opening wide. The scent of her arousal hit him hard as a body shot. God, he would have been sent to his knees if he hadn't already been sitting down.

"Touch me," she moaned.

Wrath's blood pumped as if he were in a flat-out run, his erection throbbing like it had its own heartbeat.

"That's not what I'm here for," he said.

"Touch me anyway."

He knew he should say no. This wasn't fair to her. And they needed to talk.

Maybe he should come back later in the night.

She arched up, pushing against the hand he'd clamped around her wrists. As her breasts strained against her T-shirt, he had to close his eyes.

Time to go. It was really time to—

Except he couldn't leave without at least having a taste.

Yeah, but he was a selfish bastard if he laid one finger on her. A nasty selfish bastard to take any of what she was offering in the haze of smoke.

With a curse, Wrath opened his eyes.

Man, he was so cold. Cold down to his marrow. And she was hot. Hot enough to make that ice go away, at least for a little while.

And it had been so long for him.

He willed the lights in the room off. Then he used his mind to close the back door, usher the cat into the bathroom, and slide home every lock in the apartment.

He carefully balanced the cigarillo on the edge of the table next to them and let her wrists go. Her hands grabbed his jacket, trying to push it back from his shoulders. He wrenched the thing off, and as it hit the floor with a thud, she laughed with satisfaction. His holster of daggers followed, but he kept that within reach of the futon.

Wrath bent down over her. Her breath was sweet and minty as he captured her lips with his mouth. When he felt her flinch, he pulled back immediately. Frowning, he touched the side of her mouth.

"Forget it," she told him, pulling at his shoulders.

The hell he would. God help that human who'd hurt her. Wrath was going to rip the guy's limbs off and leave him to bleed out in the street.

He dropped a soft kiss to the healing bruise and then drew his tongue down her neck. This time when she thrust her breasts out, he slid his hand under her thin shirt and onto her smooth, warm skin. Her belly was flat, and he spanned it with his hand, filling the space between her hip bones. Greedy to know the rest of her, he peeled her shirt off and tossed it aside. Her bra was pale in color, and he traced the edges of it with his fingertips before cupping the creamy swells with his hands. Her breasts filled his palms, her nipples tight buds underneath the soft satin.

Wrath's control snapped.

He bared his fangs, let out a hiss, and bit through the bra's front closure. The thing snapped back, and he latched onto one of her nipples with his lips, drawing it into his mouth. As he suckled, he shifted his body and stretched out on top of her, falling in between her legs. She absorbed his weight with a throaty sigh.

Her hands came between them as she reached for the front of his shirt, but he didn't have the patience to let her undress him. He lifted up and ripped the material off his body, popping buttons and sending them scattering across the floor. When he came back down, her breasts hit the wall of his chest and her body surged under his.

He wanted to kiss her mouth again, but he was way past anything soft and gentle, so he worshiped her breasts with his tongue and then moved down to her belly. When he got to the waistband of her boxers, he drew them off her long, smooth legs.

Wrath felt something in his head pop as her scent reached him in a fresh wave. He was perilously close to orgasm already, his release poised in his shaft, his body shaking with the need to take her. He put his hand between her thighs. She was so wet and hot that he growled.

Crazed though he was, he had to taste her before he invaded her.

Drawing off his sunglasses, he put them next to the cigarillo before pressing kisses over her hips and across the tops of her thighs. Her hands tangled in his hair as she urged him exactly where he was headed.

He kissed her softest skin, drawing her core into his mouth, and she came over and over again for him until he couldn't fight his own need any longer. He pulled back, shrugged out of his pants, and covered her with his body once more.

She wrapped her legs around his hips, and he hissed as her heat burned his erection.

He used what was left of his strength to pull back and look down into her face.

"Don't stop," she breathed. "I want to feel you inside me."

Wrath dropped his head into the fragrant hollow of her neck. And slowly drew his hips back. The tip of his erection slid into place beautifully, and he sheathed himself in her body with one powerful stroke.

He let out a bellow of ecstasy.

Heaven. Now he knew what heaven was like.

NINE

In his bedroom, Mr. X changed into black cargo pants and pulled on a black nylon shirt. He was satisfied by the way the meeting with the society had gone this afternoon. Every single *lesser* had shown up. Most of them had fallen into line well enough. A few were going to be trouble. And a small number of them had tried sucking up.

Which had gotten them nowhere.

At the conclusion of the session, he'd chosen twenty-eight more to stay in the Caldwell area, based on what he knew about their reputations and the impressions he had of them up close. Twelve of this group were on the very top of their game, and those he'd split equally into two prime squadrons. The other sixteen he'd cut into four groups of secondaries.

None of them liked the arrangement. They were used to working on their own, and the primes in particular resented being tied down. Tough. The advantage to the squadron orientation was that he could assign different parts of the city to them, establish quotas, and monitor performance more closely.

The rest he'd sent back to their outposts.

Now that he had his troops aligned and assigned, he was going to focus on the information-gathering procedure. He had an idea as to how to make it work, one he was going to beta test this evening.

Before he headed out for the night, he tossed his pit bulls two pounds of raw hamburger apiece. He liked to keep them hungry, so they were fed every other day.

He'd had the dogs, both males, for about five years, and he chained them on opposite sides of his house, one in front, one in back. It was a logical arrangement from a defense perspective, but there was also the matter of expediency. He'd tied them up together once and they'd gone for each other's throats.

He picked up his bag, locked the house, and walked across his lawn. The ranch was an early-seventies nightmare of fake-brick siding and he'd purposely kept the outside ugly. He needed to fit in, and the rural neighborhood's price point wasn't breaking a hundred thousand anytime soon.

Besides, the house was immaterial. The land was what mattered. Ten acres, so he had privacy. Plus there was an old barn in back that was surrounded by trees. He'd turned that into his workshop, and the buffer of oaks and maples was going to be important.

After all, screams could carry.

He fingered his ring of keys until he got to the right one. Because he was going to be working tonight, he was leaving his only extravagance, a black Hummer, in the garage. The four-year-old Chrysler Town & Country minivan was much better cover, and it took him ten minutes to drive the POS downtown.

Caldwell's Whore Valley was a stretch of three dimly lit, trash-strewn blocks over by the suspension bridge. Traffic was heavy tonight down the corridor of iniquity, and he pulled over to watch the action under a broken light. Cars meandered the dark street, brake lights flaring as drivers inspected what was working the pavement. In the thick summer heat, the girls were out in a big way, tottering in their mile-high shoes, their breasts and asses barely covered by easy-access clothing.

Mr. X zipped open his bag, taking out a hypodermic

needle filled with heroin and a hunting knife. He hid both in the door and put the passenger-side window down before easing into the flow of cars.

He was just one of many, he thought. Another schmo, trying to get a little.

"You lookin' for a date?" he heard one of the whores call out.

"Wanna ride?" another said, shaking her ass like it was a can of paint.

On the second pass, he found what he was looking for, a blonde with long legs and a big rack.

Just the kind of whore he would have bought for himself if he'd still had an operational phallus.

He was going to enjoy this, Mr. X thought as he hit the brakes. Killing what he couldn't have anymore carried its own special satisfaction.

"Hey, sugar," she said, coming over. She put her fore-arms on the door and leaned in through the window. She smelled like cinnamon gum and sweaty perfume. "How you doin' tonight?"

"I could be better. What's it going to cost me to buy a smile?"

She eyed the inside of the car, his clothes. "Fifty will get you off good. Any way you like."

"That's too much." But he was just playing. She was the one he wanted.

"Forty?"

"Let me see your tits."

She flashed him.

He smiled, unlocking the doors. "What's your name?"

"Cherry Pie. But you can call me anything you like."

Mr. X drove them around the corner to a secluded spot under the bridge.

He tossed the money down on the floor at her feet,

and when she bent over to pick it up, he drove the needle into the back of her neck and pushed the plunger home. Moments later she slumped like a rag doll.

Mr. X smiled and moved her back against the seat so she was sitting up. Then he tossed the needle out the window, where it joined about a dozen others, and put the van in drive.

In his underground clinic, Havers looked up from his microscope, startled out of his concentration. The grandfather clock was chiming in the corner of his lab, telling him it was time for the evening repast, but he didn't want to stop working. He put his eye back to the scope, wondering if he'd imagined what he saw. After all, desperation could be affecting his objectivity.

But no, the blood cells were living.

Breath left his lungs on a shudder.

His race was almost free.

He was almost free.

Finally, stored blood that was still viable.

As a physician, his hands had always been tied when it came to treating patients surgically and addressing certain labor and delivery complications. Real-time transfusions from vampire to vampire were possible, but as their race was scattered and their numbers small, it could be hard to find donors in a timely manner.

For centuries he'd wanted to establish a blood bank. The trouble was, vampire blood was highly unstable, and storage of it outside the body had always been impossible. Air, that life-sustaining, invisible curtain blanketing the earth, was one cause of the problem, and it didn't take a lot of those molecules to contaminate a sample. Just one or two and the plasma disintegrated, leaving the red and white blood cells to fend for themselves. Which, of course, they couldn't do.

At first it didn't make sense to him. There was

oxygen in blood. That was why it was red after leaving the lungs. The discrepancy had led him to some fascinating discoveries about vampire pulmonary function, but had ultimately gotten him no closer to his objective.

He'd tried drawing the blood and channeling it immediately into an airtight container. This most obvious solution didn't work. The disintegration occurred anyway, just at a decelerated pace. This had suggested there was another factor at work, something inherent in the corporal environment that was missing when the blood was removed from the body. He'd tried isolating samples in warmth, in cold. In suspensions of saline or human plasma.

Frustration had kept his mind burning through the permutations of his experiments. He ran more tests and tried different approaches. Retried. Walked away from the project. Came back to it.

Decades passed. And more decades.

And then personal tragedy gave him a very intimate reason to solve the problem. Following the deaths in childbirth of his *shellan* and infant son a little over two years ago, he'd become obsessed and had started from scratch.

His own need to feed was the driver.

He usually needed to drink only every six months, because his bloodline was strong. After his beautiful Evangaline's death, he'd waited as long as he could, until he had taken to his bed with the pain of the hunger. When he'd finally asked for help, he'd hated the fact that he wanted to live badly enough to drink from another female. And he'd allowed himself to consider the feeding only because he'd been convinced that it wouldn't be as it had been with Evangaline. Surely he wouldn't betray her memory by taking pleasure in someone else's blood.

There were so many whom he had helped that it

wasn't hard to find a female willing to offer herself. He'd chosen a friend who was unmated and had hoped he'd be able to keep his sadness and humiliation to himself.

It had turned out to be a nightmare. He'd held back for so long that as soon as he'd smelled blood, the predator in him had come out. He'd attacked his friend and drunk so hard, he'd had to stitch up her wrist afterward.

He'd nearly bitten her hand off.

His actions flew in the face of his notions of himself. He'd always been a gentleman, a scholar, a healer. A male not subject to the base desires of his race.

But then, he'd always been well fed.

And the terrible truth was, he'd relished the taste of that blood. The smooth, warm flow down his throat, the roaring strength that came afterward.

He'd felt pleasure. And he'd only wanted more.

The shame had made him retch. And he'd vowed never to drink of another's vein again.

It was a promise he'd kept, though as a result he'd grown weak, so weak that focusing his mind was like herding a fog bank. His starvation was a constant ache in his belly. And his body, craving sustenance that food couldn't give it, had cannibalized itself to keep him alive. He'd lost so much weight his clothes hung off of him like bags, his face turning haggard and gray.

But the state he was in had shown him the way.

The solution was obvious.

You had to feed that which was hungry.

An airtight process coupled with a sufficient quantity of human blood and he had his living cells.

Under the microscope, he watched as the vampire cells, larger and more irregularly shaped compared to the human ones, slowly consumed what he had given

86

them. The human count was decreasing in the sample, and when it was extinguished he was willing to bet the viability of the vampire component would dwindle down to nothing.

All he had to do was conduct a clinical trial. He would extract a pint from a female, mix with it an appropriate proportion of human blood, and then transfuse himself.

If everything went well, he would set up a donor and storage program. Patients would be saved. And those who chose to forgo the intimacy of drinking could live their lives in peace.

Havers looked up from the microscope, suddenly aware that he'd been staring at the cells for twenty minutes. The salad course for luncheon would be waiting on the table upstairs for him.

He removed his white coat and walked through the clinic, pausing to talk to some of his nursing staff and a couple of patients. The facility took up about six thousand square feet and was hidden deep in the earth beneath his mansion. There were three ORs, a fleet of recovery and examination rooms, the lab, his office, and a waiting area with a separate access to the street. He saw about a thousand patients a year, and made house calls for birthing and other emergencies as needed.

Although as the population had dwindled, so had his practice.

Compared to humans, vampires had tremendous advantages when it came to health. Their bodies healed fast. They were not subject to diseases such as cancer, diabetes, or HIV. But lord help you if you had an accident at high noon. No one could get to you. Vampires also died during their transitions or right afterward. And fertility was another tremendous problem. Even if conception was successful, females frequently did not survive childbirth, either from blood loss or soaring preeclampsia.

Stillborns were common, and infant mortality was through the roof.

For the sick, injured, or dying, human doctors were not a good option, even though the two species shared much of the same anatomy. If a human physician ordered a CBC on some blood from a vampire, they would find all sorts of anomalies and imagine they had something worthy of the *New England Journal of Medicine*. It was best to avoid that kind of attention.

On occasion, however, a patient would end up at a human hospital, a problem that was on the rise since the advent of 911 and fast-response ambulances. If a vampire was hurt badly enough to lose consciousness away from home, he was in danger of being picked up and taken in to a human ER. Getting him out of a facility against medical advice was always a struggle.

Havers wasn't arrogant, but he knew he was the best doctor his species had. He'd gone through Harvard Medical School twice, once in the late 1800s and then again in the 1980s. He'd stated on his application in both instances that he was disabled, and HMS had permitted him special allowances. He hadn't been able to attend the lectures because they'd taken place during the day, but his *doggen* had been allowed to take notes and hand in his examinations. Havers had read all the texts, corresponded with the professors, and even attended seminars and talks that were scheduled at night.

He'd always loved school.

When he got upstairs, he wasn't surprised to see that Marissa had not come down to the dining room. Even though luncheon was served at one A.M. every night.

He went to her rooms.

"Marissa?" he said at the door. He knocked once. "Marissa, it's time to eat."

Havers stuck his head inside. Light from the chandelier in the hall drifted in, cutting a golden slice through the blackness. The draperies were still down across the windows, and she hadn't turned any of the lamps on.

"Marissa, darling?"

"I'm not hungry."

Havers stepped through the door. He could make out her canopy bed and the small swell of her body under the covers.

"But you missed luncheon last night. As well as dinner."

"I'll come down later."

He shut his eyes, concluding that she'd been to feed the night before. Every time she saw Wrath, she would retreat into herself for days afterward.

He thought of the living cells down in his lab.

Wrath might be their race's king by birth, and he might have the purest blood of them all, but the warrior was a bastard. He seemed totally unconcerned with what he was doing to Marissa. Or perhaps he didn't even know how much his cruelty affected her.

It was hard to decide which was the worse crime.

"I've made some important progress," Havers said, going over to the bed and sitting down. "I'm going to set you free."

"From what?"

"That . . . assassin."

"Don't talk about him like that."

He gritted his teeth. "Marissa—"

"I don't want to be free of him."

"How can you say that? He treats you with no respect. I hate the idea of that brute feeding off you in some back alley—"

"We go to Darius's. He has a room there."

The idea that she was being exposed to another of

those warriors didn't make him any happier. They were all frightening, and a few were downright horrific.

He knew the Black Dagger Brotherhood was a necessary evil to defend the race, and he knew he should be grateful for their protection. Except he couldn't feel anything save dread at their existence. The fact that the world was dangerous enough, the race's enemies powerful enough, so as to mandate the likes of those warriors was tragic.

"You don't have to do this to yourself."

Marissa rolled over, turning her back to him. "Leave me."

Havers planted his hands on his knees and pushed himself to his feet. His memories of Marissa before she'd begun to service their dreadful king were so very dim. He could recall only bits and pieces of the way she'd been, and he feared the joyous, smiling young female was forever lost now.

And what was in her place? A somber, subdued shadow who floated around his house, pining for a male who treated her with no regard whatsoever.

"I hope you will reconsider luncheon," Havers said softly. "I would love to have your company."

He shut the door quietly and went down the ornate, curving staircase. The dining room table was set as he liked it, with a full complement of china, glassware, and silver. He sat down at the head of the glossy table, and one of his *doggen* came in to serve him some wine.

Looking down at the plate of Bibb lettuce before him, he forced a smile. "Karolyn, this salad is lovely."

Karolyn bowed her head, eyes glowing from his praise. "I went to a farm stand today just to find the right leaves for you."

"Well, I most certainly appreciate the effort." Havers cut into the delicate greens as she left him alone in the beautiful room.

90

He thought of his sister, curled up in her bed.

Havers was a healer by nature and profession, a male who had marked his entire life in service to others. But if Wrath were ever injured enough to come and see him, Havers would be tempted to let that monster bleed out.

Or kill him on the OR table with a slip of the scalpel.

TEN

Beth eased into consciousness slowly. It was like surfacing from a perfectly performed swan dive. There was a glow in her body, a satisfaction as she emerged from the buffered world of sleep.

Something was on her forehead.

Her eyelids flipped open. Long male fingers were moving down the bridge of her nose. They drifted across her cheek and then over to her jaw.

There was enough ambient light coming from the kitchen that she could dimly make out the man lying with her.

His concentration was fierce as he explored her face. His eyes were closed, arching brows drawn down, thick lashes against his high, regal cheekbones. He was on his side, his shoulders a mountain blocking her view to the glass door.

Good lord, he was huge. And stacked.

His upper arms were the size of her thighs. His abdomen was ribbed as if he were smuggling paint rollers under his skin. His legs were thick and corded. And his sex was as big and magnificent as the rest of him.

When he'd first come up against her naked and she'd had a chance to touch him, she'd been shocked. He had no hair on his torso or arms and legs at all. Just smooth skin over hard muscle.

She wondered why he shaved all over, even down there. Maybe he was some kind of bodybuilder.

Although why he'd go the Full Monty with a razor was a mystery.

Her memories of what had happened between them were fuzzy. She couldn't quite recall how he'd come into her apartment. Or what he'd said to her. But everything they'd done horizontally was vivid as hell.

Which made sense, since he'd given her the first orgasms she'd ever had.

The fingertips rounded her chin and came up to her lips: He brushed her lower one with his thumb.

"You are beautiful," he whispered. His subtle accent made him roll the *R* over his tongue, almost as if he were purring.

Well, that stands to reason, she thought. When he touched her, she felt beautiful.

His mouth came down on hers, but he wasn't looking for anything. The kiss was not a demand. It was closer to a thankyou.

Somewhere in the room, a cell phone went off. The ring wasn't hers.

He moved so fast she jumped. One moment he was by her side; the next he was at his jacket. He flipped open the phone.

"Yeah?" The voice that had told her she was beautiful was gone. Now he growled.

She pulled a sheet around her chest.

"We'll meet at D's. Give me ten."

He hung up the phone, put it back in the jacket, and picked up the pants he'd been wearing. The threat of re-dressing brought back some reality.

God, had she really just had sex—really, really good, mind-blowing sex—with a complete stranger?

"What's your name?" she asked.

As he pulled black leather up his thighs, she caught a terrific shot of his ass.

"Wrath." He went over to the table and got his sunglasses. When he sat down next to her, they were in place. "I've got to go. I might not get back tonight, but I'll try."

She didn't want him to leave. She liked the feel of his body taking up more than its fair share of her futon.

She reached up to him, but took her hand back. She didn't want to seem needy.

"No, touch me," he said, bending his body down, giving her all the access she could ask for.

She put her palm on his chest. His skin was warm, his heart surging in an even pump. She noticed he had a circular-shaped scar on his left pectoral.

"I need to know something, Wrath." His name felt good on her tongue even if it was an odd one. "What the hell are you doing here?"

He smiled a little, as if he liked her suspicion. "I'm here to take care of you, Elizabeth."

Well, he certainly had.

"Beth. I go by Beth."

He inclined his head. "Beth."

He stood up and reached for his shirt. He ran his hands down the front of it, as if feeling for buttons.

He wasn't going to find many, she thought. Most of them were on her floor.

"You got a wastepaper basket around here?" he asked, as if realizing the same thing.

"Over there. In the corner."

"Where?"

She stood up, keeping the sheet around her, and took the shirt. Throwing it out seemed like a lost opportunity.

When she looked at him again, he'd pulled a black holster on over his naked skin. Two daggers crisscrossed in the middle of his chest, handles down.

Oddly, as she looked at his weapons, they calmed her. The idea that there was a logical explanation to his appearance was a relief.

"Was it Butch?"

"Butch?"

"Who put you up to guard duty."

He pulled on his jacket, the heft of it widening his shoulders even more. The leather was as dark as his hair, one lapel embossed with an intricate design in black thread.

"The man who attacked you last night," he said. "He was a stranger?"

"Yes." She brought her arms around herself.

"Were the police good to you?"

"They're always good to me."

"Have they told you his name?"

She nodded. "Yeah, I couldn't believe it either. When Butch told me I thought he was joking. Billy Riddle sounds more like a Sesame Street character than a rapist, but he clearly had an MO and some practice—"

She stopped. Wrath's face had gone so vicious, she stepped back.

Jesus, if Butch was tough on perps, this guy was about two feet ahead of deadly, she thought.

But then his expression changed, as if he'd buried his emotions because he knew they scared her a little. He walked over to the bathroom and opened the door. Boo leaped up into his arms, and a low, rhythmic purring sound cut through the heavy air.

Except that sure wasn't her cat.

The throaty reverberation was coming out of the man as he held her pet in his arms. Boo ate up the attention, rubbing his head into the wide palm that was stroking him.

"I'm going to give you my cell phone number, Beth. You need to call me if you feel threatened in any way." He put the cat down and recited a bunch of digits. Made her repeat them until she had them memorized. "If I don't see you tonight, I want you to come to eight sixteen Wallace Avenue tomorrow morning. I'll explain every-thing."

And then he just looked at her.

"Come here," he said.

Her body obeyed before her mind checked in with a command to move.

As she got close to him, he put one arm around her waist and pulled her against his hard body. His lips came down hot and hungry on hers as he buried his other hand in her hair. Through his leather pants, she could feel he was ready for sex again.

And she was ready to have him.

When he lifted his head, he ran his hand leisurely over her collarbone. "This wasn't supposed to be part of it."

"Is Wrath your first or last name?"

"Both." He put a kiss on the side of her neck, sucking at her skin. She let her head fall back, and his tongue traveled up the smooth column. "Beth?"

"Hmm?"

"Don't worry about Billy Riddle. He's going to get what's coming to him."

He kissed her quickly and then walked out through the sliding glass door.

She put her hand up to her neck where he'd licked her. The skin tingled.

Beth hurried to the window and pulled up the shade.

He was already gone.

Wrath materialized in Darius's drawing room.

He hadn't expected the evening to take him where it had, and the extra layer of complication wasn't going to help the situation.

She was Darius's daughter. She was about to have her whole world turned upside down. And worse, she'd been the victim of a sexual assault the night before, for Christ's sake.

If he'd been a gentleman, he'd have left her alone.

Yeah, and when was the last time he'd lived up to his pedigree?

Rhage appeared in front of him. The vampire was wearing a long black trench coat over his leathers, and the contrast with his fair-haired beauty was no doubt a stunner. It was well-known that the brother used his looks against the opposite sex mercilessly, and that after a night of fighting, his favorite way to wind down was with a female. Or two.

If sex were food, Rhage would have been morbidly obese.

But he wasn't just a pretty face. The warrior was the best fighter the brotherhood had, the strongest, the quickest, the surest. Born with an overload of physical power, he preferred to meet *lessers* bare-handed, saving the daggers only for the end. Maintained that it was the only way to get any job satisfaction. Otherwise, the fights didn't last long enough.

Of all the brothers, Hollywood was the one the young males in the species talked about, worshiped, wanted to be. Except that was because his fan club only saw the glossy surface and the smooth moves.

Rhage was cursed. Literally. He'd gotten himself in some serious trouble right after his transition. And the Scribe Virgin, that mystical force of nature who oversaw the species from the Fade, had given him one hell of a punishment. Two hundred years of aversion therapy that kicked in whenever he didn't keep himself calm.

You had to feel sorry for the poor bastard.

"How we doing tonight?" Rhage asked.

Wrath closed his eyes briefly. A blurry image of Beth's body arching, caught as he'd looked up from between her legs, sliced through him. As he pictured himself tasting her again, his hands curled into fists, his knuckles cracking.

I'm hungry, he thought.

"I'm good to go," he said.

"Hold up. What's that?" Rhage demanded.

"What's what?"

"That expression on your face. And Christ, where's your shirt?"

"Shut up."

"What the . . . I'll be damned." Rhage laughed. "You got some grind tonight, didn't you?"

Beth was not a grind. No way, and not only because she was Darius's daughter.

"Zip it, Rhage. I'm not in the mood."

"Hey, I'm the last one to criticize. But I gotta ask, was she any good? Because you don't look particularly relaxed, my brother. Maybe I need to teach her a few things and then have her give you a try again—"

Wrath calmly introduced Rhage's back to the wall, almost taking out a mirror with the male's shoulders. "You will shut the shut up or you will be six inches shorter. Your pick, Hollywood."

His brother was just playing, but there was something unholy about taking that experience with Beth and getting it anywhere near Rhage's sex life.

And maybe Wrath was feeling just a little possessive.

"Have we made our choice?" he drawled.

"I'm feeling you." The other vampire grinned, his teeth a flash of white in his striking face. "But come on, lighten up. You don't usually waste time with the females, and I'm just glad to know you got off, that's all."

Wrath let go.

"Although Jesus, she couldn't have been all that—"

Wrath unsheathed a dagger and buried the thing into the wall an inch from Rhage's skull. The sound of steel punching through plaster had a nice ring to it, he thought.

"You do not push me on this one. Got it?"

The brother nodded slowly as the dagger handle vibrated next to his ear. "Ah, yeah. I'm thinking we're clear on that."

Tohrment's voice cut through the tension. "Whoa! Rhage, you been poppin' shit again?"

Wrath stayed still for one more moment, just to make sure the message had gotten through. Then he yanked the knife out of the wall and stepped back, prowling around the room as the other brothers arrived.

When Vishous came in, Wrath took the warrior aside. "I want you to do me a favor."

"Name it."

"Human male. Billy Riddle. I want you to work your computer magic. I need to know where he lives."

V stroked his goatee. "He in town?"

"I think so."

"Consider it done, my lord."

When they were all there, even Zsadist, who'd graced them with being on time, Wrath got the ball rolling.

"What do we have from Strauss's phone, V?"

Vishous whipped off his Sox cap and dragged a hand through his dark hair. He spoke as he repositioned the hat. "Our boy liked to hang with muscleheads, military wannabes, and Jackie Chan fans. We've got calls to Gold's Gym, a paint-ball arena, two martial-arts places. Oh, and he liked cars. There was a mechanics shop in the log, too."

"Any personals?"

"Couple. One to a landline that was disconnected two days ago. The others were cellular, untraceable, not local. I tried them all repeatedly and no one picked up. Ain't caller ID a bitch?"

"You check his priors online?"

"Yeah. Typical juvie shit with a violent edge. He fits the *lesser* profile perfectly."

"What about his home?" Wrath looked over his shoulder at the twins.

99

Phury glanced at his brother and then did all the talking. "Three-room apartment over the river. Lived alone. Didn't have a lot of shit. Couple of guns under the bed. Some silver ammo. Kevlar vest. Porn collection he obviously wasn't using anymore."

"Did you grab his jar?"

"Yeah. It's back at my place. I'll take it to the tomb later tonight."

"Good." Wrath regarded the group. "We split up. Case the businesses. I want to get inside those buildings. We're looking for their center of ops in this area."

He paired up the brothers, taking Vishous with him. He told the twins to go to Gold's and the paintball arena. Gave Tohr and Rhage the martial-arts joints. He and Vishous were going to scope out the mechanics shop, and he hoped they'd get lucky.

Because if someone were going to wire a bomb to a car, wouldn't a hydraulic lift be handy?

Before they all left, Hollywood came over, looking uncharacteristically serious.

"Wrath, man, you know I can be an asshole," Rhage said. "Didn't mean to offend. Not going there again."

Wrath smiled. The thing with Rhage was, he had piss-poor impulse control. Which explained both his fly mouth and his sex addiction.

And the problem was bad enough when he was himself. Forget about the minute the curse flipped his psycho switch and the beast came roaring to life.

"I'm serious, man," the vampire said.

Wrath clapped his brother on the shoulder. On the whole, though, the SOB was a total keeper. "Forgiven, forgotten."

"Feel free to hammer me anytime."

"Believe me, I do."

* * *

Mr. X drove to an alley downtown that was unlit and open to streets at both ends. After parking the minivan face out behind a Dumpster, he threw Cherry Pie over his shoulder and walked twenty yards away from the car. She moaned a little as she bounced on his back, as if she didn't want her high disturbed by movement.

He laid her out on the ground, and she didn't fight him as he slit her throat. He watched for a moment as her glossy blood seeped from her neck. In the darkness it looked like Quaker State motor oil. He put his finger down, getting some on the tip. His nose detected all manner of disease, and he wondered if she'd known she had an advanced case of hep C. He figured he was doing her a favor, sparing her an unpleasant, creeping death.

Not that killing her would have bothered him had she been perfectly healthy.

He wiped his finger on the edge of her skirt and then moved away to a pile of debris. An old mattress was just the ticket. Propping it up against the brick, he settled into the juncture, unbothered by the stinky, sweaty smell of the thing. He took out his dart gun and waited.

Fresh blood brought out civilian vampires like crows to roadkill.

And sure enough, not long thereafter a figure appeared at the end of the alley. It looked left and right and then rushed forward. Mr. X knew that what approached had to be who he was after. Cherry was well concealed in the darkness. There was nothing to draw anyone in her direction except for the subtle scent of her blood, something human noses could never have picked up.

The young male was greedy in his thirst, and he fell upon Cherry like someone had laid out a buffet for him. Busy drinking, he was taken by surprise when the first dart popped out of the gun and went into his shoulder. His immediate instinct was to protect his food, so he hauled Cherry's body behind some mangled trash cans.

When the second dart hit him, he wheeled around and leaped up, eyes trained on the mattress.

Mr. X tensed, but the male came forward with more aggression than competence. His body was disorganized in its movements, suggesting he was still learning how to control his limbs after his transition.

Two more darts didn't slow him down. Clearly the Demosedan, a horse tranquilizer, wasn't enough to do the job. Forced to engage the male in a fight, Mr. X stunned him easily by kicking him in the head. The male let out a howl of pain as he went down to the dirty asphalt.

The commotion attracted attention.

Fortunately, it was only two *lessers*, not curious humans or, even more annoying, the police. The *lessers* stopped at the end of the alley and, after quick consultation, moved in to investigate.

Mr. X cursed. He was not prepared to reveal himself or what he was doing. He needed to work the kinks out of the information-gathering strategy before he came forward with it and assigned his *lessers* roles. After all, a leader should never delegate that which he had not done before and done well.

There was also a matter of self-interest. There was no telling who among the slayers might try to go around him to the Omega, either copping the idea as his own or bitching about preliminary failures. God knew the Omega was always receptive to initiative and new directions. And would have benefited from some Ritalin when it came to loyalty.

Even more to the point, the Omega's version of a pink slip was quick and horrific. As Mr. X's former superior had learned three nights ago.

Mr. X plucked out the darts from the body. He would have preferred killing the vampire, but there wasn't enough time. Leaving the male still moaning on the ground, Mr. X sprinted down the alley, sticking to the wall. He kept the minivan's headlights off until he'd slid into traffic.

ELEVEN

Beth's alarm clock went off, and she slapped it into silence.

The buzzing was redundant. She'd been up for at least an hour, her mind humming like a lawn mower. With the dawn's arrival the hot night's mystery had faded, and she was forced to face what she had done.

Unprotected sex with a total stranger was one hell of a wake-up call.

What had she been thinking? She'd never done that before. She'd always been safe. Thank God she was on the pill to regulate her sporadic periods, but as for the other implications, her stomach rolled.

When she saw him again she'd ask him if he was clean, and pray the answer was the one she wanted to hear. As well as honest.

Maybe if she'd had more dating practice, she would have had some protection ready. But when was the last time she'd slept with anyone? A long time. Longer than the shelf life of a box of condoms.

The extended dry spell in her sex life was as much from lack of interest as any kind of morals thing. Men just weren't that high on her list of priorities. They ranked somewhere down around getting her teeth cleaned and having her car serviced. And she didn't have a car anymore.

She'd often wondered if there was something wrong with her, especially as she watched couples walk by on the street hand in hand. Most people her age were dating wildly, trying to find altar material. Not her. She just hadn't had any burning desire to be with a man, and had even considered the possibility that she was a lesbian. Trouble was, she wasn't attracted to women.

So last night had been a revelation.

She stretched, a delicious tightness coiled in her thighs. Closing her eyes, she felt him inside of her, his thickness surging and retreating until that final moment when his body had convulsed into hers with a powerful rush, his arms crushing her against him.

Her body arched involuntarily, the fantasy strong enough to have her throbbing between her legs. Echoes of those orgasms made her bite her lip.

With a groan she got to her feet and headed for the bathroom. When she saw the shirt he'd ripped off his chest in the wastebasket, she picked it up and held it to her nose. The black fabric smelled like him.

The throbbing got worse.

How did he and Butch know each other?

Was he on the force? She'd never seen him before, but there were a number of them she didn't know.

Vice, she thought. He must be a vice cop. Or maybe a SWAT team leader.

Because he was definitely the kind of man who looked for trouble and served asses up on a plate when he found it.

Feeling as if she were sixteen, she shoved the shirt under her pillow. And then saw the bra he'd taken off her on the floor. Good lord, the front had been cut apart, sliced by something sharp.

Weird.

After a quick shower, and a faster breakfast of two oatmeal cookies, a handful of Pepperidge Farm goldfish, and a juice box, she walked down to the office. She'd been in her cube staring at her screen saver for a half hour when her phone rang. It was José.

"We had another busy night," he said, yawning.

"Bomb?"

"Nope. Dead body. Prostitute was found with her throat cut over on Third and Trade. If you come down to the station you can see the pictures, read the reports. Off the record, of course."

She was out on the street two minutes after she'd hung up the phone. She figured she'd hit the station first and then head over to the Wallace Avenue address.

She couldn't pretend she wasn't aching to see her midnight visitor again.

As she walked to the precinct house, the morning sun was unmercifully bright, and she dug into her purse for her shades. When they weren't enough to cut the sting, she shielded her eyes with her hand. It was a relief to get inside the cool, dim police station.

José wasn't in his office, but she found Butch coming out of his.

He smiled at her dryly, the corners of his hazel eyes wrinkling. "We have to stop meeting like this."

"Heard you have a new case."

"I'm sure you have."

"Care to comment, Detective?"

"We issued a statement this morning."

"Which no doubt said absolutely nothing. Come on, can't you spare a few words for me?"

"Not if we're on the record."

"How about off?"

He took a piece of gum out of his pocket and methodically unwrapped it, folding the pale slice into his mouth and biting down. She seemed to remember him smoking at some point, but hadn't seen him lighting up recently. Which probably explained all that Wrigley's.

"Off the record, O'Neal," she prompted. "I swear."

He nodded his head over his shoulder. "We need a closed door then."

His office was about the size of her cubicle at the

paper, but at least it had a door and a window. His furniture was not as good as hers, though. His desk was an old wooden one that looked as if it had been used as a carpenter's workbench. There were hunks out of the top, and the varnish was so scratched it absorbed the fluorescent light as if thirsty.

He tossed a file at her before sitting down. "She was found behind a bunch of trash cans. Most of her blood ended up in the sewer, but the coroner thinks he found traces of heroin in her system. She'd had sex that evening, but that's not exactly news."

"Oh, my God, this is Mary," Beth said, looking at a gruesome picture and sinking into a chair.

"Twenty-one years old." Butch cursed under his breath. "What a fucking waste."

"I know her."

"From the station?"

"Growing up. We were in the same foster home for a little while. Afterward, I'd run into her sometimes. Usually here."

Mary Mulcahy had been a beautiful little girl. She'd been in the home with Beth for only about a year before she'd been sent back to her birth mother. Two years later she was back in state custody after having been left alone for a week at the age of seven. She'd said she'd lived on raw flour after the rest of the food had run out.

"I'd heard you'd been in the system," Butch said, getting thoughtful as he looked at her. "Mind if I ask why?"

"Why do you think? No parents." She closed the file and slid it onto the desk. "Did you find a weapon?"

His eyes narrowed, but not unkindly. He seemed to be debating whether to take her lead and let the subject drop.

"Weapon?" she prompted.

"Another throwing star. Had traces of blood on it,

107

but not hers. We also found some powdered residue in two different places, as if someone had lit off flares and put them on the ground. Hard to imagine the killer'd want to draw attention to the body, though."

"You think what happened to Mary and the car bomb are related?"

He shrugged, a careless lift of his broad shoulders. "Maybe. But if someone was really doing a payback on Big Daddy, they'd have hit higher up the food chain than her. They'd have gone after the pimp himself."

Beth closed her eyes, envisioning Mary as a five-year-old, a headless Barbie doll in a tattered dress tucked under her arm.

"Then again," Butch said, "maybe this is just getting started."

She heard his chair move and looked up as he came around the desk to her.

"You got any plans for dinner tonight?" he asked.

"Dinner?"

"Yeah. You and me."

Hard-ass was asking her out? Again?

Beth stood, wanting to be on an equal footing with him. "Ah, yes—no, I mean, thanks, but no."

Even if they didn't have a professional relationship of sorts, she had other things in mind. Imagine that. Keeping her calendar open just in case the man in leather wanted to see her tonight as well as this morning.

Damn, one good lay and she thought they had a thing going? She needed to get real.

Butch smiled cynically. "Someday I'm going to figure out why you don't like me."

"I do like you. You don't take shit from anyone, and even though I don't approve of your methods, I can't pretend I didn't like the fact that you broke Billy Riddle's nose again."

The harsh planes of Butch's face softened. As his eyes

bored into hers, she thought she must be crazy for not being attracted to him.

"And thanks for sending your friend over last night," she said, putting her bag up on her shoulder. "Although I have to admit, he scared the hell out of me at first."

Right before the man had showed her exactly what the highest and best use for the human body was.

Butch frowned. "Friend?"

"You know. The one who looks like some kind of Goth nightmare. Tell me, he's vice, isn't he?"

"What the hell are you talking about? I didn't send anyone over to your place."

All the blood drained out of her head.

And the growing suspicion and alarm on Butch's face kept her from trying to jog his memory.

She headed for the door. "My mistake."

Butch grabbed her arm. "Who the hell was at your apartment last night?"

She wished she knew.

"No one. Like I said, my mistake. I'll see you later."

She rushed through the lobby, her heart beating triple time. As she burst outside, she winced when the sun hit her face.

One thing was clear: There was no way she was going to meet that man this morning, even though 816 Wallace Avenue was in the best part of the city and it was broad daylight.

By four that afternoon, Wrath was about to explode.

He hadn't been able to get back to Beth's the night before.

And she hadn't shown this morning.

Her failure to come to him meant one of two things: Something had happened to her or she was blowing him off.

He checked the braille clock with his fingertips. Sundown was still hours away.

Goddamned summer days. Too long. Way too long.

He stalked to the bathroom, splashed his face with water, and braced his arms on the marble counter. In the glow from the candle set next to the sink, he stared at himself, seeing nothing more than an indistinct rush of black hair, two smudgy eyebrows, and the outline of his face.

He was exhausted. He hadn't slept all day, and the night before had been a train wreck.

Except for the part with Beth. That had been . . .

He cursed and toweled off.

God, what the hell was wrong with him? Being inside of that female was the worst of all the shit that had gone down last night. Courtesy of that stunning little interlude, his mind was wandering, his body was in a perpetual state of arousal, and his mood was in the crapper.

At least the latter was SOP for him.

Man, last night had been a total disaster.

After leaving the brothers, he and Vishous had gone across town to check out the mechanics shop. It was closed up tight as a tick, and after scoping the outside and breaking in, they'd determined it wasn't used as a center. The decrepit building was too small above ground for one thing, and there was no hidden basement that they could find. Also, the neighborhood wasn't prime. There were a couple of all-night diners around, one of which was frequented by the cops. Too much exposure.

He and Vishous were heading back to Darius's, via a quick detour through Screamer's to satisfy V's craving for Grey Goose, when they walked into a problem.

That was when things had gone from bad into the FUBAR zip code.

In an alley, a civilian vampire was gravely wounded,

with two *lessers* about to finish the job on him. Killing the *lessers* had taken some time because they were both well experienced, and the other vampire was dead when the fighting was over.

The young male had been toyed with cruelly, his body a pincushion of shallow stabs. Going by the raw patches on his knees and the gravel in his palms, he'd tried to drag himself away a number of times. There'd been fresh human blood around his mouth and the smell of it in the air, too, but they couldn't stick around to check out the female he'd bitten.

Company had been coming.

Right after the *lessers* had poofed to their royal reward, the sound of cop sirens had broken out, an acoustic rash that meant someone had called 911 after having heard the fighting or seen the flashes of light. They'd barely had time to get gone with the corpse in Vishous's Escalade.

Back at Darius's, V had searched the body. In the male's wallet there had been a slip of paper with the old language's characters on it. Name, address, age. He'd been six months out from his transition. So damn young.

An hour before dawn, they'd taken the body to the very edge of town, to a good-looking house set way back in the woods. An older civilian couple had answered the door, and their terror at finding two warriors on the other side had smelled like burning garbage to Wrath. When they'd confirmed that they had a son, Vishous had gone back to the car and picked up the remains. The father had burst from the doorway, going for his boy, taking him from Vishous's arms. Wrath had caught the mother as she'd crumpled.

The fact that the death had been avenged had calmed the father a little. But it hadn't felt like enough. Not to Wrath.

He would see all *lessers* dead before he could rest.

Wrath closed his eyes, listening to the beat of Jay-Z's *The Black Album*, trying to let go of the night before.

A rhythmic knocking broke through the music, and he willed the door open. "What's up, Fritz?"

The butler came in carrying a silver tray. "I took the liberty of preparing a repast for you, master."

Fritz put the food down on the low table in front of the couch. As he lifted the top off a covered dish, Wrath caught a whiff of herbed chicken.

Come to think of it, he was hungry.

He went over and sat down, picking up a heavy silver fork. He eyed the flatware. "Man, Darius liked expensive shit, didn't he?"

"Oh, yes, master. Only the best for my *princeps*."

The butler hovered as Wrath focused on getting some of the meat off the bone with the utensils. Fine motor skills were just not his bag, and he ended up picking the leg off the plate.

"Do you like the chicken, master?"

Wrath nodded as he chewed. "You're damned handy with the stove."

"I'm so glad you've decided to stay here."

"Not for long. But don't worry, you'll have someone to look after." Wrath pushed the fork into what looked like mashed potatoes. It was rice, and the stuff scattered. He cursed and tried to marshal some on the tines with his fore-finger. "And she'll be a hell of a lot easier to live with than I am."

"I rather like looking after you. And master, I won't prepare the rice again. I'll also make sure your meat is cut up. I didn't think."

Wrath wiped his mouth with a linen napkin. "Fritz, don't waste your time trying to please me."

There was a soft laugh. "Darius was so very right about you, master."

"That I'm a miserable son of a bitch? Yeah, he was a

perceptive one, all right." Wrath chased a piece of broccoli around with the fork. Damn it, he hated eating, especially if someone was watching him. "Never could figure out why he wanted me to come stay here so badly. No one could be that starved for company."

"It was for you."

Wrath narrowed his eyes behind his sunglasses. "Really."

"He worried that you were so alone. Living by yourself. No real *shellan*, no *doggen*. He used to say that your isolation was a self-imposed punishment."

"Well, it's not." Wrath's voice sliced through the butler's gentle tone. "And if you want to stay here, you'll keep the psych theories to yourself, got it?"

Fritz jerked as if he'd been hit. He bent at the waist and started backing out of the room. "My apologies, master. It was grossly inappropriate of me to address you as I did."

The door closed quietly.

Wrath leaned back against the sofa, Darius's fork gripped in his hand.

Ah, Christ. That damn *doggen* was enough to drive a saint crazy.

And he was not lonely. Never had been.

Vengeance was one hell of a roommate.

Mr. X eyed the two students sparring with each other. They were well matched in size, both eighteen years old and built strong, but he knew which one was going to win.

Sure enough, a side kick came out fast and hard, putting the receiver on his back.

Mr. X called an end to the match and said nothing more as the victor reached out and helped the loser struggle to his feet. The show of courtesy was irritating, and he felt like punishing them both.

The first code of the society was clear: That which you put on the ground, you kicked until it ceased to move. It was just that simple.

Still, this was class, not the real world. And the parents who were letting their sons dabble in violence would have had something to say if their precious children came home fit to be buried.

As the two students bowed to him, the loser's face was brilliant red, and not just from exertion. Mr. X let the class stare, knowing that shame and embarrassment were important parts of the corrective process.

He nodded at the victor.

"Fine job. Next time you bring him down faster though, right?" He turned to the loser. He passed his eyes from the guy's head to his feet, noting the heaving breaths, the tremble in the legs. "You know where to go."

The loser blinked rapidly as he walked over to the glass wall that looked out to the lobby. As required, he stood facing the clear panels, head up high so everyone who entered the building could see his face. If he brushed the tears off his cheeks, he would have to repeat the discipline during the next session.

Mr. X separated the class and began to put them through their exercises. He watched them, correcting stances and arm positions, but his mind was on other things.

Last night had been less than perfect. Far less.

Back home, his police scanner had informed him when the prostitute's body had been found sometime after three A.M. There had been no mention of the vampire. Perhaps the *lessers* had taken the civilian away to toy with him.

It was a shame things hadn't gone the way he'd hoped, and he wanted to get back out into the field. Using a newly slain human female as bait was going to work fine. But the tranquilizer darts needed to be calibrated better. He'd started with a relatively low dose, concerned about killing the civilian before he could work him over. Clearly the strength of the drug needed to be increased.

Tonight was a bust, though.

Mr. X eyed the loser.

This evening was all about recruiting. The ranks needed to be filled out a little following the disintegration of that new recruit two nights ago.

Back centuries ago, when there were many more vampires, the society had had hundreds of members, spread far and wide over the European continent as well as in the fledgling settlements in North America. Now that the vampire population had dwindled, however, so had the ranks of the society. It was a matter of practicality. A bored, inactive *lesser* was a bad thing. Chosen specifically for their capacity for violence, their murderous impulses couldn't be put on ice just because there weren't enough targets to go around. Quite a number of them had had to be put down for killing other *lessers* in competition for superiority in the ranks, an aggressive response more likely to occur if there was too little work. Or just as bad, they'd started taking out humans for sport.

The former was a disgrace and an inconvenience. The latter was unacceptable. It wasn't that the Omega was concerned with human fatalities. Quite the contrary. But using discretion, moving in the shadows, killing swiftly and returning to the darkness, these were the tenets of slayers. Human attention was bad news, and nothing got the Homo sapiens stirred up more than a bunch of dead people.

Which was another reason why new recruits were tricky. They tended to have more hatred than focus. Seasoning was critical so that the secret nature of the aeons-old war between vampires and the society could be preserved.

Still, their ranks needed to be filled.

He eyed the loser and smiled, looking forward to the evening.

Shortly before seven o'clock, Mr. X drove out to the suburbs, easily locating 3461 Pillar Street. He put the Hummer in park and waited, passing the time by memorizing the split-level's details. It was typical Middle America. Twenty-four hundred square feet, sitting smack-dab in the center of a tiny lot with one big tree. Neighbors were close enough to be able to read the writing on the kids' cereal boxes in the morning and the labels on the adults' domestic beer cans at night.

Happy, clean living. At least from the outside.

The screen door swung open, and the loser from this afternoon's class bounded out as if he were getting free of a sinking ship. Mom followed, lingering on the front step and regarding the SUV in front of her house as though it were a bomb ready to go off.

Mr. X put down the window and waved. She returned the greeting after a moment.

Loser leaped into the Hummer, eyes shining with greed as he looked over the leather seats and the dials on the dashboard.

"Evening," Mr. X said as he hit the gas.

The kid fumbled to get his hands up and bow his head. "Sensei."

Mr. X smiled. "Glad you could make yourself available."

"Yeah, well, my mother is a pain in my ass." Loser was trying to be cool, punching the curse words hard.

"You shouldn't talk about her like that."

Loser had a moment's confusion as he was forced to recalibrate his tough-guy act. "Ah, she wants me home by eleven. It's a weeknight, and I gotta go to work in the morning."

"We'll make sure you're back by then."

"Where are we going?"

"To the other side of town. There's someone I want you to meet."

A little later Mr. X pulled into a long, curving driveway that wound among spotlit specimen trees and ancient-looking marble sculptures. There were boxwood topiaries on the grounds, too, standing like decorations on a green marzipan cake. A camel, an elephant, a bear. The clipping had been done by an expert, so there was no question as to what each one was.

Talk about upkeep, Mr. X thought.

"Wow." Loser gave his neck a workout looking left and right. "What's this? A park? Look, at that! It's a lion. You know, I think I want to be a vet. I think that would be cool. You know, saving animals."

Loser had been in the car for less than twenty minutes, and Mr. X was ready to see the last of him. The guy was like lint in food: an irritation that made you want to spit.

And not only because he said *you know* constantly.

They came around a turn, and a great brick mansion was revealed.

Billy Riddle was out front, leaning against a white column. His blue jeans hung low on his hips, flashing the waistband of his underwear, and he was working a set of keys in his hand, whipping them around on a string. He straightened when he caught sight of the Hummer, a smile pulling at the bandage on his nose.

Loser shifted in the seat like he'd been set up.

Billy headed for the front passenger door, moving his muscular body with ease. When he saw Loser sitting there, he glowered, nailing the other guy with a vicious stare. Loser unclipped the seat belt and reached for the handle.

"No," Mr. X said. "Billy will sit behind you."

Loser settled back against the seat, picking his lip.

When Loser didn't vacate shotgun, Billy yanked open

the rear door and slid in. He met Mr. X's eyes in the mirror, and the hostility changed to respect.

"Sensei."

"Billy, how are you this evening?"

"Good."

"Fine, fine. Do me a favor and pull your pants up."

Billy jacked his waistband as his eyes shifted to the back of Loser's head. He looked as if he wanted to drill a hole in it, and going by Loser's twitchy fingers, the other guy knew it.

Mr. X smiled.

Chemistry is everything, he thought.

TWELVE

Beth leaned back in her chair, stretching her arms out. Her computer screen glowed.

Boy, the Internet was handy.

According to the title search she'd performed online, 816 Wallace Avenue was owned by a man named Fritz Perlmutter. He'd bought the property in 1978 for a little over $200,000. When she'd Googled the Perlmutter name, she'd found a number of people with *F* as a first initial, but none of them lived in Caldwell. After checking some of the government databases and coming up with nothing worth a damn, she had Tony do some hacking.

It turned out Fritz was a clean-living, law-abiding kind of guy. His credit report sparkled. He'd never had any trouble with the IRS or the police. Never been married, either. And he was a member of the private client group of the local bank, which meant he had plenty of money. But that was about all Tony could find.

Doing the math, she figured the fine and upstanding Mr. Perimutter must be in his seventies.

Why the hell would someone like him hang out with her midnight marauder?

Maybe the address wasn't legit.

Now there'd be a shocker. Guy dressed in black leather and dripping with weapons giving out false info? You don't say.

Still, 816 Wallace and Fritz Perlmutter was all she had to go on.

Going through the *Caldwell Courier Journal*'s archives,

she'd found a couple of articles on the house. The mansion was on the National Register of Historic Places, as a fantastic example of the Federal style, and there were some stories and op-eds about the work that had been done on it immediately after Mr. Perlmutter had taken possession. Evidently the local historical association had been dying to get inside the house for years to see what had changed, but Mr. Perlmutter had declined all requests. In the letters to the editor, the simmering frustration of the history buffs had been mixed with grudging approval at the accuracy of the exterior restorations.

As she reread an op-ed, Beth popped a Tums in her mouth and crunched it into a powder that filled the creases in her molars. Her stomach was sour again. And she was hungry. Great combination.

Maybe it was frustration. Essentially, she knew nothing more than she had when she started.

And the cell phone number the man had given her? Untraceable.

In the information vacuum, she was even more determined to stay away from Wallace Avenue. And feeling the echo of a need to go to confession.

She checked the time. Almost seven o'clock.

Given her hunger, she decided to go eat. Better to skip Our Lady and take nourishment of the physical variety.

Leaning to one side, she looked around the wall of her cubicle. Tony was already gone.

She really didn't want to be alone.

On a crazy impulse she picked up the phone and dialed the station. "Ricky? It's Beth. Is Detective O'Neal around? Okay, thanks. No, no message. No, I— Please don't page him. It's nothing important."

Just as well. Hard-ass was not really the uncomplicated company she was looking for.

She stared down at her watch, getting lost in the second hand's crawl around the dial. The evening hours stretched ahead of her like an obstacle course, the hours to be dodged and surmounted.

Hopefully with speed.

Maybe she'd grab some food and go see a movie afterward. Anything to delay going back to her apartment. Come to think of it, she should probably stay at a motel somewhere.

In the event that man came looking for her again.

She'd just logged off her computer when her phone rang. She picked it up on the second ring.

"Heard you were looking for me."

Butch O'Neal's voice was a gravel pit, she thought. In a good way.

"Um. Yeah." She pushed her hair back over her shoulder. "You still free for dinner?"

His laugh was a low rumble. "I'll be in front of the paper in fifteen."

He hung up before she could slide in a properly nonchalant, this-is-just-about-food comment.

After sundown Wrath walked into the kitchen, carrying the silver tray with the remnants of his meal on it. Typical of Darius, everything was the best of the best here, too. Industrial stainless-steel appliances. Plenty of cupboards and granite counter space. Lots of windows.

Too many lights.

Fritz was at the sink, scrubbing at something. He looked over his shoulder. "Master, you didn't need to bring that back."

"Yeah, I did." Wrath put the tray down on a counter and leaned into his arms.

Fritz shut off the water. "Was there something you needed?"

Well, for starters, he'd like to not be such a dick-head.

"Fritz, your job here is solid. Just wanted you to know that."

"Thank you, master." The butler's voice was very quiet. "I don't know what I would do if I didn't have someone to take care of. And I think of this as my home."

"It is. For as long as you want it to be."

Wrath turned and headed for the door. He was almost out of the room when Fritz spoke up.

"This is your home, too, master."

He shook his head. "Already got a place to sleep. Don't need another."

Wrath walked into the hall, feeling particularly ferocious. Man, Beth had better be alive and well. Or God help whoever had hurt her.

And if she'd decided to avoid him? That didn't matter. Her body was about to need something only he could provide her. So sooner or later she would come around. Or she would die.

He thought of the soft skin of her neck. Felt the sensation of his tongue stroking over the vein that ran up from her heart.

His fangs elongated as if she were before him. As if he could sink his teeth into her and drink.

Wrath closed his eyes as his body began to shake. His stomach, full with food, turned into a bottomless, achy pit.

He tried to remember the last time he'd fed. It had been a while, but surely not that long ago?

He forced himself to calm down. Get control. It was like trying to slow down a train with a hand brake, but eventually a cooling stream of sanity replaced the whacked-out, blood-lust spins.

As he came back to reality he felt uneasy, his instincts crying out for airtime.

That female was dangerous to him. If she could affect him like this without even being in the damn room, she might just be his *pyrocant*.

His detonator, so to speak. The express-lane EZ Pass to his self-destruction.

Wrath dragged a hand through his hair. How goddamned ironic that he wanted her like no other female.

But maybe it wasn't irony. Maybe that was precisely how the *pyrocant* system worked. The urge to cozy up to what could annihilate you ensured the damn thing got a chance to go to work on your ass.

After all, what kind of fun would it be if you could easily avoid your inner hand grenade?

Damn him. He needed to get Beth off his plate of responsibilities. Fast. As soon as she was through her transition, he was going to put her in the hands of an appropriate male. A civilian.

In gory flashback, he pictured that young male's bloody, beaten body.

How the hell would a civilian keep her safe?

He didn't know the answer to that one. But what other option was there? He wasn't going to keep her.

Maybe he could give her to one of his brothers.

Yeah, and who would he pick out of that bunch? Rhage? Who'd just add her to his fuck pool, or worse, eat her by mistake? V with all his problems?

Zsadist?

And did he really think he could handle knowing one of his warriors was doing her?

Not fucking likely.

God, he was tired.

Vishous materialized in front of him. The vampire

was running without his baseball cap tonight, and Wrath could dimly make out the complex markings around his left eye.

"Found Billy Riddle." V lit up one of his hand-rolled cigarettes, his gloved fingers steady. When he exhaled, the fragrance of Turkish tobacco perfumed the air. "He was arrested for sexual assault forty-eight hours ago. Lives with his daddy, who happens to be a U.S. senator."

"High-profile background."

"Hard to get higher. And I took the liberty of doing some research. Billy boy's been in and out of trouble as a juvenile. Violent stuff. Sexual shit. Got to imagine daddy's campaign manager loves the fact that the guy's hit eighteen. Everything Billy pulls now is public record."

"You nail a street address?"

"Yeah." Vishous grinned. "You gonna put a hurt on the guy?"

"Like you read about."

"So let's go."

Wrath shook his head. "I'll meet you and the rest of the brothers back here later tonight. I've got to go some-where first."

He could feel V's eyes sharpen, the vampire's fierce intellect churning over the situation. Among the brothers, Vishous had the most raw brainpower, but he paid for the privilege.

Man, Wrath sure had his own demons, and they were no walk in the park, but he wouldn't have wanted Vishous's cross to bear. Seeing what had yet to come was a terrible burden.

V drew on the hand-rolled and exhaled slowly. "I dreamed of you last night."

Wrath stiffened. He'd been kind of waiting for this. "I don't want to know, brother. I really don't."

The vampire nodded. "Just remember something, okay?"

"Shoot."

"Two guards tortured will happily fight each other."

THIRTEEN

"Dinner was great," Beth said as Butch pulled up in front of her building.

He thoroughly agreed. She was smart and funny and sit-forward-in-your-chair beautiful. And if he stepped out of line, she never failed to knock him back where he should be.

So she was also incredibly sexy.

He put the car in park, but didn't turn the engine off. He figured killing the ignition would make it look like he wanted to be invited in.

Which he did, of course. But he didn't want her to feel awkward if that wasn't where she saw things heading.

Well, wasn't he turning into a nice guy.

"You sound surprised you enjoyed yourself," he said.

"I am, a little."

Butch ran his eyes over her, starting with her knees that were just barely showing under the hem of her skirt. From the dashboard's glow, he could make out the lovely lines of her body, her long, exquisite neck, her perfect, perfect lips. He wanted to kiss her, here in this dim light, in the front seat of his unmarked, just like they were teenagers.

Then he wanted to go inside her apartment with her. And not come out again until morning.

"So thanks," she said, flashing him a smile and reaching for the door.

"Wait."

He moved quickly, so that she wouldn't have time to

think and neither would he. He took her face in his hands and put his mouth on hers.

Wrath materialized in the courtyard behind Beth's apartment and felt a prickling across his skin.

She was close by. But there were no lights on in her place.

Following a hunch, he walked around the side of the building. There was a nondescript American sedan parked in front. She was inside of it.

Wrath went down to the sidewalk and, as if he were just taking a stroll in the shadows, passed by the car.

He stopped dead.

His useless eyes worked well enough to tell him that some guy was all over her. As if the potent sexual craving of the male human wouldn't have tipped him off.

For God's sake, he could smell the bastard's lust through the sedan's glass and steel.

Wrath lunged forward. His first instinct was to rip the car door off and kill whoever had his hands on her. Just pull the guy out and tear his throat open.

But at the last second he spun away and forced himself back into the darkness.

Son of a bitch. He was literally seeing red, he was so worked up.

That some other male was kissing those lips, feeling that body under his hands . . .

A low growl vibrated through his chest and out his mouth.

She's mine.

He cursed. Yeah, and in what parallel universe was he living in? She was his temporary responsibility, not his *shellan*. She could be with whomever she wished. Wherever. Whenever.

But God, the idea that she might actually like what the guy was doing to her, that she might prefer the taste of the human's kiss, was enough to make Wrath's temples pound.

Welcome to the wonderful world of jealousy, he thought. *For the price of admission, you get a splitting headache, a nearly irresistible urge to commit murder, and an inferiority complex.*

Yippee.

Man, he couldn't wait to get his life back. The second she was through her transition, he was going to get the hell out of town. And pretend he'd never, ever met Darius's daughter.

Butch O'Neal was one hell of a kisser.

His lips were firm, but deliciously soft. Not coming on too strong, but letting her know he was prepared to take her to bed and show her he meant business.

And he smelled good up close, a mix of aftershave and fresh laundry. She reached up with her hands. His shoulders were wide and strong under her palms, his body drawn in a tight arch toward hers. He was all coiled power, and in that moment she wanted to be attracted to him. She honestly did.

Except she just didn't feel that sweet rush of desperation, that wild hunger. Not like she had the night before with . . .

Now was a hell of a time to be thinking about that other man.

When Butch pulled back, his eyes were hooded. "I'm not doing it for you, am I?"

She laughed softly. Leave it to Hard-ass. Blunt as always.

"You know how to kiss, O'Neal, I'll give you that. So it's not for lack of technique."

He returned to his side of the seat and shook his head. "Thanks a hell of a lot."

But he didn't seem terribly hurt.

And now that she was thinking more clearly, she was glad there was no spark on her end. If she had liked him, if she had wanted to be with him, he would have broken her heart. She was sure of it. In ten years, if he made it that long, he was going to implode from the stress, the ugliness, the sorrow of his job. It was eating him alive already. Every year he was wound a little tighter, and no one, but no one, was going to pull him out of that tailspin.

"Careful there, Randall," he said. "It's bad enough knowing I don't turn you on. But that pity on your face is a real ass burner."

"Sorry." She smiled at him.

"Mind if I ask you something?"

"Sure."

"What's up with you and men? Do you, ah, do you like them? Us, I mean?"

She laughed, thinking of what she'd done last night with that stranger. The question of her sexual orientation had certainly been laid to rest. Buried good and hard.

"Yeah, I like men."

"Did someone do a number on you? You know, hurt you?"

Beth shook her head. "I just like to keep to myself."

He looked down at the steering wheel, running his hand around the circumference. "That's a damn shame. Because you're terrific. You really are." He cleared his throat as if he'd made himself feel uncomfortable.

Sheepish. Good lord, Hard-ass was actually sheepish.

On impulse, she leaned over and kissed him on the cheek. "You're pretty fantastic yourself."

"Yeah. I know." He shot her his trademark mocking grin. "Now get your butt inside that building. It's late."

Butch watched as Beth crossed in front of his headlights, her hair flowing over her shoulders.

129

She was the real deal, he thought. A genuinely good woman.

And man, she knew exactly what his drill was. That look of sadness in her eyes just now meant she saw the early grave that was waiting for him.

So it was just as well there was no chemistry for her. Otherwise he might try to talk her into falling in love with him just so he didn't go to hell all by his lonesome.

He put the car in gear, but kept his foot on the brake as she went up the steps to the front lobby. She had her hand on the door and was shooting him a wave when something moved in the shadows beside the building.

He flipped the engine back into park.

There was a man dressed in black heading around to the rear.

Butch got out of the car and jogged silently across the side lawn.

FOURTEEN

Wrath's sole focus was getting to Beth. So it wasn't until he was halfway across the courtyard that he heard the human behind him.

"Police! Halt!"

And then there was that all-too-familiar sound of a gun being cocked at him.

"Let me see your hands!"

Wrath caught the man's scent and smiled. Lust had been replaced with aggression, and the fighting urge was as strong as the sexual one had been. The guy was full of juice tonight.

"I said, halt and hands!"

Wrath stopped and reached into his jacket for one of the stars. Cop or not, he was going to drop the human, put a nice little slice through his artery.

But then Beth threw open the slider.

He smelled her instantly, and wouldn't you know it, he got a hard-on.

"Hands!"

"What's going on?" Beth demanded.

"Get back in the house," the human barked. "Hands, asshole! Or I'll put a window in the back of your skull."

By this time the cop was no more than ten feet away and closing fast. Wrath lifted his palms. He wasn't about to kill in front of Beth. Besides, that gun was going to be at point-blank range in another three seconds. And not even he could survive a hit that tight.

"O'Neal—"

"Beth, get the *fuck* out of here!"

A heavy hand clamped down on Wrath's shoulder. He let the cop push him against the building.

"You want to tell me what you're doing waltzing around this place?" the human ordered.

"Out for a walk," Wrath said. "And you?"

The cop grabbed one and then the other of Wrath's arms and pulled them back. The cuffs went on quickly. The guy was an old pro with the metal.

Wrath looked over at Beth. From what he could tell, she had her arms linked tightly across her chest. Fear thickened the air around her, turning it into a blanket that covered her from head to foot.

Isn't this going well, he thought. She was scared to death of him again.

"Do not look at her," the cop said, pushing Wrath's face toward the wall. "What's your name?"

"Wrath," Beth answered. "He told me it was Wrath."

The human actually snarled at her. "Do you have a hearing problem, sweetheart? Get out of here."

"I want to know who he is, too."

"I'll phone in a fucking report tomorrow morning, how's that?"

Wrath growled. He couldn't deny that getting her inside was a damn good idea. But he did not appreciate the way the cop was talking to her.

The human reached inside Wrath's jacket and started pulling out weapons. Three throwing stars, a switch-blade, a handgun, a length of chain.

"Jesus Christ," the cop muttered as he dropped the steel links on the ground with the rest of the load. "You got some ID? Or wasn't there enough room in here for a wallet, considering you're carrying about thirty pounds of concealed weapons?"

When the cop found a thick wad of cash, he cursed again. "Am I going to find drugs, too, or have you sold out for tonight?"

Wrath allowed himself to be spun around and slammed back against the bricks. While his two daggers were stripped from their holster, he stared down at the cop, thinking how much he was going to enjoy ripping that thick throat open with his teeth. He leaned forward, leading with his head. He couldn't help it.

"O'Neal, be careful!" Beth said, as if she'd read his mind.

The cop pressed his gun muzzle into Wrath's neck. "So how about a name?"

"Are you arresting me?"

"Yeah. I am."

"For what?"

"Let me think. Trespassing. Concealed weapons. Do you have a permit for that handgun? I'm betting no. Oh, and thanks to all these throwing stars, I'm thinking murder, too. Yeah, that should do it."

"Murder?" Beth whispered.

"Your name?" the cop demanded, glaring up at him.

Wrath smiled tightly. "You must be clairvoyant."

"'Scuse me?"

"About the murder charge." Wrath laughed softly and dropped his voice. "You ever been inside a body bag, Officer?"

Rage, pure and vibrant, came out of the man's pores. "Don't threaten me."

"I'm not."

The left hook came through the air fast as a baseball, and Wrath did nothing to avoid it. The cop's meaty fist caught the side of his jaw and kicked his head back. A sunburst of pain exploded in his face.

"Butch! Stop it!"

Beth ran forward, as if she intended to put herself between them, but the cop held her off, strong-arming her.

"Jesus, you're a pain in the ass! You want to get hurt?" the human said, pushing her away.

Wrath spat out blood. "He's right. Go inside."

'Cause this was going to get ugly.

Thanks to catching a blurry eyeful of that makeout session, he didn't like the cop to begin with. But if the guy addressed Beth one more time in that tone of voice, Wrath was going to show the man's front teeth the joy of liberation. And *then* he was going to kill the son of a bitch.

"Go on, Beth," he said.

"Shut up!" the cop yelled at him.

"You going to hit me again if I don't?"

The cop crawled up into his face. "No, I'm going to shoot you."

"Fine with me. I like bullet wounds." Wrath lowered his voice. "Just not in front of her."

"Fuck you."

But the cop covered the weapons and cash by throwing his coat over them. Then he grabbed Wrath's arm and started walking.

Beth felt as though she were going to be sick as Butch led Wrath away.

Aggression was flowing between the men like battery acid, and even though Wrath was handcuffed and being held at gunpoint, she wasn't exactly sure Butch was safe. She had a feeling that Wrath was letting himself get taken into custody.

But Butch must know that, she thought. Otherwise he would have holstered his weapon instead of having its muzzle pressed up against that temple.

She knew Butch was tough on criminals, but was he crazy enough to kill one?

Going by the deadly expression on his face, she had

to think that was a big *yes*. And he might just get away with it. Violent ends came to those who lived hard lives, and Wrath was clearly not a white-collar law abider. If he turned up with a bullet in his head in some back alley, or floating facedown in the river, who would be surprised?

Giving in to a shrill instinct, she ran around the side of the building.

Butch was marching toward his car as if he were carrying an unstable load, and she rushed to catch up with them.

"Wait. I need to ask him a question."

"You want to know his shoe size or something?" Butch snapped.

"Fourteen," Wrath drawled.

"I'll remember that at Christmas, asshole."

Beth leaped in front of them so both men had to stop or run her over. She stared up into Wrath's face. "Why did you come to find me?"

She could have sworn that his gaze softened behind his sunglasses. "I don't want it to come out like this."

Butch shoved her away with a heavy hand. "I have an idea. Why don't you let me do my job?"

"Don't touch her," Wrath snarled.

"Yeah, I'm going to listen to you." Butch yanked the other man forward.

When they got to the car, Butch wrenched open the rear door and pushed Wrath's towering weight down.

"Who are you!" she yelled.

Wrath looked at her, his body becoming perfectly still in spite of the fact that Butch was all over him.

"Your father sent me," he said distinctly. And then he got into the backseat.

Beth stopped breathing.

She was dimly aware of Butch slamming the door and running around to the driver's side.

"Wait!" she called out.

But the car was already in gear, tires leaving strips of rubber on the asphalt.

FIFTEEN

Butch picked up his handset and asked Dispatch to get someone over to the courtyard immediately to pick up the weapons and cash that were under his coat. As he drove, he kept one eye on the road and the other in the rearview mirror. The suspect stared back, a slight smile on his evil-looking face.

Jesus, the guy was huge. He took up most of the backseat, his head bent at an angle so it didn't smack the roof as they sped over potholes.

Butch couldn't wait to get him out of the damn car.

Less than five minutes later, he pulled off Trade Street and into the parking lot of the station, driving up as close to the back entrance as possible. He got out and opened the rear door.

"Let's play nice, shall we?" he said as he grabbed the guy's arm.

The man rose to his feet. Butch gave him a yank.

But the suspect stepped backward, away from the station.

"Wrong way." Butch threw his anchor out, digging his heels into the pavement and pulling hard.

The suspect was inexorable. He just kept backing up, dragging Butch along with him.

"You think I won't shoot you?" Butch demanded as he reached for his gun.

And then it was all over.

Butch had never seen anyone move that fast. One second the guy had his arms behind his back; the next, the handcuffs were on the ground.

And with total economy of movement, Butch was disarmed, put in a blistering choke hold, and hauled into the shadows.

The darkness swallowed them. As Butch fought back, he realized he was in the thin alley between the station and the office building next door. It was only about five feet wide, but some sixty feet long. And it was unlit. With no windows.

When Butch was spun around and slammed into the bricks, what little breath he'd been able to steal got kicked out of his lungs in a rush. Inconceivably, he was lifted off the ground, the man holding him by the neck with only one hand.

"You should have stayed out of it, Officer," the man said in a deep, accented growl. "You should have gone along on your way and let her come to me."

Butch clawed at the iron hold. The massive hand locked around his throat was squeezing the life right out of him. He gagged, desperate for air. His vision went checkerboard, consciousness slipping out of his grasp.

He knew without a doubt that there'd be no walking away from this one. He was going to be carried out of the alley inside of a bag. Just like the man had promised.

A minute later he stopped resisting altogether, his arms dropping and hanging loose. He wanted to fight. He had the will to fight. But no longer the strength.

And as for death? He was okay with it. He was going to die in the line of duty, albeit like an idiot, because he hadn't asked for backup. Still, it was better and quicker than ending up in a hospital bed with some nasty, slow growing disease. And more honorable than shooting himself. Which was something Butch had contemplated once or twice before.

With his last lick of life, he forced his eyes to focus

on the man's face. The expression staring back at him was one of total control.

The guy's done this before, Butch thought. *And he's very comfortable with murder.*

God, Beth.

What the hell would a man like this do to Beth?

Wrath felt the cop's body go limp. He was still alive, but barely.

The human's total lack of fear was remarkable. The cop had been pissed to get jumped, and he'd fought back admirably, but he'd never been scared. And now that the Fade was upon him, he was resigned to his death. Maybe almost relieved by it.

Damn. Wrath could imagine feeling the same way.

And it was a shame to kill someone who was able to die as a warrior would. Without fear or hesitation. Such males were few and far between, be they vampires or humans.

The cop's mouth started moving. He was trying to speak. Wrath leaned down.

"Don't . . . hurt . . . her."

Wrath found himself answering, "I'm here to save her."

"No!" A voice rang out down the alley.

Wrath turned his head. Beth was running toward them.

"Let him go!"

He loosened his grip on the cop's throat. He wasn't going to kill the guy in front of her. He needed her to trust him more than he wanted to help the cop meet his maker.

As Beth skidded to a halt, Wrath dropped his hand, and the human fell to the ground. Tortured gasping sounds and hoarse gagging rang out in the shadows.

Beth knelt over the heaving policeman, glaring upward. "You almost killed him!"

Wrath cursed, knowing he had to get the hell out of there. Other cops were bound to show up.

He looked down to the other end of the alley.

"Where do you think you're going!" Her voice was scissor-sharp with anger.

"You want me to stick around so I can get arrested again?"

"You deserve to get thrown in jail!"

With a lurch the cop tried to stand up, but his legs buckled. Still, he pushed Beth's hands away when she reached for him.

Wrath needed to find a dark corner so he could dematerialize. If nearly killing someone had shaken Beth, pulling the disappearing act in front of her would only seal the deal on freaking her out.

He turned away. Began to stride off. He didn't like the idea of leaving her, but what else could he do? If he got his ass shot and killed, who would look after her? And he couldn't let himself get thrown in jail. Those cells had steel bars, which meant when dawn came, he couldn't dematerialize to safety. Faced with those two outcomes, if a bunch of cops tried to apprehend him right now, he'd have to slaughter them all.

And then what would she think of him?

"Stop right there!" she yelled.

He kept going, and her footfalls sounded out as she came running.

"I said, stop!" She grabbed onto his arm and pulled hard.

He glared at her, frustrated by the way things had gone down. Courtesy of his song and dance with her buddy, she was terrified of him, and that was going to make taking care of her a bitch. He doubted he had time to bring her around again so she would willingly go anywhere with him. Which meant he might even have to resort to taking her against her will when her transition hit.

And that wasn't going to be fun for either one of them.

As her scent drifted up into his nose, he knew she was perilously close to the change.

Maybe he needed to take her with him now.

Wrath glanced around. He couldn't very well throw her over his shoulder here, just fifteen yards from the back of the police station. Not in full view of that damned cop.

No, he was going to have to come right before dawn and abduct her. And then he'd chain her in Darius's chamber if he had to, because it was either that or she was going to die.

"Why the hell did you lie!" she yelled. "You didn't know my father."

"Yes, I did."

"Liar," she spat. "You're a killer and a liar."

"At least you got the first part right."

Her eyes widened, horror dawning on her face. "Those throwing stars . . . in your pockets. You murdered Mary. Didn't you?"

He frowned. "I haven't killed any women."

"So I'm right about the second part, too."

Wrath eyed the cop, who was still down for the count, but gaining ground.

Damn it, he thought. What if Beth didn't have until dawn? What if she took off and he couldn't find her?

He lowered his voice. "You've been really hungry lately, haven't you?"

She jerked back. "What?"

"Hungry, but not gaining any weight. And tired. So very tired. Your eyes have been stinging, too, especially in the daytime, right?" He leaned forward. "You're looking at raw meat and wondering what it tastes like. Your teeth, the upper ones in front, have been sore. Your joints ache, and your skin feels tight. And it's getting tighter."

She blinked, mouth falling open.

Behind her the cop lurched to his feet, wobbled, and did an ass plant back on the ground. Wrath spoke faster.

"You feel like you don't belong, don't you? Like everyone else is moving at a different, slower speed. You think you're abnormal, separate, apart. Restless. You sense that something is coming, something monumental, but you don't know what it is or how to stop it. You lie awake, afraid of your dreams, lost in familiar surroundings." He paused. "You've had little or no sex drive whatsoever, but men find you incredibly attractive. Those orgasms I gave you last night were the first ones you've ever had."

It was all the things he could remember about existing in the human world before his transition.

She stared at him. Dumbfounded.

"If you want to know what the hell's happening to you, you need to come with me now. You're about to get sick, Beth. And I'm the only one who can help you."

She took a step backward. Looked at the cop, who seemed to be considering the merits of lying down.

Wrath held up his hands. "I'm not going to hurt you. I promise. If I were going to kill you, I could have done it last night in ten different ways, right?"

Her head turned back to him, and he closed his eyes as he sensed her remembering exactly what he had done to her. Her desire was a sweet saturation in his nostrils before the scent was quickly cut off.

"You were going to kill Butch just now."

Actually, he wasn't so sure about that. A good opponent was hard to find.

"I didn't."

"You could have."

"Does it really matter? He's still breathing."

"Only because I came."

Wrath growled, playing the best card he had. "I'll take you to your father's house."

Her eyes popped and then narrowed with suspicion.

142

She glanced over at the cop again. Now he was back up on his feet, one hand braced against the wall, head hanging as if it were too heavy for his neck.

"My father, huh?" Her voice was dripping with disbelief. And just enough curiosity so that he knew he had her.

"We're out of time here, Beth."

There was a long silence.

The cop lifted his head and looked down the alley.

In another minute or two the guy was going to try to make another arrest. His determination was palpable.

"I'm leaving now," Wrath said. "Come with me."

Her grip tightened on her purse. "Just so we're clear, I do not trust you."

He nodded. "Why would you?"

"And those orgasms weren't my first."

"Then why were you so surprised to be having them?" he said softly.

"Hurry," she muttered, turning away from the officer. "We can get a taxi out on Trade. I didn't ask the one that got me here to wait."

SIXTEEN

As she sped down the alley, Beth knew she was gambling with her life. There was a serious chance she was being played. By a killer.

Except how did he know all those things she was feeling?

Before she turned the corner, she looked back at Butch. He was reaching out to her, one hand extended. She couldn't see his face for the shadows, but his desperate yearning crossed the distance between them. She hesitated, losing the rhythm of her steps.

Wrath took her arm. "Beth. Come on."

Heaven help her, she started running again.

The minute they got out to Trade, she hailed a passing cab. Thank God, it stopped on a dime. They jumped in, and Wrath gave out an address a couple blocks over from the one he'd told her on Wallace Avenue. Obviously as an evasion technique.

He must have a lot of those, she thought.

As the cab took off, she felt him look across the seat at her.

"That cop," he said. "Does he mean something to you?"

She grabbed her cell phone from her purse and dialed the front desk down at the station.

"I asked you a question." Wrath's tone was sharp.

"Go to hell." When Ricky's voice came through, she took a deep breath. "Is José there?"

It didn't take more than a minute for the other detective to be found, and he was already out the door to find

Butch as she ended the call. José hadn't asked many questions, but she knew they were going to come later. And just how was she going to explain to him why she'd run off with a suspect?

That made her an accomplice for aiding and abetting, didn't it?

Beth put her phone back in her purse. Her hands were shaking, and she felt light-headed. She just couldn't catch her breath either, even though the cab was air-conditioned and blissfully cool. She cracked the window. The breeze was hot and damp as it blew through her hair.

What had she done? To her body last night. To her life right now.

What was next? Setting her apartment on fire?

She hated that Wrath had dangled the one carrot she couldn't resist in front of her. That he was obviously a criminal. That he terrified her, but she still got hot thinking about how he'd kissed her.

And she despised the fact that he knew those were her first orgasms.

"Drop us off here," Wrath told the driver ten minutes later.

Beth paid with a twenty-dollar bill, thinking they were lucky she had the cash on her. Wrath's money, that big bank roll of the stuff, was on the ground in her back-yard. So it wasn't like he could cover the fare.

Was she really going home with this man?

The taxi left, and they walked down a perfectly kept sidewalk in a well-maintained, ritzy neighborhood. It was an absurd switch in scenery. From the violence in that back alley, to rolling lawns and flower beds.

She was willing to bet the people who lived in these houses had never run from the police.

She glanced back at Wrath, who was slightly behind her. He was scanning around them as if he were looking to get jumped, although how he could see anything with those black glasses on, she had no idea. She just didn't get why he wore them. Aside from compromising his vision, those flashy lenses were a serious identifying feature. If anyone clapped their eyes on him, they'd be able to describe him accurately in a heartbeat.

Not that the long black hair and the sheer size of him wouldn't have done the job well enough.

She turned her head away. The sound of his boots hitting the concrete behind her was like fists thudding on a solid door.

"So the cop." Wrath's voice was close, deep. "Is he your lover?"

Beth almost laughed. God, he sounded jealous.

"I'm not going to answer that."

"Why?"

"Because I don't have to. I don't know you, I don't owe you."

"You got to know me pretty damn well last night," he said in a low growl. "And I got to know you *very* well."

Let's not go there, she thought, getting instantly wet between her legs. God, the things that man could do with his tongue.

She crossed her arms over her chest and stared at a well-kept Colonial. Lights glowed in various windows, making it look inviting and somehow familiar. Probably because homey-looking places were universal. And universally appealing.

She could use a week in one right about now.

"Last night was a mistake," she said.

"Didn't feel that way to me."

"Then you felt wrong. You felt *all* wrong."

He reached for her before she even sensed he'd moved. She was walking along and then she was in his arms. One of his hands clamped onto the base of her neck.

The other pulled her hips tight against him. His erection was a thick rope on her belly.

She closed her eyes. Every inch of her skin came alive, her temperature soaring. She hated the reaction to him, but like the man, she had no control over it.

She waited for his mouth to come down on hers, except he didn't kiss her. He bent his lips to her ear instead.

"Don't trust me. Don't like me. I could give a shit. But don't you *ever* lie to me." He took a deep breath, as if he were drawing her into him. "I can smell the sex coming off you right now. I could take you down on this sidewalk and be up that skirt of yours in a heartbeat. And you wouldn't fight me, would you?"

No, she probably wouldn't.

Because she was an *idiot*. Who evidently had a death wish.

His lips brushed the side of her neck. And then his tongue licked her skin lightly. "Now, we can be civilized and wait until we get home. Or we can get down to it right here. Either way, I'm dying to come inside of you again, and you're not going to say no."

Beth gripped his shoulders through his leather jacket. She was supposed to push him away, but she didn't. She brought him closer, arching her breasts to his chest.

A sound of male desperation broke free of him, halfway between a groan of satisfaction and a dark plea.

Ha, she thought, regaining some power.

She broke their contact with grim satisfaction. "The only thing that makes this god-awful situation remotely bearable is the fact that you want me more."

She kicked her chin up and started walking. She could actually feel his eyes on her body as he followed, as if he were touching her with his hands.

"You're right," he said. "I would kill to have you."

Beth wheeled around, pointing a finger at him. "So

147

that was it. You saw Butch and me kissing in the car. Didn't you?"

Wrath cocked an eyebrow at her. Smiled tightly. Didn't answer.

"Is that why you attacked him?"

"I was merely resisting arrest."

"Yeah, that's what it looked like," she muttered. "So did you? Did you see him kiss me?"

Wrath closed the space between their bodies, menace flowing out of him. "Yeah, I saw. And I *hated* that he was touching you. Does knowing that get you off? Do you want to nail me a good one and tell me he's a better lover than I am? It would be a lie, but it would still hurt like hell."

"Why do you care so much?" she demanded. "You and I spent one night together. Not even! It was a couple of hours."

He clamped his jaw shut. She knew his teeth were grinding by the way the hollows under his cheekbones moved. And she was glad he was wearing the sunglasses. She had a feeling his eyes would have scared the hell out of her.

When a car passed by on the street, she remembered he was a fugitive from the police, and technically so was she. What the hell were they doing, arguing on the sidewalk . . . like lovers?

"Look, Wrath, I don't want to be arrested tonight." Like she'd ever thought those words would come out of her mouth? "Let's just keep going. Before someone finds us."

She turned, but he took her arm in a sure grip.

"You don't know this yet," he said grimly. "But you are *mine*."

For a split second, she swayed toward him.

But then she shook her head. She put her hands up to her face, trying to shut him out.

148

She felt marked, and the crazy thing was, she didn't really mind. Because she wanted him, too.

Which was not going to win her any prizes in the mental health department.

God, she needed to take another shot at the last couple of days. If she could only go back forty-eight hours, back to when she was sitting at her desk with Dick doing his leering-boss routine.

She'd do two things differently. She'd order a cab instead of walking home, so she never met up with Billy Riddle. And the instant she went into her apartment, she'd pack some clothes and go to a motel. So when this leather-clad, drug-lord lothario came looking for her she wouldn't have been found.

She just wanted her pathetic, boring life back. And how ridiculous was that? Considering she'd thought that getting out of it was the only way to save herself only a little while ago.

"Beth." His voice had lost most of its edge. "Look at me."

She shook her head, only to have her hands peeled back from her eyes.

"You're going to be okay."

"Yeah, right. There's probably a warrant being issued for my arrest at this very moment. I'm running around in the dark with the likes of you. And this is all happening because I'm so desperate to know my dead parents, I'm willing to put my life in danger on the *remote* chance I could learn something about them. I'm telling you, it's one hell of trip from where I am to 'okay.'"

His fingertip stroked down her cheek. "I'm not going to hurt you. I'm not going to let anything hurt you."

She rubbed her forehead, wondering whether she was ever going to feel normal again. "God, I wish you'd never shown up at my back door. I wish I'd never seen your face."

He dropped his hand.

"We're almost there," he said tersely.

Butch gave up trying to stand and sank to the ground.

He sat there for a while, just breathing in and out. He couldn't seem to move.

It wasn't because his head hurt, although it did. And it wasn't because his legs felt weak, although they did.

He was ashamed.

Getting beaten by a bigger man wasn't the problem, although his ego had certainly taken one on the chin.

No, it was the knowledge that he'd screwed up and endangered a young woman's life. When he'd called about the weapons pickup, he should have had two officers waiting for him at the door to the station. He'd known that suspect was especially dangerous, but he'd been sure he could handle it himself.

Yeah, well, he'd handled jack shit. He'd had his ass kicked. And now Beth was in the company of a killer.

God only knew what would become of her.

Butch closed his eyes and put his chin down on his knee. His throat was killing him, but it was his head that he was really worried about. The damn thing wasn't working right. His thoughts were incoherent, his cognitive processes shot to hell. Maybe he'd gone without oxygen long enough to get brain-fry.

He tried to pull it together, but only managed to sink deeper into the fog.

And then, because his masochistic side had terrific timing, the past reared its thorny skull.

Out of the messy jumble of images clanging around his mind, one popped forward that brought tears to his eyes. A young girl, no more than fifteen. Getting into an unfamiliar car. Waving at him from the window as she disappeared down their street.

His older sister. Janie.

Her body had been found in the woods behind the local baseball field the following morning. She'd been raped, beaten, and strangled. Not in that order.

After she'd been abducted, Butch had stopped sleeping through the night. Two decades later, he still hadn't picked up the habit again.

He thought of Beth, looking over her shoulder as she'd run away with the suspect. The fact she'd disappeared with that killer was the only thing that got Butch to plant his feet on the ground and drag his body toward the station.

"Yo! O'Neal!" José came pounding down the alley. "What happened to you?"

"We need to get out an APB." Was that his voice? It sounded hoarse, like he'd been to a football game and screamed for two hours. "White male, six-six, two seventy. Dressed in black leather, wearing sunglasses, shoulder-length dark hair." Butch threw out a hand, steadying himself against the building. "Suspect not armed. Only because I stripped him. He'll be restocked within the hour, no doubt."

When he stepped forward, he swayed.

"Jesus." José grabbed his arm, holding him up.

Butch tried not to lean on the guy, but he needed the help. He couldn't make his legs move right.

"And a white female." His voice cracked. "Five-nine, long black hair. Wearing a blue skirt and a white button-down." He paused. "Beth."

"I know. She called." José's face tightened. "I didn't ask for details. From the sound of her voice, she wasn't about to give me any."

Butch's knees wobbled.

"Whoa, Detective." José hoisted him up. "We're going to take this slow."

The instant they came through the station's back door, Butch weaved. "I need to go look for her."

"Let's just chill on this bench."

"No . . ."

José loosened his hold, and Butch went down like a piano.

Just as half the freaking precinct came up in a rush. The fleet of concerned guys in dark blue and badges made him feel pathetic.

"I'm fine," he snapped. Then he had to put his head between his knees.

How could he have let this happen?

If Beth turned up dead in the morning . . .

"Detective?" José got down on his haunches, putting his face in Butch's line of sight. "We've called an ambulance."

"Don't need one. Is the APB out?"

"Yeah, Ricky's doing it right now."

Butch brought his head up. Slowly.

"Man, what happened to your neck?" José breathed.

"It was used to hold my body off the ground." He swallowed a couple of times. "Did the weapons get picked up from the address I called in?"

"Yeah. We got 'em and the cash. Who the hell is this guy?"

"I have no fucking clue."

SEVENTEEN

Wrath walked up the front steps of Darius's house. The door swung open before he could reach the brass handle.

Fritz was on the other side. "Master, I didn't know you were—"

The *doggen* froze as he saw Beth.

Yeah, you know who she is, Wrath thought. *But let's be cool.* She was jumpy enough as it was.

"Fritz, I'd like you to meet Beth Randall." The butler kept staring. "You going to let us in?"

Fritz bent down low and bowed his head. "Of course, master. Ms. Randall, it is an honor to finally meet you in person."

Beth seemed taken aback, but managed a smile as the *doggen* straightened and moved from the doorway.

When she stuck her hand out, Fritz gasped and looked to Wrath for permission.

"Go ahead," Wrath muttered as he shut the front door. He never could understand the strict traditions of the *doggens*.

Fritz reached out reverently, clasping her palm in both of his and dropping his forehead to their joined hands. Words in the old language were spoken in a quiet rush.

Beth was clearly astonished. But then she had no way of knowing that by offering her hand to him, she had paid him the highest honor of his species. As the daughter of a *princeps*, she was a high-bred aristocrat in their world.

Fritz was going to be glowing for days.

"We'll be in my chamber," Wrath said when the contact was broken.

The *doggen* hesitated. "Master, Rhage is here. He had a . . . little accident."

Wrath cursed. "Where is he?"

"In the downstairs bathroom."

"Needle and thread?"

"In there with him."

"Who's Rhage?" Beth asked as they started down the hall.

Wrath paused by the drawing room. "You wait here."

But she followed when he walked on.

He turned around, pointing over her shoulder. "That wasn't a request."

"And I'm not waiting anywhere."

"Damn it, do as I say."

"No." The word was spoken without heat. She defied him with total calmness and strength of purpose.

As if he were no more an obstacle in her path than a throw rug.

"Jesus *Christ*. Fine, lose your dinner."

As he stalked down to the bathroom, he could smell the blood all the way out in the hall. This was a nasty one, and he really wished Beth weren't so hell-bent on seeing for herself.

He pushed the door open, and Rhage looked up. The vampire's arm was hanging over the sink. There was blood everywhere, a dark pool on the floor, a little pond on the counter.

"Rhage, man, what's up?"

"Sliced and diced. *Lesser* got me a good one, right through a vein, down to the bone. I'm leaking like a sieve."

In a blurry composite, Wrath caught the movement of Rhage's hand going down to his shoulder and up into the air. Down to his shoulder, up into the air.

"Did you get him?"

"Hell, yeah."

"Oh . . . my . . . God," Beth said. "Oh, dear God. Is he stitching—"

"Hey, who's the cutie?" Rhage said, pausing on the up-stroke.

There was a strangled sound, and Wrath moved, blocking Beth's view with his body.

"Need help?" he asked, even though both he and his brother knew he had nothing to offer. He couldn't see well enough to close his own wounds, much less someone else's. The fact that he had to rely on his brothers or Fritz to tend to him was a weakness he despised.

"No, thanks." Rhage laughed. "I'm a good little sewer, as you know firsthand. Now who's your friend?"

"Beth Randall, this is Rhage. An associate of mine. Rhage, this is Beth, and she doesn't do movie stars, got it?"

"Loud and clear." Rhage leaned to one side, trying to see around Wrath. "Nice to meet you, Beth."

"Are you sure you don't want to go to a hospital?" she said weakly.

"Nah. This one's just messy. When you can use your large intestine as a belt loop, that's when you hit the pros."

A croaking sound came out of Beth's mouth.

"I'm going to take her downstairs," Wrath said.

"Oh, yes, please," she murmured. "I'd really like to go down . . . stairs."

He put his arm around her, and he knew how affected she was by the way she melted into his body. It felt so good to have her relying on him for strength.

Too good, actually.

"You cool?" Wrath said to his brother.

"Damn straight. I'm leaving as soon as this is done. Got three jars to collect."

"Nice tally."

"Would have been more if this little gift hadn't come

by air mail. No wonder you like those stars so much."
Rhage moved his hand around, as if he were tying a
knot. "You should know Tohr and the twins are"—he
grabbed a pair of scissors off the counter and snipped
the thread—"continuing our work from last night. They
should be back in a couple hours to report in, just as
you asked."

"Tell them to knock first."

Rhage nodded and had the sense not to follow up
with any commentary.

As Wrath led Beth down the hall, he found himself
stroking her shoulder. Her back. Then he curled his hand
around her waist, his fingers sinking into her soft flesh.
She fit well against him, her head coming up to his
chest, resting on his pectoral as they moved together.

Too comfortable. Too familiar, he thought. Way too
good.

He held on to her anyway.

And even as he did, he wished he could take back
what he'd said to her on that sidewalk. About her being
his.

Because that wasn't true. He didn't want to take her
as his *shellan*. He'd been worked up, jealous. Picturing
that cop's hands all over her. Pissed off that he hadn't
killed the human after all. The words had slipped out.

Ah, hell. The female did something to his brain.
Somehow managed to unplug his well-developed self-
control and put him in touch with his inner fricking
psycho.

It was a connection he wanted to avoid.

After all, fits of insanity were Rhage's specialty.

And the brothers didn't need another hair-trigger
loose cannon in the group.

Beth closed her eyes and leaned against Wrath, trying
to shut out the picture of that gaping wound. The effort

was like blocking sunlight with her hands: Parts of the image kept seeping through. All that bright red, shiny blood, the raw, dark pink muscle, the shocking white of bone. And that needle. Puncturing the skin, pulling the flesh out to a point, breaking through with the black thread—

She opened her eyes.

Open was better.

No matter what the man said, that was no little scrape he was dealing with. He needed to go to the hospital. And she would have argued the point more strenuously, except she'd been a little busy trying to convince her pad thai to stay put.

Besides, that guy seemed pretty darned competent at fixing himself up.

He was also one hell of a looker. Even though the gore was distracting, she couldn't help but notice his dazzling face and body. Short blond hair, iridescent blue eyes, a face that belonged on the big screen. He'd been dressed as Wrath was, in black leather pants and shit-kickers, but his shirt had been cast aside. The muscles of his upper torso had stood out in sharp relief beneath the overhead light, an impressive display of strength. And the multicolored tattoo of a dragon that covered his whole back was a total stunner.

But then, it wasn't as if Wrath were going to hang out with some scrawny tax accountant-looking nancy.

Drug dealers. They were clearly drug dealers. Guns, weapons, huge amounts of cash. And who else got into a knife fight and played doctor on themselves?

She recalled that the man had borne the same circular-shaped scar on his chest that Wrath did.

They must be in a gang, she thought. Or the mob.

She suddenly needed some space, and Wrath let her go as they walked into a lemon-colored room. Her feet slowed. The place looked like a museum or something

157

she'd expect to see in *Architectural Digest*. Thick, pale drapery framed wide windows, rich oil paintings gleamed from the walls, objets d'art were tastefully arranged. She glanced down at the carpet. The thing was probably worth more than her apartment.

Maybe they didn't just deal in crack, X, and heroin, she thought. Maybe they worked the antiques black market as well.

Now there was a combo you didn't run across very often.

"This is nice," she murmured, fingering an antique box. "Very nice."

She eyed Wrath when she got no response. He was standing just inside the room, arms folded across his pecs, at the ready even though he was home.

But then, when did he ever relax? she thought.

"Have you always been a collector?" she asked, trying to buy some time so her nerves could settle. She walked over to a Hudson River School painting. Good lord, it was a Thomas Cole. Probably worth hundreds of thousands. "This is beautiful."

She glanced over her shoulder. He was focused on her, paying no attention to the painting. And there was no expression of pride or ownership on his face.

Which was not the way someone looked when their things were admired.

"This is not your house," she said.

"Your father lived here."

Yeah, sure.

But what the hell. She'd come this far. She might as well play along.

"Then he obviously had plenty of money. What did he do for a living?"

Wrath walked across the room, toward an exquisite, full-length portrait of what looked like a king.

"Come with me."

"What? You want me to walk through that wall—"

He pushed one side of the painting, and it swiveled outward to reveal a dark corridor.

"Oh," she said.

He gestured with his arm. "After you."

Beth approached carefully. The glow of gas lanterns flickered over black stone. She leaned in, seeing a set of stairs that disappeared around a turn far below.

"What's down there?"

"A place where we can talk."

"Why don't we stay up here?"

"Because you're going to want to do this privately. And my brothers are likely to show up soon."

"Your brothers?"

"Yes."

"How many of them are there?"

"Five, now. And you're stalling. Go on. Nothing will hurt you down there, I promise."

Uh-huh. Sure.

But she put her foot over the gilded edge of the frame. And stepped into the darkness.

EIGHTEEN

Beth took a deep breath and hesitantly put her hands out to the stone walls. The air wasn't musty; there was no creepy coating of moisture on anything; it was just very, very dark. She went down the stairs slowly, feeling her way. The lanterns were more like fireflies, lights unto themselves rather than illumination for someone using the stairwell.

And then she reached the bottom. To the right there was an open door, and she caught the warm glow of candlelight.

The room was just like the passageway: black walled, dimly lit, but clean. The candles were soothing as they flickered at their posts. While she put her purse down on the coffee table, she wondered if Wrath slept here.

God knew the bed was big enough for him.

And were those black satin sheets?

She figured he'd taken a lot of women down to this lair of his. And it didn't take a genius to figure out what happened once he closed the door.

A lock clicked into place, and her heart seized up.

"So about my father," she said briskly.

Wrath walked past her, taking off his jacket. He was wearing a muscle shirt under it, and she couldn't ignore the raw power of his arms, his biceps and triceps rippling as he put the leather aside. The tattoos running down his inner forearms flashed as he peeled the empty holster from his shoulders.

He went into the bathroom and she heard water splashing. When he came back out, he was drying his face with a towel. He put his sunglasses on before looking at her.

"You're father, Darius, was a worthy male." Wrath casually tossed the towel back into the bathroom and walked over to the couch. He sat forward, elbows on his knees. "He was an aristocrat from the old country before he became a warrior. He's . . . he *was* my friend. My brother in the work I do."

Brother. He kept using that word.

They were in the Mafia. Definitely.

Wrath smiled a little, as if remembering something that pleased him. "D had skills. He was fast on his feet, smart as hell, good with a knife. But he was cultured. A gentleman. He spoke eight languages. Studied everything from world religions to art history to philosophy. He could talk your ear off about Wall Street and then tell you why the Sistine Chapel ceiling is actually a Mannerist work, not from the Renaissance."

Wrath leaned back, running a hefty arm across the top of the sofa. His knees fell out to the sides, his thighs spreading.

He looked damn comfortable as he pushed his long black hair back.

Sexy as hell.

"Darius never lost his temper, no matter how nasty things got. He just stuck to the job at hand until it was finished. He died with the full respect of his brothers."

Wrath actually seemed to miss her father. Or whatever man he was channeling for the purpose of . . .

What exactly was he trying to pull here? she wondered. Where did it get him to throw out this crap?

Well, she was in his bedroom, wasn't she?

"And Fritz tells me he loved you very deeply."

Beth pursed her lips. "Assuming I even buy any of this, I've got to wonder. If my father cared so much, why didn't he bother to introduce himself to me?"

"It's complicated."

"Yeah, it's really hard to walk up to your daughter, stick your hand out, and say your name. Real tough stuff." She walked across the room, only to find herself next to the bed. She quickly paced elsewhere. "And what's up with the warrior rhetoric? Was he in the mob, too?"

"Mob? We're not the mob, Beth."

"So you're just freelance killers as well as drug dealers? Hmmm . . . Come to think of it, diversification is probably a good business strategy. And you need a lot of cash to keep up a house like this. As well as fill it full of art that belongs in the Met."

"Darius inherited his money and he was very good at taking care of it." Wrath leaned his head back, as if he were looking up at the house. "As his daughter, all of this is yours now."

She narrowed her eyes. "Oh, really."

He nodded.

What a crock, she thought.

"So where's the will? Where's some executor ready to pass papers? Wait, let me guess, the estate's been in probate. For the last thirty years." She rubbed her aching eyes. "You know, Wrath, you don't have to lie to get me in bed. As much as I'm ashamed of myself, all you have to do is ask."

She took a deep, sad breath. Until now she hadn't realized that a small part of her had believed she'd get some answers. Finally.

Then again, desperation could make a fool out of anyone.

"Look, I'm going to take off. This was just—"

Wrath was in front of her faster than she could blink. "I can't let you go."

Fear licked her heart, but she put up a good front. "You can't *make* me stay."

His hands lifted to her face. She jerked back, but he wouldn't let go.

The pad of his thumb stroked her cheek. Whenever he got too close, she became spellbound and it happened again. She felt her body swaying toward his.

"I'm not lying to you," he said. "Your father sent me to you because you're going to need my help. Trust me."

She yanked away. "I don't want to hear that word on your lips."

Here he was, a criminal who'd almost killed a cop in front of her, and he was expecting her to buy a line of bull that she knew was false.

While he was stroking her face like a lover.

He must think she was a moron.

"Look, I've seen my records." Her voice didn't waver. "My birth certificate lists my father as unknown, but there was a note in the file. My mother told a nurse in the delivery room that he'd passed away. She was unable to disclose a name because she went into shock from blood loss thereafter and died herself."

"I'm sorry, but that's just not what happened."

"You're sorry. Yeah, I bet you are."

"I'm not playing games—"

"The hell you aren't! God, to think for even a moment that I might know one of them, even secondhand . . ." She stared at him with disgust. "You are *so* cruel."

He swore, a nasty, frustrated sound. "I don't know how to get you to believe me."

"Don't bother trying. You have no credibility." She grabbed her purse. "Hell, it's probably better this way. I would almost rather he'd died than know that he was a criminal. Or that we'd lived in the same town all my life but he never came to see me, wasn't even curious enough to know what I looked like."

"He knew." Wrath's voice was very near again. "He knew you."

163

She spun around. He was so close he overwhelmed her with his size.

Beth leaped away. "Stop this right now."

"He knew you."

"Stop saying that!"

"*Your father knew you*," Wrath shouted.

"Then why didn't he want me?" she yelled back.

Wrath winced. "He did. He watched over you. All your life he was never far away."

She closed her eyes, wrapping her arms around herself. She couldn't believe she was tempted to fall under his spell again.

"Beth, look at me. Please."

She lifted her lids.

"Give me your hand," he said. "Give it to me."

When she didn't respond, he placed her palm on his chest, over his heart.

"On my honor. I have not lied to you."

He became utterly still, as if giving her a chance to read every nuance of his face and his body.

Could this be the truth? she wondered.

"He loved you, Beth."

Don't believe this. Don't believe this. Don't—

"Then why didn't he come for me?" she whispered.

"He hoped you wouldn't have to know him. That you'd be spared the kind of life he lived." Wrath stared down at her. "And he ran out of time."

There was a long silence.

"Who was my father?" she breathed.

"He was as I am."

And then Wrath opened his mouth.

Fangs. He had fangs.

Her skin shrank in horror. She shoved him away. "You bastard!"

"Beth, listen to me—"

"So you can tell me you're a fucking *vampire?*" She

lunged at him, punching his chest with her hands. "You sick bastard! You sick . . . *bastard!* If you want to role-play your fantasies, do it with someone else."

"Your father—"

She slapped him, hard. Right across the face.

"Do *not* go there. Don't even try it." Her hand stung, and she tucked it in against her belly. She wanted to cry. Because she was hurting. Because she'd tried to hurt him back and he seemed utterly unaffected by the fact that she'd hit him.

"God, you almost had me, you really did," she moaned. "But then you had to take it one step too far and flash those fake teeth."

"They're real. Look closely."

More candles came on in the room, lit by no one.

Her breath left her in a rush. Abruptly, she had the sense that nothing was as it seemed. The rules were off. Reality was sliding into a different realm.

She raced across the room.

He met her at the door and she crouched, as if she had a prayer of keeping him away from her.

"Don't come near me." She grabbed for the handle. Threw her whole body into it. The thing wouldn't budge.

Panic ran like gasoline through her veins.

"Beth—"

"Let me go!" The door handle cut into the skin of her palms as she wrenched it.

When his hand came down on her shoulder, she screamed. "Don't touch me!"

She leaped away from him. Careened around the room. He tracked her, coming at her slowly, inexorably.

"I'm going to help you."

"Leave me alone!"

She dashed around him and dove for the door. This time it opened before she even got to the handle.

As if he'd willed it so.

She looked back at him in horror. "This isn't real."

She bolted up the stairs, tripping only once. When she tried to work the latch on the painting, she broke a nail, but eventually got it open. She ran through the drawing room. Burst out of the house and—

Wrath was there, standing on the front lawn.

Beth skidded to a halt.

Terror flooded her body, fright and disbelief seizing her heart in a fist. Her mind slipped into madness.

"No!" She took off, running in any direction as long as it was away from him.

She felt him following her, and she threw her legs out harder and faster. She ran until she couldn't breathe, until she was blinded by exhaustion and her thighs were screaming. She ran flat-out and still he followed.

She fell down onto grass, sobbing.

Curling into a ball, as if to shield herself from blows, she wept.

When he picked her up she didn't fight him.

What was the use? If this was a dream, she would wake up eventually. And if it was the truth . . .

She was going to need him to explain a hell of a lot more than just her father's life.

As Wrath carried Beth back down to the chamber, fear and confusion poured out of her in waves of distress. He laid her down on the bed and yanked the top sheet free so he could wrap her up. Then he went to the couch and sat down, thinking she'd appreciate the space.

Eventually she shifted around, and he felt her eyes on him.

"I'm waiting to wake up. To have the alarm go off," she said hoarsely. "But it's not going to, is it?"

He shook his head.

"How is this possible? How . . ." She cleared her throat. "Vampires?"

"We're just a different species."

"Bloodsuckers. Killers."

"Try persecuted minority. Which was why your father was hoping you wouldn't go through the change."

"Change?"

He nodded grimly.

"Oh, God." She clamped her hand over her mouth as if she were going to be sick. "Don't tell me I'm going to . . ."

A shock wave of panic came out of her, creating a breeze through the room that reached him in a cool rush. He couldn't bear her anguish and wanted to do something to ease her. Except compassion wasn't among his strengths.

If only there were something he could fight for her.

Yeah, well, there was nothing at the moment. Nothing. The truth wasn't a target he could eliminate. And it wasn't her enemy, even though it hurt her. It just . . . was.

He stood up and approached the bed. When she didn't shrink away from him, he sat down. The tears she shed smelled like spring rain.

"What's going to happen to me?" she murmured.

The desperation in her voice suggested she was talking to God, not him. But he answered anyway.

"Your change is coming fast. It hits all of us sometime around our twenty-fifth birthday. I'll teach you how to take care of yourself. I'll show you what to do."

"Good God . . ."

"After you go through it, you're going to need to drink."

She choked and jerked upright. "I'm not *killing* anyone!"

"It's not like that. You need the blood of a male vampire. That's all."

"That's all," she repeated in a dead tone.

167

"We don't prey on humans. That's an old wives' tale."

"You've never taken a . . . human?"

"Not to drink from them," he hedged. "There are some vampires who do, but the strength doesn't last long. To thrive, we need to feed off our own race."

"You make it all sound so normal."

"It is."

She fell silent. And then, as if it just dawned on her, "You're going to let me—"

"You're going to drink from me. When it's time."

She let out a strangled sound, like she'd wanted to cry out, but her gag reflex had kicked in.

"Beth, I know this is hard—"

"You do not."

"—because I had to go through it, too."

She looked at him. "Did you learn you were one out of the blue also?"

It wasn't a challenge. More like she was hoping she had common ground with someone. Anyone.

"I knew who my parents were," he said, "but they were dead by the time my transition hit. I was alone. I didn't know what to expect. So I know what the confusion feels like."

Her body fell back against the pillows. "Was my mother one, too?"

"She was human, from what Darius told me. Vampires have been known to breed with them, although it's rare for the infants to survive."

"Can I stop the change? Can I stop this from happening?"

He shook his head.

"Does it hurt?"

"You're going to feel—"

"Not me. Will I hurt you?"

Wrath swallowed his surprise. No one worried about him. Vampires and humans alike feared him. His race worshiped him. But none were ever concerned for him. He didn't know how to handle the sentiment.

"No. It won't hurt me."

"Could I kill you?"

"I won't let you."

"Promise?" she said urgently, sitting up and gripping his forearm.

He couldn't believe he was taking a vow to protect himself. At her request.

"I promise you." He reached his hand out to cover hers, but stopped before he made contact.

"When will it happen?"

"I can't tell you that for sure. But soon."

She let go, settling against the pillows. Then she curled on her side away from him.

"Maybe I'll wake up," she murmured. "Maybe I'll still wake up."

NINETEEN

Butch drank his first Scotch in one swallow. Big mistake.

His throat was raw, and it felt like he'd French-kissed a blowtorch. As soon as he stopped coughing, he ordered another from Abby.

"We're going to find her," José said, putting his beer down.

The other detective was sticking to the light stuff, but then José had to go home to his family. Butch, on the other hand, was free to behave as badly as he wished.

José played with his mug, twisting it around in circles on the bar. "You shouldn't blame yourself, Detective."

Butch laughed and threw back Scotch number two. "Yeah, there's a huge list of people who were in my car with that suspect." He lifted his finger to get Abby's attention. "I'm dry again."

"Not for long." She jiggled right over with the single-malt, smiling at him while she tipped the bottle into his glass.

José shifted in his bar stool as if he didn't approve of Butch's Scotch velocity and the effort of keeping his lip zipped was making him squirm.

As Abby went over to another customer, Butch glanced at José.

"I'm going to get ugly wasted tonight. You shouldn't stick around."

José popped some peanuts into his mouth. "I'm not leaving you here."

"I'll cab it home."

"Naw. I'll hang until you're through. Then I'll drag you

back to your apartment. Watch you throw up for an hour. Push you into bed. Before I leave I'll get the coffee machine set up. Aspirin will be right next to the sugar bowl."

"I don't have a sugar bowl."

"So it'll be next to the bag."

Butch smiled. "You'd have made a great wife, José."

"That's what mine tells me."

They were silent until Abby poured number four.

"The throwing stars I peeled off that suspect," Butch said. "Where do we stand with them?"

"Same as the ones we found at the car bomb and around Cherry's body. Typhoons. Three-point-one ounces of four-forty stainless steel. Four-inch diameter. Removable center weight. You can get 'em off the Internet for about twelve bucks a pop or buy them through martial-arts academies. And no, there were no prints."

"The other weapons?"

"Flashy set of knives. The boys in the lab got a real hard-on for them. Composite metal, diamond hard, beautifully made by hand. No identifying manufacturer. Gun was your standard nine-millimeter Beretta, model 92G-SD. Real well cared for, and naturally the serial number had been etched off. The freaky thing was the bullets. Never seen anything like 'em. Hollow, filled with some kind of liquid. The boys think it's just water. But why would someone do that?"

"You gotta be kidding me."

"Uh-huh."

"And no prints."

"Nope."

"On anything."

"Nope." José finished the bowl of peanuts and trolled his hand to get Abby's eye for more. "That suspect's slick. Neat as a pin. A real professional. Wanna bet he's moved up north from the Big Apple? He doesn't sound Caldwell home-grown."

"Tell me that while I was wasting time with those damn EMTs we checked with the NYPD."

Abby came over with more nuts and more Scotch.

"We're doing ballistics on the gun, just to see if there are any unusual characteristics," José said evenly. "Checking the money to see if it's hot. First thing in the morning we'll give the New York boys everything we got, but it's not going to be much."

Butch cursed as he watched the bowl get refilled.

"If anything happens to Beth . . ." He didn't finish the sentence.

"We'll find them." José paused. "And God help him if he hurts her."

Yeah, Butch would personally go after the guy.

"God help him," he vowed, making room in his glass for another shot.

Wrath was exhausted as he sat on the couch and waited for Beth to speak again. His body felt as though it were sinking in on itself, his bones weakening under their burden of flesh and muscle.

As he replayed the scene in the station house's alley, he realized he hadn't stripped the cop of his memory. Which meant the police were going to be looking for him with an accurate description.

Damn it. He'd been so caught up in the fricking drama, he'd forgotten to protect himself.

He was getting sloppy. And sloppy was dangerous.

"How did you know about the orgasms?" Beth asked abruptly.

He stiffened. And so did his cock, just at hearing the word leave her lips.

Moving his body around to make some room in his pants, he wondered if he could avoid answering her. He didn't want to talk right now about the sex they'd had. Not with her lying in that bed. Mere feet away from him.

He thought of her skin. Soft. Smooth. Warm.

"How did you know?" she prompted.

"It's the truth, isn't it?"

"Yes," she whispered. "Was it different with you because you're not . . . you're a . . . Hell, I can't even say the word."

"Maybe." He brought his palms together, linking his fingers tight. "I don't know."

Because it had been different for him, too, even though technically she was still a human.

"He's not my lover. Butch. The cop. He's not."

Wrath felt his breath ease out of him. "I'm glad."

"So if you see him again, don't kill him."

"Okay."

There was a long pause, and then he heard her shifting around on the bed. The satin sheets made a soft sound as she moved.

He pictured her thighs rubbing against each other and then saw himself opening them with his hands. Nudging them farther apart with his head. Kissing a path down to where he so desperately wanted to be.

He swallowed, his skin turning into shrink-wrap.

"Wrath?"

"Yeah."

"You really didn't mean to sleep with me last night, did you?"

Hazy images of her had him closing his eyes. "No, I didn't."

"So why did you?"

How could he not have? he thought, jaw clenching. He'd been powerless to leave her alone.

"Wrath?"

"Because I had to," he replied, stretching his arms, trying to find some ease. His heart thundered in his chest, his instincts coming alive, as if he were in battle.

He could hear the breath leave her lips, her heart as it pumped, her blood as it flowed.

"Why?" she whispered.

He should go. He should leave her alone.

"Tell me why."

"You made me realize how cold I am."

More shifting on the bed.

"I liked warming you," she said huskily. "I liked the feel of you."

Dark hunger curled in his gut, cramping up his stomach.

Wrath stopped breathing. Waited to see if it would pass. The gnawing sensation grew stronger.

Shit, that sinful need wasn't just about sex. It was about blood.

Hers.

He stood up quickly and put more space between them. He definitely needed to get out of here. Hit the streets. Find a fight.

And he needed to feed.

"Look, I've got to take off. But I want you to crash here."

"Don't go."

"I have to."

"Why?"

His mouth opened, his fangs throbbing as they elongated.

And his teeth weren't the only thing demanding to be used. His erection was a painful, rigid length straining against his fly. He felt himself get stretched between the two needs. Sex. Blood.

Both hers.

"Are you running away?" she whispered. It was mostly a question. Only a little bit of a taunt.

"Be careful, Beth."

"Why?"

"I'm about to crack over here."

She got off the bed and came to him. Her hand landed squarely on his chest, right above his heart. And then her other one wrapped around his waist.

He hissed as she stepped into his body.

But at least the sexual need cut through his other hunger.

"Are you going to tell me no?" she asked.

"I don't want to take advantage of you," he said through gritted teeth. "You've been through enough tonight."

She gripped his shoulders. "I'm angry. Scared. Confused. I want you to make love to me until I don't feel, until I'm numb. If anything, I'd be using you." She looked down. "God that sounds awful."

The hell it did. He was more than willing to be used like that by her.

He tilted her chin up with his forefinger. Even though her rich scent told him exactly what her body needed from him, he wished he could see her face clearly.

"Don't leave," she whispered.

He didn't want to, but his bloodlust put her in danger. She needed to be strong for her change. And he was thirsty enough to drain her dry.

Her hand left his waist. And found his erection.

His body jerked wildly, breath slamming into his lungs. His gasp shattered the silence in the room.

"You want me," she said. "And I want you to take me."

She rubbed her palm over his length, the friction passing with aching clarity through the second skin of his leathers.

Just sex. He could do it. He could hold back the other need. He could.

But was he willing to bet her life on his control?

"Don't say no, Wrath."

And then she lifted up onto her tiptoes and put her lips to his.

Game over, he thought, crushing her to him.

He thrust his tongue into her mouth as he grabbed her hips and ground himself into her hand. Her moan of satisfaction cranked him even higher, and as her nails bit into his back, he loved the little bursts of pain he felt because they meant she was as hungry as he was.

He had her on the bed and under him in a flash of movement, and he pushed up her skirt and tore off her panties with vicious impatience. He didn't treat her blouse or bra any better. There would be time to savor later. Now was all about raw sex.

While he worked her breasts with his mouth, her hands were rough as she pulled his shirt from his chest. He left her only long enough to undo his pants and spring his erection. Then he linked his forearm behind one of her knees, stretched her leg up, and plunged himself into her body.

He heard her gasp at his powerful entry, and her slick heat grabbed onto him, pulsating as she came. He froze in place, absorbing the sensation of her release, feeling her core stroke him.

An overwhelming, possessive instinct flashed through him.

With dread, he realized he wanted to mark her. Mark her as his. He wanted that special scent all over her so no other male would come near her. So that they would know whom she belonged to. So that they would fear the repercussions of wanting to possess her for themselves.

Except he knew he had no right to do that. She wasn't his.

He felt her body go still underneath him, and he looked down.

"Wrath?" she whispered. "Wrath, what's wrong?"

He made a move to pull out of her, but she caught his face in her hands.

"Are you all right?"

The concern for him in her voice was what did it.

With an awesome surge, his body leaped out of reach of his mind. Before he could think any further, before he could stop, he propped himself up on his arms and pounded into her, taking her hard, drilling her. The bed's headboard banged against the wall to the beat of his thrusts, and she grabbed onto his straining wrists, trying to hold herself in place.

A low sound shot through the room, growing louder and louder, until he realized the growl was coming from him. As a fevered heat broke out all over his skin, his nose registered that dark fragrance of possession.

He was powerless to stop himself.

His lips peeled off his teeth as his muscles churned and his hips thrashed against her. Drenched in sweat, head spinning, mindless, breathless, he took everything she was offering him. Took it and demanded more, becoming an animal as she became one, too, until they were nothing but wildness.

He came violently, filling her up, pumping into her, his orgasm going on and on and on, until he realized she was climaxing right along with him, the two of them holding on to each other for dear life against shattering waves of passion.

It was the most perfect union he'd ever known.

And then everything turned into a nightmare.

As the last shudder left his body and went into hers, at that moment when he was finally spent, the balance of his desires was thrown. His bloodlust surged forward in a wicked, consuming rush, as powerful as the lust had been.

He bared his teeth and went for her neck, for the vein deliciously close to the surface of her pale skin. His fangs were about to sink deep, his throat dry with thirst for her, his gut spasming with a starvation that cut to his soul, when he pulled himself up short, horrified by what he was about to do.

He pushed himself away from her, scrambling across the bed until he fell to the floor, landing on his ass.

"Wrath?" In alarm she started for him.

"No!"

The hunger for her blood was too strong, the instinct undeniable. If she got too close . . .

He moaned, trying to swallow. His throat was like sandpaper. Sweat broke out all over him again, but this time it was in a sickening flush.

"What happened? What did I do?"

Wrath crawled backward, his body aching, his skin on fire. The smell of her sex on him was like a whip against his self-control.

"Beth, leave me. I've got to . . ."

But she was still coming at him. His body slammed into the couch.

"Get the fuck back!" He bared his fangs and hissed loudly. "You get any closer and I'm going to bite you, got it?"

She stopped immediately. Terror clouded the air between them, but then she shook her head.

"You wouldn't hurt me," she said with a conviction that struck him as dangerously naive.

He struggled to speak. "Get dressed. Go upstairs. Ask Fritz to take you home. I'll send someone to watch over you."

He was panting now, the pain ripping through his stomach, almost as bad as it had been that first night of his transition. He'd never needed Marissa like this.

Jesus. What was happening to him?

"I don't want to leave."

"You have to. I'll send someone to keep you safe until I can get back to you."

His thighs shook, the muscles straining against the hold he'd clamped down on his body. His mind and his physical needs had declared war, had marched onto the battlefield with swords drawn. And he knew which one was going to win if she didn't get away from him.

"Beth, *please*. It hurts. And I don't know how long I can hold myself back."

She hesitated. And then yanked her clothes on.

She went to the door and looked back at him.

"*Go.*"

And she did.

TWENTY

It was a little after nine when Mr. X hit the drive-through at McDonald's. "I'm glad you both liked the movie. And I have in mind something else tonight, although we'll have to be quick about it. One of you needs to be home by eleven."

Billy cursed under his breath as they pulled up in front of the lit menu. He ordered twice as much as Loser did. Loser offered to pay for his share.

"That's all right. My treat," Mr. X said. "Just don't spill anything."

While Billy ate and Loser played with his food, Mr. X drove them over to the War Zone. The laser-tag place was pickup central for the under-eighteen crowd, its dim interior perfect for obscuring both acne as well as pathetic adolescent yearning. The sprawling one-story was hopping tonight, filled with twitchy teenage boys and the bored, overdressed girls they were trying to impress.

Mr. X got three guns and target halters, passing one to each of the guys. Billy was ready to go in under a minute, his weapon resting in his hands easily as if it were an extension of his arms.

Mr. X eyed Loser, who was still trying to get the halter straps to fit his shoulders. The guy looked miserable, his lower lip slack as his fingers worked the plastic catches. Billy watched him, too. As if Loser were food.

"So I thought we'd have a little friendly competition," Mr. X said when they finally stepped through the turnstiles. "See which one of you can hit the other the most."

As they entered the fighting arena, Mr. X's eyes quickly adjusted to the velvet blackness and the neon flashes from other players. The space was large enough for the thirty or so who were dancing around the obstacles, laughing and shouting as they fired beams of light.

"Let's split up," Mr. X said.

While Loser blinked myopically, Billy took off, moving with the swiftness of an animal. A moment later the sensor in the middle of Loser's chest went off. The guy looked down at it as if he didn't know what had happened.

Billy retreated into the darkness.

"Better take cover, son," Mr. X murmured.

Mr. X stayed out of their way while watching everything they did. Billy hit Loser over and over again from countless angles, shifting in and out of the obstacles, coming fast, now slow, then shooting from far away. Loser's confusion and anxiety ratcheted up every time the light on his chest flashed, and desperation made him move with childlike uncoordination. He dropped his gun. Tripped over his own feet. Knocked his shoulder into a barrier.

Billy was resplendent. Though his target was failing, weakening, he showed no mercy. Even when Loser dropped his gun to his side and leaned up against a wall with exhaustion, Billy hit him again.

And then took off into the shadows.

This time Mr. X followed Billy, tracking the guy's movements with a purpose other than measuring performance. Riddle was fast, shifting around the foam obstacles, doubling back to where Loser was so he could ambush from behind.

Mr. X anticipated where Billy was headed. With a quick shift to the right, he put himself in Riddle's path.

181

And shot Billy at point-blank range.

Billy looked down in shock at his chest. It was the first time his receptor had gone off.

"Pretty good job tonight," Mr. X said. "You played the game well, son. Until just now."

Billy's eyes lifted, his hand coming to rest over the blinking target. Over his heart.

"Sensei." The word was spoken like a lover, with a lover's awe and adoration.

Beth wasn't about to ask the butler for a ride, because she was too shaken to carry on a polite conversation with anyone. As she walked down to the street, she took out her cell phone to call a cab. She was dialing when the purr of a car engine brought her head up.

The butler got out of the Mercedes and bowed his head. "Master called me. He would like me to take you home, mistress. And I . . . I would like to drive you."

He was so earnest, almost hopeful, as if she'd be doing him a favor if she let him take care of her. But she needed some space. After everything that had happened, she was rattling around in her own head.

"Thank you, but no." She forced a smile. "I'm just going to . . ."

The man's face fell. He looked like a dog who'd been whipped.

Where good manners failed her, guilt stepped up to the plate.

"Ah, okay."

Before he could come around the car, she opened the passenger-side door and slid into the front seat. The butler seemed flustered at her initiative, but recovered quickly, that beaming smile back on his wrinkled face.

As he got behind the wheel and put the engine in gear, she said, "I live at—"

"Oh, I know where you live. We've always known

182

where you were. First at St. Francis Hospital in the neonatal intensive-care unit. Then you went home with the nurse. We had hoped she would keep you, but the hospital made her give you back. Then you went into the system. We didn't like that. First you were assigned to the McWilliamses on Elmwood Avenue, but you became ill and went back into the hospital with pneumonia."

He put the blinker on and turned left at a stop sign.

She could barely breathe, she was listening so hard.

"After that you were sent to the Ryans, but there were too many children. And then you went to the Goldrichs, who lived in that split-level off Raleigh Street. We thought the Goldrichs were going to keep you, but then she got pregnant. Finally to that orphanage. We hated when you were there, because they didn't let you out to play enough."

"You keep saying 'we'," she whispered, afraid to believe. Wanting to.

"Yes. Your father and I."

Beth covered her mouth with the back of her hand, her eyes capturing the butler's profile as if it were something she could keep.

"He knew me?"

"Oh, yes, mistress. All along. Kindergarten and elementary school and high school." His eyes met hers. "We were so proud of you when you went to college on that academic scholarship. I was there when you graduated. I took pictures so your father could see."

"He knew me." She tried the words out, feeling like she must be talking about someone else's parent.

The butler looked across the seat and smiled. "We have every column you've ever written. Even the ones you wrote in high school and college. When you started at the *Caldwell Courier Journal*, your father refused to go to sleep in the morning until after I brought the

183

paper to him. No matter how hard his night had been, he wouldn't rest until he read what you wrote. He was so proud of you."

She fumbled through her bag, trying to find a Kleenex.

"Here," the butler said, handing her a small package of tissues.

Beth blew her nose as delicately as she could.

"Mistress, you must understand how hard it was for him to stay away from you. It was just that he knew it would be dangerous to get too close. Families of warriors need to be guarded carefully, and you were unprotected because you were raised human. He'd also hoped you'd be spared the transition."

"Did you know my mother?"

"Not well. They weren't together long. She disappeared shortly after they started seeing each other because she found out he was not a human. She didn't tell him she was pregnant, and it wasn't until she was about to give birth that she reached out to him. I think she was scared of what she was bringing into the world. Unfortunately she went into labor and was taken to a human hospital before we could get to her. But you should know that he loved her. Very deeply."

Beth absorbed the information, her mind soaking it up, filling in holes.

"My father and Wrath, they were close?"

The butler hesitated. "Your father loved Wrath. We all do. He is our lord. Our king. That is why your father sent him to you. And you mustn't fear him. He will not hurt you."

"I know that."

When her apartment building came into view, she wished she had more time with the butler.

"And here we are," he said. "Eleven eighty-eight Redd Avenue, apartment one-B. Although I have to say, neither your father nor I approved of the fact that you're living in a ground-floor unit."

The car came to a stop. She didn't want to get out. "May I ask you more? Later?" she said.

"Oh, mistress, yes. Please. There is so much I want to tell you." He got out of the car, but she was already shutting her door by the time he came around to her.

She thought about putting out her hand and thanking him formally.

Instead she threw her arms around the little old man and hugged him.

After Beth left the chamber, Wrath's thirst called out for her and then stung him hard, as if it knew he was the one who had sent her away.

He pulled up his pants and dragged himself to the phone, calling Fritz, then Tohrment. His voice kept cracking, and he had to repeat himself to be understood.

As soon as he hung up with Tohr, the dry heaves started. He staggered to the bathroom, calling out for Marissa with his mind. He lurched over the toilet, but there was nothing much in his stomach.

He'd waited too long, he thought. Ignored the signals his body had been giving him for quite some time. And then Beth had come along, and his internal chemistry had taken another series of hits. No wonder he was crazed.

Marissa's scent drifted in from the chamber.

"My lord?" she called out.

"I need . . ."

Beth, he thought, hallucinating. He saw her in front of him, heard her voice in his head. He put his hand out. Touched nothing.

"My lord? Shall I come to you?" Marissa asked from the other room.

Wrath wiped the sweat from his face and came out,

185

weaving like a drunk. He reached blindly into the air, pitching forward.

"Wrath!" Marissa rushed to him.

He let himself fall onto the bed, taking her down with him. Her body came up against his.

He felt Beth's.

And his face landed in sheets that were marked with Beth's scent. As he took a deep breath to try to stabilize himself, all he smelled was Beth.

"My lord, you need to feed." Marissa's voice came from far away, as if she were out in the stairway.

He looked to the sound and saw nothing. He was totally blind now.

Marissa's voice grew curiously strong. "My lord, here. Take my wrist. Now."

Warm skin was in his palm. He opened his mouth, but couldn't get his arms to work properly. He reached out, touched a shoulder, a collarbone, the curve of a neck.

Beth.

The hunger took over, and he reared up across the female body. With a roar he sank his teeth into the soft flesh above an artery. He drank deep and hard, seeing visions of the dark-haired woman who was his, picturing her giving herself to him, imagining it was her in his arms.

Marissa gasped.

Wrath's arms were nearly snapping her in half, his massive body a cage around hers as he drank. For the first time she felt every hard line of him.

Including what she realized must be an erection, something she'd never been anywhere near before.

The possibilities were exciting. And terrifying.

She went limp and tried to breathe. This was what she'd always wanted from him, though his passion was

186

shocking. But what could she expect? He was a full-blooded male. A warrior.

And he'd finally realized he needed her.

Satisfaction took the place of any discomfort, and she tentatively ran her hands over his wide, bare shoulders, a liberty she'd never taken before. He made a sound deep in his throat, as if he wanted her to do more. With delicious pleasure she sank her hands into his hair. It was so soft. Who could have guessed? Such a hard male, but oh, how soft the dark waves were. Like her satin dresses.

Marissa wanted to see into his mind, an invasion she'd never risked for fear of his taking offense. But now everything was different. Maybe he would even kiss her after he finished. Make love to her. Maybe she could stay with him now. She would like to live at Darius's with him. Or wherever. It didn't matter.

She closed her eyes and reached out to his thoughts.

Only to see the female he was really thinking of. The *human* female.

It was a dark-haired beauty with her eyes half-closed. She was on her back, breasts exposed. His fingers were caressing her tight, pink nipples as he kissed the skin of her stomach, moving downward.

Marissa dropped the image as if it were broken glass.

Wrath wasn't here with her now. It wasn't her neck he was drinking from. It wasn't her body he was drawing hard into his.

And that erection wasn't because of her.

Wasn't for her.

As he sucked at her neck, his thick arms crushing her against him, Marissa cried out at the unfairness.

Of her hopes. Of her love. Of him.

How fitting that he was draining her. And how she wished he would finish the job. Drink her dry. Let her die.

It had taken her years and years, aeons, to realize the truth.

He never had been hers. He never would be.

God, she had nothing now that the fantasy was gone.

TWENTY-ONE

Beth put her purse down on the hall table, said hello to Boo, and went into the bathroom. She eyed the shower, but decided against having one. Even though her stiff body could have used some time under a hot spray, she loved the lingering smell of Wrath on her skin. It was a wonderful, erotic perfume, a dark spice. Like nothing she'd ever come across before, nothing she could possibly forget.

Turning on the sink, she cleaned up, exquisitely sensitive and more than a little tender between her legs. Not that she cared about the ache. Wrath could do that to her anytime he wanted.

He was . . .

No words came to mind. Just an image of him releasing into her, his massive, sweat-covered shoulders and chest seizing up as he gave himself to her. As he branded her as his.

Which was what it had seemed like. She felt as though she'd been dominated and imprinted by a man. Taken.

And she wanted that again. Wanted him now.

But she shook her head, thinking that the unprotected sex had to stop. Bad enough it had been twice. Next time they were going to be safe.

On her way out of the bath, she caught her reflection in the mirror and stopped moving. She bent at the waist, bringing her face closer to the glass.

She still looked exactly as she had this morning. But she felt like a stranger.

Opening her mouth, she examined her teeth. When she probed the two canines in front, sure enough, they were sore.

Dear God, who was she? *What* was she?

She thought about Wrath, after they'd been together. Pushing himself away from her, his half-naked body straining, his muscles looking as if they were going to break through his skin. When he'd bared his teeth, his fangs had been longer than when she'd first seen them. As if they'd grown.

His beautiful face had been contorted with agony.

Was that what she was in for?

A rapping noise came from the other room, as though someone was knocking on a window. She heard Boo meow in welcome.

Beth put her head cautiously around the doorjamb.

There was someone at the slider. Someone big.

"Wrath?" She rushed over and opened the door before she really looked.

When she saw what was on the other side, she wished she'd checked more carefully first.

It wasn't Wrath, although the man looked a little like him. Black hair was cut short. Harsh face. Intense dark blue eyes. A whole lot of leather.

His nostrils flared and he frowned, staring at her hard. But then he seemed to catch himself.

"Beth?" His voice was deep, but friendly. And as the man smiled, fangs were revealed.

She didn't even jump.

Damn, she was getting used to the weirdness already.

"I'm Tohrment, a friend of Wrath's." The guy stuck his hand out. "You can call me Tohr."

She shook it, not sure what to say.

"I'm here to hang for a while. I'll just be outside if you need anything."

190

The man . . . vampire—shit, whatever he was—turned away and headed for the picnic table.

"Wait," she said. "Why don't you . . . Please come in."

He shrugged. "Okay."

As he stepped through the door, Boo meowed loudly and pawed at the man's shitkickers. The two greeted each other like long-lost friends, and when the vampire straightened, his leather jacket fell open. Daggers. Just like Wrath's. And she had a feeling that the kind of weapons Butch had peeled off Wrath were hiding in this man's pockets, too.

"Would you like something to drink?" She winced. *Not blood. Please don't say blood.*

He grinned at her, as if he knew what she was thinking. "You got any beer?"

Beer? He drank beer?

"Ah, yeah. Actually, I think I do." She disappeared into the kitchen. Brought back two Sam Adamses. She needed a belt right about now, too.

After all, she was playing hostess to a vampire. Her father had been a vampire.

Her lover *was* a vampire.

She tilted the beer back and drank hard.

Tohrment laughed softly. "Long night?"

"You have no idea," she replied, wiping her mouth.

"Oh, I might." The vampire sat down in her wing chair, his big body overflowing the arms and dwarfing the high back. "I'm glad I finally met you. Your father talked about you a lot."

"He did?"

"He was so damn proud of you. And you've got to know—he stayed away to protect you, not because he didn't love you."

"That's what Fritz said. Wrath, too."

"How're you getting along with him?"

"Wrath?"

191

"Yeah."

She felt a blush hit her cheeks and headed to the kitchen so he didn't catch her reaction. She grabbed a bag of cookies from the top of the fridge and put some on a plate.

"He's . . . he's . . . How do I put it?" She tried to think of a good answer.

"Actually, I think I know."

She came back and held out the plate. "Would you like some?"

"Oatmeal raisin," he said, taking three. "My favorite."

"You know, I thought vampires only drank blood."

"Nah. Necessary nutrients in it, but we need food, too."

"How about garlic?"

"Bring it on." He leaned back in the chair, munching happily. "I love the stuff roasted with a little olive oil."

Jeez. The guy was almost easygoing, she thought.

No, that wasn't right. His sharp eyes kept scanning the windows and the glass door, as if he were monitoring the periphery. She knew without a doubt that if he didn't like something he saw, he was going to be out of that chair in a heartbeat. And it wouldn't be to check locks. It'd be to attack.

He put another cookie in his mouth.

But at least he was relaxing to be around. Relatively speaking.

"You're not like Wrath," she blurted.

"No one's like Wrath."

"Yeah." She bit into her own cookie and sat down on the futon.

"He's a force of nature," Tohr said, tilting back his beer. "And he's deadly, no mistaking that. But there's no one who will take better care of you, assuming he chooses to do so. Which he has with you."

"How do you know?" she whispered, wondering what Wrath had told him.

Tohr cleared his throat, a flush hitting his cheeks. "He's marked you."

She frowned, looking down at herself.

"I can smell it," Tohr said. "The warning's all over you."

"Warning?"

"As if you were his *shellan*."

"His what?"

"His mate. That scent on your skin sends a powerful message to other males."

So she'd been right. About the sex they'd had and what it meant.

That really shouldn't please me as much as it does, she thought.

"You don't mind it, do you?" Tohr said. "Being his."

She didn't want to answer that. On one level she wanted to be Wrath's. On another, she felt much safer being as she had always been. On her own.

"Do you have one?" she asked. "A mate?"

The vampire's face lit with devotion. "Her name's Wellsie. We were promised to each other before our transitions. It was dumb luck that we fell in love. Truth is, if I'd met her on the street, I would have chosen her. How's that for fate?"

"Occasionally it works for us," she murmured.

"Yeah. Some males take more than one *shellan*, but I can't imagine ever being with another female. Which is evidently why Wrath called me."

She cocked an eyebrow at him. "Sorry?"

"The other brothers, they have females they drink from, but they don't have any emotional ties. There'd be nothing to prevent them—" He stopped and bit into another cookie. "Well, given that you're . . ."

"I'm what?" She felt as though she hardly knew herself.

And she was willing to even take hints from strangers at this point.

"Beautiful. Wrath wouldn't have wanted to put you in any of the others' care, because if they'd been tempted to make a move on you, there would be serious trouble." Tohr shrugged. "Well, and a couple of the brothers are just flat-out dangerous. You wouldn't want to leave any female alone with them, at least not one you cared about."

She wasn't sure she wanted to meet any of the brothers.

Wait a minute, she thought.

"Does Wrath have a *shellan* already?" she asked.

Tohr finished his beer. "I think you'd better talk to him about that."

Which was not a no.

A sick feeling of disappointment set up shop in the middle of her chest, and she went back into the kitchen.

Damn. She was getting emotional over Wrath. They'd had sex twice, and already her head was a mess.

This one is going to hurt, she thought as she cracked open another beer. When things went sour between them, it was going to hurt like hell.

Notwithstanding the whole turning-into-a-vampire thing.

Oh, God.

"More munchies?" she called out.

"That would be great."

"Beer?"

"Naw. I'm good."

She brought the bag in from the kitchen, and they were silent as they polished off the cookies. Even the broken ones at the bottom.

"You got anything else around here to eat?" he asked.

She stood, feeling peckish herself. "I'll see what I can dig up."

"You have cable?" He nodded toward her TV.

She tossed him the clicker. "Sure do. And if I remember, there's a Godzilla marathon on TBS tonight."

"*Sweet*," the vampire said, kicking his legs out. "I always root for the monster."

She smiled at him. "Me, too."

TWENTY-TWO

Butch woke up because someone was driving a gutter spike into his head.

He cracked open one eye.

No, that was the phone ringing.

He picked up the receiver and put it in the vicinity of his ear. "Yeah?"

"Good morning, sunshine." José's voice brought back the spike.

"Time?" he croaked.

"Eleven o'clock. Thought you'd want to know that Beth just called here looking for you. She sounded okay."

Butch's body went limp with relief. "Guy?"

"Didn't mention him. But she did say she wanted to talk with you sometime today. I canceled the APB on her because she was calling from home."

Butch sat up.

And then lay right back down.

He wasn't going anywhere for a while.

"Not feeling too good," he muttered.

"I figured that. Which is why I told her you'd be tied up until this afternoon. Just so you know, I left your place at seven this morning."

Ah, Christ.

Butch tried the whole vertical thing again, forcing himself to stay upright. The room swam. He was still drunk as shit. And he had a hangover.

Talk about multitasking.

"Coming in now."

"I wouldn't do that. The captain's gunning for your ass.

Internal Affairs showed up here asking about you and Billy Riddle."

"Riddle? Why?"

"Come on, Detective."

Yeah, he knew why.

"Listen, you're in no condition to run into the captain." José's voice was even, pragmatic. "You need to sober up. Get your shit together. Come in later. I'll cover for you."

"Thanks."

"And I left the aspirin next to the phone with a tall glass of water. Figured you weren't going to be able to make it to the coffeepot. Take three, turn your ringer off, and sleep. If anything exciting happens, I'll come and get you."

"I love you, honey."

"So buy me a mink and a nice pair of earrings for our anniversary."

"You got it."

He hung up the phone after two tries and closed his eyes. Just a little more sleep. And then he might feel like a human again.

Beth scribbled her last edit on a piece about a rash of identity thefts. The article looked like it was bleeding, it had so many corrections and she saw a trend setting in. Dick's big boys were getting sloppier and sloppier as they relied on her. And it wasn't just background mistakes; now they were making grammatical and structural errors. As if they'd never heard of the *Chicago Manual of Style*.

She didn't mind line editing when she was collaborating. As long as the person who'd drafted the article had done even a modest amount of proofreading.

Beth put the article in her out box and focused on her computer screen. She called up a file she'd been in and out of all day long.

Okay, what else did she want to know?

She reviewed her list of questions.

Will I be able to go outside during the day? How often will I have to feed? How long will I live?

Her fingers flew over the keyboard.

Who are you fighting?

And then, *Do you have a . . .*

What was that word? *Shellan?*

She typed *wife* instead.

God, she cringed at what Wrath's answer might be. And even if he didn't have one, who did he feed from?

And what would that feel like? To have him unleash his hunger on her?

She knew instinctively it would be the same as the sex. Half-savage. All-consuming. Probably leaving her bruised and weak.

As well as in a state of total bliss.

"Hard at work, Randall?" Dick drawled.

She changed screens so her e-mail account showed. "Always."

"You know, I heard a rumor about you."

"Really?"

"Yeah. Heard you went out with that homicide detective, O'Neal. Twice."

"So?"

Dick leaned over her desk. She was wearing a loose crew-neck shirt, so there was little for him to see. He straightened.

"So good job. Work a little magic on him. See what you can get. We could do a cover story on police brutality with him as the poster child. Keep this up, Randall, and I might be persuaded to promote you."

Dick sauntered off, obviously enjoying his role as dispenser of patronage.

What an ass.

Her phone rang, and she barked her name into the receiver.

There was a pause. "Mistress? Are you all right?"

The butler.

"Sorry—and yes, I'm fine." She put her head down on her free hand. After dealing with the likes of Wrath and Tohr, Dick's pasty version of male arrogance seemed absurd.

"If there's anything I can do . . ."

"No, no, I'm okay." She laughed. "It's nothing I haven't dealt with before."

"Well, I probably shouldn't be calling"—Fritz's voice dropped to a whisper—"but I didn't want you to be unprepared. Master has requested a special dinner tonight. For you and he, alone. I thought perhaps I would pick you up and we would find you a dress."

"A dress?"

For a date kind of thing with Wrath?

The idea struck her as a terrific one, but then she reminded herself to be careful about reading romance into things. She didn't really know the lay of the landscape.

Or who else he was laying, as it were.

"Mistress, I know this is presumptuous of me. He's going to call you himself—"

At that moment the second line on her phone started to ring.

"I just wanted you to be ready for tonight."

Caller ID flashed the number Wrath had made her memorize. She grinned like an idiot.

"I would love to get a dress. I would absolutely love to."

"Good. We shall go to the Galleria. They have a Brooks Brothers there as well. Master has put in a request for clothing. I believe he wants to look his best for you as well."

As she hung up, that stupid smile stuck to her face like glue.

Wrath left a message on Beth's voice mail and rolled over in bed, reaching out for the braille clock. Three in the afternoon. He'd slept for about six hours, which was more than usual, but what his body typically needed after a feeding.

God, he wished she were with him.

Tohr had called at dawn with a report. The two of them had stayed up all night watching Godzilla movies, and by the sound of the male's voice, he was half in love with her.

Which Wrath simultaneously understood and resented the hell out of.

But man, he'd made the right call sending Tohr over. Rhage definitely would have come on to her, and then Wrath would have had to break something of the brother's. An arm, maybe a leg. Maybe both. And Vishous, while he didn't have Hollywood's outrageous good looks, had plenty of pimp juice. Phury's vow of celibacy was strong, but why put him in the path of temptation?

Zsadist?

He hadn't even considered that option. The scar down that brother's face would have scared the shit out of her. Hell, even Wrath could see the damn thing. And mortal terror in a female was Z's favorite turn-on. He got off on it like most males favored crap from Victoria's Secret.

No, Tohr would be on sentry duty if the need ever arose again.

Wrath stretched. Feeling the satin sheets against his naked skin made him yearn for Beth. Now that he'd fed, his body felt stronger than ever, as though his bones were shafts of carbon and his muscles were steel cables. He was back to himself again, and the whole lot of him was itching to be used hard.

Except he bitterly regretted what had happened with Marissa.

He thought back to the night. As soon as he'd lifted his head from her neck, he knew he'd nearly killed her. And not from drinking too much.

She'd pushed herself away, her body shaking from misery as she'd floundered off the bed.

"Marissa—"

"My lord, I release you. From the covenant. You are free of me."

He'd cursed, feeling like hell for what he'd done to her.

"I don't understand your anger," she'd said weakly. "This is what you have always wanted, and I grant it to you now."

"I never wanted—"

"Me," she'd whispered. "I know."

"Marissa—"

"Please don't say the words. I couldn't bear to hear the truth from your lips, even though I know it well. You have always been ashamed to be tied to me."

"What the hell are you talking about?"

"I disgust you."

"What?"

"Do you think I haven't noticed? You can't wait to be free of me. I drink and then you bolt up, as if you've had to force yourself to endure my presence." She'd started to sob then. "I've always tried to be clean when I come to you. I spend hours soaking in the tub, washing myself. But I cannot find the dirt that you see."

"Marissa, stop. Just stop. It isn't about you."

"Yes, I know. I saw the female. In your mind." She'd let out a shudder.

"I'm sorry," he'd said. "And you have never disgusted me. You're beautiful—"

"Don't say that. Not now." Marissa's voice had hardened then. "If anything, just be sorry that it took this long for me to see what has always been true."

"I will still protect you," he'd vowed.

"No, you won't. I'm no longer your concern. Not that I've ever been."

And then she'd left, the fresh scent of the ocean lingering a moment before dissipating.

Wrath rubbed his eyes. He was determined to make it up to her somehow. He wasn't sure exactly how he'd pull that off, considering the hell she'd been put through. But he wasn't prepared to have her drift off into the ether thinking that she'd been utterly nothing to him. Or that he'd found her in some way unclean.

He'd never loved her, true. But he hadn't wanted to hurt her, which was why he'd told her to leave him so often. If she pulled out, if she made it clear she didn't want him, she would still be able to hold her head up in the catty aristocratic circle she was from. In her class, a *shellan* who was rejected by her mate was perceived as damaged goods.

Now that she had left him, she'd be spared any ignominy. And he had a feeling that when word got out, no one would be surprised.

Funny, he'd never really considered how he and Marissa would part, perhaps because after all these centuries, he'd assumed they never would. But he'd certainly never expected it to be because he was forming some kind of attachment to another female.

And that was what was happening. With Beth. After marking her last night as he had, he couldn't pretend he wasn't getting emotionally tied to her.

He cursed out loud, knowing enough about male vampire behavior and psychology to realize he was in trouble. Hell, they were both in trouble now.

A bonded male was a dangerous thing.

Especially when he was going to have to leave his female.

And give her into the keeping of another.

Trying to push the implications out of his mind, Wrath reached for the phone and dialed upstairs, thinking he needed something to eat. When there was no answer, he assumed Fritz must have gone to the store to buy food.

Good thing. Wrath had asked the brothers to come later in the evening, and they liked to eat big. It was time to reconnoiter, catch up with their investigations.

The need to avenge Darius burned.

And the closer Wrath got to Beth, the hotter the fire.

TWENTY-THREE

Butch walked out of the captain's office. His holster felt too light without his gun in it. Wallet was too flat without his badge. It was like being naked.

"What happened?" José asked.

"I'm taking a vacation."

"What the hell does that mean?"

Butch started down the hall. "Did the NYPD have anything on that suspect?"

José grabbed his arm and pulled him into an interrogation room. "What happened?"

"I'm suspended without pay, pending the conclusion of an internal investigation. Which we both know is going to find that I acted with inappropriate force."

José buried a hand in his hair. "I told you to back off those suspects, man."

"That Riddle guy deserved worse."

"Not the point."

"Funny, that's what the captain said."

Butch walked over to the two-way mirror and looked at himself. God, he was getting old. Or maybe he was just tired of the only job he'd ever wanted to do.

Police brutality. Screw that. He was a protector of the innocent, not some self-impressed skull-cracker who got off on being a tough guy. The trouble was, there were just too many rules favoring criminals. The victims whose lives were shattered by violence should be half so lucky.

"I don't belong here anyway," he said softly.

"What?"

There was just no place for men like him in the world anymore, he thought.

Butch turned around. "So. The NYPD. What did we find out?"

José stared at him for a long time. "Suspended from the force, huh?"

"At least until they officially can me."

José put his hands on his hips and looked down, shaking his head as if he were remonstrating with his shoes. But he answered.

"*Nada.* It's like he came out of nowhere."

Butch cursed. "Those stars. I know you can get them on the Web, but they can be bought locally, right?"

"Yeah, through martial-arts academies."

"We've got a couple of those in town."

José nodded slowly.

Butch took his keys out of his pocket. "I'll see ya."

"Hold up—we already sent someone out to ask around. Both academies said they don't remember anyone buying them who fit the suspect's description."

"Thanks for the tip." Butch started for the door.

"Detective. Yo, *O'Neal.*" José grabbed Butch's forearm. "Damn it, will you stop for a minute?"

Butch glared over his shoulder. "Is this where you warn me to stay out of police business? 'Cause you might as well save the speech."

"Christ, Butch, I'm not your enemy." José's dark brown eyes were penetrating. "The boys and I are behind you. As far as we're concerned, you do what you need to do, and you've never been wrong. Anyone you've knocked around has deserved it. But maybe you've just been lucky, you know? What if you'd hurt someone who wasn't—"

"Cut the preacher routine. I'm not interested." He clamped his hand on the doorknob.

José squeezed hard. "You're off the force, O'Neal.

And going half-cocked into an investigation you've been removed from won't bring Janie back."

Butch expelled his breath like he'd been punched. "You want to kick me in the nuts now, too?"

José removed his hand, looking as if he were throwing in the towel. "I'm sorry. But you gotta know that getting deeper in the weeds is only going to screw you. It's not going to help your sister. It's never helped her."

Butch slowly shook his head. "Shit. I know that."

"You sure?"

Yeah, he was. He'd really liked hurting Billy Riddle, and that was about vengeance for what had been done to Beth. It had nothing to do with bringing his sister back to life. Janie was gone. And she'd been gone for a long, long time.

Still, José's sad eyes made him feel like he had a terminal illness.

"It's gonna be fine," he found himself saying. Although he didn't really believe it.

"Just don't . . . don't push your luck out there, Detective."

Butch threw open the door. "Pushing's all I know how to do, José."

Mr. X leaned back in his office chair, thinking about the night ahead. He was ready to try again, even though the downtown area was hot right now, what with the car bombing and the discovery of the whore's body. Trolling for vampires in the vicinity of Screamer's was going to be risky, but the risk of being caught added to the challenge.

Even more to the point, however, if you wanted to catch a shark, you didn't fish in freshwater. He had to go to where the vampires were.

Anticipation shot through him.

He'd been brushing up on his torture techniques.

And this morning, before leaving for the academy, he'd visited the workspace he'd set up in his barn. His tools were gathered and gleaming: a dentist's drill set; knives of various sizes; a ball-peen hammer and a chisel; a Sawzall.

A melon baller. For the eyes.

The trick was, of course, walking that fine line between pain and death. Pain you could stretch out for hours, days. Death was the ultimate off switch.

There was a knock at the door.

"Enter," he said.

It was the receptionist, the jacked woman who had arms big as a man's and no breasts to speak of. Her contradictions never ceased to amaze him. In spite of the fact that a raging case of penis envy caused her to take steroids and pump iron like a gorilla, she insisted on wearing makeup. And doing her hair. In her cropped T-shirt and leggings, she looked like a bad drag queen.

She disgusted him.

You should always know who you are, he thought. *And who you aren't.*

"A guy's here to speak with you." Her voice was about an octave and a half too low. "O'Neal, I think that's the name. Acts like a cop, but didn't pop a badge."

"Tell him I'll be right out." *You freak of nature*, he added to himself.

Still, Mr. X had to laugh as the door shut behind her. Him. Whatever.

Here he was, a man with no soul who killed vampires, and he was calling her a freak?

Yeah, well, at least he had a purpose. And a plan.

She was just going to Gold's Gym again tonight. Right after she got rid of her five-o'clock shadow.

It was a little before six when Butch pulled the unmarked up in front of Beth's building. He'd have to return the vehicle eventually, but suspended wasn't fired. The captain was going to have to ask for the damn car back.

He'd gone to both martial-arts academies and talked with the directors. One guy had been obnoxious. Your typical ass-kiss-craving, self-defense lunatic who'd convinced himself he was actually Asian. In spite of the fact that he was as white as Butch was.

The other man had been just plain weird. He'd looked like a 1950s milkman, with blond hair that had obviously been hit with some pomade and a bright, annoying smile that had missed its Pepsodent ad by nearly half a century. The guy had bent over to be helpful, but something was off. Butch's bullshit detector had spiked a serious woody the minute Mr. Mayberry had opened his mouth.

And the guy had smelled like a sissy, besides.

Butch leaped up Beth's front steps and rang her buzzer. He'd left her a voice mail at work and at home telling her he was coming over. He was about to hit the button again when he saw her through the glass door, coming into the lobby.

Goddamn.

She had on a wraparound black dress that just about brought his headache back, it was so perfect for her. The vee in front dipped down and showed a little of her breasts. The tight waist set off her slim hips beautifully. And the slit up one side showed a flash of thigh with every step she took. Her heels were tall, making her ankles look fragile and lovely.

She looked up from the purse she'd been rummaging around in and seemed surprised to see him.

Her hair was up. He thought about what it would be like to take it down.

She opened the door. "Butch."

"Hi." He felt tongue-tied as a kid.

"I got your messages," she said softly.

208

He stepped back so she could come outside. "You got time to talk?"

Even though he knew what her answer was going to be.

"Ah, not right now."

"Where are you going?"

"I have a date."

"With whom?"

She met his eyes with such deliberate calmness, he knew the next thing she said was going to be a lie.

"No one special."

Yeah, right.

"What happened to the man last night, Beth? Where is he?"

"I don't know."

"You're lying."

Her eyes never wavered from his. "If you'll excuse me—"

He gripped her arm. "Do not go to him."

The low sound of an engine filled the silence between them. A large black Mercedes with tinted windows pulled up. Real drug-lord time.

"Ah, fuck, Beth." He squeezed her arm, desperate to get her attention. "Don't do this. You're aiding and abetting a suspect."

"Let go of me, Butch."

"He's *dangerous*."

"And you aren't?"

He dropped his hold.

"Tomorrow," she said, stepping back. "We'll talk tomorrow. Meet me here after work."

Getting frantic, he put his body in her path. "Beth, I can't let you—"

"Are you going to arrest me?"

Not as a cop, he couldn't. Not unless he was reinstated to the force.

"No. I won't take you in."

"Thank you."

"I'm not doing it as a favor," he said bitterly as she walked around him. "Beth, *please*."

She paused. "Nothing is as it seems."

"I don't know. I've got a pretty fucking clear picture. You're protecting a killer, and there's a serious chance you're going to get stuffed into a pine box. Do you understand what this guy is? I've seen his face up close. When his hand was around my neck and he was squeezing the life right out of me. A man like that has murder in his blood. It's his nature. How can you go to him? Hell, how can you let him walk the streets?"

"He's not like that."

But the words were phrased as a question.

The car door opened, and a little old man in a tuxedo got out.

"Mistress, is there a difficulty?" the man asked her solicitously, while at the same time shooting Butch the evil eye.

"No, Fritz. No problem." She smiled, but it was a shaky one. "Tomorrow, Butch."

"If you live that long."

She paled, but rushed down the stairs, sliding into the car.

After a moment Butch got into his. And trailed them.

When Havers heard footsteps coming toward the dining room, he looked up from his plate with a frown. He'd been hoping to make it through his meal without an interruption.

But it wasn't one of the *doggen* coming in with news that a patient had arrived to be treated.

"Marissa!" He rose from his chair.

She marshaled a smile for him. "I thought I would come down. I'm tired of spending so much time in my room."

"I'm very pleased to have your company."

As she came up to the table, he pulled out her chair. He was happy that he'd insisted her place was always set, even after he'd lost hope she would join him. And tonight it seemed as though she was making an effort with more than just coming to eat. She was wearing a beautiful dress made of black silk that had a jacket with a stiff, stand-up collar. Her hair was down around her shoulders, flashing spun gold in the candlelight. She looked lovely, and he felt a flush of animosity. It was a total insult that Wrath couldn't appreciate all she had to offer, that this exquisite female of noble blood was not good enough for him.

Other than for use as a feeding trough.

"How is your work?" she asked as she was served wine by one *doggen*. A plate of food was set in front of her by another. "Thank you, Phillip. Karolyn, this looks wonderful."

She picked up a fork and gently prodded the roast beef.

Good heavens, Havers thought. This was almost normal.

"My work? Fine. Actually better than fine. As I mentioned, I've had a bit of a breakthrough. Feeding may soon be a thing of the past." He lifted his glass and drank. The burgundy should have been a perfect accompaniment to the beef, but it tasted off to him. Everything on his plate was sour on his tongue as well. "I transfused myself with stored blood this afternoon, and I feel fine."

Actually, that was a bit of an overstatement. He didn't feel sick, but something wasn't right. That normal rush of strength had yet to hit him.

"Oh, Havers," she said softly. "You still miss Evangaline, don't you?"

"Painfully. And the drinking is simply not . . . agreeable to me."

No, he would no longer stay alive the old-fashioned way. From now on it would be clinical. A sterilized needle in his arm, hooking him up to a bag.

"I'm so very sorry," Marissa said.

Havers reached out, laying his palm faceup on the table. "Thank you."

She put her hand in his. "And I'm sorry that I've been so . . . preoccupied. But it will be better now."

"Yes," he said urgently. Wrath was just the kind of barbarian who would want to continue to drink from the vein, but at least Marissa could be spared the indignity. "You could try the transfusion as well. It will free you, too."

She took her hand back and reached for her wineglass. As she lifted the burgundy to her mouth, she spilled some on her jacket.

"Oh, bother," she muttered, brushing the wine off the silk. "I'm terribly uncoordinated, aren't I?"

She removed the jacket and laid it on the empty chair next to her.

"You know, Havers, I would like to try it. Drinking is no longer palatable to me, either."

A delicious relief, a feeling of possibility, overtook him. The sensation seemed wholly unfamiliar because he hadn't felt it in so very long. The idea that something might change for the better had become a foreign concept to him.

"Truly?" he whispered.

She nodded, pushing her hair over her shoulder and picking up her fork. "Yes, truly."

And then he saw the marks on her neck.

Two inflamed puncture wounds. A red blaze where she had been sucked. Purple contusions on the skin of her collarbone where she'd been gripped by a heavy hand.

Horror curdled his appetite, blurred his vision.

"How could he have treated you so roughly?" Havers breathed.

Marissa's hand went to her neck before she quickly pulled some hair forward. "It's nothing. Truly, it's not . . . anything."

His eyes stayed in place as he continued to see clearly what she had hidden.

"Havers, please. Let's just eat." She picked up her fork again, as if she were prepared to demonstrate exactly how one did that. "Come now. Eat with me."

"How can I?" He threw down his silverware.

"Because it's over."

"What is?"

"I have broken the covenant with Wrath. I am no longer his *shellan*. I will see him no more."

Havers could only stare for a moment. "Why? What has changed?"

"He has found a female he wants."

Anger congealed in Havers's veins. "And just who does he prefer to you?"

"You do not know her."

"I know all females of our class. Who is it?" he demanded.

"She is not of our class."

"She is one of the Scribe Virgin's Chosen, then?" In the vampire social hierarchy, they were the only ones above a female of the aristocracy.

"No. She is human. Or at least half-human, from what I could tell from his thoughts about her."

Havers turned to stone in his chair. Human. A *human?*

Marissa had been forsaken for a . . . Homo sapiens?

"Has the Scribe Virgin been contacted?" he asked in a brittle voice.

"That is his duty, not mine. But make no mistake, he will go to her. It is . . . over."

Marissa took a small piece of beef and put it between her lips. She chewed carefully, as if she'd forgotten how.

Or perhaps the humiliation she was obviously feeling made it difficult to swallow.

Havers gripped the arms of his chair. His sister, his beautiful, pure sister, had been ignored. Used. Brutalized as well.

And all that was left of her mating with their king was the shame of being cast aside for a human.

Her love had never meant anything to Wrath. Neither had her body or her impeccable bloodlines.

And now the warrior had done away with her honor.

The hell it was over.

TWENTY-FOUR

Wrath pulled on the Brooks Brothers jacket. It was tight in the shoulders, but he was hard to fit, and he'd given Fritz no notice.

Then again, the thing could have been custom-tailored and he would still have felt shackled. He was much more comfortable in leather and weapons than this worsted-wool crap.

He walked into the bathroom and squinted at himself. The suit was black. So was the shirt. That was all he could really see.

Good God, he probably looked like a lawyer.

He stripped off the jacket and put it on the marble counter. Pulling his hair back with impatient hands, he tied the length with a strap of leather.

Where was Fritz? The *doggen* had left to get Beth nearly an hour ago. The two of them should be back by now, but the house above still felt empty.

Ah, hell. Even if the butler had been gone for only a minute and a half, Wrath would have been restless. He was pumped to see Beth, itchy and distracted. All he could think about was burying his face in her hair as he drove the hardest part of himself deep inside her body.

God, those sounds she made when she came for him.

He glanced at his reflection. Put the jacket back on.

But sex wasn't everything. He wanted to treat her with respect, not just throw her on her back. He wanted to slow down. Eat with her. Talk with her. Hell, he wanted to give her what females liked: a little TLC.

215

He tried out a smile. Widened it. His cheeks felt like they were going to crack.

Yeah, okay, so he wasn't exactly Hallmark-card material. But he could pull off some romance. Couldn't he?

He rubbed his jaw. What the hell did he know about romance?

Abruptly, he felt like a fool.

No, it was worse than that. The fancy new suit exposed him, and the truth he saw was a nasty surprise.

He was changing himself for a female. For no other reason than to try to please her.

This was bonding at work, he thought. This was precisely why he never should have marked her, why he never, ever should have let himself get that close.

He reminded himself yet again that when she was through her transition, he was finished with her. He would go back to his life. And she would . . .

God, why did he feel like he'd been shot through the chest?

"Wrath, man?" Tohrment's voice boomed through the chamber.

The sound of his brother's baritone was a relief, bringing Wrath back to center.

He stepped out into the bedroom and scowled when he heard his brother's low whistle.

"Look at you," Tohr said, moving around him.

"Bite me."

"No, thanks. I prefer the females." The brother laughed. "Although I have to say you clean up nice."

Wrath crossed his arms over his chest, but the jacket pulled so tightly he worried he was going to split the seam in the back. He dropped his hands.

"You're here why?"

"I called your cell and you didn't answer. You said you wanted us all to meet here tonight. When?"

"I'm busy until one."

"One?" Tohr drawled.

Wrath planted his hands on his hips. A feeling of deep uneasiness, like someone had broken into his home, sneaked up on him.

This was so wrong, he thought. The date. With Beth.

But it was too damn late to cancel.

"Make that midnight," he said.

"I'll tell the brothers to be ready then."

He had a feeling Tohr was sporting a little grin, but the vampire's voice was steady. There was a pause.

"Yo, Wrath?"

"What."

"She's as beautiful as you think she is. Just thought you'd want to know."

If any other male had said that, Wrath would have given the idiot a nose job. And even though it was Tohr, his temperature still rose. He didn't like being reminded how irresistible she was. It made him think about the male she'd end up with for life.

"You got a point or are you just shooting your lip off?"

It wasn't an invitation to elaborate, but Tohr marched right through the opening anyway. "You're way into her."

He should have stuck with "Fuck you" as a response, Wrath thought.

"And I think she feels the same way," Tohr tacked on.

Oh, great. That made him feel better. Like he might end up breaking her heart or something.

Man, this date thing was a *really* bad idea. Just where did he think he was taking them with all the hearts-and-flowers shit?

Wrath bared his fangs. "I'm only hanging in until she goes through the change. That's it."

"Yeah, sure." When Wrath growled deep in his throat, the other vampire shrugged. "I've never seen you dress for a female before."

"She's Darius's daughter. You want me to be like Zsadist with one of his whores?"

"Dear God, no. And damn, I wish he'd stop that. But I like what I'm seeing with you and Beth. You've been alone for too long."

"That's your opinion."

"And others'."

Sweat broke out across Wrath's forehead.

Tohr's honesty made him feel trapped. As did the fact that he was only supposed to be protecting Beth, but instead was busy trying to make her feel as if she were more special to him than she really was.

"Don't you have somewhere you need to be?" he demanded.

"Nope."

"Just my luck."

Desperate to move around, he walked over to the couch and picked up his biker jacket. He needed to restock it with weapons, and since Tohr didn't seem in a big hurry to get his ass in gear, the distraction was better than screaming.

"The night Darius died," Tohr said, "he told me you'd turned him down when he asked you to take care of her."

Wrath opened the closet and reached into a storage bin full of throwing stars, daggers, and chains. He made his selections with rough hands. "So?"

"What changed your mind?"

Wrath clapped his molars together, biting down hard, a breath away from lashing out.

"He's dead. I owe him."

"You owed him when he was alive, too."

Wrath whirled around. "Do you have any other business with me? If not, get the hell out of here."

Tohr lifted his hands. "Easy, brother."

"Fuck easy. I'm not talking about her with you or

218

anyone else. Got it? And keep your mouth shut with the brothers, too."

"Okay, okay." Tohr backed over to the door. "But do yourself a favor. Cop to what's going on with that female. An unacknowledged weakness is deadly."

Wrath growled and leaned into his attack pose, upper body jutting forward on his hips. "Weakness? This coming from a male who's dumb enough to love his *shellan*? You gotta be kidding me."

There was a long silence.

And then Tohr said softly, "I'm lucky to have found love. I thank the Scribe Virgin every day that Wellsie is in my life."

Wrath's temper surged, set off by something he couldn't put his finger on. "You're *pathetic*."

Tohr hissed. "And you've been dead for hundreds of years. You're just too mean to find a grave and lie down."

Wrath threw the leather jacket to the floor. "At least I'm not pussy-whipped."

"Nice. Fucking. Suit."

Wrath crossed the distance between them in two strides, and the other vampire met the approach head-on. Tohrment was a big male, with thick shoulders and long, powerful arms. Menace pulsated between them.

Wrath grinned coldly, his fangs lengthening. "If you spent half the amount of time defending our race that you do chasing after that female of yours, we might not have lost Darius. Ever think of that?"

Anguish came out of the brother like blood from a chest wound, and the vampire's white-hot agony thickened the air. Wrath drew in the scent, taking the burn of misery down deep into his lungs, into his very soul. The knowledge that he'd laid out a male of honor and courage with such a low blow filled him with self-loathing. And while he waited for Tohr

219

to attack, he welcomed the inner hatred as an old friend.

"I can't believe you said that." Tohr's voice throbbed. "You need to—"

"I don't want any of your worthless advice."

"*Fuck you*." Tohr knocked him a good one in the shoulder. "You're gonna get it anyway. You'd better learn who your enemies really are, you arrogant asshole. Before you're standing alone."

Wrath barely heard the door slam shut. The voice screaming in his head that he was a worthless piece of shit overrode just about everything else.

He drew in a great breath and emptied his lungs with a vicious yell. The sound vibrated around the room, rattling the doors, the loose weapons, the mirror in the bathroom. Candles flared wildly in response, their flames licking up the walls, greedy to get free of their wicks and destroy what they could. He roared until his throat felt as if it were going to tear apart, until his chest burned.

When he finally closed his mouth, he felt no relief. Just remorse.

He marched over to the closet and took out a nine-millimeter Beretta. After he loaded it, he tucked the gun into the waistband of his slacks at the small of his back. Then he headed for the door and took the stairs two at time, his thighs eating up the distance to the first floor.

Stepping into the drawing room, he listened. The silence was probably a good thing for everybody. He needed to get ahold of himself.

Prowling around the house, he stopped at the dining room table. It had been set as he'd asked. Two places at one end. Crystal and silver. Candles.

And he'd called his brother pathetic?

If it hadn't been all Darius's priceless crap, he'd

have swept the table clean with his arm. His hand shot out, as if it were ready to follow through on the impulse anyway, but the jacket confined him. He gripped the lapels, prepared to rip the thing off his back and burn it, but the front door opened. He wheeled around.

There she was. Coming across the threshold. Walking into the hall.

Wrath's hands dropped to his sides.

She was dressed in black. Her hair was up. She smelled . . . like night-blooming roses. He breathed in through his nose, his body hardening, his instincts demanding that he get her under him.

But then her emotions hit him. She was wary, nervous. He could sense her mistrust with clarity, and he took perverse satisfaction as she hesitated to look at him.

His temper returned, nice and sharp.

Fritz was busy closing the door, but the *doggen*'s happiness was obvious in the air around him, shimmering like sunshine. "I've put out some wine in the drawing room. I'll serve the first course in about thirty minutes, shall I?"

"No," Wrath commanded. "We'll sit down now."

Fritz seemed confused, but then clearly caught the drift of Wrath's emotions.

"As you wish, master. Right away." The butler disappeared as though something were on fire in the kitchen.

Wrath stared at Beth.

She took a step back. Probably because he was glaring.

"You look . . . different," she said. "In those clothes."

"If you think they've civilized me, don't be fooled."

"I'm not."

"Good. Now let's get this over with."

221

Wrath went into the dining room, thinking she'd follow if she wanted. And if she chose not to, hell, it was probably for the better. He wasn't in a big hurry to get trapped at the table anyway.

TWENTY-FIVE

Beth watched Wrath saunter away as if he didn't give a rat's ass whether or not she ate with him.

If she hadn't been having second thoughts herself, she would have been totally insulted. He'd invited her to dinner. So why was he all bent out of joint when she showed up? She was tempted to hightail it right back out the front door.

Except she followed because she felt like she had no choice. There were so many things she wanted to know, things only he could explain.

Although as God was her witness, if there were any way to get the information from someone else, she would have.

As he walked in front of her, she shot a glare at the back of his head and tried to ignore his powerful stride. The latter was an abject failure. He just moved too superbly. With each sharp impact of his heel, his shoulders shifted under the expensive jacket, counterbalancing the thrust of his legs. As his arms swung loosely, she knew that his thighs were clenching and releasing with every step. She pictured him naked, his muscles flexing under his skin.

Butch's voice bounced around in her head. *A man like that has murder in his blood. It's his nature.*

And yet Wrath had sent her away last night when he'd been a danger to her.

She told herself to forget attempting to reconcile the contradictions. She was just trying to read tea leaves with all the mental aerobics. She needed to go with her gut, and her gut said Wrath was the only help she had.

As she stepped into the dining room, the beautiful table that had been set for them was a surprise. There were flowers in the center, tuberoses and orchids. And ivory candles. And gleaming china and silver.

Wrath went around and pulled out a chair, waiting for her to sit in it. Looming over the thing.

God, he looked fantastic in the suit. And the open collar of his shirt showed off his throat, the black silk making his skin look tanned. Too bad he was flat-out pissed. His face was as harsh as his temper, and with his hair pulled back, the aggressive thrust of his jaw was even more prominent.

Something had set him off. Big-time.

Perfect date material, she thought. A vampire with the social equivalent of road rage.

She approached cautiously. As he slid the seat under her, she could have sworn he bent down to her hair and inhaled deeply.

"Why were you so late?" he demanded while sitting at the head of the table. When she didn't answer, he cocked an eyebrow at her, the dark arch rising over the rim of his black sunglasses. "Did Fritz have to talk you into coming?"

To give herself something to do, she took her napkin and unfolded it in her lap. "It was nothing like that."

"So tell me what it was."

"Butch followed us. We had to wait until we got free of him."

She sensed the space around Wrath darkening as if his anger sucked the light right out of the air.

Fritz came in with two small plates of salad. He put them down.

"Wine?" he asked.

Wrath nodded.

After the butler had finished pouring and left, she picked up a heavy silver fork and forced herself to eat.

224

"Why are you afraid of me now?" Wrath's voice was sardonic, as if he were bored by her fear.

She jabbed at the greens. "Hmmm. Could it be because you look like you want to strangle someone?"

"You walked into this house scared of me again. Before you even saw me, you were frightened. I want to know why."

She kept her eyes on her plate. "Maybe I was reminded that last night you almost killed a friend of mine."

"Christ, not that again."

"You asked," she shot back. "Don't get mad if you don't like my answer."

Wrath wiped his mouth impatiently. "I didn't kill him, did I?"

"Only because I stopped you."

"And that bothers you? Most people like to be heroes."

She put her fork down. "You know what? I don't want to be here with you right now."

He kept eating. "So why did you come?"

"Because you asked me to!"

"Believe me, I can handle the rejection." As if she were of no concern to him whatsoever.

"This was a mistake." She put her napkin down next to her plate and stood.

He cursed. "Sit down."

"Don't tell me what to do."

"Let me amend that. Sit down and shut up."

She gaped at him. "You arrogant ass—"

"Someone's already called me that tonight, thank you very much."

Fritz picked that moment to breeze in with some warm rolls.

She glared at Wrath and pretended she was only reaching across the table for the wine bottle. She wasn't about to march off in front of Fritz. And besides, she suddenly felt like sticking around.

225

So she could yell at Wrath a little longer.

When they were alone again, she hissed, "Where do you get off talking to me like that?"

He took a final bite of salad, placed his fork on the edge of his plate, and dabbed the corners of his mouth with his napkin. Like he'd been trained by Emily Post herself.

"Let's get one thing straight," he said. "You need me. So get over your hangups about what I *might* have done to that cop. Your good buddy Butch is still above ground, right? So what's the problem?"

Beth stared at him, trying to read through his sunglasses, searching for some softness, something she could connect to. But the dark lenses shut her out of his eyes completely, and the tight lines of his face gave her nothing to go on.

"How can life mean so little to you?" she wondered aloud.

The smile he gave her was cold. "How can death mean so much to *you?*"

Beth sank back in her chair. Cringed from him, was more like it. She couldn't believe she'd made love—no, had sex—with him. He was utterly callous.

Abruptly, her heart hurt. Not because he was being hard on her, but because she was disappointed. She'd really wanted him to be different than he appeared. She'd wanted to believe the flashes of warmth he'd shown her were as big a part of him as those hard edges.

She rubbed the raw patch at her sternum. "I'd really like to go, if you don't mind."

There was a long pause.

"Ah, hell . . ." he muttered, letting out his breath. "This isn't right."

"No, it isn't."

"I thought that you deserved . . . I don't know. A date. Or something. Something normal." He laughed harshly as she looked at him with surprise. "Dumb idea, I know. I should stick to what I'm good at. I'd be better off teaching you how to kill."

Underneath his thick pride, she sensed a kernel of something else. Insecurity? No, that wasn't it. Naturally with him, it would be more intense.

Self-hatred.

Fritz came in, picked up their salad plates, and reappeared with soup. It was cold vichyssoise. *Interesting*, she thought absently. Usually it was soup first, then salad, wasn't it? But then, she had to imagine vampires had lots of different social traditions. Like the men having more than one woman.

Her stomach lurched. She wasn't going to think of that. She simply refused to.

"Look, just so you know," Wrath said as he picked up his spoon, "I fight to protect, not because I've got a jones for murder. But I've killed thousands. Thousands, Beth. Do you understand? So if you want me to pretend I'm not comfortable with death, I can't do that for you. I just can't."

"Thousands?" she mumbled, overwhelmed.

He nodded.

"Who in God's name are you fighting?"

"Bastards who would kill you as soon as you go through the transition."

"Vampire hunters?"

"*Lessers*. Humans who have traded their souls to the Omega in return for a free reign of terror."

"Who—or what—is the Omega?" As she spoke the word, the candles flickered wildly, as if tormented by invisible hands.

Wrath hesitated. He actually seemed uncomfortable with the subject. He, who wasn't afraid of anything.

"You mean the devil?" she prompted.

"Worse. You can't compare them. One's just a metaphor.

227

The other's very, very real. Fortunately, the Omega has a counterpart, the Scribe Virgin." He smiled wryly. "Well, maybe *fortunately* is too strong a word. But there is a balance."

"God and Lucifer."

"Maybe according to your lexicon. Our legend has it that vampires were created by the Scribe Virgin as her one and only legacy, as her chosen children. The Omega resented her ability to generate life, and he despised the special powers she gave to the species. The Lessening Society was his defensive response. He uses humans because he is incapable of creation and because they are a readily available source of aggression."

This is just too strange, she thought. Trading souls. The undead. The stuff just didn't exist in the real world.

Then again, she was having dinner with a vampire. So was anything really all that impossible?

She thought of the gorgeous blond man who'd stitched himself up.

"You have others who fight with you, right?"

"My brothers." He took a drink from his wineglass. "As soon as the vampires recognized they were under siege, the strongest and most powerful males were weeded out. Trained to fight. Turned loose against the *lessers*. Those warriors were then bred to the strongest females over generations until a separate subspecies of vampires emerged. The most powerful of this class were indoctrinated into the Black Dagger Brotherhood."

"Are you brothers by blood?"

He smiled tightly. "In a matter of speaking."

His face shuttered, as if the matter were private. She had the sense that he would say no more about the brotherhood, but she was still curious about the war he was fighting.

Especially because she was about to turn into one of those he protected.

228

"So it's humans you kill."

"Yes, although they're basically dead already. In order to give his fighters the longevity and strength they would need to fight us, the Omega had to strip them of their souls." Distaste flickered across his harsh features. "Not that having a soul ever prevented a human from coming after us."

"You don't like . . . us, do you?"

"First of all, half of what's in your veins is from your father's side. And secondly, why would I like humans? They beat the crap out of me before my transition, and the only reason they don't fuck with me now is because I scare the hell out of them. And if it got widely known that vampires existed? They'd come after us even if they weren't in the society. Humans are threatened by anything different, and their response is to fight. They're bullies, picking on the weak, cowering from the strong." Wrath shook his head. "Besides, they irritate me. Look at how their folklore portrays our species. There's Dracula, for Christ's sake, an evil blood-sucker who preys on the defenseless. There's piss-poor B movies and porn. And don't get me started on the whole Halloween thing. Plastic fangs. Black capes. The only things the idiots got right are that we drink blood and that we can't go out in the daylight. The rest is bullshit, fabricated to alienate us and stimulate fear in the masses. Or just as offensive, the fiction is used to create some kind of mystique for bored humans who think the dark side is a fun place to visit."

"But you don't really hunt us, right?"

"Don't use that word. It's *them*, Beth. Not *us*. You are not wholly human right now, and soon you won't be human at all." He paused. "And no, I don't hunt them. But if they get in my way, they've got a serious problem."

She considered what he'd said, trying to ignore the

panic that rose every time she thought about the transition she was supposedly about to go through.

"When you went after Butch like that . . . Surely he's not a . . . whatever, a *lesser*."

"He tried to keep me from you." Wrath's jaw clenched. "I will level anyone and anything before I'd let that happen. And whether he's your lover or not, if he does it again—"

"You promised me you wouldn't kill him."

"I won't take him out. But I'm not going to go easy on him."

Something worth giving Hard-ass a heads-up on, she thought.

"Why aren't you eating?" Wrath demanded. "You need food."

She looked down. Food? Her life was suddenly a Stephen King novel and he was worried about her diet?

"Eat." He nodded at her bowl. "You want to be as strong as possible for the change."

Beth picked up her spoon, just to get him off her back. The soup tasted like Elmer's glue even though she imagined it was perfectly made, perfectly seasoned.

"You're armed right now, aren't you?" she asked.

"Yes, I am."

"Do you ever put down your weapons?"

"No."

"But when we were . . ." She shut her mouth before the words *making love* popped out.

He leaned forward. "There's always something within my reach. Even when I take you."

Beth swallowed. Hot thoughts warred with the horrible realization that he was either paranoid or evil was truly always close.

And damn, she thought. Wrath was a lot of things. But he sure wasn't the hysterical type.

There was a long silence between them, until Fritz

cleared the soup bowls and brought in plates of lamb. She noticed that Wrath's meat had been cut up for him into bite-sized pieces. *Odd*, she thought.

"I have something I want to show you after dinner." He picked up his fork, and it took him two tries to spear some meat with the tines.

And that was when she realized he wasn't even bothering to look at his plate. His gaze was focused down the table.

A chill went through her. Something was very off.

She looked carefully at the sunglasses he wore.

She remembered his fingertips searching her face that first night they were together, as if he'd been trying to see her through touch. And then thought of the fact that he always wore those lenses, as if he weren't just blocking out light, but covering his eyes.

"Wrath?" she said softly.

He reached out for his wineglass, his hand not closing around it until the crystal hit his palm.

"What?" He brought the glass to his lips, but put it back down. "Fritz? We need red."

"Right here, master." Fritz came in with another bottle. "Mistress?"

"Ah, yes, thank you."

When the door to the kitchen flapped shut, Wrath said, "You have something else to ask me?"

She cleared her throat. She had to be reading into things. Desperate to find a weakness in him, she was now trying to convince herself that he was blind.

If she were smart, and that was seriously debatable, she'd quickly run through her list of questions. And then go home.

"Beth?"

"Yeah . . . ah, so it's true you can't go out during the day?"

"Vampires do not do sunlight."

"What happens?"

"Second- to third-degree burns will immediately pop up upon exposure. Incineration occurs not long afterward. The sun is not something you want to screw with."

"But I can go outside now."

"You haven't gone through the change. Although who knows? Afterward you might still be able to tolerate it. It's different for people who have a human parent. Vampire characteristics can be diluted." He took a drink from his glass, licking his lips. "Then again, you're going to go through the transition, so Darius's blood is strong in your veins."

"How often will I have to . . . feed?"

"In the beginning, fairly frequently. Maybe twice, three times a month. Although again, there's no way of knowing."

"After you help me through the first time, how will I be able to find a man who I can drink—"

Wrath's growl stopped her. When she looked up, she shrank into the chair. He was back to being pissed.

"I'll take care of finding you someone," he said, his accent thicker than usual. "Until then, you will use me."

"Hopefully that won't be for long," she muttered, thinking that he didn't look happy about getting stuck with her.

His mouth curled as he looked her way. "So eager for someone else?"

"No, I just thought that . . ."

"What? You thought what?" His tone was hard, hard as the stare shooting out from behind the sunglasses.

The fact that he clearly didn't want to be tied to her was difficult to put into words. The rejection hurt even though she'd no doubt be better off without him.

"I . . . ah, Tohr said you were the king of the vampires. I kind of figure that would make you busy."

"My boy's got to learn to zip it."

"Is it true? That you're the king?"

"No," he snapped.

Well, if that wasn't a door getting slammed in her face.

"Are you married? I mean, do you have a mate? Or two?" she said quickly, figuring she might as well let it all fly. His mood was already back in black. It wasn't like she could make it worse.

"Christ. No."

Well, that was a relief of sorts. Although it was clear what he thought of relationships.

She took a sip of wine. "Do you have a woman in your life at all?"

"No."

"So who do you feed from?"

Long silence. Not an encouraging one.

"There was someone."

"Was?"

"Was."

"Since when?"

"Recently." He shrugged. "We were never close. It was a bad match."

"Who do you go to now?"

"God, you really are a reporter, aren't you?"

"Who?" she pushed.

He looked at her for a long time. And then his face changed, the aggression seeming to bleed out of him. His fork came gently down to his plate and his other hand was placed palm up on the table. "Ah, hell."

In spite of his curse, the air suddenly seemed softer.

She didn't trust the change in his mood at first, but then he whipped off his sunglasses and rubbed his eyes. When he put the lenses back in place, she watched his chest expand, as if he were collecting himself.

"God, Beth, I think I wanted it to be you. In spite of the fact that I'm not going to be around for long after

233

your change." He shook his head. "Man, I am one stupid SOB."

Beth blinked, feeling a kind of sexual heat that he would drink her blood to survive.

"But don't worry," he said. "That's not going to happen. And I'll find you another male fast."

He pushed his plate away, food left half-eaten on the china.

"When was the last time you fed?" she asked, thinking of the powerful craving she'd watched him battle.

"Last night."

Pressure in her chest made her feel as if her lungs were clogged. "But you didn't bite me."

"It was after you left."

She pictured him with another woman in his arms. When she reached for her wineglass, her hand shook.

Wow. Her emotions were breaking all kinds of land speed records tonight. She'd been terrified, pissed off, insanely jealous.

She had to wonder what was next.

Happiness, she had a feeling, probably wasn't it.

TWENTY-SIX

Beth put the wineglass back down, wishing she had more control over herself.

"You don't like that, do you?" Wrath said in a low voice.

"What?"

"Me drinking from another female."

She laughed darkly, despising herself. Him. The whole situation. "You want to rub my nose in it?"

"No." He paused. "The idea you will someday score another male's skin with your teeth and take his blood inside of you makes me want to stab something."

Beth stared at him.

So why don't you stay with me? she thought.

Wrath shook his head. "But I can't let myself think like that."

"Why not?"

"Because you cannot be mine. No matter what I said before."

Fritz came in, cleared, and then served dessert. Whole strawberries on a gold-rimmed plate. Some chocolate sauce on the side to dip them in. A little cookie.

Normally, Beth would have polished the lot of it off in high gear, but she was too shaken to eat.

"You don't like strawberries?" Wrath asked as he put one into his mouth. His bright white teeth bit through the red flesh.

She shrugged, forcing herself to look away from him. "I do."

"Here." He picked a berry off his plate and leaned toward her. "Let me feed you."

His long fingers held the stem firmly, his arm poised in the air.

She wanted to take what he offered. "I can feed myself."

"Yes, you can," he said softly. "But that's not the point."

"Did you have sex with her?" she asked.

His eyebrows flickered. "Last night?"

She nodded. "When you feed, do you make love to her?"

"No. And let me answer your next question. I'm not sleeping with anyone but you right now."

Right now, she thought.

Beth looked down at her hands, feeling stupidly hurt.

"Let me feed you," he murmured. "Please."

Oh, grow up, she told herself. They were adults. They were tremendous in bed together, and that was more than she'd ever had from a man before. Was she really going to walk away just because she was going to lose him?

Besides, even if he promised her a rosy future, a man like him wasn't going to stick around. He was a fighter who ran with a pack of guys just like himself. Home-and-hearth stuff would be boring as hell to him.

She had him now. She wanted him now.

Beth tilted forward in her chair, opened her mouth, and put her lips around the strawberry, taking it whole. Wrath's nostrils flared as he watched her bite down. When some of the sweet juice escaped and dripped onto her chin, he hissed.

"I want to lick that off," he muttered under his breath. He reached forward and took hold of her jaw. Lifted his napkin.

She put her hand on his. "Use your mouth."

A low sound, from deep inside his chest, cut through the room.

Wrath leaned toward her, tilting his head. She caught

a flash of his fangs as his lips opened and his tongue came out. He stroked the juice from her skin and then pulled away.

He stared at her. She looked back at him. The candles flickered.

"Come with me," he said, holding out his hand.

Beth didn't hesitate. She put her palm against his and let herself get drawn up from the table. He took her into the drawing room, over to the picture and through the wall. Down the stone staircase they went, his presence immense in the darkness.

When they got to the bottom landing, he led her into his chamber, and she looked at the bed. It had been made, the pillows neatly lined up against the headboard, the satin sheets smooth as still water. Her body flushed as she remembered what it had felt like to have him on top of her, moving inside of her.

They were headed there again, she thought. And she couldn't wait.

A deep growl made her look over her shoulder. Wrath's gaze was leveled on her as if she were a target.

He'd read her thoughts. He knew what she wanted. And he was prepared to deliver.

He walked up to her, and she heard the door shut and lock. She looked around, wondering if there was someone else in the room. There wasn't.

His hand went to her neck, and he angled her head back with his thumb. "I've wanted to kiss you all night long."

She braced herself for a hard one, ready for all he could give her, except that when his lips came down on hers they were languorous. She could feel the passion in the taut lines of his body, but he clearly refused to be hurried. When he lifted his head, he smiled at her.

She was totally used to the fangs, she thought.

"We're going to take this slow tonight," he said.

But she stopped him before he kissed her again. "Wait. I have something I have to . . . Do you have any condoms?"

He frowned. "No. Why?"

"Why? Ever hear of safe sex?"

"I don't carry those kinds of diseases, and you can't give me anything."

"How do you know?"

"Vampires are not susceptible to human viruses."

"So you can have sex all you want? Without worrying about anything?"

When he nodded, she found herself feeling a little ill. God, how many women he must have—

"And you're not fertile," he said.

"How do you know that?"

"Trust me. We'd both know if you were. Besides, you won't have your first needing for another five years or so after the change. And even when you're in it, conception isn't guaranteed because—"

"Hold on. What's this needing thing?"

"Females are fertile only every ten years or so. Which is a blessing."

"Why?"

He cleared his throat. Actually seemed a little embarrassed. "It's a dangerous time. All males respond on some level if they're in the vicinity of a female in her need. They can't help themselves. Fights can break out. And the female, she, ah . . . the cravings are intense. Or so I've heard."

"You don't have children?"

He shook his head. Then frowned. "God."

"What?"

"To think of you going through the needing." His body swayed, as if he'd closed his eyes. "To be the one you used."

Sexual heat came out of him in a rush. She could actually feel a hot gust move the air.

"How long does it last?" she asked in a husky voice.

"Two days. If the female is . . . serviced well and fed properly, she rebounds quickly."

"And the man?"

"The male's totally used up when it's over. Milked dry. Drained of blood, too. It takes longer for him to recover, but I've never heard one complain. Ever." There was a pause. "I'd love to be the one who relieves you."

Abruptly, he stepped back. She felt a cold draft as his mood changed and the shifting heat dissipated.

"But that will be some other male's duty. And privilege."

His cell phone started ringing.

As he tore it out of his inner pocket with a snarl, she felt for whoever it was.

"What?" There was a pause.

She headed for the bathroom to give him some privacy. And because she needed a little herself. The images in her head were enough to make her dizzy. Two days. Of nothing but him?

When she came back out, Wrath was sitting on the couch, elbows on his knees, brooding. He'd taken off his jacket, and his shoulders looked very wide in that black shirt. As she approached, she caught a glimpse of a handgun under the coat and shivered a little.

He looked up as she sat beside him. She wished she could read him better and blamed the dark lenses. Reaching out to his face, she stroked the harsh cut of his cheek, the strong length of his jaw. His mouth opened slightly, as if her touch made him short of breath.

"I want to see your eyes," she said.

He pulled back a little. "No."

"Why not?"

"Why do you care what they look like?"

She frowned. "You can be hard to read with those

239

glasses on. And right now I wouldn't mind knowing what you're thinking."

Or feeling, even more important.

Finally, he shrugged. "Suit yourself."

When he made no move to take off the lenses, she reached up to the temple pieces and slid the sunglasses from his face. His eyelids were down, his lashes dark against his skin. He didn't open his eyes.

"Won't you show me?"

His jaw tightened.

She looked at the glasses. When she lifted them to the candlelight, she could barely see through them at all, they were so dark.

"You're blind, aren't you?" she said softly.

His lips curled back, but not in a smile. "Worried that I can't take care of you now?"

She wasn't surprised by the hostility. She imagined a man like him would hate any weakness he had.

"No, I'm not worried about that at all. But I would still like to see your eyes."

With a flash of movement, Wrath dragged her across his lap, holding her off balance so it was only the strength of his arms that kept her from hitting the floor. His mouth was set in a grim line.

Slowly, he lifted his lids.

Beth gasped.

His irises were the most extraordinary color. A luminescent pale green, so pale they were almost white. Framed by his thick, dark lashes, set deeply beneath his brows, his eyes gleamed like they were lit from inside his skull, all but popping out of his face like lightbulbs.

Then she noticed his pupils. They were all wrong. Tiny, unfocused pinpricks of black.

She caressed his face. "Your eyes are beautiful."

"Useless."

"Beautiful."

She watched as he scanned her face. He was straining, as if trying to get his vision to work.

"Have they always been like this?" she whispered.

"I was born visually impaired. My sight got worse after my transition and will probably degenerate even more as I age."

"So you can see something?"

"Yeah." His hand lifted to her hair. When waves of it landed on her shoulder, she realized he was picking the pins out of her chignon. "I know I like your hair down, for instance. And I know you are very beautiful."

His fingers traced the contours of her face, then brushed lightly down her neck to her collarbone. They kept going, marking a path between her breasts.

Her heart pounded. Her thoughts slowed down. The world receded until there was only Wrath.

"Sight is seriously overrated, though," he murmured, flattening his palm over her sternum. The weight was heavy. Warm. A foretaste of what his body would feel like pressing hers down into the mattress. "Touch, taste, smell, hearing. The other four senses are just as important."

He leaned forward, nuzzled her neck, and she felt a soft scratching. *His fangs*, she thought. Running up her throat.

She wanted him to bite her.

Wrath breathed in deeply. "You have a perfume to your skin that makes me hard. Instantly. All I have to do is smell you."

She arched in his arms, rubbing herself against his thighs, thrusting her breasts up. Her head fell back, and she let out a little moan.

"God, I love that sound," he said, moving his hand up to the base of her throat. "Make it for me again, Beth."

He sucked her neck. She obliged.

241

"That's it," he groaned. "Sweet heaven, that is *so* it."

His fingers started traveling again, this time over to the tie on her dress. He loosened the bow.

"I wouldn't let Fritz change the sheets."

"What?" she mumbled.

"On the bed. After you left. I wanted to smell you when I lay down in them."

The front of her dress slid open, and cool air hit her skin as his hand drifted up her rib cage. When he got to her bra, he drew a circle around the edges of one lace cup, gradually working his way inward until he brushed against her nipple.

Her body jerked, and she grabbed onto his shoulder. His muscles were rock solid from holding her off balance. She looked up into his fearsome, magnificent face.

His eyes literally glowed, the irises throwing off light that cast her breasts in shadows. The promise of raw, pounding sex and his ferocious hunger for her were obvious in the grinding of his jaw. The heat coming off his tremendous body. The tension in his legs and chest.

But he was utterly in control of himself. And her.

"You know, I've been too greedy with you," he said, bringing his head down to her collarbone. He bit her lightly, not breaking her skin. Then his tongue licked over the spot, stroking, satin smooth. He moved lower, to her breastbone. "I really haven't taken you properly yet."

"I'm not so sure about that," she said roughly.

He laughed with a deep rumble, his breath warm and moist over her skin. He kissed up the top of her breast, and then he took her nipple into his mouth, through the lace. She arched again, feeling like a dam had broken between her legs.

His head lifted, a smile of anticipation pulling at his mouth.

He gently slid the bra strap down and peeled the lace

away. Her nipple puckered even more for him, and she watched as his dark head went down to her pale skin. His tongue, glossy and pink, came out of his mouth and licked her.

As her thighs parted without any demand from him, he laughed again, a thick, male sound of satisfaction.

His hand slipped in between the folds of her dress, brushing against her hip, moving slowly over to her lower belly. He found the edge of her panties and slid his forefinger underneath the lace. Just a little.

He moved that fingertip back and forth, a sensuous tickle inches from where she wanted it to be. Needed it to be.

"More," she demanded. "I want more."

"And you'll get it." His whole hand disappeared under the black lace. She cried out as he came into contact with her hot, wet core. "But Beth?"

She was barely conscious. Completely consumed by his touch. "Umm?"

"Do you want to know what you taste like?" he said against her breast.

One long finger dipped into her body. As if he wanted her to know he wasn't talking about her mouth.

She gripped his back through his silk shirt, scoring him with her nails.

"Peaches," he said, shifting her body, moving downward with his mouth, kissing the skin of her stomach. "Like eating peaches. Silky flesh on my lips and tongue as I suck. Smooth and sweet down the back of my throat when I swallow."

She moaned, close to orgasm and far, far away from sanity.

With a quick motion, he scooped her up and carried her over to the bed. As he laid her down, he parted her legs with his head and put his mouth over the black lace between her thighs.

She gasped and pushed her hands into his hair, only to get tangled up. He yanked away the leather tie. Black waves fell down across her belly, like the flutter of a hawk's wings.

"Just like peaches," he said, stripping off her panties. "And I love peaches."

That eerie, beautiful illumination from his eyes washed over her body. And then he lowered his head again.

TWENTY-SEVEN

Havers went down into his lab and paced around, loafers slapping against the white linoleum tile. After two trips around the room, he came to rest in front of his work-station. He stroked the graceful enameled neck of his microscope. Looked up at the fleets of glass beakers and the battalions of vials on the shelves overhead. He heard the humming of refrigerators, the droning purr of the ventilation unit in the ceiling. Caught the lingering, medicinal specter of Lysol disinfectant.

The scientific environment reminded him of his intellectual pursuits.

Of the pride he took in the strength of his mind.

He considered himself civilized. Capable of shelving his emotions. Good at responding logically to stimuli. But this hatred, this anger was not something he could sit with. The feeling was too violent, too energizing.

Plans spun in his head, plans involving bloodshed.

Except who was he kidding? If he raised so much as a Swiss army knife at Wrath, he was the one who'd be left bleeding.

He needed someone who knew how to kill. Someone who could get close to the warrior.

When the solution came to him, it was obvious. He knew just whom to go to and where to find him.

Havers turned to the door, satisfaction bringing a smile to his lips.

But when he caught his reflection in the mirror over the deep-bellied lab sink, he froze. His shifty eyes were too bright, too eager. The nasty grin was one he'd never worn before. The fevered flush on his face was in anticipation of a vile result.

He didn't recognize himself in the mask of vengeance.

He hated the way he looked.

"Oh, God."

How could he even think such things? He was a physician. A healer. He'd devoted himself to saving lives, not taking them.

Marissa had said it was over. She'd broken the covenant. She wasn't going to see Wrath again.

Yet didn't she still deserve to be avenged for the way she'd been treated?

And now was the time to strike. The approach to Wrath was uncluttered by the threat that Marissa might get caught in the crossfire.

Havers felt a shudder go through him, and he assumed it was horror at the magnitude of what he was considering. But then his body lurched, and he had to reach out to steady himself. Vertigo threw the world around him into a blender, and he tumbled over to a chair.

Wrenching free the knot of his bow tie, he struggled to breathe.

The blood, he thought. The transfusion.

It wasn't working.

In despair, he fell from the chair to his knees. Brought to the ground by his failure, he closed his eyes and let himself sink into blackness.

Wrath rolled onto his side and took Beth with him, keeping them joined. With his erection still twitching inside of her, he brushed her hair back. It was damp with her delicate sweat.

Mine.

As he kissed her lips, he noted with satisfaction that she was still breathing hard.

He'd made love to her properly, he thought. Slow and deliberate.

"Will you stay?" he asked.

She laughed huskily. "I'm not sure I can walk right now. So, yeah, I think lying here is a good option."

He pressed his lips to her forehead. "I'll return just before dawn."

As he withdrew from the warm cocoon of her body, she looked up. "Where are you going?"

"I'm meeting with my brothers and then we're going out."

He left the bed and went to the closet, dressing in his leathers, pulling his holster onto his shoulders. He slipped in a dagger on each side and grabbed his jacket.

"Fritz will be here," he said. "If you need anything, pick up the phone and dial star forty. It'll ring upstairs."

She wrapped a sheet around herself and rose from the bed.

"Wrath." She touched his arm. "Stay."

He dipped down for a quick kiss. "I'm coming back."

"Are you going to fight?"

"Yes."

"But how can you? You're . . ." She stopped.

"And I've been blind for three hundred years."

Her breath sucked in. "You're that old?"

He had to laugh. "Yeah."

"Well, I've got to say you're holding up just fine." Her smile faded. "How long will I live?"

A shot of cold dread hit him, stealing a couple of heartbeats from his chest.

What if she didn't make it through the transition?

Wrath felt his stomach lurch. He, who was all chummy with the Grim Reaper, suddenly got cracked in the gut with some base mortal fear.

But she was going to make it, right? *Right?*

He realized he was looking at the ceiling, and

wondered who the hell he was talking to. The Scribe Virgin?

"Wrath?"

He yanked Beth against him, holding her tight, as if he could physically bar her from her fate if it was a bad one.

"Wrath," she said into his shoulder. "Wrath, honey, I can't . . . I can't breathe."

He loosened his hold immediately and looked down into her eyes, trying to force his to focus. The strain pulled the skin of his temples tight.

"Wrath? What's wrong?"

"Nothing."

"You didn't answer my question."

"That's because I don't know the answer."

She seemed taken aback, but then arched up onto her tiptoes. She kissed his lips. "Well, however long I've got, I wish you would stay with me tonight."

There was a pounding on the door.

"Yo, Wrath?" Rhage's voice carried through the steel. "We're all here."

Beth stepped back, wrapping her arms around herself. He could sense she was closing up on him again.

He was tempted to lock her in, but he couldn't bear to keep her as a prisoner. And his instincts told him that however much she might wish things were different, she was resigned to her fate, as well as his role in it. She was also safe from the *lessers* at this point, as they would see her only as a human.

"Will you be here when I get back?" he asked, drawing on his jacket.

"I don't know."

"If you leave, I need to know where to find you."

"Why?"

"The change, Beth. The change. Look, it'll be safer if you stay."

"Maybe."

He kept his curse to himself. He wasn't going to beg.

"The other door out in the hall," he said. "It opens into your father's bedroom. I thought you might like to go in there."

Wrath left before he embarrassed himself.

Warriors did not beg. They rarely even asked. They took what they wanted and killed for it if they had to.

But he really hoped she'd be there when he got back. He liked the thought of her sleeping in his bed.

Beth went into the bathroom and took a shower, letting the hot water soothe her nerves. When she got out, she dried off and noticed a black robe hanging on a hook. She put it on.

She sniffed the lapels and closed her eyes. Wrath's smell was all over it, a combination of soap and after-shave and . . .

Male vampire.

Good lord. Was she actually living this?

She walked out into the chamber. Wrath had left the closet open, and she went over to look at his clothes. What she found was a cache of weapons that petrified her.

She eyed the door that led out into the stairwell. She thought about leaving, but as much as she wanted to go, she knew Wrath was right. Staying was safer.

And her father's bedroom was an enticement.

She would go there and hope that whatever she found didn't give her palpitations. God knew, her lover was providing one shock after another.

As she stepped out onto the bottom landing, she pulled the lapels of the robe closer together. The gas lanterns flickered, making the walls seem alive as she stared at the door across the way. Before she lost her nerve, she walked over, grabbed its handle, and pushed.

Darkness greeted her on the other side, a wall of black that suggested either a bottomless pit or an infinite space. She reached past the jamb and patted the wall, hoping she'd hit a light switch and not something that would bite her.

No luck on the switch. But a minute later her hand was still attached to her arm.

Stepping into the void, she moved slowly to the left until her body hit something big. Given the clapping of brass pulls, and the smell of lemon wax, she figured the thing was probably a highboy. She kept going, feeling her way around until she found a lamp.

It came on with a clicking sound, and she blinked at the glow. The lamp's base was a fine Oriental vase, and the table under it was made of mahogany, and very ornate. No doubt the room was done in the same fabulous style as the upstairs.

When her eyes adjusted, she looked around.

"Oh . . . my . . . God."

There were pictures of her everywhere. Black-and-whites, close-ups, colored ones. She was all ages, from infancy through childhood and into her teens. In college. One was very recent, having been taken while she was leaving the *Caldwell Courier Journal*'s office. She remembered that day. It had been the first snowfall of the winter, and she'd been laughing as she'd looked up at the sky.

Eight months ago.

The idea that she had missed knowing her father by a margin of seasons struck her as tragic.

When had he died? How had he lived?

One thing was clear: He had great taste. Great style. And he obviously liked the finer things. Her father's vast private space was resplendent. The walls were a deep red that set off another spectacular collection of Hudson River School landscapes set in gilt frames. The floor was covered with blue, red, and gold Oriental rugs that glowed like stained glass. But the bed was the most magnificent thing in the room. It was a massive, hand-carved antique with dark red velvet drapes hanging from a canopy. On the bedside table to the left, there was a lamp and yet another picture of her. On the right, there was a clock, a book, and a glass.

He'd slept on that side.

She went over and picked up the hardcover. It was in French. Underneath the book there was a magazine. *Forbes*.

She put them back and then looked at the glass. There was still an inch of water in it.

Either someone was sleeping here . . . or her father had died very recently.

She looked around, searching for clothes or a suitcase that would suggest a guest. The mahogany desk across the room caught her eye. She went over and sat in its thronelike chair, getting swamped by carved arms. Next to the leather blotter there was a small stack of papers. They were bills for the house. Electric. Phone. Cable. All in Fritz's name.

So . . . normal. She had the same things on her desk.

Beth eyed the glass on the bedside table.

His life had been abruptly interrupted, she thought.

Feeling like an interloper, but unable to resist, she pulled open the shallow drawer under the desktop. Montblanc pens, binder clips, a stapler. She slid it back into place, then reached down and looked into a larger drawer. It was full of files. She picked one out. They were financial records—

Holy shit. Her father was loaded. Really loaded.

She glanced at another page. As in millions and millions and millions loaded.

She put the file back and shut the drawer.

Certainly explained the house. The art. The car. The butler.

Next to a phone there was a picture of her in a silver frame. She picked it up, trying to imagine him looking at it.

Where was a photo of him? she wondered.

Could you even take a photograph of a vampire?

She went around the room again, looking in each of the frames. Just her. Just her. Just . . .

Beth bent down.

And with a shaky hand reached out for a gold frame.

Inside was a black-and-white picture of a dark-haired woman looking shyly into the camera. Her hand was on her face, as if she were embarrassed.

Those eyes, Beth thought with wonder. She'd been staring at an identical pair in the mirror every day of her life.

Her mother.

She brushed her forefinger down the glass.

Sitting blindly on the bed, she brought the picture as close as her eyes would bear without her vision blurring. As if proximity to the image would close the distance of time and circumstance, bringing her to the lovely woman in the frame.

Her mother.

TWENTY-EIGHT

This was more like it, Mr. X thought as he humped an unconscious civilian vampire up onto his shoulder. He carried the male quickly through the alley, opened the back of the minivan, and laid his prey down like a sack of potatoes. He was careful to tuck a black wool blanket over his cargo.

He knew his procurement system would work, and upgrading the strength of the tranquilizer from Demosedan to Acepromazine had made the difference. His instinct of using horse tranqs instead of sedatives calibrated for humans had been correct. The vampire had still required two darts of the Acepro before he went down.

Mr. X looked over his shoulder before getting behind the wheel. The prostitute he'd killed was lying across a storm drain, her heroin-saturated blood seeping into the sewage system. The dear girl had even helped him with the needle. Of course, she hadn't been expecting 100 percent pure H.

Or having enough of it pumped into her vein to put a moose into a deep nod.

The police would find her by morning, but he'd been very neat, just like before. Latex gloves. Hat pulled down over his hair. Densely woven nylon clothes that should leave no fibers.

And God knew, she hadn't struggled at all.

Mr. X calmly started the engine and eased out onto Trade Street.

A fine shine of anticipatory sweat broke out above

his upper lip. The arousal, all the adrenaline pumping through him, made him miss the days when he could still have sex. Even if the vampire had no information to give, the rest of the evening was going to be enjoyable

He'd start with the hammer, he thought.

No, the dental drill would be better. Under the fingernails.

That should wake the male right up. After all, there was no sense torturing the unconscious. Like kicking a corpse, that would just be an aerobic workout, and even then, only a mild one. He should know.

Considering what he'd done to his father's body when he'd found it.

From the back he heard a flopping sound. He glanced over his shoulder. The vampire was moving under the blanket.

Good. He was alive.

Mr. X looked back out to the road and frowned. Leaning forward in his seat, he gripped the wheel.

Up ahead, there was the flare of brake lights.

Cars were stopped in a line. A bunch of orange cones were set out. And blue and white flashes announced a police presence.

An accident?

No. A roadblock. Two cops with flashlights looking into cars. A sign that read, INTOXICATION CHECKPOINT.

Mr. X hit his brakes. He reached into his black bag, took out the dart gun, and fired another two into the vampire to keep the noise down. With the windows darkened and the black blanket as cover, they had a shot at making it through. As long as the male didn't move.

When it was Mr. X's turn, he put the window down as the cop approached. The man's flashlight hit the dashboard, casting a glow.

"Evening, Officer." Mr. X assumed a pleasant expression.

"You been drinking tonight, sir?" The cop was your basic middle-aged nobody. Doughy around the middle. Fuzzy mustache that needed a better trim job. Gray hair poofing out from under his hat like a weed. He had all the aspects of a sheep-dog except for the flea collar and the tail.

"No, Officer, I have not."

"Hey, I know you."

"Do you?" Mr. X smiled more broadly while eyeing the man's throat. Frustration made him think of the knife he had in the car door. He reached down and ran his finger over the handle, soothing himself.

"Yeah, you teach jujitsu to my son." When the cop leaned back, his flashlight swung to the side, hitting the black bag in the passenger seat. "Darryl, come meet Phillie's sensei."

While the other cop ambled over, Mr. X checked to make sure the bag was zipped up. No sense flashing the dart gun or the nine-millimeter Glock he had inside of it.

For a good five minutes, he made nice-nice with the boys in blue while fantasizing about the ways he could shut them up.

When he finally put the minivan in gear, he discovered the knife was in his hand and almost in his lap.

He had some serious aggression to work off.

Wrath stared hard at the blurry contours of the single-story commercial building. For the past two hours, he and Rhage had been watching the Caldwell Martial Arts Academy, waiting to see if it got any nocturnal action. The facility was located at the far end of a strip mall, on the edge of a stretch of woods. Rhage, who had cased the place the night before, estimated it was about twenty thousand square feet in size.

Plenty big enough to be a center for the *lessers*.

The parking lot ran down the front of the academy, and there were about ten to fifteen spaces on one side. There were two entrances. Double glass doors in front. Side ingress with no window. From their vantage point in the woods, they could see both the empty lot and the ways in and out of the building.

The other sites had been dead ends. The Gold's Gym hadn't yielded anything other than a revolving membership of steak-heads. It closed at midnight, opened at five A.M., and had been quiet for the past couple of nights. The paintball arena was the same, just an empty building from the moment it closed its doors. The best bets were the two academies, and Vishous and the twins were across town at the other one.

Although *lessers* could go out in the day, they did their hunting at night because that was when their targets moved around. As dawn got close, the society's recruitment and training centers were often used as places to congregate, but not always. Also, because the *lessers* shifted locales frequently, one spot could be hot for a month or a season or a year and then be deserted.

As Darius had been dead for only a few days, Wrath was hoping the society hadn't moved on yet.

He felt for his watch. "Damn it, it's almost three."

Rhage shifted against the tree he was behind. "So I guess Tohr isn't showing up tonight."

Wrath shrugged, hoping like hell the subject would get dropped.

It didn't.

"That's not like him." Rhage paused. "But you're not surprised."

"No, I'm not."

"Why?"

Wrath cracked his knuckles. "I took a piece out of him. When I shouldn't have."

"I'm not gonna ask."

"Wise of you." And then for some absurd reason, he tacked on, "I need to apologize to him."

"That'll be a surprise."

"Am I that awful?"

"No," Rhage said without his usual bravado. "You're just not wrong that often."

Candor was a surprise coming from Hollywood.

"Well, I sure as hell did a number on Tohr."

Rhage clapped him on the back. "Lemme tell you, as someone who offends folks regularly, there ain't much that can't be fixed."

"I brought Wellsie into it."

"Not a good idea."

"And how he feels about her."

"Shit."

"Yeah. Pretty much."

"Why?"

"Because I . . ."

Because he'd felt like an idiot trying to pull off even a sliver of what Tohrment had managed to do so successfully for two centuries. In spite of Tohr's calling as a warrior, he'd sustained a relationship with a female of worth. And it was a good, strong, loving union. He was the only one of the brothers who'd been able to do that.

Wrath thought about Beth. Pictured her coming up to him, asking him to stay.

Man, he was desperate to find her in his bed when he got home. And not because he wanted to take her. It was because then he could sleep beside her. Rest a little, knowing that she was safe and with him.

Ah, hell. He had a terrible feeling he was going to have to stick around that female. For a while.

"Because?" Rhage prompted.

Wrath's nose tingled. A faint whiff of sweetness, like baby powder, floated by on the breeze.

"Get out your welcome mat," he said, opening his jacket.

"How many?" Rhage asked, pivoting around.

The sounds of sticks snapping and leaves rustling softly broke the night. Got louder.

"Three. At least."

"Yee-haw."

The *lessers* were coming straight at them, through a clearing in the woods. They were loud, talking and walking without care, until one of them stopped. The other two pulled up, shut up.

"Evening, boys," Rhage said, sauntering out into the open.

Wrath took the stealth approach. As the *lessers* circled his brother, crouching, drawing knives, Wrath skirted around the edge of the trees.

Then he reached out of the shadows and plucked one of the *lessers* off the ground, starting the fight. He slit its throat, but there was no time to polish off the kill. Rhage had engaged two, but the third was about to nail the brother in the head with a baseball bat.

Wrath fell upon the undead Sammy Sousa, taking it down to the ground and stabbing it in the throat. Juicy, strangled noises bubbled up into the air. Wrath looked around, in case there were more or his brother needed help.

Rhage was doing just fine.

Even to Wrath's poor eyesight, the warrior was a thing of beauty when he fought. All fists and kicks. Rapid motion. Animal reflexes. Power and endurance. He was a master of hand-to-hand combat, and the *lessers* hit the ground again and again, the length of time it took them to get up growing longer and longer.

258

Wrath went back to the first *lesser* and knelt over the body. It writhed as he went through its pockets and took all the ID he could find.

He was about to stab it in the chest when he heard a shot-gun go off.

TWENTY-NINE

"So Butch, you gonna hang around until I get off tonight?"

Abby smiled as she poured him another Scotch.

"Maybe." He didn't want to, but after a couple more he might change his mind. Assuming he could still get it up while he was drunk.

With a shift to the left, she looked behind him at another guy, shooting the man a little wink while flashing some cleavage.

Covering her bases. Probably a good idea.

Butch's cell phone vibrated on his belt, and he grabbed it. "Yeah?"

"We've got another dead prostitute," José said. "Thought you'd want to know."

"Where?" He leaped off the bar stool like he had somewhere to go. Then sat back down, slowly.

"Trade and Fifth. But don't come over. Where are you?"

"McGrider's."

"Ten minutes?"

"I'll be here."

Butch pushed the Scotch away as frustration tore through him.

Was this how he was going to end up? Getting drunk every night? Maybe working a PI or a security job until he got fired for being a derelict? Living alone in that two-room apartment until his liver kicked it?

He'd never been one for plans, but maybe it was time he made some.

"You didn't like that one?" Abby said, framing the shot glass with her breasts.

Reflexively, he reached for the damn thing, brought it to his lips, and tossed it back.

"That's my man."

But when she went to pour him another, he covered the top with his hand. "I think I'm done tonight."

"Yeah, right." She smiled when he shook his head. "Well, you know where to find me."

Yeah, unfortunately.

José took longer than ten minutes. It was a good half hour before Butch saw the detective cutting through the crowd of drinkers, a grim figure in his casual clothes.

"Do we know her?" Butch asked before the man could sit down.

"Another one of Big Daddy's. Carla Rizzoli. A.k.a. Candy."

"Same MO?"

José ordered a vodka straight up. "Yup. Throat slit, blood everywhere. There was some residue on her lips like she'd been foaming at the mouth."

"H?"

"Probably. The medical examiner's going to do the autopsy first thing tomorrow."

"Anything found at the scene?"

"A dart. Like you'd shoot an animal with. We're having it analyzed." José polished off the vodka with a quick tilt of his head. "And I heard Big Daddy's pissed. He's looking for revenge."

"Yeah, well, hopefully he'll take it out on Beth's boyfriend. Maybe a war will drive that bastard out of hiding." Butch set his elbows onto the bar. Rubbed his achy eyes. "Goddamn it, I can't believe she's protecting him."

"Man, I never saw that one coming. She finally picks someone—"

"And he's a total lowlife."

José looked over. "We're going to have to call her in."

"I figured." Butch focused his eyes by squinting. "Listen, I'm supposed to meet her tomorrow. Give me a crack at her first, will ya?"

"I can't do that, O'Neal. You're not—"

"Yeah, you can. You just schedule her for the day after."

"The investigation is moving forward—"

"Please." Butch couldn't believe he was begging. "Come on, José. I've got a better shot than anyone at getting through to her."

"Why's that?"

"Because she watched him almost kill me."

José looked down at the grotty bar top. "You've got one day. And nobody'd better find out, because the captain will have my head. Then no matter what, I gotta interrogate her at the station."

Butch nodded while Abby came dancing back over with a Scotch bottle in one hand and a liter of vodka in the other.

"You're looking dry, boys," she said with a giggle. The message in her lusty smile and her vacant eyes was getting louder, more desperate, as the night crawled to an end.

Butch thought of his empty wallet. His empty holster. His empty apartment.

"I gotta get out of her," he muttered, sliding off the stool. "I mean, here."

Wrath's arm absorbed the shotgun's load, and the impact twisted his torso like rope. He went with the force of the hit, spinning to the ground, but he didn't stay down. Moving fast and low, he got the hell out of the way, not giving the shooter a chance to nail him again.

The fifth *lesser* had come out of nowhere. And it was packing a heavy load in that sawed-off.

Behind a pine tree, Wrath quickly took stock of the injury. Nothing too deep. Some skin and muscle stripped off his biceps. Bone was intact. He could still fight.

He took out a throwing star and stepped into the open.

And that was when a tremendous flash of light illuminated the clearing.

He leaped back into the shadows. "Aw, *Christ!*"

Now they were all in for it. The beast was coming out of Rhage. And the shit was going to hit the fan.

Rhage's eyes glowed white as headlights as his body mutated in a ghastly display of tearing and ruptures. Something horrible took his place, its scales glistening in the moonlight, its claws slicing through the air. The *lessers* didn't know what hit them as the creature attacked with a full set of fangs, going after them until their blood ran down its huge chest in a river.

Wrath stayed back. He'd seen this before, and the beast didn't need help. Hell, if you got too close, you were liable to get a body trim.

When it was all over, the creature let out a howl so loud, the trees bowed away, their branches blown asunder.

The slaughter was absolute. There was no hope of getting any identification off the *lessers* because there were no bodies. Even their clothes had been consumed.

Wrath stepped into the clearing.

The creature swung around, panting.

Wrath kept his voice low and his hands at his sides. Rhage was in there somewhere, but until he came out again, you couldn't assume the beast would remember who the brothers were.

"We're cool," Wrath said. "You and me, we've done this before."

The beast's chest pumped up and down, nostrils quivering as it sniffed the air. Glowing eyes fixated on the blood running down Wrath's arm. A snort came out. The claws lifted.

"Forget it. You did your thing. You're fed. Now, let's have Rhage back."

The great head shook back and forth, but its scales started to vibrate. A high-pitched protest breached the creature's throat, and then there was another flash.

Rhage fell naked to the ground, landing face-first in the dirt.

Wrath ran over and dropped to his knees, reaching out. The warrior's skin was slick with sweat, and he was shaking like a newborn in the cold.

Rhage shifted at the touch. Tried to lift his head. Failed.

Wrath took the brother's hand and squeezed it. The burn on reentry was always a bitch.

"Relax, Hollywood, you're good. You're doing good." He took off his jacket and gently covered his brother. "You're just going to hang here and let me take care of you, dig?"

Rhage mumbled something and curled into a ball.

Wrath flipped open his cell phone and dialed. "Vishous? We need a car. Now. You're kidding me. No, I gotta move our boy. We just had a visit from his other side. But you tell Zsadist not to fuck around."

He hung up and looked at Rhage.

"Hate this," the brother said.

"I know." Wrath moved the sticky, blood-soaked hair out of the vampire's face. "We're going to get you home."

"Didn't like seeing you shot."

Wrath smiled softly. "Clearly."

Beth stirred, burrowing deeper into the pillow.

Something wasn't right.

She opened her eyes just as a deep male voice broke the silence. "What the fuck do we have here?"

She bolted upright. Looked frantically to the sound.

The man towering over her had black, lifeless eyes. A harsh face with a jagged scar running down it. Hair that was practically shaved it was so short. And long, white fangs that were bared.

She screamed.

He smiled. "My favorite sound in all the world."

She clamped a hand over her mouth.

God, that scar. It ran down his forehead, over his nose, across his cheek, and back around to his mouth. The tail end of the S distorted his upper lip, pulling one side into a permanent sneer.

"Admiring my artwork?" he drawled. "You should see the rest of me."

Her eyes darted to his broad chest. He was wearing a skintight, long-sleeved black shirt. On both his pecs, small rings were evident beneath the material, as if he had his nipples pierced. As she looked back up at his face, she saw he had a black band tattooed around his neck and a plug in his left earlobe.

"Pretty, aren't I?" His cold stare was the stuff of nightmares, of dark places where no hope could be found, of hell itself.

Forget the scar, she thought. Those eyes were the scariest thing about him.

And they were fixated on her as if he were sizing her up for a shroud. Or for some sex.

She moved her body away from him. Started looking around for something she could use as a weapon.

"What, you don't like me?"

Beth eyed the door, and he laughed.

"Think you can run fast enough?" he said, pulling the bottom of his shirt free from the leather pants he had on. His hands moved to his fly. "I'm damn sure you can't."

"Get away from her, Zsadist."

Wrath's voice was a sweet relief. Until she saw that he had no shirt on and his arm was in a sling.

He barely looked at her. "Time to go, Z."

Zsadist smiled coldly. "Not willing to share the female?"

"You only like it if you pay for it."

"So I'll flip her a twenty. Assuming she lives through the sex."

Wrath kept coming at the other vampire, until they stood nose-to-nose. The air crackled around them, super-charged by their aggression.

"You're not touching her, Z. You're not looking at her. You're going to say good-night and walk the fuck out of here." Wrath removed the sling, exposing a bandage on his biceps. There was a red blush in the center as if he were bleeding, but he looked ready to take on the other man.

"Bet you're pissed you needed a ride home tonight," Zsadist said. "And that I was the closest one with a car."

"Don't make me regret it more."

Zsadist took a step to the left, and Wrath went with him, using his body to shield her.

Zsadist chuckled, a deep, evil rumble. "You're actually willing to fight for a human?"

"She's Darius's daughter."

Zsadist's head snapped to the side, those black pits of his probing her features. After a moment, there was a subtle softening in his brutal face, a drop in the sneer. And then he made a point to tuck in his shirt while looking her in the eye. As if he were apologizing.

Wrath did not step off, however.

"What's your name?" Zsadist asked her.

"Her name's Beth." Wrath put his head into the path of Zsadist's vision. "And you're leaving."

There was a long pause.

"Yeah. Sure. Whatever."

Zsadist strode over to the door, moving with the same lethal prowl Wrath did. Before he left, he stopped and looked back.

He must have been truly handsome once, Beth thought. Although it wasn't the scar that made him unattractive. It was the hellfire inside of him.

"Nice to meet you. Beth."

She let her breath out as the door closed and the locks flipped into place.

"Are you okay?" Wrath asked. She could feel his eyes running over her body, and then he gently put his hands on her. "He didn't . . . he didn't touch you, did he? I heard you scream."

"No. No, he just scared me. I woke up and he was in the room."

Wrath sat down on the bed, still passing his palms over her as if he didn't believe she was okay. When he seemed satisfied, he pushed his hair back. His hands were shaking.

"You're hurt," she said. "What happened?"

He put his good arm around her and pulled her against his chest. "It's nothing."

"Then why do you need a sling? And a bandage? And why are you still bleeding?"

"Shhh." He put his chin on the top of her head. She could feel his body trembling.

"Are you ill?" she asked.

"I just have to hold you for a minute. Okay?"

"Absolutely."

As soon as his body calmed, she pulled away. "What's the matter?"

He took her face in his hands. Pressed his lips to hers. "I couldn't bear it if he'd . . . taken you away from me."

"That guy? Don't worry, I'm not going anywhere with him." And then she realized Wrath wasn't talking about a date. "You think he was going to kill me?"

Not that she couldn't see how that might have been possible. So cold. Those eyes had been so cold.

Instead of answering, Wrath's mouth came down on hers. She stopped him.

"Who is he? And what happened to him?"

"I don't want you near Z again. Ever." He tucked a strand of hair behind her ear. His touch was tender. His voice was not. "Are you listening to me?"

She nodded. "But what—"

"He walks into a room and I'm in the house, you come and find me. If I'm not around, you lock yourself in one of these rooms down here. The walls are made of steel, so he can't materialize inside. And don't ever touch him. Not even inadvertently."

"Is he a warrior?"

"Do you understand what I'm telling you?"

"Yeah, but it would help if I knew a little more."

"He's one of the brothers, but he's nearly soulless. Unfortunately, we need him."

"Why, if he's so dangerous? Or is it only toward women?"

"He hates everyone. Except maybe his twin."

"Oh, great. There are two like him?"

"Thank God for Phury. He's the only one who can get through to Z, although even then, it's not a sure thing." Wrath kissed her forehead. "I don't want to scare you, but I need you to take this seriously. Zsadist's an animal, but I think he respected your father, so he may leave you alone. I just can't take any chances with him. Or you. Promise me that you'll stay away from him."

"Okay." She closed her eyes and leaned into Wrath. His arm came around her, but then he shifted back.

"Come on." He pulled her up to her feet. "Come to my chamber."

When they walked into Wrath's room, Beth heard the shower shut off. A moment later, the door opened.

The warrior she'd met before, the movie-star-handsome one who'd been stitching himself up, came out slowly. He had a towel wrapped around his waist, and his hair was dripping. He moved as if he were eighty, as if every muscle in his body hurt.

Good lord, she thought. He didn't look at all well, and there was something way wrong with his stomach. It was swollen, like he'd swallowed a basketball. Unsure what to make of his midsection, she wondered whether his wound was infected. He looked feverish.

She glanced at his shoulder and frowned when she could barely see a mark. It was as if the injury had occurred months ago.

"Rhage, man, how we feeling?" Wrath asked, leaving her side.

"Belly hurts."

"Yeah. I can imagine."

Rhage swayed as he looked around the room, eyes barely open. "Going home. Where my clothes?"

"You lost them." Wrath put his good arm around his brother's waist. "And you're not leaving, you're crashing in D's room."

"Am not."

"Don't start. And we're not waltzing here. Will you lean on me, for Christ's sake?"

The other man sagged, and Wrath's back muscles tightened as he absorbed the weight. The two of them slowly made their way out to the landing and then into her father's chamber. She stayed at a discreet distance, watching as Wrath helped Rhage slide into bed.

As the warrior leaned back against the pillows, his eyes squeezed shut. His hand moved to his stomach, but he winced and let it fall to the side, as if the slightest pressure were torture.

"Feel sick."

"Yeah, indigestion's a bitch."

"Do you want some Tums?" Beth blurted out. "Alka-Seltzer?"

Both vampires looked over at her, and she felt as if she'd intruded on the moment.

Of all the stupid things—

"Yeah," Rhage muttered as Wrath nodded.

Beth walked back to her purse and decided on Alka-Seltzer because it had aspirin in it for his aches. She went into Wrath's bathroom, grabbed a glass, and did the plop-plop, fizz-fizz thing.

When she returned to her father's bedside, she offered the glass to Wrath. He shook his head.

"You'll spill less than I will."

She flushed. It was so easy to forget he couldn't really see.

She leaned over Rhage, but couldn't reach his mouth. Hiking up the robe, she climbed onto the mattress and knelt next to him. She felt awkward being so close to a naked, virile man in front of Wrath.

Considering what had happened to Butch.

But come on, Wrath had nothing to worry about here. No matter how sexy the other vampire was, she didn't feel any heat as she sidled up to the guy.

And he sure as hell wasn't about to come on to her. Not given the kind of shape he was in.

She gently lifted Rhage's head and put the edge of the glass to his beautifully shaped lips. It took him five minutes to sip the liquid down. When he was finished, she started to get off the bed. She didn't get far. With a great lurch, he pitched over onto his side and put his head in her lap, throwing one muscular arm around behind her.

He was seeking comfort.

Beth didn't know what she could really do for him, but she put the glass aside and stroked his back, running her hand over his fearsome tattoo. She murmured things she wished someone had whispered to her when she felt ill. Hummed a little for him.

After a while, the tension left his skin and bones. He began breathing deeply.

When she was sure he was out cold, she carefully extracted herself from his grasp. As she turned to meet Wrath's gaze, she braced herself. Surely he'd know there was nothing—

Shock stilled her.

Wrath wasn't mad. Far from it.

"Thank you," he said hoarsely. The bow of his head was almost humble. "Thank you for caring for my brother."

He took his sunglasses off.

And looked at her with total adoration.

THIRTY

Mr. X tossed the Sawzall on to his workbench and wiped his hands on a towel.

Well, hell, he thought. The damn vampire was dead.

He'd tried everything to wake the male up, even the chisel, and he'd made a mess out of his barn in the process. There was vampire blood all over the place.

At least cleanup was easy.

Mr. X walked over to the double doors and threw them open. Straight ahead, the sun was coming up over the far ridge, lovely gold light spilling across the landscape. He stood back as the interior of the barn was illuminated.

The vampire's body exploded into flames, the pool of blood underneath the table going up in a cloud of smoke. A soft morning breeze carried the stench of incinerated flesh away.

Mr. X stepped into the morning glow, looking at the mist that hung over the back meadow. He wasn't prepared to declare failure. The plan would have worked if he hadn't come up to those cops and had to plow the extra darts into his captive. He just needed to get back out there again.

His jones for torture had a serious case of the blue balls.

For the time being, though, he had to cool it with the prostitutes. Those fool cops were a good reminder that he wasn't working in a vacuum. That he could be caught.

Not that getting tangled up with the law would

be anything other than an inconvenience. But he prided himself on the smoothness of his operations.

Which was why he'd chosen the whores as bait. First, he figured if one or two turned up dead, it wouldn't cause an uproar. They were less likely to have family mourning them, so there wouldn't be added pressure on the police to nail a suspect. As for the inevitable investigation, there was a ready pool of suspects, thanks to the pimps and lowlifes who worked the back alleys. There were plenty for the police to chose from and chase after.

But that didn't mean he could get sloppy. Or overuse Whore Valley.

He went back in the barn, put his tools away, and headed for the house. He checked his messages before going to shower.

There were several.

The most important of which was from Billy Riddle. Evidently, the guy had had a disturbing interaction the night before and had called just after one A.M.

It was good that he was seeking comfort, Mr. X thought. And probably time that they had a conversation about his future.

An hour later, Mr. X drove to the academy, opened its doors, and left them unlocked.

The *lessers* he'd ordered to report in started to arrive shortly thereafter. He could hear them talking in the hall next to his office, their voices low. The moment he came up to them, they quieted down, looking at him. Dressed in black fatigues, their faces grim, there was only one whose coloring had yet to fade. Mr. O's brunette brush cut stood out, as did his dark brown eyes.

The longer a *lesser* stayed in the society, the more he lost his individual physical characteristics. The browns, the blacks, the reds of the hair turned to a pale ash; the tints of yellow or crimson or tan in the skin blanched out to a blushless white. The process typically took about a decade, although he had yet to see any strands of blond appear around O's face.

He did a quick head count. As all of the members of his two prime squadrons were there, he locked the academy's outside door and escorted the group into the basement. Their boots were loud and sharp on the metal stairwell, a drumroll of the power in their bodies.

Mr. X had set up the war room as nothing special, nothing unusual. Just a regular old classroom with twelve chairs, a chalkboard, a TV, and a podium in front.

The unremarkable decor wasn't just subterfuge. He didn't want any high-tech distractions. Group dynamics were the purpose and focus of these meetings.

"So tell me about last night," he said, eyeing the slayers. "How did it go?"

He listened to the reports, unimpressed with the excuses. There had been two kills the night before. He'd given them a quota of ten.

And it was a disgrace that O, who was so new, had been responsible for both deaths.

Mr. X crossed his arms over his chest. "What's the problem?"

"We couldn't find any," Mr. M said.

"I found one last night," Mr. X snapped. "Quite easily, I might add. And Mr. O found two."

"Well, the rest of us couldn't." M looked at the others. "The numbers in this area have thinned."

"The problem is not geography," a voice muttered from the back.

Mr. X's eyes shifted through the *lessers*, focusing on O's dark head in the back of the room. He was not surprised that the slayer had spoken up.

274

O was proving to be one of the best they had, even though he was a new recruit. With terrific reflexes and stamina, he was a great fighter, but like all powerful things, he was hard to control. Which was why Mr. X had put him in with others who had centuries of experience. O was liable to dominate any group made up of individuals even remotely inferior to himself.

"Would you care to elaborate, Mr. O?" Mr. X was not at all interested in the man's opinion. But he was very prepared to show up the new recruit in front of the others.

O shrugged carelessly, and his drawl was just short of insulting. "The problem is motivation. There are no consequences for failure."

"And what exactly would you suggest?" Mr. X asked.

O reached forward, grabbed M by the hair, and slit the other man's throat with a knife.

The other *lessers* leaped away, crouching into attack positions, even as O sat back down and calmly wiped his blade off with his fingers.

Mr. X bared his teeth. And then got himself under control.

He walked across the room to M. The *lesser* was still alive, gasping for breath, trying to stem the blood loss with his hands.

Mr. X knelt down. "The rest of you will leave. Now. We will reconvene tomorrow morning, when you will have better news for me. Mr. O, you stay."

When O defied the order and made a move to get up, Mr. X froze the man in the chair, stealing control of the large muscles in his body. O seemed momentarily shocked, clearly trying to fight the hold that was on his arms and legs.

It was a battle he wouldn't win. The Omega always

provided a few extra benefits to the *Fore-lesser*. This kind of mental dominion over fellow slayers was one of them.

As soon as the room had emptied, Mr. X took out a knife and stabbed M in the chest. There was flare of light and then a popping sound as the *lesser* disintegrated.

Mr. X glared up at O from the floor. "If you ever pull something like that again, I will turn you over to the Omega."

"No, you won't." In spite of his being at another's mercy, O's arrogance was unchecked. "You wouldn't want to look as if you can't control your own men."

Mr. X stood up.

"Careful, O. You underestimate the Omega's affection for sacrifices. If I were to give you to him as a gift, he would be most grateful." Mr. X walked over and ran a finger down O's cheek. "If I were to tie you down and call him to you, he would enjoy unwrapping you. And I would enjoy watching it."

O snapped his head back, more angry than frightened. "Don't touch me."

"I'm your leader. I can do anything I want with you." Mr. X clamped a hand on O's jaw and forced his thumb in between the man's lips and teeth. He jerked the *lesser*'s face forward. "So mind your manners, don't ever take another society member out without my express permission, and we'll get along fine."

O's brown eyes burned.

"Now what do you say to me?" Mr. X murmured, reaching out and stroking the man's hair back. The color was a deep, rich chocolate.

O mumbled.

"I didn't hear you." Mr. X pressed his thumb into the soft, fleshy plot under O's tongue, digging in until tears formed in the other man's eyes. When he removed his grip, he ran a quick, wet caress over O's lower lip. "I said, I didn't hear you."

"Yes, sensei."

"Good boy."

THIRTY-ONE

Marissa could not get comfortable in her bed. No matter which way she turned or where she put the pillows, she was irritated.

Somehow, her mattress had been filled with rocks, and her sheets had turned into sandpaper.

Throwing back the covers, she went over to the bank of windows that were shuttered and covered in thick satin drapery. She wanted some fresh air, but there would be no opening them. It was morning.

As she settled onto her chaise longue, she covered her bare feet with the hem of her silk nightgown.

Wrath.

She couldn't stop thinking about him. And every time another image of them together came to mind, she wanted to curse. Which was shocking.

She was the docile one. The lovely one. All female perfection and gentleness. Anger went totally against her nature.

Except the more she thought of Wrath, the more she wanted to punch something.

Assuming she could make a fist.

She glanced down at her hand. Yup, she could. Though it was pathetically small.

Especially compared to his.

God, she'd endured so much. And he had no appreciation of how difficult her life had been.

Being the untouched spinster *shellan* of the most powerful vampire of them all was hell on earth. Her failures as a female had burned out any sense of self-worth she'd had. The isolation had preyed on her sanity. The embarrassment at living with her brother because she had no home of her own had stung.

And she'd been horrified to be stared at by others and talked about behind her back. She was very aware that she was a constant topic of conversation, envied, pitied, spied upon, the stuff of fable. She knew young females were told of her story, although whether it was as warning or inducement, she didn't want to know.

Wrath was totally unaware of how she'd suffered.

Part of that fault she had to lay at her own feet. Playing the good little female had felt like the right thing to do, the only way to be worthy, the only chance at finally sharing a life with him.

Except how had it turned out?

With him finding a dark-haired human he cared about more.

God, the payoff for all her efforts went beyond not fair and right into cruel.

And she wasn't the only one who'd suffered. Havers had been worried sick about her for centuries.

Wrath, on the other hand, had always been just fine. And he was no doubt doing just fine right now. In all likelihood he was, at this very moment, lying naked with that female. Putting that hard length at his hips to good use.

Marissa closed her eyes.

She thought about being pulled against his body, held in those crushing arms, consumed by him. She'd been too shocked to feel much heat. There'd been so much of him, all over her, his hands tangling in her hair, his mouth sucking hard at her throat. And that thick rod of his had scared her a little.

Which was ironic.

She'd dreamed about what it would be like for so

long. To be taken by him. To leave her virginal state behind and know what it was to have a male inside.

Whenever she'd imagined them together, her body had always warmed, her skin had tingled. But the reality had been overwhelming. She'd been totally unprepared, and she wished it had lasted longer and been a little less intense. She had a feeling she would have liked it if he'd gone more slowly.

But then, he hadn't been thinking of her.

Marissa recurled her hand, making that fist again.

She didn't want him back. What she wanted was for him to have a taste of the pain she'd been through.

Wrath put his arms around Beth and drew her close, looking at Rhage over the top of her head. Watching her ease the male's suffering had broken down all sorts of barriers.

Care for his brothers, care for him, he thought. It was the oldest code in the warrior class.

"Come to my bed," he whispered in her ear.

She let him take her hand and lead her to his room. Once inside, he shut and locked the door and extinguished all the candles but one. Then he pulled the sash of the robe she wore free and stripped the satin from her shoulders. Her naked skin gleamed in the light of the single wick that burned.

He took his leather pants off. And then they were lying together.

He didn't want sex from her. Not now. He just wanted to share some comfort. He wanted her warm skin against his, her breath brushing lightly over his chest, her heart beating mere inches from his own. And he wanted to give her the same kind of peace back.

He stroked her long, silky hair and breathed deeply.

"Wrath?" Her voice was lovely in the dim quiet, and he liked the vibration of her throat against his pecs.

"Yeah." He kissed the top of her head.

"Who did you lose?" She shifted, putting her chin on his chest.

"Lose?"

"Who did the *lessers* take from you?"

The question seemed out of the blue. And then it didn't. She'd seen the aftereffects of a fight. Somehow knew that he fought not only for his race, but for himself.

It was a long time before he could answer. "My parents."

He felt her emotions shift from curiosity to sorrow. "I'm sorry."

There was a long silence.

"What happened?"

Now that was an interesting question, he thought. Because there were two versions. In vampire lore, that bloody night had taken on all sorts of heroic implications, being heralded as the birth of a great warrior. The fiction wasn't his doing. His people needed to believe in him, so they created that which sustained their misplaced faith.

He alone knew the truth.

"Wrath?"

His eyes went to the hazy beauty of her face. It was difficult to deny the gentle tone she used. She wanted to offer him compassion, and for some godforsaken reason, he wanted it from her.

"It was before my transition," he murmured. "A long time ago."

His hand paused on her hair, the memories coming back gruesome and vivid.

"We thought as the First Family we were safe from the *lessers*. Our homes were well defended, well hidden in the forests, and we moved all the time."

He found that if he continued to smooth her hair, he could keep talking.

281

"It was winter. A cold night in February. One of our servants betrayed our location. The *lessers* came in a pack of fifteen or twenty and slaughtered their way through our estate before breaching our stone battlements. I'll never forget the sound when they pounded on the door to our private quarters. My father shouted for his weapons while forcing me into a crawl space. He locked me inside just before they broke through the door with a battering ram. He was good with a sword, but there were so many of them."

Beth's hands came to his face. He dimly heard soft words falling from her lips.

Wrath closed his eyes, seeing the ghastly images that still had the power to rip him from sleep. "They massacred the servants before killing my parents. I saw it all through a knothole in the wood. As I said, my eyes were better back then."

"Wrath—"

"While it was happening, they made so much noise, no one heard me screaming." He shuddered. "And I fought to get free. I pushed against the latch, but it was solid and I was weak. I tore at the wood, scratched at it until my fingernails splintered and bled. I kicked with my feet . . ." His body responded to the remembered horror of being confined, his breath growing ragged, his skin breaking out in a cold sweat. "After they left, my father tried to drag himself over to me. They had stabbed him in the heart, and he was . . . He gave out two feet from the crawl space, reaching for me. I kept calling his name over and over again until I lost my voice. I begged for him to live even as I watched the light in his eyes dim and then go out. I was trapped there for hours with their bodies, watching the pools of blood get bigger. Some civilian vampires came the following night and let me out."

He felt a soothing stroke down his shoulder, and he

brought Beth's hand to his mouth, kissing the skin of her palm.

"Before the *lessers* left, they pulled back all the tapestries from the windows. The moment the sun rose and came into the room, all the bodies burned up. I had nothing to bury."

He felt something hit his face. A tear. Beth's.

He reached out and stroked her cheek. "No crying."

Though he cherished her for her sympathy.

"Why not?"

"It changes nothing. I cried while I watched, and still they all died." He turned on his side and gathered her close. "If only I could have . . . I still have dreams about that night. I was such a coward. I should have been out there with my father, fighting."

"But you would have been killed."

"As a male should. Protecting his own. That's honorable. Instead I was sniveling in a crawl space." He hissed with disgust.

"How old were you?"

"Twenty-two."

She frowned, as if she'd assumed he'd been much younger. "You said it was before your transition?"

"Yeah."

"So what were you like then?" She smoothed his hair back. "It's hard to imagine you fitting in a crawl space, the size you are now."

"I was different."

"You said you were weak."

"I was."

"So maybe you needed to be protected."

"*No.*" His temper flared. "A male protects. Never the other way around."

Abruptly, she backed off.

As the silence stretched between them, he knew she was thinking through his actions. Shame made him remove his hands from her body. He rolled away, onto his back.

He never should have said a thing.

He could just imagine what she thought of him now. After all, how could she not be revolted by his failure? By the reality that he'd been weak when his family had needed him most?

With a shrinking feeling, he wondered if she'd still want him. If she'd still welcome him into her slick heat. Or would that be gone for her? Now that she knew?

He waited for her to put her clothes on and leave.

She stayed in the bed.

But of course she did, he thought. She understood that her transition was coming no matter what, and she needed his blood. It was a matter of necessity.

He heard her sigh in the darkness. As if she were giving up on something.

He wasn't sure how long they lay together, side by side but not touching. It must have been hours. He fell asleep briefly, only to wake up when Beth shifted against him, her bare leg moving over his.

A jolt of lust went through him, but he beat it back savagely.

Her hand brushed over his chest. Drifted down his stomach and across his hip. He held his breath as he got hard in a rush, his erection achingly close to where she was touching him.

Her body moved nearer to his, her breasts caressing his ribs, her core rubbing on his thigh.

Maybe she was still asleep.

And then she took him into her hand.

Wrath moaned, arching his back.

Her fingers were steady as she stroked him.

He went for her instinctively, craving what she seemed to be offering, but she stopped him. Rising to her knees, she pressed him down to the mattress with her palms on his shoulders.

"This time is for you," she whispered, kissing him softly.

He could barely speak. "You still want . . . me?"

Confusion spiked her brows. "Why wouldn't I?"

With a pathetic groan of relief and gratitude, Wrath lurched for her again. Except she didn't let him get anywhere near her body. She pushed him back down and gripped his wrists, bringing his arms over his head.

She kissed his neck. "When we were together last, you were very . . . generous. You deserve the same kind of treatment."

"But your pleasure is mine." His voice was rough. "You can't know how much I like to make you come."

"I'm not so sure about that." He felt her shift, and then her hand brushed against his erection. He bowed off the mattress, a low sound rumbling up through his chest. "I might have some idea."

"You don't have to do this," he said hoarsely, fighting once more to touch her.

She leaned into his wrists forcefully, holding him still. "Relax. Let me be in control."

Wrath could only stare up in disbelief and breathless anticipation as she pressed her lips to his.

"I want to do you," she whispered.

In a silky rush, her tongue entered his mouth. Penetrated him. Slid in and out as if she were fucking him.

His whole body went rigid.

With each one of her thrusts, she got farther inside of him, into his skin and his brain. Into his heart. She was possessing him, taking him. Leaving her mark on him.

When she left his mouth, she moved down his body. She licked his neck. Sucked his nipples. Raked her nails gently across his belly. Tested his hip bones with her teeth.

He gripped the headboard and pulled, making the whole bed frame shift and creak in protest.

Waves of stinging heat made him feel as if he were going to pass out. Sweat bloomed over his skin. His heart hammered so hard it started skipping beats.

Words fell from his lips, a stream of consciousness spoken in the old language, a guttural expression of what she was doing to him, how beautiful she was to him.

The second she took his erection into her mouth, he nearly came. He cried out, body spasming. She pulled back, gave him time to settle.

And then she put him through torture.

She knew just when to bring it on, just when to pause. The combination of her wet mouth at his thick tip and her hands moving up and down his shaft was a one-two punch he could barely withstand. She brought him to the brink over and over again until he was reduced to begging.

Finally, she straddled his hips and hovered above him. He looked down between their bodies. Her thighs were wide open over his swollen, throbbing erection, and he almost lost it.

"Take me," he moaned. "God, *please*."

She slid him inside of her, and his whole body felt the sensation. Tight, wet, hot, she enveloped him. She began to move in a slow, pumping rhythm, and he didn't last long. When he came, he felt like he'd been ripped in two, the bursts of energy creating a shock wave that went through the room, shaking the furniture, blowing out the candle.

On the slow float back to earth, he realized it was the first time anyone had ever taken such care to pleasure him.

He wanted to weep that she would still have him at all.

Beth smiled in the darkness at the sound Wrath made as his body rocked under hers. The force of his orgasm took her over the edge, and she fell onto his heaving chest as her own delicious waves took her breath away.

Afraid that she was too heavy, she made a move to get off him, but he stopped her, holding on to her hips. He spoke to her in a beautiful tumble of sounds she didn't understand.

"What?"

"Stay just where you are," he said in English.

She settled onto his body, relaxing completely.

She wondered what he'd said to her as she'd made love to him, but the tone of his voice, reverent, praising, told her a lot. Whatever he'd uttered, they'd been a lover's words.

"Your language is beautiful," she said.

"There are no words worthy of you."

His voice sounded different. He felt different to her.

No barriers, she thought. There were no barriers between them right now. That deadly guard, that ever-watchful, predatory defense of his was gone.

Unexpectedly, she felt herself growing protective of him.

It was odd, feeling that way about someone so much more physically powerful than herself. But he needed safeguarding. She could sense the vulnerability in him in this quiet moment, in this dense darkness. His heart was almost in her reach.

God, that horrific story of his family's deaths.

"Wrath?"

"Hmm?"

She wanted to thank him for telling her. But she

didn't want to ruin the fragile communion between them.

"Has anyone ever told you how beautiful you are?" she said.

He chuckled. "Warriors are not beautiful."

"You are. To me. You are utterly beautiful."

He stopped breathing. And then moved her off of him. With a quick motion, he left the bed, and moments later there was a soft light on in the bathroom. She heard water running.

She should have known it wasn't going to last. But she wanted to cry at the loss, anyway.

Beth fumbled around for her clothes, found them, dressed.

When he came out of the bathroom, she was heading for the door.

"Where are you going?" he demanded.

"Work. I don't know what time it is, but I usually get in around nine, so I'm sure I'm late."

She couldn't see very well, but eventually found the door.

"I don't want you to go." Wrath was right next to her, his voice making her jump.

"I have a life. I need to get back to it."

"Your life is here."

"No, it isn't."

Her hands felt around for the locks, but she couldn't budge them, even when she threw her body into the effort.

"Are you going to let me out of here?" she muttered.

"Beth." He took her hands in his, forcing her to stop. Candles flared to life, as if he wanted her to see him. "I'm sorry I can't be . . . easier to get along with."

She pulled away. "I didn't mean to embarrass you. I wanted you to know how I felt. That's all."

"And I find it hard to believe that I don't disgust you."

Beth stared at him in disbelief. "Good God, why would you?"

"Because you know what happened."

"With your parents?" Her mouth fell open. "Let me get this straight. You think I'm going to be disgusted because you were forced to endure the slaughter of your mother and father?"

"I did nothing to save them," he bit out.

"You were *locked* in."

"I was a coward."

"You were *not*." Getting pissed at the man probably wasn't fair, but why couldn't he see the past more clearly? "How can you say—"

"I stopped screaming!" His voice ricocheted around the room, startling her.

"What?" she whispered.

"I stopped screaming. After they were finished with my parents and the *doggen*, I stopped screaming. The *lessers* were looking through our quarters. They were searching for *me*. And I stayed quiet. I clamped my hand over my mouth. I prayed they wouldn't find me."

"Of course you did," she said gently. "You wanted to live."

"No," he shot back. "I was *afraid* of dying."

She wanted to reach out to him, except she was certain he would pull away.

"Wrath, can't you see? You were a victim as much as they were. The only reason you're here today is because your father loved you enough to keep you safe. You stayed silent because you wanted to survive. That's nothing to be ashamed of."

"I was a coward."

"Don't be ridiculous! You'd just seen your parents murdered!" She shook her head, frustration making her tone sharp. "I'm telling you, you need to reexamine what happened. You've let those horrible hours mark you, and who could blame you for that, but you're looking at it all wrong. *All* wrong. Put down this warrior-honor crap and give yourself a break!"

Silence.

Ah, hell. Now, she'd done it. The guy opens up to her and she throws his shame back at him. Way to encourage intimacy.

"Wrath, I'm sorry, I shouldn't have—"

He cut her off. Both his voice and his face were like stone.

"No one has ever spoken to me as you just did."

Shit.

"I'm really sorry. I just can't understand why—"

Wrath dragged her into his arms and hugged her hard, talking in that other language again. When he pulled back, he ended the monologue with something like *leelan.*

"Is that vampire talk for *bitch*?" she asked.

"No. Far from it." He kissed her. "Let's just say I respect the hell out of you. Even though I can't agree with your take on my past."

She put her hand on his neck, giving his head a little shake. "You will, however, accept the fact that what happened doesn't in any way change my opinion of you. Although I do feel tremendous sorrow for you and for your family and what you all had to endure."

Long pause.

"Wrath? You will repeat after me. 'Yes, Beth, I understand and will trust your honesty about your feelings for me.'" She shook his neck again. "Let's say it together." Another pause. "Now, not later."

"Yes," he gritted out.

God, if those lips of his were any tighter, they'd snap off his front teeth.

"Yes, what?"

"Yes, Beth."

"'I trust you to be honest with me about how you feel.' Come on. Say it."

He grumbled his way through the words.

"Good man."

"You're tough, you know that?"

"I'd better be if I'm going to hang around with you."

Abruptly, he took her face into his hands. "I want that," he said fiercely.

"What?"

"For you to be around."

Her breath caught. A tenuous hope took fire in her chest. "Really?"

He closed his glowing eyes and shook his head. "Yeah. It's fucking stupid. It's crazy. It's dangerous."

"So it'll fit right into your life script."

He laughed and looked down at her. "Yeah, pretty much."

God, his eyes were breaking her heart, they were so tender.

"Beth, I want to stay with you, but you have to understand, you'll be a target. And I don't know how to keep you safe enough. I don't know how the hell to—"

"*We'll* figure it out," she said. "We can do it together."

He kissed her. Long. Slowly. With precious care.

"So you'll stay now?" he asked.

"No. I really do need to get to work."

"I don't want you to go." His hand cupped her chin. "I hate that I can't be with you outside during the day."

But the locks sprang free and the door opened.

"How do you do that?" she asked.

"You will be back before dusk." It wasn't a request, not by a long shot.

"I'll be back sometime after sunset."

He growled.

"And I promise to call if anything weird happens."

She rolled her eyes. Man, she was going to have to re-calibrate her standards for that word. "I mean, *weirder*."

"I don't like this."

"I'll be careful." She kissed him and then headed up the stairs. She could still feel his eyes on her as she pushed open the painting and stepped into the drawing room.

THIRTY-TWO

Beth went to her apartment, fed Boo, and got into the office just after noon. For once, she wasn't famished, and she worked through lunch. Well, sort of. She couldn't really concentrate and mostly engineered a rotation of the paper piles on her desk.

Butch left her two messages during the day, confirming they were going to rendezvous at her apartment around eight.

By four o'clock, she decided to cancel her meeting with him.

Nothing good could come out of it. There was no way she was turning Wrath over to the police, and if she thought Hard-ass was going to go easy on her because he liked her and they were in her home, she was just lying to herself.

Still, she wasn't going to put her head in the sand. She knew she was going to be called in for questioning. How could she not be? As long as Wrath was a suspect, she was on the hot seat. She needed to get herself a good lawyer and wait to be called down to the station.

On her way back from a trip to the copier, she glanced out a window. The late-afternoon sky was cloudy, with the promise of thunderstorms hanging in the creamy, thick air. She had to look away. Her eyes ached, and the discomfort didn't fade as she blinked repeatedly.

Back at her desk, she popped two aspirin and called the station house looking for Butch. When she was told by Ricky that he'd been put on administrative leave, she demanded to talk to José. He got right on the phone.

"Butch's suspension. When did it happen?" she asked.

"Yesterday afternoon."

"Are they going to fire him?"

"Off the record? Probably."

So Butch wasn't going to show up at her place after all.

"Where are you, B-lady?" José asked.

"Work."

"You lying to me?" His voice was more sad than confrontational.

"Check your caller ID."

José let out a long sigh. "I need to bring you in."

"I know. Can you give me some time to get a lawyer?"

"You think you're going to need one?"

"Yeah."

José cursed. "You gotta get away from that man."

"I'll call you later."

"Another prostitute was killed last night. Same MO."

The news gave her a moment of pause. She couldn't have said what Wrath had been doing when he'd been out. But what possible purpose could a dead prostitute have for him?

Make that two dead prostitutes.

Anxiety spiked, making her temples throb.

Except she just couldn't see Wrath slitting some poor, defenseless woman's throat and leaving her to die in an alley. He was lethal, not evil. And though he operated outside of the law, she didn't imagine he'd take the life of someone who hadn't threatened him. Especially after what had happened to his parents.

"Listen, Beth," José said. "I don't need to tell you how serious this situation is. That man is our prime suspect for three murders, and obstruction of justice is a serious charge. It'll kill me, but I will put you behind bars."

"He didn't murder anyone last night." Her stomach rolled.

"So you admit you know where he is."

"I gotta go, José."

"Beth, please don't protect him. He's dangerous—"

"He did not kill those women."

"That's your opinion."

"You've been a good friend, José."

"Goddamn it." He added a couple of words in Spanish. "Get that lawyer fast, Beth."

She hung up the phone, grabbed her purse, and shut down her computer. The last thing she wanted was for José to come to her office and take her away in handcuffs. She needed to go home, pick up some clothes, and get to Wrath's as soon as she could.

Maybe they could just disappear together. It might be their only choice. Because sooner or later the police would find them in Caldwell.

As she walked out onto Trade Street, her belly was in knots, and the heat sucked the energy right out of her. The minute she walked into her apartment, she poured some ice-cold water into a glass, but as she tried to drink it, her intestines cramped up. Maybe she had a stomach bug. She popped two Tums and thought of Rhage. She might have picked up something from him.

God, her eyes were killing her.

And even though she knew she needed to start packing, she got out of her work clothes, put on a T-shirt and shorts, and sat down on the futon. She only meant to take a little breather, but once she was off her feet, she couldn't seem to get her body moving again.

Sluggishly, like the channels in her brain were clogging up, she pictured Wrath's injury. He'd never told her how he'd gotten hurt. What if he'd attacked the prostitute and the woman had fought back?

Beth pressed her fingers to her temples as a wave of nausea brought bile into her throat. Lights flickered in front of her eyes.

No, this wasn't the flu. She was coming down with the Godzilla of migraines.

Wrath dialed his phone again.

Tohrment was obviously using caller ID and avoiding his ass.

Hell. He sucked at apologies, but he really wanted to get this one out on the table. Because it was going to be a doozy.

He took the cell phone with him to bed and leaned back against the headboard. He wanted to call Beth. Just to hear her voice.

Yeah, and he'd thought he was just going to waltz away after her transition? He could barely stand being away from her for a couple of *hours*.

Man, he had it bad for that female. He couldn't believe what had come out of his mouth when she'd been making love to him. And then he'd topped off the simpering praise by calling her his *leelan* before she left.

He might as well admit it. He was probably falling in love.

And if that wasn't enough of a shocker, she was half-human. As well as Darius's daughter.

But how could he not adore her? She was so strong, with a will to match his own. He thought of her standing up to him, confronting him about his past. Few would have dared, and he knew where she got her courage from. Her father probably would have done the same thing.

When his cell phone went off, he flipped it open. "Yeah?"

"We got issues." It was Vishous. "I just read the paper. Another dead prostitute. In an alley. Bled out."

"So?"

"I hacked into the coroner's database. In both cases, the females had had their necks chewed on."

"Shit. Zsadist."

"That's what I'm thinking. I keep telling him he's got to pull back. You have to talk with him."

"Tonight. Tell the brothers to come here first. I'm going to set him straight in front of everyone."

"Good plan. Then the rest of us can peel your hands from his throat when he mouths off."

"Hey, you know where Tohr is? I can't reach him."

"No idea, but I'll go to his house on the way over to D's if you want."

"Do that. He needs to be here tonight." Wrath hung up.

Damn it. Someone was going to have to put a muzzle on Zsadist.

Or a dagger in his chest.

Butch let the car roll to a stop. He had no real hope Beth was going to be at the apartment, but he went to the lobby door and hit the buzzer anyway. No answer.

Surprise, surprise.

He walked around the side of the apartment building and through the courtyard. It was after dark, so he was not encouraged by her lights being off. He cupped his hands and leaned into the sliding glass door.

"*Beth!* Oh, God! Sweet Jesus!"

Her body was facedown on the floor, one arm extended in front of her toward a phone that was just out of reach. Her legs were sprawled, as if she'd been writhing in pain.

"*No!*" He pounded on the glass.

She moved a little, as if she'd heard him.

Butch went over to a window, whipped off his shoe, and pushed his hand deep inside the sole. He punched at the glass until it cracked and then shattered. As he reached in to free the lock, he cut himself, but he didn't care if he lost an arm getting to her. He threw his body inside and knocked over a table as he lunged forward.

"Beth! Can you hear me?"

She opened her mouth. Worked it slowly. No words came out.

He looked for blood and found none, so he gingerly rolled her onto her back. She was pale as a grave marker, clammy, barely conscious. When she opened her eyes, her pupils were totally dilated.

He extended her arms, searching for track marks. There were none, but he wasn't about to waste time stripping off her shoes and checking between her toes.

Butch flipped open his cell phone and dialed 911.

When the service picked up, he didn't wait for the greeting. "I have a probable drug overdose."

Beth's hand fluttered up, and she started to shake her head. She was trying to bat the phone away.

"Baby, be still. I'm going to take care—"

The operator's voice cut him off. "Sir? Hello?"

"Take me to Wrath," Beth moaned.

"Fuck him."

"Excuse me?" the operator said. "Sir, can you tell me what's happening?"

"Drug overdose. I think it's heroin. Her pupils are fixed and dilated. She hasn't vomited yet—"

"Wrath, I need to go to Wrath."

"—but she's going in and out of consciousness—"

And then Beth jerked up from the floor and snatched the phone out of his hand. "I'm going to die . . ."

"The hell you are!" he yelled.

She gripped the front of his shirt. Her body shook, sweat staining the front of her T-shirt. "I *need* him."

Butch stared into her eyes.

He'd been wrong. So very wrong. This wasn't an OD. It was withdrawal.

He shook his head. "Baby, no."

"*Please.* I need him. Going to die." Suddenly, she jack-knifed into the fetal position, like a wave of pain had snapped her in half. The cell phone skittered out of her hand, out of reach. "Butch . . . please."

Fuck. She looked bad. As in death's-doorstep bad.

If he took her to an ER, she might die on the way over or while waiting to be treated. And methadone was meant to ease cravings, not pull an addict out of a free fall.

Fuck.

"Help me."

"God*damn* him," Butch said. "How far away?"

"Wallace."

"Avenue?"

She nodded.

Butch couldn't allow himself to think. He scooped her up in his arms and carried her out through the courtyard.

He was *so* going to nail that bastard.

Wrath crossed his arms and leaned back against the wall in the drawing room. The brothers stood around, waiting for him to speak.

And Tohr was there, though from the minute he'd come through the door with Vishous, he'd refused to meet Wrath's eyes.

Fine, Wrath thought. *We'll just do this in public.*

"My brothers, we've got two pieces of business." He stared at Tohr's face. "I have gravely injured one of you. Accordingly, I offer Tohrment a *rythe.*"

Tohr snapped to attention. The brothers likewise were surprised.

It was an unprecedented action, and he knew it. A *rythe* was essentially a free shot, and the one to whom it was offered could choose the weapon. Fist, dagger, gun, chains. It was a ritual way of assuaging honor, both for the offended and the offender. Both could be cleansed.

The shock in the room didn't come from the act itself.

The brothers were quite familiar with the ritual. Given their aggressive natures, every one of them at some time or another had offended the hell out of someone else.

But Wrath, for all his sins, had never offered a *rythe* before. Because according to vampire law, anyone who raised an arm or weapon to him could be condemned to die.

"In front of these witnesses, hear me now," he said loudly and clearly. "I absolve you of the repercussions. Do you accept?"

Tohr's head went down. He put his hands in the pockets of his leathers and slowly shook his head. "I cannot strike you, my lord."

"And you cannot forgive me, can you?"

"I don't know."

"I can't blame you for that." But man, he wished Tohr had accepted. They needed to be healed. "I will offer again at another time."

"And I will ever decline."

"So be it." Wrath pegged Zsadist with a dark glare. "Now about your goddamned love life."

Z, who'd been standing behind his twin, sauntered forward. "If anyone nailed Darius's daughter, it was you, not me. What's the problem?"

A couple of the brothers muttered curses under their breath.

Wrath bared his fangs.

"I'm going to let that pass, Z. But only because I know how much you like to get hit, and I'm not in the mood to make you happy." He straightened, in case the brother lunged. "I want you to chill with the whores. Or at the very least, clean up after yourself."

"What are you talking about?"

"We don't need the heat."

Zsadist glanced back at Phury, who said, "The bodies. The cops found them."

"What bodies?"

Wrath shook his head. "Christ, Z. Do you think the cops are going to let two dead women left to bleed out in alleys slide?"

Zsadist came forward, getting so close their chests touched. "I don't know dick about that. Smell me. I'm telling the truth."

Wrath breathed deep. He caught the scent of outrage, a tangy flare in his nose like someone had blasted him with citrus air freshener. But there was no anxiety, no emotional subterfuge.

Trouble was, Z not only was a black-souled cutthroat, he was an accomplished liar.

"I know you too well," Wrath said softly, "to believe any word you say."

Z started to growl, and Phury moved fast, wrapping a thick forearm around his twin's neck and hauling the brother back.

"Easy, Z," Phury said.

Zsadist grabbed onto his twin's wrist and yanked free. He glowed with hatred. "One of these days, *my lord*, I'm going to—"

A noise like cannonballs hitting a wall cut him off.

Someone was pounding the holy hell out of the front door.

The brothers left the drawing room and went to the foyer in a group. The sounds of weapons being drawn and cocked followed their heavy footfalls.

Wrath checked the video monitor that was mounted on the wall.

When he saw Beth in the cop's arms, he stopped breathing. He threw open the front door and grabbed for her body as the man rushed inside.

This is it, he thought. She was in the transition.

The cop was vibrating with anger as Beth's weight was transferred between them. "You goddamn son of a bitch. How can you do this to her?"

Wrath didn't bother responding. Cradling Beth in his arms, he strode quickly through the knot of brothers. He could feel their astonishment, but he wasn't about to stop and explain.

"Nobody kills the human but me," he barked. "And he does not leave this house until I come back."

Wrath sped into the drawing room. Pushed the painting aside. Ran down the stairs as fast as he could go.

Time was of the essence.

Butch watched the drug dealer disappear with Beth. Her head bounced as they rushed away, her hair a silken flag trailing behind them.

For a moment, he was utterly immobilized, caught between wanting to scream and needing to cry.

The waste. The horrible waste.

Then he heard the door shut and lock behind him. And realized he was surrounded by five of the meanest, biggest bastards he'd ever seen.

A hand landed on his shoulder like an anvil. "How'd you like to stay for dinner?"

Butch looked up. The guy was wearing a baseball cap and had some kind of marking—was that a tattoo, on his *face*?

"How'd you like to *be* dinner?" said another one, who looked like some kind of model.

Anger returned to Butch, thickening his muscles, strengthening his bones.

He jacked up his pants.

These boys wanna play? he thought. *Fine. We'll fucking dance.*

To show he wasn't afraid, he met each of them in the eye. The two who'd spoken. A relatively normal-looking one who was hanging back. Another guy with an outrageous mane of hair, the kind of stuff women would pay hundreds for at some ritzy salon.

And then the last man.

Butch stared at the scarred face. Black eyes glared back.

This fella, he thought, *was the one to really watch out for.*

With a deliberate shrug, he stepped free of the hold on his shoulder.

"Tell me something, boys," he drawled. "Do you wear that leather to turn each other on? I mean, is it a dick thing with you all?"

Butch got slammed so hard against the door that his back teeth rattled.

The model shoved his perfect face into Butch's. "I'd watch your mouth, if I were you."

"Why bother, when you're keeping an eye on it for me? You gonna kiss me now?"

A growl like none Butch had ever heard came out of the guy.

"Okay, okay." The one who seemed the most normal came forward. "Back off, Rhage. Hey, come on. Let's relax."

It took a minute before the model let go.

"That's right. We're cool," Mr. Normal muttered, clapping his buddy on the back before looking at Butch. "Do yourself a favor and shut the hell up."

Butch shrugged. "Blondie's dying to get his hands on me. I can't help it."

The guy launched back at Butch, and Mr. Normal rolled his eyes, letting his friend go this time.

The fist that came sailing at jaw level snapped Butch's head to one side. As the pain hit, Butch let his own rage fly. The fear for Beth, the pent-up hatred of these lowlifes, the frustration about his job, all of it came out of him. He tackled the bigger man, taking him down onto the floor.

The guy was momentarily surprised, as if he hadn't

expected Butch's speed or strength, and Butch took advantage of the hesitation. He clocked Blondie in the mouth as payback and then grabbed the guy's throat.

One second later, Butch was flat on his back with the man sitting on his chest like a parked car.

The guy took Butch's face into his hand and squeezed, crunching the features together. It was nearly impossible to breathe, and Butch panted shallowly.

"Maybe I'll find your wife," the guy said, "and do her a couple of times. How's that sound?"

"Don't have one."

"Then I'm coming after your girlfriend."

Butch dragged in some air. "Got no woman."

"So if the chicks won't do you, what makes you think I'd want to?"

"Was hoping to piss you off."

Stunning electric-blue eyes narrowed.

They had to be contacts, Butch thought. No one really had peepers that color.

"Now why'd you want to do that?" Blondie asked.

"If I attacked first"—Butch hauled more breath into his lungs—"your boys wouldn't have let us fight. Would've killed me first. Before I had a chance at you."

Blondie loosened his grip a little and laughed as he stripped Butch of his wallet, keys, and cell phone.

"You know, I kind of like this big dummy," the guy drawled.

Someone cleared a throat. Rather officiously.

Blondie leaped to his feet, and Butch rolled over, gasping. When he looked up, he was convinced he was hallucinating.

Standing in the hall was a little old man dressed in livery. Holding a silver tray. "Pardon me, gentlemen. Dinner will be served in about fifteen minutes."

"Hey, are those the spinach crepes I like so much?" Blondie said, going for the tray.

"Yes, Sire."

"Hot damn."

The other men clustered around the butler, taking what he offered. Along with cocktail napkins. Like they didn't want to drop anything on the floor.

What the hell was this?

"Might I ask a favor?" the butler said.

Mr. Normal nodded with vigor. "Bring out another tray of these and we'll kill anything you want for you."

Yeah, guess the guy wasn't really normal. Just relatively so.

The butler smiled as if touched. "If you're going to bloody the human, would you be good enough to do it in the backyard?"

"No problem." Mr. Normal popped another crepe in his mouth. "Damn, Rhage, you're right. These are awesome."

THIRTY-THREE

Wrath was getting desperate. He couldn't get Beth to come around.

And her skin was getting colder by the moment.

He shook her on the bed again. "Beth! Beth! Can you hear me?"

Her hands twitched, but he had a feeling the spasms were involuntary. He put his ear down to her mouth. Air was still coming out, but the intervals were alarmingly long. And the force of the exhale was alarmingly weak.

"Damn it!" He bared his wrist and was about to score himself with his fangs when he realized he wanted to hold her if she was able to drink.

When she was able to drink.

He stripped off his holster, pulled out a dagger, and removed his shirt. He felt around his neck until he found his jugular. Placing the point of his knife against his skin, he cut himself. Blood came out in an obliging rush.

He took his fingertip, got it wet, and brought it to her lips. When he dipped it inside her mouth, her tongue did not respond.

"Beth," he whispered. "Come back to me."

He brought more of his blood to her.

"Damn it, don't you die!" Candles flared in the room. "I love you, *damn you! Goddamn you, don't you let go!*"

Her skin was turning blue now; even he could see the color change.

Frantic prayers fell from his lips, ancient ones in the old language. Ones he'd assumed he'd forgotten.

She wasn't moving. She was far too still.

The Fade was upon her.

Wrath screamed in fury and grabbed her body. He shook her until her hair tangled. "Beth! *I will not let you go! I will come after you before I let you . . .*"

A moan came out of him, and he pulled her against him. As he rocked her cold body back and forth, his blind eyes stared at the black wall before him.

Marissa took special care as she got dressed, determined to go down to the first meal of the night looking her best. After reviewing her wardrobe, she chose a long gown made of cream-colored chiffon. She'd purchased it the season before from the Givenchy collection, but had never worn it. The bodice was tighter and a little more revealing than she usually favored, though the Empire waist ensured that the overall effect was entirely modest.

She brushed out her hair, leaving it free to fall over her shoulders. It was so long now, reaching her hips.

The sight of it brought Wrath to mind. He'd once mentioned its softness, so she'd grown it out under the assumption that the more of it there was, the more he'd like it. And the more he'd like her.

Maybe she would cut off the blond waves. Hack them free of her head.

Her anger, which had simmered down, flared again.

Abruptly, Marissa came to a decision. She was through keeping everything inside. It was time to share.

But then she pictured Wrath's towering height. His cold, hard features. That awesome presence of his. Could she really confront him?

She'd never know if she didn't try. And she wasn't about to let him waltz off into whatever future waited for him without speaking her mind.

She glanced at her Tiffany clock. If she didn't show for dinner and then help out in the clinic as she'd promised, Havers would be suspicious. Better to wait until later in the night to go to Wrath. She had sensed he was staying at Darius's. She would go there.

And she would bide her time until he came home.

Some things were worth waiting for.

"Thanks for meeting me, sensei."

"Billy, how are you?" Mr. X put aside the menu he'd been idly looking at. "I was worried when I got your call. And then you didn't make it to class."

As Riddle slid into the booth, he didn't look so hot. His eyes were still black and blue, and exhaustion hung off his face like loose skin.

"Someone's after me, sensei." Billy crossed his arms over his chest. There was a pause, as if he wasn't sure how far to go with the story.

"This have something to do with your nose?"

"Maybe. I dunno."

"Well, I'm glad you came to me, son."

Another pause.

"You can trust me, Billy."

Riddle sucked in a breath, as if he were about to dive into a pool. "My dad's in D.C., as usual. So last night I had a few friends over. We were smoking some blunts—"

"You shouldn't do that. Illegal drugs are bad news."

Billy shifted uncomfortably, fiddling with the platinum chain around his neck. "I know."

"Go on."

"So me and my friends were by the pool, and one wants to go hit it with his girlfriend. I tell them they can use the cabana, but when they go over, the door's locked. I go up to get the key from the house, and when I'm walking back, a guy steps in front of me, like from out of nowhere. He was fuck—er, freakin' huge. Long black hair. Dressed in leather—"

The waitress came hopping over. "What can I getcha—"

"Later," Mr. X snapped.

As she disappeared in a huff, he nodded to Billy.

Riddle grabbed Mr. X's glass of water and drank. "Anyway, he scared the hell out of me. He was looking at me like he wanted to have me for lunch. But then my friend calls out, because he's wondering where I am with the key. The man said my name and then just kind of disappeared, right as my friend came up the lawn." Billy shook his head. "Thing is, I don't know how he got over the wall. My dad put one all around the back of the grounds last year because he's been getting terrorist threats or something. It's, like, twelve feet tall. And the house was all locked up in front with the security system on."

Mr. X looked down at Billy's hands. They were gripped tightly together.

"I . . . ah, I'm kinda scared, sensei."

"You should be."

Riddle looked vaguely nauseated at having his fears confirmed.

"So, Billy. I want to know. You ever kill something?"

Riddle frowned at the abrupt change of subject. "What are you talking about?"

"You know. A bird. Squirrel. Maybe a cat or a dog?"

"No, sensei."

"No?" Mr. X leveled his eyes on Billy's. "I got no time for liars, son."

Billy cleared his throat. "Yeah. Maybe. When I was younger."

"How'd that make you feel?"

A flush crept up Billy's neck. His hands came apart. "*Nada.* I didn't feel anything."

"Come on, Billy. You've got to trust me."

Billy's eyes flashed. "Okay. Maybe I liked it."

"Yeah?"

"Yeah." Riddle drew out the word.

"Good." Mr. X lifted his hand and caught the waitress's eye. She took her time coming over. "We'll talk about that man later. First, I want you to tell me about your father."

"My dad?"

"You ready to order now?" the waitress said in a snotty tone.

"What do you want, Billy? It's on me."

Riddle recited half the menu.

When the waitress left, Mr. X prompted him. "Your dad?"

Billy shrugged. "I don't see him a lot. But he's . . . you know . . . whatever. A dad. I mean, who cares what he's like?"

"Listen, Billy." Mr. X leaned forward. "I know you ran away from home three times before you turned twelve. I know your father sent you to prep school the minute your mom was in the ground. And I know when you got yourself kicked out of Northfield Mount Hermon, he packed you off to Groton, and when you were tossed out of there, he put you in a military academy. It sounds to me like he's been trying to get rid of you for the last decade."

"He's busy."

"And you've been a lot to handle, haven't you?"

"Maybe."

"So would I be right in assuming that you and Daddy Dearest don't have some kind of *Leave It to Beaver* thing going?" Mr. X waited. "Tell me the truth."

310

"I hate him," Riddle blurted.

"Why?"

Billy crossed his arms over his chest again. His eyes went cold.

"Why do you hate him, son?"

"Because he breathes."

THIRTY-FOUR

Beth stared off into a vast white distance. She was in some kind of dreamscape, with hazy edges that suggested there was no end to what was before her.

A lone figure, lit from behind, approached out of the vapor. She sensed that it was male, whatever it was, and she didn't feel threatened. She felt as if she knew him.

"Father?" she whispered, not sure whether she meant her own or God Himself.

The man was still quite far away, but his hand lifted in greeting, as if he'd heard her.

She stepped forward, but her mouth was suddenly flooded with a taste she didn't recognize. She put her fingertips to her lips. When she looked down at them, she saw red.

The figure dropped his hand. As if he knew what the stain meant.

Beth slammed back into her body. It was like being catapulted and landing on gravel. Everything hurt.

She cried out. As her mouth opened, she got a rush of that taste. She swallowed reflexively.

Something miraculous happened. Like a balloon re-inflating, her skin filled with life. Her senses came alive.

She blindly grabbed onto something hard. Latched on to the source of the taste.

Wrath felt Beth jerk like she'd been electrocuted. And then she started to drink at his neck with great, urgent pulls of her mouth. Her arms tightened around his shoulders, her nails digging into his flesh.

His roar was one of triumph as he eased back on the bed, lying down so the blood flow would be better. He kept his head to one side, exposing his neck to her, and she crawled up onto his chest, her hair spilling all over him. The wet sound of her sucking, the knowledge he was giving her life, gave him a monstrous hard-on.

He held her loosely, stroking her arms. Encouraging her to take more of him. Take all that she needed.

Much later, Beth lifted her head. Licked her lips. Opened her eyes.

Wrath was staring up at her.

And he had a gaping wound in his neck.

"Oh, God . . . what have I done to you?" She reached to stanch the blood seeping from his vein.

He grabbed her hands and brought them to his lips. "Will you have me as your *hellren*?"

"What?" Her mind was having difficulty turning over.

"Marry me."

She looked at the hole in his throat and her stomach lurched. "I-I . . ."

The pain came hard and fast. Tackling her. Taking her into a shadow box of agony. She doubled over, rolling onto the mattress.

Wrath shot up and cradled her in his lap.

"Am I dying . . . ?" she moaned.

"Oh, no, *leelan*. You're not. This will pass," he whispered. "But it's not going to be fun."

Her entire digestive tract convulsed in waves, and she flopped over onto her back. She could barely make out Wrath's face through the pain, but his eyes were wide with worry. He took her hand in his and she squeezed as the next blast of torture overtook her.

Her vision dimmed. Came back. Dimmed again.

Sweat dripped from her body, soaking the sheets. She gritted her teeth and arched. Turned this way and then another. Trying to escape.

She didn't know how long it lasted. Hours. Days.

Wrath stayed with her the whole time.

Wrath took his first deep breath sometime after three A.M.

Finally, she was still.

And not dead still. Calm still.

She'd been so brave. She'd taken the pain with no whimpering, no crying. Even he had begged for his transition to be over.

A croak came out of her.

"What, my *leelan*?" He put his head down to her mouth.

"Shower."

"Right."

He left the bed, got the water started, and came back for her. Gently lifting her into his arms, he carried her to the bathroom. She couldn't stand, so he sat her on the marble counter, stripped her clothes off, and then picked her up again.

He stepped under the water, shielding her body with his back. He wanted to see if the change in temperature and humidity was unpleasant for her. When she didn't protest, he let the rush hit her feet first in case the sensation was too much. Gradually, he eased her under the showerhead.

She seemed to like the water, craning her neck and opening her mouth.

He saw her fangs, and they were beautiful to him.

Bright white. Sharply pointed. He remembered the sensation of her drinking.

Wrath pulled her against him for a moment, just hugging her. And then he dropped her feet to the ground and held her body with one arm. With his free hand, he picked up a jar of shampoo and squeezed a little on the top of her head. He rubbed her hair into a lather and then rinsed it clean. With a bar of soap, he gently massaged her skin as best he could without dropping her and then made sure every last sud was washed off.

Scooping her up into his arms again, he shut off the water, got out, and grabbed a towel. He wrapped her up and put her back on the counter, propping her against the wall and the mirror. Carefully, he blotted the water from her hair, her face, her neck, her arms. Then her feet, calves, and knees.

Her skin was going to be hypersensitive for a while. Her eyes and hearing, too.

During her transition, he'd watched for signs that her body was changing and had seen none. She was the same height as before. She fit the same way against him. He wondered if she'd even be able to go out during the day.

"Thank you," she whispered.

He kissed her and carried her to the sofa. Then he stripped the bed of the wet sheets and mattress pad. He struggled with remaking it. He had a tough time finding the other set of sheets, and getting them on right was hard as hell for him. When he was finally finished, he picked her up and settled her against the fresh satin.

Her deep sigh was the best compliment he'd ever been paid.

Wrath knelt by the side of the bed, suddenly aware

that his leather pants and his shitkickers were soaking wet.

"Yes," she whispered.

He kissed her forehead. "Yes what, my *leelan*?"

"I will marry you."

THIRTY-FIVE

Butch paced around the drawing room again, stopping at the fireplace. He looked down at the logs that were banked in the hearth. He imagined how nice a fire would be in there during the winter. How you could sit on the silk couches and watch the flickering flames. How that butler would serve you hot toddies or something.

What the hell was that bunch of thugs doing in a place like this?

From down the hall, he heard the sounds of the men. They'd been in what he assumed must be a dining room for hours, just running their mouths. At least their choice of dinner music was appropriate. Hard-core rap thumped through the house, 2Pac, Jay-Z, D-12. Occasionally, he heard shouts of laughter over the beats. Taunts of the macho variety.

He eyed the front door for the one millionth time.

When the men had shoved him into the drawing room and then headed down the hall a lifetime ago, his first thought was of escaping, even if he had to put a chair through a window. He'd call José. Bring the whole station house to their front door.

But before he could act on the impulse, a voice had filled his ear. "I hope you decide to run."

Butch had spun around, crouching. The skull-trimmed, scarred one was right next to him, though he hadn't heard the guy move.

"Go 'head." Those freaky-ass black eyes had stared at Butch with the dead intensity of a shark. "Crack open that door. Run your little heart out. Run fast, run smart, call for help. Just know that I'll come after you. Like a hearse."

"Zsadist, leave him alone." The guy with the great hair had stuck his head out into the room. "Wrath wants the human alive. For the time being."

The scarred man had spared Butch one last look. "Try it. Just try it. I'd rather hunt you down than eat dinner with them."

Then he'd sauntered out.

Threat notwithstanding, Butch had cased what he could see of the house. There wasn't a phone that he could find, and judging by the security system panel he'd spied in the front hall, all the windows and doors in the place had to be wired for sound. Busting out discreetly wasn't an option.

And he didn't want to leave Beth behind.

God, if she died . . .

Butch inhaled. Frowned.

What the hell was that?

The tropics. He smelled the ocean.

He turned around.

A breathtaking woman was standing in the doorway. Waif-like, elegant, she was dressed in a filmy gown, and her gorgeous blond hair drifted to her hips in waves. Her face was all delicate perfection, her eyes the pale blue color of sea glass.

She took a step back, as if in fear of him.

"No," he said, lurching forward, thinking of the men in the room down the hall. "Don't go back there."

She looked around, as if she wanted to call for help.

"I'm not going to hurt you," he said quickly.

"How do I know that?"

She had a subtle accent. Like all of them did. Maybe Russian?

He held his hands out, palms up, to show he didn't have a weapon. "I'm a cop."

Yeah, okay, so that was no longer exactly true, but he wanted to reassure her.

She gathered the skirt of her dress up, as if she were going to take off.

Hell, he shouldn't have used the *C*-word. If she was the moll of one of them, then she was even more likely to bolt if she thought he was the law.

"I'm not here in an official capacity," he said. "No gun, no badge."

Abruptly, she dropped the gown, and her shoulders straightened as if she were drafting her courage into service. She came forward a little, moving fluidly, gracefully. Butch kept his mouth shut and tried to look smaller than he actually was, less threatening.

"He doesn't normally let your kind be around," she said.

Yeah, he could imagine cops didn't hang out too often in this house. "I'm waiting for . . . a friend."

Her head tilted to the side. As she got closer, her beauty nearly blinded him. Her facial structure was the stuff of fashion magazines, her body the kind of long, lovely sweep he imagined trotted down runways. And that perfume she wore. It got into his nose, into his brain. She smelled so good his eyes watered.

She was unreal, he thought. So pure. So clean.

He felt like he should brush his teeth and shave before saying one more word to her.

What the hell was she doing hanging out with those lowlifes?

Butch's heart cramped with the idea of how useful she'd be to them. *Dear God*. On the sex market, you could get thousands and thousands and thousands for just an hour with a woman like this one.

No wonder the house was so well tricked out.

Marissa was leery of the human, especially considering his size. She'd heard so many stories about them. How

319

they hated the vampire race. How they hunted her species.

But this one seemed to be taking great pains not to frighten her. He didn't move; he barely breathed. All he did was stare at her.

Which was unnerving, and not only because she wasn't used to being looked at. His hazel eyes gleamed out of his harsh face, missing nothing, taking in all of her.

He was smart, this one. Smart and . . . sad.

"What's your name?" he asked quietly.

She liked his voice. Deep and low. Rough around the edges, as if he were perpetually a little hoarse.

She was getting very close to him now, just feet away, so she stopped.

"Marissa. I am called Marissa."

"Butch." He touched his broad chest. "Er . . . Brian. O'Neal. People call me Butch, though."

He stuck his hand out. Then retracted it, rubbed it vigorously on his pant leg, and offered it again.

She lost her nerve. Touching him was too much, and she took a step back.

He dropped his hand slowly, not looking at all surprised that she'd rejected him.

And still, he stared.

"What are you looking at?" She brought her hands up to the bodice of the gown, covering herself.

A flush ran up his neck and into his cheeks. "Sorry. You're probably sick of men gawking at you."

Marissa shook her head. "No males look at me."

"I find that very hard to believe."

It was true. They were all terrified of what Wrath might do.

God, if those others had only known how little she'd been wanted.

"Because . . ." The human's voice trailed off. "Man, you are so . . . totally . . . beautiful."

And then he cleared his throat, like he wished he could take the words back.

She tilted her head, considering him. There was something she couldn't decipher in his tone. An achy pitch.

He dug his hand into his thick, dark hair. "And I'm going to shut up now. Before I make you feel even more uncomfortable."

His eyes stayed on her face.

They were really nice eyes, she thought. So warm. And they held a lonely yearning as he looked at her. As if he couldn't have something he wanted.

She knew all about that.

The human laughed, a burst of sound that came from deep inside his chest. "And how 'bout I try not to stare? That'd be good." He crammed his hands in the pockets of his pants and focused on the floor. "Look at me. Not staring. Not staring at all. Hey, this is a nice rug. You ever notice it before?"

Marissa smiled in a small way and took a step closer to him. "I think I like the way you look at me."

Those hazel eyes snapped back to her face.

"I'm just not used to it," she explained. Her hand went to her neck, but she dropped it.

"Man, you cannot be real," the human said softly.

"Why not?"

"You just can't."

She laughed a little. "Well, I am."

He cleared his throat again. Offered her a lopsided grin. "Mind if I ask you to prove it?"

"How?"

"Can I touch your hair?"

Her first thought was to back away again. But then, why should she? She was tied to no male. If this human wanted to touch her, why couldn't he?

Especially because she kind of wanted him to.

She dropped her head down so some of her hair fell

forward. She thought about holding a section out to him. But no. She would let him come closer.

And the human did.

His hand was big as it reached out, and her breath caught, but he didn't go for the blond wave hanging in front of her. Instead, his fingertips made contact with a lock resting on her shoulder.

She felt a blast of heat through her skin, as though he'd touched her with a lit match. In no time, the sensation traveled throughout her body, as if she'd spiked a fever.

What was this?

The human's finger moved her hair aside, and then his whole hand brushed against her shoulder. His palm was warm. Solid. Strong.

She lifted her eyes to him.

"I can't breathe," she whispered.

Butch nearly fell over.

Good God, he thought. She wanted him.

And her innocent amazement at his touch was better than the best sex he'd ever had.

His body shot into overdrive, his erection straining his jeans, demanding to get out.

But this couldn't be real, he thought. She had to be playing him. No one looked like she did, and hung out with those boys, without knowing every trick in the book. And pulling a lot of them on her back.

He watched as she took an unsteady breath. And then licked her lips. The tip of her tongue was pink.

Sweet Jesus.

She might only be a fantastic actress. She might only be the best whore anyone had ever come across. But as she looked up at him, she had him in the palm of her hand. He was buying what she was selling in a big fricking way.

He let his finger run up the side of her neck. Her skin was so soft, so pale, he was afraid he'd leave a mark just by touching her.

"Do you live here?" he asked.

She shook her head. "I live with my brother."

He was relieved. "That's good."

He brushed her cheek lightly. Stared at her mouth.

What would she taste like?

His eyes dipped lower, to her breasts. They seemed to have swelled and were pushing against the bodice of her fine gown.

Her voice was tremulous. "You look at me as if you're thirsty."

Oh, God. She had that right. He was parched.

"Except I thought humans didn't feed?" she said.

Butch frowned. She had an odd way with words, but then English was clearly her second language.

His fingers moved over to her mouth. He paused, wondering if she would pull away if he touched her lips. *Probably*, he thought. Just to keep the game going.

"Your name," she said. "It's Butch?"

He nodded.

"What are you thirsty for, Butch?" she whispered.

His eyes slammed shut as his body swayed.

"Butch?" she said. "Did I hurt you just now?"

Yeah, only if you consider raging lust a kind of pain, he thought.

THIRTY-SIX

Wrath got out of bed and drew on a fresh set of leathers and a black T-shirt.

Beth was sleeping soundly on her side. When he went over and kissed her, she stirred.

"I'm going upstairs," he said, stroking her cheek. "But I'm not leaving the house."

She nodded, brushed her lips against his palm, and sank back down into the healing rest she needed so badly.

Wrath put on his sunglasses, locked the door behind him, and mounted the stairs. He knew there was a stupid, satisfied grin on his face and that his brothers were going to ride him hard for it.

But what the hell did he care?

He was taking a true *shellan*. He was going to be mated. And they could kiss his ass.

He pushed open the painting and stepped into the drawing room.

He couldn't believe what he saw.

Marissa in a long creamy gown. The cop in front of her, stroking her face, evidently poleaxed. All around them, the delicious scent of sex in the air.

And then Rhage burst into the room, dagger drawn. The brother was clearly ready to field dress the human for touching what he presumed was Wrath's *shellan*.

"Take your hands—"

Wrath leaped forward. "Rhage! Hold up!"

The brother caught himself as Butch and Marissa looked around frantically.

Rhage smiled and tossed the dagger across the room

at Wrath. "Go for it, my lord. He deserves death for putting his hand to her, but can we play with him a little first?"

Wrath caught the knife. "Go back to the table, Hollywood."

"Ah, come on. You know it's better with an audience."

Wrath smirked. "Only for you, my brother. Now leave us."

He threw the dagger back and Rhage sheathed it while leaving. "Man, Wrath, you can be a real buzz kill, you know that? A total fucking buzz kill."

Wrath looked over at Marissa and the cop. He had to approve of the way the human was using his body to protect her.

Maybe the guy was more than just a good opponent.

Butch glared at the suspect and put his arms out, trying to corral Marissa. She refused to stay behind him. Actually side-stepped his body, placing hers in front.

Like she was protecting him?

He grabbed her thin arm, but she resisted.

As that black-haired murderer came forward, she addressed the man sharply and they started talking in a language Butch didn't recognize. She grew heated. The man nodded a lot. Gradually she calmed.

And then the man put his hand on her shoulder and turned his head to look at Butch.

Good God, the guy's neck had a raw wound on one side, like something had chewed on him.

The man spoke. Marissa's reply was hesitant, but then she repeated it in a stronger tone.

"So be it," the bastard said, smiling tightly.

Marissa moved so she was standing side by side with Butch. She looked at him and blushed.

Something had been decided. Something—

325

With a quick movement, the man grabbed Butch's throat.

Marissa screamed. "Wrath!"

Ah, shit, not this again, Butch thought as he struggled.

"She seems to be intrigued by you," the murderer said in Butch's ear. "So I'm going to let you keep breathing. But you hurt her and I'll skin you alive."

Marissa was talking rapidly in that foreign language, cursing the man, no doubt.

"We understand each other?" the man demanded.

Butch narrowed his eyes on those sunglasses. "She's got nothing to fear from me."

"Keep it that way."

"You're another story, however."

The man let go. Straightened Butch's shirt. Smiled.

Butch frowned.

Man, there was something seriously wrong with that guy's teeth.

"Where's Beth?" Butch demanded.

"She's safe. And healthy."

"No thanks to you."

"Thanks only to me."

"Then you've got some weird-ass ways of defining those words. I want to see her for myself."

"Later. And only if she wants to see you."

Butch's anger flared, and the bastard seemed to sense the surge in his body.

"Watch it, cop. You're in my world now."

Yeah, fuck you, buddy.

Butch was about to open his mouth when he felt something grab onto his arm. He looked down. Fear was shining in Marissa's eyes.

"Butch, please," she whispered. "Don't."

The suspect nodded.

"You be polite, and you stay with her," the man said,

voice softening as he looked at Marissa. "She's happy to have your company, and she deserves a good shot of happy. We'll see about Beth. Later."

Mr. X took Billy back to the Riddle estate after they'd driven around the city for hours, talking.

Billy's past was perfect, and not just because of the violence he'd perpetrated on others. His father was just the kind of male role model Mr. X liked to see. A total, raving lunatic with a God complex. The man was a former NFL player, big, aggressive and competitive, and he'd ridden Billy since birth.

Nothing the son ever did was good enough. Mr. X's personal favorite was the story of Billy's mother's death. The woman had fallen into the pool after drinking too much one afternoon, and Billy had found her floating facedown. He'd pulled her out of the water and attempted CPR before calling 911. At the hospital, as the toe-tagged body had been wheeled to the morgue, the distinguished senator from the great state of New York had suggested his son had killed her. Evidently, Billy should have known to get an ambulance on the scene first rather making a half-assed attempt to play paramedic himself.

Mr. X didn't question the merits of matricide. It was just that in Billy's case, the kid had been trained as a lifeguard and had actually tried to save the woman.

"I hate this house," Riddle muttered, staring up at the beautifully lit bricks and columns and shutters.

"Too bad you're on all those waiting lists. College would have gotten you out."

"Yeah, well, I might have gotten in to one or two. If he hadn't forced me to apply to only Ivies."

"So what are you going to do?"

Billy shrugged. "He wants me to move out. Get a job. It's just . . . I don't know where I can go."

"Tell me something, Billy, you got a girlfriend?"

He smiled, a little half pull at the corners of his lips. "I got a couple."

Yes, Mr. X could imagine the guy did, handsome as he was. "Someone special?"

Billy's eyes slid over. "They're good for getting off. But they're all over me. Calling and shit, wanting to know where I am, what I'm doing. They want too much, and I, ah . . ."

"You what?"

Billy's eyes narrowed.

"Go on, son. There's isn't anything you can't tell me."

"I, ah, I like them better when they're hard to get . . ." He cleared his throat. "Actually, I like it when they're trying to get away."

"You like to catch them?"

"I like to take them. You know what I mean?"

Mr. X nodded, thinking that was one more vote in Riddle's favor. No ties to family. No ties to a girlfriend. And his sexual dysfunction would be taken care of during the induction ceremony.

Riddle grabbed for the door handle. "Anyway, thanks, sensei. This was really great."

"Billy."

Riddle paused, glancing back expectantly. "Yes, sensei?"

"What if you came to work for me?"

Riddle's eyes flared. "You mean at the academy?"

"Sort of. Let me tell you a little about what you would be doing and then you can think it over."

THIRTY-SEVEN

Beth rolled over, looking for Wrath, and then remembered that he'd gone upstairs.

She sat up, bracing herself in case the pain came back. When nothing hurt, she got to her feet. She was naked, and she looked down at her body. Everything seemed the same. She did a little jig. Seemed to work okay, too.

Except she couldn't see very well.

She went into the bathroom. Removed her contacts. And saw perfectly.

Well, there's one benefit.

Whoa. Fangs. She had fangs.

She leaned in, prodded them a little. Eating with those puppies was going to take some getting used to, she thought.

On impulse, she brought up her hands, turned her fingers into claws. Hissed.

Cool.

Halloween was going to be a real kick in the pants from now on.

She brushed out her hair, pulled on Wrath's robe, and headed for the stairs. When she got to the top, she wasn't breathless at all.

And wasn't this going to make her workouts a snap?

As she stepped out of the painting, she saw Butch sitting across the sofa from a stunning blonde. In the distance, she heard male voices and heavy music.

Butch looked up.

"Beth!" He rushed over, wrapping her in a bear hug. "Are you all right?"

"I'm fine. Truly, I'm fine." Which was amazing, considering what she'd felt like earlier.

Butch pulled back, taking her face in his hands. He stared at her eyes. Frowned. "You don't look high."

"Why would I be?"

He shook his head sadly. "Don't hide it from me. I brought you here, remember?"

"I shall go," the blonde said, getting up.

Butch immediately turned to her. "No. Don't."

He went back to the couch. As he looked down at the woman, his expression was unlike any Beth had ever seen on his face. He was clearly enthralled.

"Marissa, I want you to meet my *friend*"—he emphasized the word—"Beth Randall. Beth, this is Marissa."

Beth lifted a hand. "Hello."

The blonde stared across the room, scrutinizing Beth from head to foot.

"You are Wrath's female," Marissa said with a kind of awe. As if Beth had pulled off some great feat. "The one he wants."

Beth felt her cheeks warm. "Ah, yeah. I guess I am."

There was an awkward silence. Butch looked back and forth between the two of them, frowning like he wanted in on the secret.

Yeah, well, Beth wanted to know what it was, too.

"Do you know where Wrath is?" she asked.

Butch scowled, as if he didn't want her near the man. "He's in the dining room."

"Thanks."

"Listen, Beth. We need to—"

"I'm not going anywhere."

He took a deep breath, blowing it out in a slow hiss.

"Somehow, I thought that's what you would say." He looked at the blonde. "But if you need me, I, ah . . . I'll be here."

She smiled to herself as Butch sat back down with the woman.

As she went out to the hall, the sound of men talking and the deep rumble of rap music got louder.

"So what'd you do to the *lesser?*" a male voice said.

"I lit his cigarette with a sawed-off," another one answered. "He didn't come down for breakfast, you feel me?"

There was a loud chorus of laughter. A couple of bangs, like heavy fists hitting a table.

She pulled the lapels of the robe closer together. It probably would've been smart to get dressed first, but she hadn't wanted to wait to see Wrath.

She rounded the corner.

The instant she appeared in the doorway, all talk ceased. Heads turned; eyes stared. Hard-core rap expanded to fill the silence, bass thumping, lyrics chanting.

My God. She'd never seen so many big men in leather before in her life.

She took a step backward just as Wrath shot to his feet from the head of the table. He came at her, looking intense. No doubt she'd interrupted some kind of sacred guy time.

She tried to think of something to say to him. He was probably going to want to play it cool in front of his brothers, do that whole I'm-a-tough-guy, this-broad-is-just-a—

Wrath wrapped his whole body around hers, putting his face in her hair.

"My *leelan,*" he whispered in her ear. He ran his hands up and down her back. "My beautiful *leelan.*"

He pulled away and kissed her on the lips. His smile was tender as he smoothed her hair.

Beth grinned. Evidently, her man didn't have a problem with public displays of affection. Good to know.

She tilted her head, looking around his shoulder.

And they were definitely in public. The men were gaping. Positively gaping.

She nearly laughed. Seeing a bunch of guys who looked like violent offenders sitting around a table set with silver and china was incongruous enough. But having them be so totally flabbergasted seemed downright absurd.

"You want to introduce me?" she said, nodding at the group.

Wrath put his arm around her shoulders, tucking her against him.

"This is the Black Dagger Brotherhood. My fellow warriors. My brothers." He nodded to the blindingly handsome one. "Rhage, you know. Tohr also. The one with the goatee and the Sox hat is Vishous. The Rapunzel over there is Phury." Wrath's voice dropped to a snarl. "And Zsadist has already introduced himself."

The two she'd spent some time with smiled at her. The others nodded, except for the scarred one. He just stared.

That guy had a twin, she recalled. But she'd have been hard-pressed to pick out his real brother.

Though the one with the absolutely delicious hair and the fantastic yellow eyes did look a little like him.

"Gentlemen," Wrath said. "This is Beth."

And then he switched over to that language she didn't understand.

When he ended, there was an audible gasp.

He looked down, smiling. "Do you need anything? Are you hungry, *leelan?*"

She put her hand on her stomach. "You know, I am. I have the weirdest craving for bacon and chocolate. Go figure."

"I will serve you. Sit down." He indicated his chair and then headed off through a swinging door.

She eyed the men.

Great. Here she was, naked in a bathrobe, alone with well over a thousand pounds of vampire. Pulling off the nonchalant thing was impossible, so she just headed over for Wrath's seat. She didn't get far.

There was a loud scraping noise as five chairs slid backward. The men rose as a unit. And started coming for her.

She looked to the faces of the two she knew, but their grave expressions weren't encouraging.

And then the knives came out.

With a metallic *whoosh*, five black daggers were unsheathed.

She backed up frantically, hands in front of herself. She slammed into a wall and was about to scream for Wrath when the men dropped down on bended knees in a circle around her. In a single movement, as if they'd been choreographed, they buried the daggers into the floor at her feet and bowed their heads. The great *whoomp* of sound as steel met wood seemed both a pledge and a battle cry.

The handles of the knives vibrated.

The rap music continued to pound.

They seemed to be waiting for some kind of response from her.

"Umm. Thank you," she said.

The men's heads lifted. Etched into the harsh planes of their faces was total reverence. Even the scarred one had a respectful expression.

And then Wrath came in with a squeeze bottle of Hershey's syrup.

"Bacon's on the way." He smiled. "Hey, they like you."

"And thank God for that," she murmured, looking down at the daggers.

THIRTY-EIGHT

Marissa smiled, thinking that the human got more handsome the longer she was around him. "So you protect your kind for a living. That is good."

He shifted beside her on the couch. "Well, actually, I don't know what I'm going to do now. I have a feeling I'm about to be between jobs."

The chiming of a clock made her wonder how much time they'd spent together. And when the sun was coming up. "What time is it?"

"Just after four A.M."

"I must go."

"When can I see you again?"

She stood. "I don't know."

"Can we have dinner?" He leaped up. "Lunch? What are you doing tomorrow?"

She had to laugh. "I don't know."

She'd never been pursued before. It was nice.

"Ah, hell," he muttered. "I'm blowing it with this overeager sh—stuff, aren't I?" He put his hands on his hips and stared at the carpet as if disgusted with himself.

She stepped forward. His head snapped up.

"I would touch you now," she said softly. "Before I go."

His eyes flared.

"May I? Butch?"

"Anywhere," he breathed.

She lifted her hand, thinking she would just put it on his shoulder. But his lips fascinated her. She'd watched them move while he enunciated his words and wondered what they felt like.

"Your mouth," she said. "It's rather . . ."

"What?" His voice was hoarse.

"Lovely."

She put her fingertip on his lower lip. His gasp drew air over her skin, and when he exhaled on a shudder, it came back warm and moist.

"You're soft," she said, brushing her forefinger back and forth.

He closed his eyes.

His body was throwing off the most intoxicating scent. She'd caught the heady fragrance the moment he'd first seen her. Now, it saturated the air.

Curious, she slipped her finger into his mouth. His eyes flipped open.

She felt his front teeth, finding the absence of fangs odd. When she went in farther, it was slick, wet, warm.

Slowly, his lips closed around her finger. And then his tongue ran around the tip in a circle.

A surge went through her body. "Oh . . ."

Her breasts tingled at the tips, and something was happening between her legs. She felt achy. Hungry.

"I want . . ." She didn't know what to say next.

He covered her hand with his and pulled his head back, sucking the length of her finger until it popped out of his mouth. With his eyes boring into hers, he turned her palm over, licked the center of it with his tongue, and pressed his lips to her skin.

She leaned into him.

"What do you want?" he asked in a low voice. "Tell me, baby. Tell me what you want."

"I . . . don't know. I've never felt this before."

Her answer seemed to crack the spell. His face grew dark, and he dropped her hand. A curse, soft and vile, floated out of him as he put some space between them.

Marissa's eyes burned at his rejection. "Have I displeased you?"

God knew, it was something she seemed to excel at when it came to males.

"Displeased? No, you're doing just fine. You're a real pro." He pushed a hand through his hair. He seemed to be struggling with himself, as if he were trying to get back to normal from some faraway place. "It's just that the innocent act is freaking me out a little."

"Act?"

"You know, the doe-eyed-virgin routine."

She stepped forward while trying to frame a response, but he held out his hands. "That's close enough right now."

"Why?"

"Please, baby. Give it a rest."

Her face fell. "You make no sense."

"Oh, *really*," he said. "Look, you can turn me on just standing there. You don't have to pretend you're something you're not. And I . . . ah, I don't have a problem with what you do. I'm not going to arrest you for it, either."

"Why would you arrest me?"

As he rolled his eyes, she had no clue what he was talking about.

"I will go now," she said abruptly. His aggravation was growing with each passing moment.

"Wait." He reached out and took her arm. The instant he made contact, he dropped his hand. "I still want to see you."

She frowned, eyeing the hand he'd touched her with. He was rubbing the thing like he wanted to get rid of a sensation.

"Why?" she asked. "You obviously don't like the feel of me right now."

"Uh-huh. Yeah, sure." He regarded her cynically. "Look, how much is it going to cost me to get you to play normal?"

She glared back at him. Before she'd had it out with Wrath, she might have just skulked off. But no more.

"I don't understand you," she said.

"Whatever, baby. Tell me, are some guys so hard up to pop cherries that they actually buy this act?"

Marissa didn't understand all the vernacular he used, but the gist of what he was thinking finally got through to her. Appalled, she threw her spine into a straight line.

"I beg your pardon!"

He stared at her, jaw set hard. Then he exhaled.

"Ah, hell." He rubbed his face with his hand. "Look, forget it, okay? Let's just forget we ever met——"

"I have *never* been taken. My *hellren* did not favor my company. So I have not once been kissed or touched or even held by a male who felt passion for me. But I am not . . . I am not unworthy." Her voice quavered at the end. "I've just never been wanted before."

His eyes went wide, like she'd slapped him or something.

She looked away. "And I've never touched a male," she whispered. "I just don't know what to do."

The human let out a long breath, as if all the oxygen in his body were being expelled.

"Holy Mary, mother of God," he murmured. "I'm sorry. I'm really, really sorry. I'm . . . I'm a total asshole, and I totally misjudged you."

His horror at what he'd said to her was so palpable, she smiled a little. "You truly mean that."

"Hell, yeah. I mean, yes, I do. I hope I haven't completely offended you. Well, how could I not have? Jesus Christ . . . I'm very sorry." He looked positively pale.

She put her hand on his arm. "I forgive you."

He laughed in disbelief. "You shouldn't. You should stay pissed at me for a while. At least a week, maybe a month. Probably longer. I was way out of line."

"But I don't want to be angry at you."

There was a long pause. "Will you still see me tomorrow?"

"Yes."

He seemed stunned by his good fortune. "Really? Man, you're going for sainthood, you know that?" He reached out and stroked her cheek with his fingertip. "Where, baby? Where's good for you?"

She thought for a moment. Havers would have a fit if he knew she was seeing a human.

"Here. I will meet you here. Tomorrow night."

He smiled. "Good. Now, how're you getting home? Do you need a ride? A taxi?"

"No, I will do that myself."

"Wait—before you go." He moved toward her. That lovely scent of his hit her nose and she breathed him in. "Can I kiss you good-night? Even though I don't deserve it?"

Per custom, she offered him the back of her hand.

He took it and pulled her forward. That throbbing in her blood and between her legs came back.

"Close your eyes," he whispered.

She did as he'd said.

His lips softly brushed her forehead. Then her temple.

Her mouth opened as the sweet suffocation returned.

"You could never displease me," he said in his gravelly voice.

And then his lips touched her cheek.

She waited for more. When nothing came, she opened her eyes. He was staring down at her remotely.

"Go," he said. "I'll see you tomorrow."

She nodded. And dematerialized right out of his hand.

* * *

338

Butch shouted and leaped back. *"Shit!"*

He looked at his hand. He could still feel her palm against his. Still smell her perfume.

But she was goddamned gone. Poof. One minute in front of him and then the next . . .

Beth came running into the room. "Are you okay?"

"No, I'm not fucking okay," he snapped.

The suspect strode in. "Where's Marissa?"

"How should I know! She fucking disappeared! In front . . . She was . . . I held her hand and then she—"
He sounded like a frantic idiot and clapped his trap shut.

But why wouldn't he be freaked out? He liked the laws of physics just as he knew them. Gravity keeping everything on the flipping planet where it should be.
$E = mc^2$ telling him how fast he could get to a bar.

People not poofing the hell out of a goddamned room.

"May I tell him?" Beth asked her man.

The suspect shrugged. "Usually I'd say no, because it's better they don't know. But considering what he saw—"

"Tell me what? That you're a bunch of—"

"Vampires," Beth murmured.

Butch looked at her, annoyed. "Yeah, right. Try that one again, sweetheart."

But then she started talking, telling him things he couldn't believe.

When Beth fell silent, he could only stare at her. His instincts were telling him she wasn't lying. But it was all just too hard to accept.

"I don't believe this," he said to her.

"It was hard for me to comprehend, too."

"I'll bet."

He paced around the room, wishing he had a drink. The two of them just stared at him.

Finally, he stopped in front of Beth. "Open your mouth."

He heard a low, nasty sound behind him just as a cold draft hit him in the back.

"Wrath, it's okay," Beth said. "Calm down."

She parted her lips, revealing two long canines that had very certainly not been there before. Butch felt his knees wobble as he reached out to touch her teeth.

A thick hand clamped on his arm, tight enough to bend the bones in his wrist.

"Don't even think about it," Beth's man growled.

"Let him go," she commanded gently, though she didn't offer her mouth again after the guy had released his grip. "They're real, Butch. This whole thing . . . it's all real."

Butch looked up at the suspect. "So you're actually a vampire, is that it?"

"You'd better believe it, cop." The big, dark bastard smiled, flashing a monstrous set of fangs.

Now that's some serious hardware, Butch thought.

"Did you bite her and turn her into one?"

"Doesn't work that way. You're either born our kind or you're not."

Well, weren't all those Dracula fans going to be bummed? No two-pronged conversions.

Butch let himself fall down onto the sofa. "Did you kill those women? To drink their . . ."

"Blood? No. What's in human veins wouldn't keep me alive for long."

"So you're telling me you had nothing to do with those deaths? I mean, we found throwing stars at the scenes that match the ones you were packing the night I arrested you."

"I didn't kill them, cop."

"How about the one in the car?"

The guy shook his head. "My prey is not human. What I fight's got nothing to do with your world. And the bomb? We lost one of ours in it."

Beth made a quick, hard sound. "My father," she whispered.

The man drew her into his arms. "Yeah. And we're looking for the bastard who did it."

"Any idea who pushed the button?" Butch asked, the cop in him coming out.

The guy shrugged. "We got a bead on something. But that's our business, not yours."

Yeah, and Butch had no reason to ask anyway. Because he wasn't on the force.

The guy stroked Beth's back and shook his head. "I won't lie to you, cop. Occasionally, a human gets in the way of what we do. And if anyone threatens our race, I will kill them, no matter who or what they are. But I'm not going to tolerate human casualties the same way I used to, and not just because it risks our exposure." He pressed a kiss onto Beth's mouth, meeting her eyes.

At that point, the rest of the gang members filed into the room. Their cold stares made Butch feel like a bug under glass. Or a roast beef about to be carved up.

Mr. Normal stepped forward and offered him a Scotch bottle. "You look like you could use some."

Yeah, you think?

Butch took a swig. "Thanks."

"So can we kill him now?" said the one with the goatee and the baseball hat.

Beth's man spoke harshly. "Back off, V."

"Why? He's just a human."

"And my *shellan* is half-human. The man doesn't die just because he's not one of us."

"Jesus, you've changed your tune."

"So you need to catch up, *brother*."

Butch got to his feet. If his death was going to be debated, he wanted in on the discussion.

"I appreciate the support," he said to Beth's boy. "But I don't need it."

He went over to the guy with the hat, discreetly switching his grip on the bottle's neck in case he had to crack the damn thing over a head. He moved in tight, so their noses were almost touching. He could feel the vampire heating up, priming for a fight.

"I'm happy to take you on, asshole," Butch said. "I'll probably end up losing, but I fight dirty, so I'll make you hurt while you kill me." Then he eyed the guy's hat. "Though I hate clocking the shit out of another Red Sox fan."

There was a shout of laughter from behind him. Someone said, "This is gonna be fun to watch."

The guy in front of Butch narrowed his eyes into slits. "You true about the Sox?"

"Born and raised in Southie. Haven't stopped grinning since '04."

There was a long pause.

The vampire snorted. "I don't like humans."

"Yeah, well, I'm not too crazy about you bloodsuckers."

Another stretch of silence.

The guy stroked his goatee. "What do you call twenty guys watching the World Series?"

"The New York Yankees," Butch replied.

The vampire laughed in a loud burst, whipped the baseball cap off his head, and slapped it on his thigh. Just like that, the tension was broken.

Butch let out a long breath, feeling like he'd just been missed by an eighteen-wheeler. As he took another swig from the bottle, he decided it had been one weird fucking night.

"Tell me that Curt Schilling was not a god," the vampire said.

There was a collective groan from the other men. One of them muttered, "If he starts going on about Varitek, I'm outta here."

"Schilling was a true warrior," Butch said, taking

another hit of the single-malt. When he offered the Scotch to the vampire, the guy grabbed the bottle and took a hard pull.

"Amen to that," the vampire said.

THIRTY-NINE

When Marissa walked into her bedroom, she took a little spin, feeling her gown splay out around her.

"Where have you been?"

She stopped midtwirl. The dress came to a heel in a swirling rush.

Havers was sitting on the chaise, his face in shadow. "I asked, *where were you*?"

"Please don't take that tone—"

"You saw the brute."

"He's not a—"

"Do not defend him to me!"

She wasn't going to. She was going to tell her brother that Wrath had listened to her recriminations and accepted all blame for the past. That he'd apologized and his regret had been tangible. That although his words couldn't make up for what had happened, she felt that she had been heard.

And that even if her former *hellren* was the reason she'd gone to Darius's, he wasn't why she'd stayed.

"Havers, please. Things are much different." After all, Wrath had told her he was to be mated. And she had . . . met someone. "You must hear me out."

"No, I mustn't. I know that you go to him still. That is enough."

Havers got off the chaise, moving without his usual grace. As he stepped into the light, she was horrified. His skin was gray, his cheeks hollow. He'd been getting thinner and thinner of late. Now, he looked like a skeleton.

"You are ill," she whispered.

"I am perfectly well."

"The transfusion didn't work, did it?"

"Do not try to change the subject!" He glared at her. "God, I never thought it would come to this. I never thought you would hide from me."

"I have hidden nothing!"

"You told me you had broken the covenant."

"I did."

"You *lie*."

"Havers, listen to me—"

"No longer!" He did not meet her eyes as he opened the door. "You are all I have left, Marissa. Do not ask me to politely sit aside and play witness your destruction."

"Havers!"

The door slammed.

With grim determination, she ran out to the hall. "Havers!"

He was already at the head of the stairs, and he refused to look back at her. His hand slashed violently in the air behind him, as if he were dismissing her.

She went back to her room and sat down at her dressing table. It was a long while before she could take a full breath.

Havers's anger was understandable, but frightening because of its intensity and rarity. She'd never seen her brother in such a state. It was clear there would be no reasoning with him until he calmed down.

Tomorrow she would talk with him. She would explain everything, even the new male she had met.

She looked at herself in the mirror and thought of how the human had touched her. She brought her hand up, feeling again the sensation of him sucking her finger. She wanted more of him.

Her fangs elongated slightly.

What would his blood taste like?

* * *

345

After settling Beth in her father's bed, Wrath went to his chamber and dressed himself in a white shirt and long, baggy white pants. He grabbed a string of enormous black pearls out of an ebony box and knelt on the floor next to his bed, settling back on his heels. He put the necklace on, laid his hands palms-up on his thighs, and closed his eyes.

As he marshaled his breath, his senses came alive. He could hear Beth shifting in the bed across the hall, sighing as she burrowed into the pillows. The rest of the house was fairly quiet, only subtle vibrations coming down to him. As some of the brothers were crashing in the upstairs bedrooms, male feet were moving around.

He was willing to bet Butch and V were still talking baseball.

Wrath had to smile. That human was a trip. One of the most aggressive men he'd ever come across.

And as for Marissa liking the cop? Well, they'd all just have to see where that went. Having any kind of relationship with someone of the other species was dangerous. Sure, the brothers slept with a lot of human women, but those were one night only, so the memories were easy to erase. Once emotions got involved, and time passed, it was harder to do a good scrub job on the human brain. Things lingered. Surfaced later. Got people into trouble.

Hell, maybe Marissa was just going to play with the guy and then suck him dry. Which was fine. But until either she killed him or took him for her own, Wrath was going to watch the situation carefully.

Wrath harnessed his thoughts and started to chant in the old language, using the sounds to wipe out his cognitive processes. He was rusty at first, tripping over words. The last time he'd said the prayers, he'd been nineteen or twenty years old. Memories of his father sitting next to him and telling him what to say were a seductive diversion, but he forced his mind to be blank.

The pearls began to warm against his chest.

And then he found himself in a courtyard. The Italianate architecture was white; the marble fountain, the marble columns, the marble floor, all had a pale glow to them. The only splash of color came from a flock of songbirds sitting in a white tree.

He stopped praying and got to his feet.

"It has been a long time, warrior." The regal female voice came from behind him.

He turned around.

The diminutive figure approaching him was completely draped in black silk. Her head and face were covered, her hands and feet, everything. She glided over to him, not walking, just moving through the still air. Her presence made him uneasy.

Wrath bowed his head. "Scribe Virgin, how are you?"

"More to the point, how fare you, warrior? You have come seeking change, have you not?"

He nodded. "I—"

"You wish the covenant with Marissa to be broken. You have found another and you would take her as your *shellan*."

"Yes."

"This female you want. She is the daughter of your brother Darius, who is in the Fade."

"Have you seen him?"

She laughed slightly. "Do not make inquiries of me. I let your first question slide because you were being polite, but remember your manners, warrior."

Shit.

"My apologies, Scribe Virgin."

"I grant you and Marissa freedom from your covenant."

"Thank you."

There was a long pause.

He waited for her ruling on the second part of his request. He sure as hell wasn't going to ask.

"Tell me something, warrior. Do you think your species is unworthy?"

He frowned and then quickly smoothed his face into neutral. The Scribe Virgin wasn't going to put up with being glowered at.

"Well, warrior?"

He had no idea where she was going with this. "My species is a fierce and proud race."

"I didn't ask you for a statement of definition. I asked you what you *thought* of them."

"I protect them with my life."

"And yet you will not lead your people. So I can only surmise that you do not value them and therefore fight because you like to or because you wish to die. Which is it?"

This time he let his frown stay in place. "My race survives because of what the brothers and I do."

"Barely. In fact, its numbers dwindle. It does not thrive. The only localized colony is the one that settled on the United States' East Coast. And even they live isolated from one another. There are no communities. The festivals are no longer held. Rituals are observed privately, if at all. There is no one to mediate disputes, no one to give them hope. And the Black Dagger Brotherhood is cursed. There are none left in it who do not suffer."

"The brothers have their . . . problems. But they are strong."

"And should be stronger." She shook her head. "You have failed your bloodline, warrior. You have failed your purpose. So tell me, why should I grant your wish to take the half-breed as queen?" The Scribe Virgin's robes moved as if she were shaking her head. "Better that you continue to merely service her with your staff

348

than to have your people saddled with yet another meaningless figurehead. Go now, warrior. We are finished."

"I would have a word in my defense," he said, gritting his teeth.

"And I would deny you." She turned away.

"I beg of your mercy." He hated saying the words, and he guessed by the sound of her laugh that she knew it.

The Scribe Virgin came back to him.

When she spoke, her tone was hard, hard as the black lines of her robe against all the white marble. "If you're going to beg, warrior, do it properly. Get on your knees."

Wrath forced his body down to the ground, hating her.

"I rather like you like this," she murmured, back to being relatively pleasant. "Now, what were you saying?"

He swallowed the hostile words in his throat, forcing himself to affect an even temper that was an absolute lie. "I love her. I want to honor her, not just have her to warm my bed."

"So treat her well. But there is no need to have a ceremony."

"I disagree." He tacked on, "Respectfully."

There was a long pause.

"You have sought no counsel from me over these centuries."

He lifted his head. "Is that what bothers you?"

"Do not question me!" she snapped. "Or I will have that half-breed taken from you faster than your next breath."

Wrath put his head down and ground his fists into the marble.

He waited.

Waited so long, he was tempted to look and see if she had gone.

"I will require a favor," she said.

"Name it."

"You will lead your people."

Wrath looked up, his throat squeezing shut. He couldn't save his parents, he could barely do right by Beth, and the Scribe Virgin wanted him to be responsible for his whole goddamned race?

"What say you, warrior?"

Yeah, like *no* was an option. "As you wish, Scribe Virgin."

"That is my command, warrior. It is not my wish and not the favor I will ask of you, either." She let out an exasperated noise. "Do get to your feet. Those knuckles of yours are bleeding on my marble."

He stood and leveled his eyes on her. He stayed silent, figuring she was probably going to lay some more conditions on him.

She addressed him sharply. "You have no wish to be king. That is obvious. But it is your birth obligation, and it is about time you lived up to your legacy."

Wrath dragged a hand through his hair, creeping anxiety tensing his muscles.

The Scribe Virgin's voice softened. A little. "Worry not, warrior. I will not leave you to find your way alone. You will come to me and I will help you. Being your counsel is part of my purpose."

Which was a good thing, because he was going to need the help. He had no clue how to rule. He could kill a hundred different ways, handle himself in any kind of battle, keep his head cool when the goddamned world was on fire. But ask him to address a thousand of his people in a crowd? His stomach rolled.

"Warrior?"

"Yeah, you'll be hearing from me."

"But that's still not the favor you owe."

"What is—" He brushed a hand through his hair. "I take that back."

She laughed softly. "You always did learn fast."

350

"I'd better." If he were going to be king.

The Scribe Virgin floated closer to him, and he smelled lilacs. "Put your hand out."

He did.

The black folds shifted as her arm came up. Something fell into his hand. A ring. A heavy gold ring set with a ruby the size of walnut. It was so hot he almost had to drop the thing.

The Saturnine Ruby.

"You will give her this from me. And I will attend the ceremony."

Wrath gripped the gift so hard, it bit into his palm. "You honor us."

"Yes, but I have another purpose in coming."

"The favor."

She laughed. "Good one. A question posed in the form of a statement. You will, of course, not be surprised when I do not indulge you. Go now, warrior. Go to your female. Let us hope she is a good choice for you."

The figure turned and moved away.

"Scribe Virgin?"

"We are through."

"Thank you."

She paused by the fountain.

Black folds shifted as she reached out to the tumbling water. When the silk fell back, a blinding light was revealed, as if her bones glowed and her skin were translucent. The moment she touched the water, a rainbow sprang from the contact, filling the white courtyard.

Wrath hissed in shock as his vision suddenly cleared. The courtyard, the columns, the colors, *her*, all of it came into sharp focus. He latched onto the rainbow. Yellow, orange, red, violet, blue, green. The jewellike colors were so brilliant, they sliced through the air, and yet their vivid beauty didn't hurt him. He drank in the sight, wrapped his mind around it, held on to it.

351

The Scribe Virgin faced him, dropping her hand. Instantly, the colors vanished and his vision faded again.

She'd given him a small gift, he realized. Just as she'd put the ring in his hand for Beth.

"You are right," she said softly. "I had hoped to be closer to you. Your father and I, we were bonded, and these lonely centuries have been long and hard. No one worshiping, no one chanting, no history to be kept. I am useless. Forgotten.

"But far worse," she went on, "I see the future, and it is grim. The survival of the race is not ensured. You will not be able to do this alone, warrior."

"I'll learn to ask for help."

She nodded. "We will start anew, you and I. And we will work together, as it should be."

"As it should be," he murmured, trying out the words.

"I will come to you and your brothers tonight," she said. "And the ceremony will be performed accordingly. We will set you into a covenant that is right, warrior, and we will do it in the right way. Assuming the female will have you."

He had a feeling the Scribe Virgin was smiling.

"My father told me your name," he said. "I would use it, if you wish."

"Do."

"We'll see you then, Analisse. And the preparations will be made."

FORTY

Mr. X watched Billy Riddle walk into the office. Riddle was dressed in a dark blue polo shirt and a pair of khaki shorts, looking tanned, healthy, strong.

Strapping, to use an old-fashioned word from Mr. X's youth.

"Sensei." Billy bowed his head.

"How are you doing, son?"

"I've thought it over."

Mr. X waited for the answer, surprised by how much he cared about what it was going to be.

"I want to work for you."

Mr. X smiled. "That's good, son. That's real good."

"So what do I have to do? Are there papers I have to fill out for the academy?"

"It's a bit more involved than that. And the academy isn't really going to be your employer."

"But I thought you said—"

"Billy, there are a few more things you're going to have to understand. And there's the little detail of an initiation."

"You mean hazing? Because that's no problem. I've been through a couple already. For football."

"It's a little more hard-core than that, I'm afraid. But don't worry, I got through it and I know you'll do fine. I'll tell you what you have to bring with you, and I'll be by your side. The whole time."

After all, watching the Omega go to work was not something to be missed.

"Sensei, I, ah . . ." Riddle cleared his throat. "I just want you to know, I'm not going to let you down."

Mr. X smiled slowly, thinking this was the very best part of his job.

He stood up and approached Billy. Putting a hand on Riddle's shoulder, he squeezed the bones and stared into the wide blue eyes that met his.

Billy slipped nicely into a trance.

Mr. X leaned forward and carefully removed Riddle's diamond earring. Then he took the soft lobe between his thumb and forefinger, massaging it.

His voice was low and quiet.

"I want you to call and tell your father that you are moving out, effective immediately. Tell him that you've found a job and that you are going into an intensive training program."

Mr. X took off Riddle's stainless-steel Rolex and then pulled the collar of the guy's shirt open. He reached inside, following the platinum chain Billy wore around to the back. He released the necklace, sliding the links free until he captured them in his palm. The metal was warm from lying against skin.

"When you speak with your father, you will remain calm no matter what he says to you. You will reassure him that your future is a promising one and that you have been chosen out of many applicants for a very important role. You will tell him that he may always reach you on your cell phone, but that it will be impossible for him to see you, as you will be traveling."

Mr. X ran his hand over Billy's chest, feeling the pads of muscle, the warmth of life, the hum of youth. Such power in this body, he thought. Such marvelous force.

"You will not mention the academy. You will not reveal my identity. And you will not tell him that you are coming to live with me." Mr. X spoke right into

Billy's ear. "You will tell your father that you are sorry for all the evil things you did. You will tell him that you love him. And then I will pick you up and take you away."

As Billy breathed deeply in peaceful surrender, Mr. X remembered his own induction ceremony. For a brief, passing instant, he wished that he'd thought more carefully about the offer he'd accepted decades ago.

He'd be an old man now. An old man with grandchildren, maybe, if he'd ever found a woman he could have stood to be around for any length of time. And he would have had an average life, maybe worked at one of the paper mills or at a gas station. He would have been one of a hundred million other anonymous men who were bitched at by their wives and who drank with their buddies and who passed their precious days in a haze of ambient dissatisfaction because they were nothing special.

But he would have been alive.

Looking into Billy's vivid blue eyes, Mr. X wondered whether he had in fact come out on the money side of the exchange. Because he was no longer his own man. He was a servant of the Omega's whims. The top servant, as it were, but a servant nonetheless.

And he would never be mourned.

Either because he never stopped breathing . . . or because no one would miss him after he took his last lungful.

He frowned.

Not that any of that mattered, however, because there was no going back. Which was something Riddle was going to learn firsthand tonight.

Mr. X released Riddle's mind and body.

"So are we clear?" he said softly.

Billy nodded, dazed. He looked down at himself, as if wondering what had happened.

355

"Good, now give me your cell phone." After Billy had handed the thing over, Mr. X smiled. "What do you say to me, son?"

"Yes, sensei."

FORTY-ONE

Beth woke up in Wrath's bed. Sometime during the day, he must have come and carried her to his chamber.

His chest was against her back. His arm was snaked around her body. His hand was between her legs.

His erection, heavy and hot, lay against her hip.

She rolled over. His eyes were shut, his breathing deep and slow. She smiled, thinking that even in his sleep, he wanted her.

"I love you," she whispered.

His lids flipped open. It was like getting hit with spotlights.

"What, *leelan*? Are you all right?" And then he snatched his hand back, as if he had just realized where it was. "Sorry. I, ah . . . You're probably not ready to . . . so soon after . . ."

She took his hand and guided it between her thighs, pressing his fingers against herself.

His fangs came down on his lower lip as he took a sharp breath.

"I'm more than ready for you," she murmured, taking his thick length into her palm.

When he moaned and moved toward her, she actually felt his heart beating, his blood rushing, his lungs as they filled. It was the oddest thing. She could sense exactly how much he wanted her, and not just because she was stroking his arousal.

And when he moved his fingers, sliding into her, her own body responded, and she could feel him getting even more turned on. Each kiss, each caress, every lick and shiver, was magnified.

Wrath forced them to take it slowly. When she would have straddled him, he put her on her back and pleasured her even though his own body was raging for a release. He was so gentle with her, so loving.

Finally, he was poised over her open thighs, his great arms supporting his weight above her. His long dark hair fell around her, mingling with her own.

"I wish I could see your face clearly," he said, frowning as if trying to focus his eyes. "Just once, I wish . . ."

She put her hands on his cheeks, feeling the rough stubble of his beard growth.

"I'll tell you what you'd see," she murmured. "I love you. That's what you'd see."

He closed his eyes and smiled. The expression transformed his face. He glowed.

"Ah, *leelan*, you please me no end."

He kissed her. And slowly entered her body with his. When he had filled her, stretched her out, joined them completely, he became still. He spoke in his language and then hers.

The "I love you, wife" made her beam back at him.

Butch flopped around, half-awake. The bed wasn't his. The thing was a twin, not a king. And the pillows weren't his. They were supersoft, as if his head were on Wonder bread. Sheets were likewise way too fine.

But the snoring beside him really confirmed it. He was definitely not at home.

He opened his eyes. Thick draperies were down over the windows, but the glow from a light in the bathroom was enough for him to see some things. The room was decked out in high-class everything. Antiques, paintings, fancy-schmancy wallpaper.

He looked to the snoring. In the other twin bed, a

man was sound asleep, dark head buried in a pillow, sheets and blankets pulled up to his chin.

Everything came back.

Vishous. His new buddy.

Fellow Red Sox fan. Wicked smart IT guy.

Fricking vampire.

Butch put a hand to his forehead. There'd been many times that he'd rolled over and been unnerved by who was next to him.

But this was a goddamned chart topper.

How'd they . . . That's right. They'd crashed after kicking Tohr's bottle of Scotch.

Tohr. Short for Tohrment.

God, he even knew their names. Rhage. Phury. And that scary-ass Zsadist guy.

Yeah, no Tom, Dick, and Harry names for the vampire types.

But come on, could you actually imagine some lethal bloodsucker named Howard? Eugene?

Oh, no, Wallie, please don't bite my—

Holy Christ, he was totally losing it.

What time was it?

"Yo, cop, what time is it?" Vishous asked, groggy.

Butch reached for the bedside table. Next to his watch was a Red Sox hat, a gold lighter, and a black driving glove.

"Five thirty."

"Cool." The vampire rolled away. "Don't crack the drapes for another two hours. Or I'm up in flames and my brothers will leave you shitting in a bag."

Butch smiled. Vampires or not, he understood these guys. They spoke his language. Related to the world like he did. He felt comfortable around them.

It was damn eerie.

"You're smiling," Vishous said.

"How'd you know?"

"I'm damn handy with emotions. You one of those annoying, cheerful-in-the-morning types?"

"Hell, no. And this isn't morning."

"It is to me, cop." Vishous turned onto his side and looked at Butch. "You know, you handled yourself last night. Don't know many humans who would have taken on Rhage or me. Much less in front of all the brothers."

"Ah, now, don't get all mushy on me. We ain't dating." Except the truth was, Butch was kind of moved by the respect.

But then Vishous narrowed his eyes. His intellect was so fierce, getting assessed by him was like being plucked naked and sandblasted.

"You got one hell of a death wish." It wasn't a question.

"Yeah, maybe," Butch said. He waited to be asked why. When the inquiry didn't come, he was surprised.

"We all do," Vishous murmured. "That's why I'm not asking for details."

They were silent for a moment.

Vishous's eyes narrowed again. "You're not going back to your old life, cop. You know that, right? Because you've seen too much of us. We wouldn't be able to scrub your memories clean enough."

"You telling me to pick out a casket?"

"Hope not. But it's not my call. Depends a lot on you." There was a pause. "You don't have much to go back to, do you?"

Butch looked up at the ceiling.

When the brothers had let him check his messages this morning, there'd been only one. It had been the captain, telling him to come in for the results of Internal's investigation.

Yeah, like that was an appointment he needed to keep. He knew damn well what the outcome would be. He was going to be fired and served up as a sacrificial lamb to

360

combat the image of police brutality. Or he was going to be put out to pasture at a desk job.

As for his family? Ma and Pop, bless them, were still in their row house in Southie, surrounded by the surviving sons and daughters they loved so much. Though still mourning Janie, they were happy in their retirement years. And Butch's brothers and sisters were so busy having babies, raising babies, and thinking about having more babies, that they were totally tied up with their family obligations. In the O'Neal clan, Butch was just a footnote. The Dark One Who Had Failed to Procreate.

Friends? José was the only one he could even remotely consider a friend. Abby wasn't even that. She was just a screw every now and again.

And after meeting Marissa last night, he'd lost his interest in casual sex.

He glanced over at the vampire. "Naw, I don't have anything."

"I know what that feels like." Vishous rustled around as if he were trying to get comfortable. When he settled on his back, he threw one heavy arm over his eyes.

Butch frowned as he caught sight of the vampire's left hand. It was covered with tattoos, dense, intricate designs that ran down the back of it, onto the palm, and around each finger. It must have hurt like a bitch to have done.

"V?"

"Yeah?"

"What's doing with the tats?"

"I didn't pester you about your curse, cop." Vishous put the arm away. "If I'm not up by eight, wake me, true?"

"Yeah. True." Butch closed his eyes.

361

FORTY-TWO

In the chamber downstairs, Beth turned off the shower, reached for a towel, and clonked her new engagement ring on the marble counter.

"Oh, not good. *Really* not good . . ." She cradled her hand, thinking she was lucky Wrath was upstairs checking on preparations for the ceremony. Although maybe that cracking sound had carried to the first floor.

She braced herself before she looked down, convinced she'd either knocked the ruby loose or taken a hunk out of the stone. But it was fine.

Not that she was in a big hurry to bash it around again. Never one for rings, she was going to have to get used to wearing the thing.

Would that all of life's little adjustments be so hard, she thought wryly. *Fiancé slides a priceless hunk of geology on your finger. What a bummer.*

She had to smile as she dried off. Wrath had been so proud to put that ring on her. He'd told her it was a gift from someone whom she'd meet tonight.

At her wedding.

She paused with the towel. God, that word. Wedding. Who'd have ever thought she'd—

Someone knocked on the chamber door.

"Hello, Beth? Are you in there?" The unfamiliar female voice was muffled.

Beth drew on Wrath's robe and went over, but didn't open the door. "Yes?"

"It's Wellsie. I'm Tohr's *shellan*. I thought you might like someone to help you get through tonight, and I've brought a gown for you, in case you don't have one already. Well, I'm also just your average nosy female, so I wanted to meet you."

Beth cracked the door.

Whoa.

There was nothing average about Wellsie. She had flame red hair, a face like a Greco-Roman goddess, and an aura of total self-possession. Her bright blue gown set off her coloring like an autumn sky over changing leaves.

"Ah, hi," Beth said.

"Hi, yourself." Wellsie's sherry-colored eyes were shrewd without being cold. Especially as she started to smile. "Aren't you gorgeous. No wonder Wrath fell as hard as he did."

"Would you like to come in?"

Wellsie marched into the room, carrying a long flat box and a big bag. She gave off an air of being in charge, but somehow, she didn't seem pushy.

"Tohr almost didn't tell me what was going on. He and Wrath are in a thing."

"Thing?"

Wellsie rolled her eyes, shut the door from across the room, and put the box down on the coffee table.

"Males like them, they get all riled up and take a hunk out of each other every once in a while. It's inevitable. Tohr won't tell me what it's all about, but I can guess. Honor, prowess on the field, or us, their females." Wellsie flipped open the box, revealing folds of red satin. "They're good-hearted, our boys. But they can blow their stacks and say something stupid every now and again."

She turned and smiled. "Enough of them. Are you ready for this?"

Beth was normally reticent around strangers. But this straight-talking woman with the no-nonsense eyes felt like someone worth taking a gamble on.

"Maybe not." Beth laughed. "I mean, I haven't known Wrath for long, but he feels like he's mine. I'm going with my gut on this. Not my head."

"I was the same way with Tohr." Wellsie's face softened. "Took one look at him and I knew I was done for."

Her hand absently went to her stomach.

She's pregnant, Beth thought. "When are you due?"

Wellsie flushed, but it seemed to be out of anxiety more than happiness.

"Long time. A year. If I can hold it." She bent down and took out the gown. "So would you like to try this on? We're almost the same size."

The dress was an antique, with black beading over lace on the bodice and a tremendous waterfall of a skirt. The red satin positively smoldered, catching the light from the candles and holding the glow deep within its folds.

"That's . . . spectacular." Beth reached out and stroked the skirting.

"My mother had it made for me. I was mated in it almost two hundred years ago. We can skip the corset if you want, but I brought the petticoats. They're such fun. And listen, if you don't like it or have something else you were planning to wear, I will absolutely not take offense."

"Are you crazy? Like I'm going to turn that down so I can get married in my shorts?"

Beth gathered up the dress and nearly ran to the bathroom. Stepping into the gown was like stepping back in time, and when she came back out into the chamber, she couldn't stop herself from fluffing the skirt. It was a little tight in the bodice, but she didn't care if she never took a full breath.

"You look great," Wellsie said.

"Yeah, because this is the most beautiful thing I've ever had on. Can you do the last buttons up the back?"

Wellsie's fingers were cool and quick. When she was finished, she tilted her head to one side, clasping her hands together. "You do it justice. The whole red-and-black combo really works with your hair. Wrath's going to pass out when he sees you."

"Are you sure you want to lend it to me?" What if she spilled on the thing?

"Clothes are meant to be worn. And that gown hasn't been on a body since 1814." Wellsie checked her diamond watch. "I'm going to go upstairs and see how the prep's coming. Fritz is probably going to need help. The brothers sure know how to eat, but their kitchen skills are deplorable. You'd think they'd be better with knives, considering what they do for a living."

Beth turned around. "Give me a hand undoing these buttons and I'll go with you."

After helping her out of the dress, Wellsie hesitated. "Listen, Beth . . . I'm happy for you. I truly am. But I feel like I should be honest. Having one of these males as a mate isn't easy. I hope you'll call me if you need someone to vent to."

"Thanks," Beth said, thinking she actually might do that. She could see Wellsie giving good advice. Probably because the woman looked like she had everything under control in her own life. She just seemed so . . . competent.

Wellsie smiled. "And maybe I'll be able to call you once in a while, too. God, I've waited so long to have someone to talk to who understands."

"None of the other brothers have wives, right?"

"You and I are it, dearie."

Beth smiled. "So we'd better stick together."

Wrath went upstairs, wondering who'd slept where. He knocked on one of the guest room doors, and Butch

365

answered. The human was drying his hair with a towel. Had another wrapped around his waist.

"You know where V is?" Wrath asked.

"Yeah, he's shaving." The cop nodded over his shoulder and stepped aside.

"You need me, boss?" V called out from the bathroom.

Wrath chuckled. "Well, isn't this cozy."

The "fuck off" came from both of them as Vishous sauntered into the bedroom, boxers hanging low on his hips. His cheeks were white, and he was dragging an old-fashioned razor across his jawbone. Both his hands were bare.

Oh, man. V's left hand was actually in the breeze, its sacred tattoos spelling out the dire consequences if anyone came into contact with it. Wrath wondered whether the human had any conception what V could do with that thing.

Probably not, or the cop wouldn't be so damned relaxed dancing around the room half-naked.

"So, V," Wrath said, "there's a little issue I need to settle before I'm mated."

Usually he worked alone, but if he was going to take care of Billy Riddle, he wanted Vishous as backup. Humans didn't obligingly disintegrate when you stabbed them, but his brother's left hand would take care of the body. Work of a moment and that corpse would be ether.

V grinned. "Give me five and I'm ready."

"Good deal." Wrath could feel Butch's eyes on him. Clearly, the guy wanted to know what was up. "You don't want to get tangled in this one, cop. Especially given your vocation."

"I'm off the force. Just so you know."

Interesting, Wrath thought. "Mind telling me why?"

"I broke a suspect's nose."

"In a fight?"

"During questioning."

Somehow that was not a surprise. "Now why'd you do that?"

"He tried to rape your future wife, vampire. I wasn't inclined to be gentle when he said she was asking for it."

Wrath felt a growl come out of his throat. The sound was like a living thing as it rose up from his gut. "Billy Riddle."

"Beth told you about the guy?"

Wrath stalked to the door. "Haul ass, V," he snapped.

When he got downstairs, he sensed Beth's presence and found her coming through the painting. He walked up and put his arms around her, hugging her fiercely. He would have her avenged before they were joined. She deserved no less from her *hellren*.

"Are you okay?" she whispered.

He nodded against her hair and then looked at Tohr's *shellan*. "Hey, Wellsie. Good of you to come."

The female smiled. "I thought she deserved some support."

"And I'm glad you're here." He pulled back from Beth long enough to kiss Wellsie on the hand.

Vishous strode into the room, fully armed. "Wrath, man, we off?"

"Where are you going?" Beth asked.

"I need to take care of something." He ran his hand down her arm. "The other brothers are staying here to help get things ready. The ceremony will start at midnight, and I'll be back before then."

She looked like she wanted to argue, but then glanced at Wellsie. Something seemed to pass between the two females.

"Be safe," Beth finally said to him. "Please."

"Don't worry." He kissed her long and slow. "I love you, *leelan*."

367

"What does that word mean?"

"Something close to 'dearest one'." He picked his jacket off a chair and gave her one more peck on the lips before leaving.

FORTY-THREE

Butch combed his hair, slapped on a little cologne, and slipped into a suit that wasn't his. Just as the medicine cabinet in the bathroom was lined with different aftershaves and shaving creams, the closets were full of brand-new men's clothes of various large sizes. All top-drawer, designer stuff.

He'd never worn Gucci before.

And though he didn't like being a mooch, he just couldn't see Marissa in the same clothes he'd been wearing last night. Even if they'd been particularly sharp—and they weren't—he was sure they now smelled like a bar: V's Turkish tobacco and booze combined.

He wanted to be fresh as a daisy for her. He really did.

Butch took a turn in front of a full-length mirror, feeling like a pansy, but unable to help himself. The black pinstripe fit him well. The bright white, open-collared shirt made his tan come out. And the sweet pair of Ferragamo loafers he'd found in a box were just the right amount of flash.

He was almost handsome, he thought. As long as she didn't look too closely at his bloodshot eyes.

The four hours of sleep and all that Scotch showed.

A soft rapping noise sounded.

Feeling like a poser and hoping it wasn't one of the brothers, he opened the door.

The butler looked up with a smile. "Sire, you look quite dashing. Fine choices, fine choices."

Butch shrugged, fussing with the shirt collar. "Yeah, well."

"But you need a handkerchief in your breast pocket. May I?"

"Ah, sure."

The little old man buzzed right over to a bureau, pulled out a drawer, and rifled around. "This should be perfect."

His knobby hands worked the white square into some kind of origami masterpiece and stuffed the thing into place on Butch's chest.

"Now, you are ready for your guest. She is here. Are you receiving?"

Receiving? "Hell, yeah."

As they went out into the hall, the butler laughed softly.

"I look stupid, don't I?" Butch said.

Fritz's face grew serious. "No, not at all, sire. I was just thinking how much Darius would have enjoyed all this. He liked a full house."

"Who's Dar—"

"Butch?"

Marissa's voice brought them both to a halt. She was at the head of the stairs, and she took Butch's breath away. Her hair was up high on her head, and her gown was a pale pink sheath. Her shy pleasure at seeing him made his chest swell.

"Hey, baby." He walked forward, aware that the butler was beaming with delight.

She fidgeted with her dress, as if she were a little nervous. "I probably should have waited downstairs. But everyone's so busy. I felt like I was in the way."

"You want to hang up here for a while?"

She nodded. "If you don't mind. It's quieter."

The butler chimed in. "There's a second-floor sitting porch. Just go down the hall. It's at the end."

Butch offered her his arm. "That okay with you?"

She slipped her hand through his elbow. As her eyes

370

skittered away from his, her blush was enchanting. "Yes. Yes, it is."

So she wanted to be alone with him.

This was a good sign, Butch thought.

As Beth carried a heaping platter of crudités into the dining room, she decided that Fritz and Wellsie could have run a small country together. They had the brothers racing around, setting the dining room table, putting fresh candles out, helping with the food. And God only knew what was happening in Wrath's chamber. The ceremony was going to take place there, and Rhage had been down in the room for an hour.

Beth put the platter on the sideboard and headed back into the kitchen. She found Fritz struggling to reach a large crystal bowl high up in the cupboard.

"Here, let me get that."

"Oh, thank you, mistress."

She put it down on the counter and then watched as he filled it with salt.

That's some serious hypertension right there, she thought.

"Beth?" Wellsie called out. "Can you go into the pantry and grab three jars of peach preserves for the ham basting?"

Beth went inside the boxy little room and flipped on the light switch. Cans and jars ran from floor to ceiling in an overwhelming array of options. She was looking for the peach section when she heard the door open.

"Fritz, do you know—"

She pivoted around. And slammed right into Zsadist's hard body.

He hissed, and they both leaped back as the door shut them in together.

He closed his eyes as if in pain, his lips drawing back from his fangs and teeth.

"I'm sorry," she whispered, trying to move farther

away. There wasn't much room, and there was no escape. He was standing in front of the door. "I didn't see you. I'm really sorry."

He was wearing another tight long-sleeved shirt, so as his hands curled into fists, the flexing of his arms and then his shoulders was obvious. He was big to begin with, but the power in his body made him seem huge.

His lids opened. When those black eyes touched her face, she cringed.

Cold. So very cold.

"Christ, I know I'm ugly," he snapped. "But don't fear me. I'm not a total savage."

Then he grabbed something and left.

Beth sagged against the jars and cans, looking up at the empty space he'd left on the shelf. Chutney. He'd taken chutney.

"Beth, did you find—" Wellsie stopped short in the doorway. "What happened?"

"Nothing. It was . . . nothing."

Wellsie gave her a level stare while adjusting the apron over her blue dress. "You're lying to me, but it's your mating day, so I'll let you get away with it." She located the jam and took down some jars. "Hey, why don't you go to your father's room and have a lie-down? Rhage has finished, so you can take a deep breath down there. You need to pamper yourself a little before you're mated."

"You know, I think that's a good idea."

Butch leaned back in the wicker rocker, crossing his legs and pushing at the floor with one foot. The chair made a creaking sound.

In the distance, heat lightning flashed. The night smelled of the garden down below.

And of the sea.

Across the shallow porch, Marissa tilted her head back

to scan the sky. A slight summer breeze touched the tendrils of hair around her face.

He decided he could look at her for a lifetime and not get enough.

"Butch?"

"Sorry. What was that?"

"I said, you look quite beautiful in that suit."

"This old thing? I just threw it on."

She laughed, exactly as he'd meant her to, but as the sound tingled his ears, he grew serious.

"You're the beautiful one."

Her hand went up to her neck. She didn't seem to know how to handle compliments, as though she hadn't gotten many of them.

He found that so hard to believe.

"I did my hair for you," she said. "I thought maybe you would like it this way."

"I like it any way. All ways."

She smiled. "I chose this dress for you, too."

"I like it. But you know something, Marissa? You don't have to try with me."

Her eyes dipped down. "I'm used to trying."

"So get unused to it. You're perfect."

She beamed. Absolutely beamed. And all he could do was stare.

The breeze picked up a little, sweeping her chiffon skirting around the graceful curve of her hips. And suddenly he wasn't just thinking about how lovely she was.

Butch nearly laughed. He'd never considered lust the kind of thing that could ruin a moment, but his body's needs were something he wouldn't mind shelving for the night. Or even longer. He really wanted to treat her right. She was a woman worthy of being worshiped and held and made happy.

Butch frowned. Yeah, and just how would he be able

to do that? The happy part, that was. He was confident he had the worshiping and the holding down pat.

It was just . . . a virgin vampire was a category of female he knew absolutely nothing about.

"Marissa, you know I'm not one of your kind, don't you?"

She nodded. "From the moment I first saw you."

"And that doesn't"—*turn you off?*—"bother you?"

"No. I like the way I feel around you."

"And how's that?" he asked, getting quiet.

"I feel safe. I feel pretty." She paused and eyed his lips. "And sometimes other things."

"Like what?" In spite of his good intentions, he really wanted to hear about the other things.

"I get hot. Especially here"—she touched her breasts—"and here." Her hands brushed over the juncture between her thighs.

Butch saw double, his heart kicked so hard. As he blew out a lungful of hot air, he was sure his head was going to explode.

"Do you feel anything?" she asked.

"You better believe it."

His voice sounded Scotch-raw. *Which is what desperation will do to a guy.*

Marissa crossed the porch, coming toward him. "I would kiss you now. If you wouldn't mind."

Wouldn't mind? He was willing to beg just to keep looking at her.

He uncrossed his legs and sat up, thinking that the fact someone could walk in on them at any time would help keep him in check. He was about to get to his feet when she knelt in front of him.

And moved her body right between his legs.

"Whoa. Easy there." He stopped her before she came in contact with his erection. He wasn't sure she was ready for that. Hell, he wasn't sure *he* was ready for that.

"If we're going to . . . We need to take this slow. I want it to be good for you."

She smiled, and he caught sight of the tips of her fangs. His erection throbbed.

Now who'd have thought that'd be a turn-on?

"I dreamt of doing this last night," she murmured.

Butch cleared his throat. "Did you?"

"I imagined that you came to my bed. You bent over me."

Oh, God, he could just picture that. Except in his fantasy they were both naked.

"You were naked," she whispered, leaning into him. "And so was I. Your mouth was hard on mine. You tasted tangy, like Scotch. I liked it." Her lips hovered mere inches from his. "I liked you."

Holy heaven. He was actually about to come. And they hadn't even kissed yet.

She moved to close the distance, but he held her off at the last moment. She was too much for him. Too lovely. Too sexy. Way, way too innocent.

God, he'd let down so many people over the course of his life. He didn't want to add her to the list.

And she deserved a prince for her first. Not some washed-up ex-cop, wearing someone else's gigolo armor. He had no idea how vampires ran their private lives. But he was damn sure she could do a hell of a lot better than him.

"Marissa?"

"Hmmm?" Her eyes didn't stray from his lips. In spite of her inexperience, she looked like she was ready to devour him.

And he wanted to be eaten.

"Do you not desire to?" she whispered, pulling back. Looking worried. "Butch?"

"Oh, no, baby. Not that. Never that."

He shifted his hands from her shoulders up to her

neck, holding her head steady. Then he tilted his to one side and put his lips right on her mouth.

She gasped, drawing his breath into her lungs, taking something of him inside of her. He rumbled in satisfaction, but kept control, stroking her mouth gently, caressing her softly. When she swayed toward him, he traced the outside of her lips with his tongue.

She was going to taste so sweet, he thought, preparing to go deeper while still keeping a chain on himself.

But Marissa jumped the gun. She captured his tongue with her mouth and sucked on it.

Butch groaned, his hips jerking up from the chair.

She broke off the kiss. "You didn't like that? I liked it when you did that to my finger last night."

He yanked at his collar. Where the hell was all the air in this part of North America?

"Butch?"

"I liked it," he said in a guttural croak. "Trust me. I *really* liked it."

"Then I would do it again."

She lunged forward and took his mouth in a blazing kiss, pressing him back into the wicker, hitting him like a ton of bricks. He was in such shock, all he could do was grip the chair's arms. Her onslaught was powerful. Erotic. Hotter than Hades. She practically crawled onto his chest as she explored his mouth, and he braced his body, throwing his weight into his palms.

Suddenly, there was a loud snapping sound.

And then he rolled onto the floor with her.

"What the f—" Butch lifted his left hand. And up came the wicker arm he'd taken hold of.

He'd ripped the side off the chair.

"You okay?" he said breathlessly, tossing the thing away.

"Oh, yes." She smiled up at him. Her dress was caught

in his legs. And her body was tight against him. Almost where he needed it to be.

As he looked at her, he was ready for it all, ready to get under that dress, part her thighs with his hips, and bury himself in her heat until they were both totally lost.

Except in his current state, he was liable to take her hard, not make love to her properly. And he was crazed enough to do it here, on the porch, in the open.

So it was *way* time for a break.

"Let's get you off the floor," he said roughly.

Marissa moved faster than he did, practically springing to her feet. When she held her hand out to help him up, he took it to humor her. Only to find himself plucked from the floor as if he weighed no more than a newspaper.

He smiled as he brushed off his jacket. "You're stronger than you look."

She seemed embarrassed and took care to check her dress. "Not really."

"That's not a bad thing, Marissa."

Her eyes came back to his and then slowly drifted down his body.

With a shot of embarrassment, he realized his raging erection made a tent out of his pants. He turned away so he could rearrange himself.

"What are you doing?"

"Nothing." He faced her, wondering if his pulse was ever going to slow down.

Man, he wasn't going to need a stress test anytime soon. If his heart could get through a kiss from her, he could probably run a marathon.

While dragging a car behind him.

Sideways to the road.

"I liked that," she said.

He had to laugh. "So did I. But it's hard to believe you're a vir—"

Butch slammed his mouth closed. Rubbed his thumb over his eyebrows.

No wonder he didn't date. He had the social skills of a chimp.

"Just so you know," he muttered, "I put my foot in it sometimes. But I'll work on this for you."

"Foot in it?"

"Blurt shit out. Stuff. I mean . . . Hell." He looked to the door. "Listen, how about we head down and see what's doing with the party?"

Because if he stayed up here one minute longer, he was going to be all over her.

"Butch?"

He glanced back at her. "Yeah, baby?"

Her eyes flashed, and she licked her lips. "I want more of you."

Butch stopped breathing. And wondered if she was thinking about his blood.

Looking into her beautiful face, he relived what it felt like to get pushed back into that chair. And he imagined that instead of kissing him, she was sinking those pearly white fangs of hers deep into his neck.

He could think of no better way to go than in her arms.

"Whatever you want of me," he murmured, "you can have."

FORTY-FOUR

Wrath watched as Billy Riddle walked out of the mansion and struck a pose against the columns in front. The guy put down a duffel bag and looked up at the sky.

"Perfect," Wrath said to Vishous. "Enough time to kill him and get back."

But before he and V stepped out of the shadows, a black Hummer came up the circular drive. As it passed them, the sweet smell of baby powder floated out one of its windows.

"You've got to be kidding me," Wrath murmured.

"That's a *lesser*, my brother."

"And what do you want to bet he's doing some recruiting?"

"Good candidate."

Billy hopped inside, and the SUV began to move.

"We should have taken my car," V hissed. "Then we could have followed them."

"There's no time for a trail. The Scribe Virgin's showing up at midnight. We do this now. Here."

Wrath leaped in front of the Hummer, planting his hands on the hood and pushing the SUV to a stop. He glared through the front windshield while Vishous approached from the lateral, sidling up to the driver's door.

Wrath smiled as the engine was put in park. Inside, he could detect both fear and anticipation. He knew which one was Billy Riddle's. The guy was edgy. The *lesser*, on the other hand, was ready to fight.

But there was something else. Something that didn't feel quite right.

Wrath quickly glanced around. "Watch yourself, V."

The roar of a car engine broke through the night, and the whole lot of them got blasted with headlights.

A nondescript American sedan heaved to a stop, and two men jumped out with guns drawn.

"State police. Put your hands up. You in the car. Get out."

Wrath watched the driver's-side door. What emerged was big and intense. And under the scent of baby powder, the *lesser* stank of evil.

As the society member lifted his hands, it stared at the insignia on Wrath's jacket. "My God. I thought you were a myth. The Blind King."

Wrath bared his fangs. "Nothing you've heard about me is a myth."

The *lesser*'s eyes flashed. "I'm positively inspired."

"And I'm heartbroken that we gotta split now. But we'll be seeing you and that new recruit again. Soon."

Wrath nodded to Vishous, swept clean the memories of the humans, and dematerialized.

Mr. X was in awe.

The Blind King lived.

There had been stories circulating for centuries about him, legends really, but there hadn't been a confirmed sighting since Mr. X had joined the society. In fact, rumors had even abounded that the regal warrior had died, extrapolations based primarily on the disintegration of vampire society.

But no, the king was alive.

Good God. Now that would be a prize to lay at the Omega's altar.

"I told you he was coming," Billy was saying to the staties. "He's my martial-arts teacher. Why did you pull us over?"

The officers holstered their guns, focusing on Mr. X.

"May I see some identification, sir?" one of them asked.

Mr. X smiled and handed over his driver's license. "Billy and I are just going out for dinner. Maybe a movie."

The man studied the picture and then his face. "Mr. Xavier, here's your license back. Sorry for the inconvenience."

"Not a problem, Officer."

Mr. X and Billy got back into the Hummer.

Riddle cursed. "They're such idiots. Why did they stop us?"

Because we got jumped by two vampires, Mr. X thought. *You just don't remember it, and neither do those two guys with the badges.*

Tricky mind games. Tricky, tricky.

"What are the state police doing here?" Mr. X asked as he put the SUV in gear.

"My dad got another terrorist threat, and he's decided to leave D.C. for a little while. He's coming home tonight, and they'll be crawling all over the place until he goes back to the capital."

"Did you talk with your father?"

"Yeah. He actually seemed relieved."

"I'm sure he is."

Billy reached into his duffel bag. "I got what you said I needed."

He held up a wide-necked ceramic jar with a lid.

"That's good, Billy. Perfect size."

"What's going in it?"

Mr. X smiled. "You'll find out. Are you hungry?"

"Naw. Too pumped for food." Billy clapped his palms together and squeezed, flexing his muscles. "Just so you know, I don't crack easy. Whatever goes down tonight, I'll stay tight."

We'll just see about that, Mr. X thought as he headed for his house. They were going to do the ceremony in the barn, and the torture table was going to be a big help. He could tie Billy down easier that way.

As the city dissolved and the farm country eased up around the road, Mr. X found himself smiling.

The Blind King.

In Caldwell.

Mr. X glanced over at Riddle.

In Caldwell and looking for Billy.

Now why would that be?

FORTY-FIVE

Beth was back in The Dress. And loving it.

"I don't have shoes," she said.

Wellsie took another hairpin out of her mouth and slid it into Beth's chignon.

"You're not supposed to be wearing any. Okay, let me see how you look." Wellsie smiled as Beth danced around her father's bedroom, red satin skirting flaring like fire around her.

"I'm going to cry." Wellsie covered her mouth with her hand. "I know it. As soon as he sees you, I'm going to start crying. You're just too beautiful, and this is the first happy thing since . . . I don't know when."

Beth stopped, the gown fluttering to rest. "Thank you. For everything."

Wellsie shook her head. "Don't be nice to me, or I'll start with the tears right now."

"I mean it. I feel like . . . I don't know, I'm marrying into a family. And I've never really had one before."

Wellsie's nose reddened. "We are your family. You're one of us. Now stop it, will you? Before you get me going."

Someone pounded on the door.

"Is everything okay in there?" came a male voice from the other side.

Wellsie went over and put her head out, keeping the door mostly shut. "Yes, Tohr. Are the brothers all lined up?"

"What the— Have you been crying?" Tohrment demanded. "Are you all right? Dear God, is it the baby?"

"Tohr, relax. I'm a female, I cry at matings. It's in the job description."

There was the sound of a kiss.

"I just don't want anything to upset you, *leelan*."

"Then tell me the brothers are ready."

"We are."

"Good. I'll bring her out."

"Leelan?"

"What?"

There were low words spoken in their beautiful language.

"Yes, Tohr," Wellsie whispered. "And after two hundred years, I'd mate you again. In spite of the fact that you snore and you leave your weapons all over our bedroom."

The door shut, and Wellsie turned around. "They're ready for you. Shall we?"

Beth tugged at the bodice. Looked down at her ruby ring. "I never thought I'd do this."

"Life is full of wonderful surprises, isn't it?"

"It certainly is."

They walked out of her father's bedroom and into Wrath's chamber.

All the furniture had been emptied out, and where the bed had been, Wrath's brothers were lined up against the wall. They were a magnificent sight, wearing identical black satin jackets and loose pants with jeweled daggers hanging on their hips.

There was a collective inhale as the assembly noticed her. The brothers shifted, looked down. Looked back at her. Bashful smiles actually broke out across those harsh faces.

Well, except for Zsadist's. He glanced at her once and then just stared at the floor.

Butch, Marissa, and Fritz stood to one side. She gave them a little wave. Fritz took out a handkerchief.

And there was someone else in the room.

A tiny person draped in black from head to toe. Even the face was covered.

Beth frowned. Under the folds of black, there was a pool of light on the floor. As if the figure were glowing.

But where was Wrath?

Wellsie led her over until she was standing in front of the men. The one with the gorgeous hair, Phury, stepped forward.

Beth glanced down, trying to collect herself, and noticed that he had a prosthesis where one foot should have been.

She looked up into his yellow eyes, not wanting to stare. When he smiled, she found herself calming a little.

His voice was rich, his words evenly spoken. "We're going to do as much of this in English as we can, so you'll understand. Are you ready to start?"

She nodded.

"My lord, come forward," he called out.

Beth looked over her shoulder.

Wrath materialized in the hall doorway, and she put her hand to her mouth. He was resplendent, wearing a sashed black robe that was embroidered with dark thread. A long, gold-handled dagger hung at his side, and there was a circle of rubies set in some kind of matte-finished metal on his head.

As he strode forward, moving with the grace she loved, his hair flared in waves that fell past his thick shoulders.

He looked at no one but her.

When he was standing before her, he whispered, "You take my breath away."

She started to cry.

Wrath's face was worried as he reached out. "*Leelan*, what's the matter?"

Beth shook her head and felt Wellsie tuck a Kleenex into her hand.

"She's fine," the woman said. "Trust me, she's fine. Aren't you?"

Beth nodded and blotted under her eyes. "Yes."

Wrath touched her cheek. "We can stop this."

"No!" she shot back. "I love you, and we're going to get married. Right now."

Some of the brothers laughed softly. "Guess we're straight on that," one of them said with respect in his voice.

When she was under control again, Wrath looked over at Phury and nodded.

"We're going to make the presentation to the Scribe Virgin first," the brother said.

Wrath took her hand and led her over to the robed figure. "Scribe Virgin, this is Elizabeth, daughter of the Black Dagger warrior Darius, granddaughter of the *princeps* Marklon, great-granddaughter of the *princeps* Horusman . . ."

The list went on for a while. When Wrath fell silent, Beth impulsively reached out to the figure, offering her hand.

There was a shout of alarm and Wrath grabbed her arm, hauling her back. Several of the brothers leaped forward.

"That's my fault," Wrath said, splaying his arms out as if to protect her. "I didn't adequately prepare her. She meant no offense."

A laugh—low, warm, and feminine—came out of the robes. "Fear not, warrior. She's fine. Come here, female."

Wrath moved aside, but stayed close.

Beth approached the figure, worried about every move she made. She could feel herself being surveyed.

"This male asks that you accept him as your *hellren*, child. Would you have him as your own if he is worthy?"

"Oh, yes." Beth looked at Wrath. He was still tense. "Yes, I will."

The figure nodded. "Warrior, this female will consider you. Will you prove yourself for her?"

"I will." Wrath's deep voice carried throughout the room.

"Will you sacrifice yourself for her?"

"I will."

"Will you defend her against those who would seek to harm her?"

"I will."

"Give me your hand, child."

Beth reached out tentatively.

"Palm up," Wrath whispered.

She flipped her wrist. The folds moved and covered her hand. She felt an odd tingling, like a low-level electrical charge.

"Warrior."

Wrath put his hand out, and it too was obscured by the black robe.

Suddenly, warmth surrounded her, enveloped her. She looked at Wrath. He was smiling back at her.

"Ah," the figure said. "This is a good mating. A very good mating."

Their hands were dropped, and then Wrath had his arms around her and was kissing her.

People started to clap. Someone blew a nose.

Beth held on to her new husband as hard as she could. It was done. It was real. They were—

"Almost finished, *leelan*."

Wrath stepped back, pulling the sash on his robe free. He took the garment off, revealing his bare chest.

Wellsie came up and took Beth's hand. "It's going to be okay. Just breathe with me."

Beth glanced around nervously as Wrath knelt before his brothers and dropped his head. Fritz brought over a small table with the crystal bowl full of salt, a pitcher of water, and a small lacquer box on it.

Phury stood over Wrath. "My lord, what is the name of your *shellan*?"

"She is called Elizabeth."

With a rasping sound, Phury unsheathed his black dagger.

And bent down over Wrath's bare back.

Beth gasped and lunged forward as the blade descended. "No—"

Wellsie held her in place. "Stay here."

"What is he—"

"You're mating a warrior," Wellsie whispered fiercely. "Let him have his honor in front of his brothers."

"No!"

"Listen to me—Wrath is giving his body, himself, to you. All of it is yours now. That's the purpose of the ceremony."

Phury stepped back, and Beth caught a trickle of blood running down Wrath's side.

Vishous came forward. "What is the name of your *shellan*?"

"She is called Elizabeth."

As the brother leaned down, Beth shut her eyes and squeezed Wellsie's hand hard. "He doesn't need to do this to prove himself to me."

"Do you love him?" Wellsie demanded.

"Yes."

"Then you must accept his ways."

Zsadist stepped forward next.

"Easy, Z," Phury said softly, staying close beside his twin.

Oh, God, not more.

The brothers came forward again and again, asking him the question. When they were finished, Phury took the pitcher of water and poured it into the bowl of salt. Then he dumped the thick, briny liquid on Wrath's back.

Beth weaved on her feet as she watched his muscles spasm. She couldn't imagine the agony, but except for bearing down onto the floor, Wrath didn't cry out. As he endured the pain, his brothers growled their approval.

Phury bent down and opened the lacquer box, taking out a pristine white cloth. He dried the wounds, then rolled the material up and put it back inside.

"Rise, my lord," he said.

Wrath stood. Across his shoulders, in an arch of Old English letters, was her name in his skin.

Phury presented Wrath with the box. "Take this to your *shellan* as a symbol of your strength, so she will know that you are worthy of her and that your body, your heart, and your soul are now hers to command."

Wrath turned around. As he came toward her, she anxiously scanned his face. He was fine. Better than fine. He was positively glowing with love.

Dropping to his knees before her, he bowed his head and held up the box.

"Will you take me as your own?" he asked, looking at her over the top of the sunglasses. His pale, blind eyes were sparkling.

Her hands shook as she accepted the box from him. "Yes. I will."

Wrath rose, and she threw her arms around him, careful not to reach too far up his back.

A chant began with the brothers, a low beat of words she didn't understand.

"Are you okay?" he said into her ear.

She nodded, wondering why couldn't she have been named Mary. Or Sue.

But *no*, she had to be nine-letter Elizabeth.

"Can we not do that again?" she asked, burying her head into his shoulder.

Wrath laughed softly. "You'd better brace yourself if we have children."

The chanting grew louder, deep male voices pumping.

She looked to the brothers, the tall, fierce men who were now a part of her life. Wrath pivoted and put his arm around her. Together, they swayed to the rhythm that swelled, filling the air. The brothers were as one as they paid homage in their language, a single powerful entity.

But then, in a high, keening call, one voice broke out, lifting above the others, shooting higher and higher. The sound of the tenor was so clear, so pure, it brought shivers to the skin, a yearning warmth to the chest. The sweet notes blew the ceiling off with their glory, turning the chamber into a cathedral, the brothers into a tabernacle.

Bringing the very heavens close enough to touch.

It was Zsadist.

His eyes closed, his head back, his mouth wide open, he sang.

The scarred one, the soulless one, had the voice of an angel.

FORTY-SIX

During the wedding dinner, Butch went easy on the alcohol.

It wasn't hard. He was too busy enjoying Marissa's company.

As well as watching Beth with her new husband. God, she was so happy. And that mean-ass-looking vampire she'd signed on for was just the same. He wouldn't let go of her, couldn't stop staring at her. All night long, he'd had her sitting on his lap at the table, feeding her from his hand while he stroked her neck.

As the party wound down, Marissa stood up from her chair. "I have to go back to my brother's. He's expecting me for dinner, actually."

So that was why she hadn't eaten anything.

Butch frowned, not wanting her to go. "When will you be back?"

"Tomorrow night?"

Damn, that was forever.

He put his napkin down. "Well, I'll be here. Waiting for you."

Jeez, talk about whipped, he thought.

Marissa said her good-byes, and then disappeared.

Butch reached for his wineglass and tried to pretend his hand wasn't shaking. The whole blood/fang thing he could almost handle. The poofing stuff was going to take some time.

Ten minutes later, he realized he was sitting at the table alone.

He had no interest in going home. In the space of a

day, he'd managed to shelve his real life, just push it into a corner of his mind. And like a gadget that had been broken, he had no interest in pulling it back out, examining it, using it again.

He looked around at all the chairs and thought of the people—er, vampires—who'd filled them.

He was an outsider in their world. An interloper.

Although it wasn't like being the odd man out was a new one for him. The other cops had been good guys, but he'd never been more than work-tight with them, even José. He'd never gone over to the de la Cruzes' for dinner or anything.

As he stared at the empty plates and the half-full wine-glasses, he realized he had nowhere to go. Nowhere he wanted to be. The isolation had never bothered him before. Actually, it had made him feel safer somehow. So it was kind of funny that being on his own didn't seem like such a great thing now.

"Yo, cop. We're heading for Screamer's. You wanna come?"

Butch looked up at the doorway. Vishous was in the hall with Rhage and Phury behind him. The vampires had expectant looks on their faces, like they honestly wanted to hang with him.

Butch found himself grinning like the new kid who didn't have to sit alone at lunch after all.

"Yeah, I could do with a bar crawl."

As he stood up, he wondered if he should get casual. The brothers had changed into leathers, but he was loath to let the suit go. He loved the thing.

Screw it. He liked the threads; he was going to wear the threads. Even if they weren't really him.

Butch buttoned the jacket, smoothing it down over his chest. He checked to make sure the handkerchief was still in a perfect fold.

"Come on, cop, you're fabulous," Rhage said with a

burning smile. "And I'm itching for some company, know what I mean?"

Yeah, he could guess.

Butch came around the table. "'Cept I gotta warn you boys. Some folks I sent up the river, they hang at Screamer's. Might get ugly."

Rhage clapped him on the back. "Why do you think we want you to come?"

"Hell, yeah." V grinned and pulled his Sox cap down low. "Bar fight's a perfect chaser to some Grey Goose."

Butch rolled his eyes and then looked at Phury seriously. "Where's your boy?"

Phury stiffened. "Z's not coming."

Good. Butch had no problem going out with the others. He was sure that if they were going to kill him, he'd be in the ground by now. But that Zsadist guy . . . you had to wonder when he was going to lose it. And what he was going to take out with him when he did.

But man, he could sing.

As they headed to the front door, Butch murmured, "Helluva set of pipes on that SOB. Some serious beautiful."

The brothers nodded, and Rhage slipped a meaty arm around Phury's shoulders. Phury's head dipped down low for a moment, as if he were carrying something heavy and was desperate to give his back a rest.

They went outside, heading toward a black Escalade ESV. Its lights flashed when the security system was disarmed.

"Oh, damn. I forgot." Butch pulled up short. The vampires stopped and looked at him. "Shotgun!"

As he bolted around the car, Phury and Rhage snapped into gear while cursing him to hell and back. On the other side, he got an argument, but his hand was on the door, and he wasn't budging.

"Humans ride in the back!"

393

"On the hood!"

"Listen, bloodsuckers, I called it—"

"V, I'm going to bite him!"

Vishous's laughter cut through the thick night air as he slid behind the steering wheel. His first move was to crank the stereo so loud, the entire SUV pulsed.

Notorious BIG's "Hypnotize."

And they could hear Biggie in Montreal, Butch thought as he climbed in.

"Damn, my brother," Rhage said, getting into the back. "This a new system?"

"Worship me, gentlemen." V lit a hand-rolled. Flipped the gold lighter shut. "And I might let you play with the buttons."

"That'd almost be worth the ass-kissing."

The headlights came on.

And Zsadist walked into the beams.

Phury immediately opened his door and made room. "You gonna bounce with us, after all?"

Zsadist gave Butch a nasty stare as he slid into the back, but Butch didn't take it personally. The vampire didn't look happy to see any of the others, either.

V threw them into reverse and gunned it.

The conversation kept up in spite of the music, but the atmosphere had changed.

Which made sense, considering there was now a live grenade in the car.

Butch glanced back at Zsadist. Black eyes glittered in return. The smile on the vampire's face was greedy for sin and ready for evil.

Havers lowered his fork as Marissa entered the dining room. He'd been worried when she was not at the table, but afraid to check her rooms. In his current frame of mind, he wouldn't have handled her being gone at all well.

"Forgive my tardiness," she said, kissing him on the cheek. She settled into her chair like a bird, arranging herself and her dress with grace. "I'm hoping we can talk."

What was that smell on her? he wondered.

"This lamb looks wonderful," she murmured as Karolyn brought in another plate of food.

Aftershave, he thought. His sister smelled like aftershave. She had been with a male.

"Where did you spend the evening?" he asked.

She hesitated. "Darius's."

He laid his napkin on the table and got to his feet. His rage was so complete, it rendered him curiously numb.

"Havers, why are you leaving?"

"As you can see, I am finished eating. I bid you good rest, sister."

She grabbed his hand. "Won't you stay?"

"I have something to take care of."

"Surely it can wait." Her eyes implored him.

"No, no longer."

Havers went into the front hall, taking pride in how calm he was. Shoring up his nerve, he dematerialized.

As he took shape again, he shuddered.

Parts of downtown were foul. Truly foul.

The alley he'd chosen was right next to one of the clubs, Screamer's. He'd heard from some of the civilian vampires whom he had treated that the brothers frequented the place. As he considered the human crowd waiting to get in, he could see why. They were an aggressive herd, reeking of lust. Depravity.

Up to the brothers' low standards for companionship, no doubt.

Havers started to lean back against the building, but thought better of it. The bricks were filthy and dripping with some kind of condensation. He could well imagine what kind of culture might be running on the slime.

He looked up and down the alley. Sooner or later, he would find what he was looking for.

Or it would find him.

Mr. X locked his front door and stepped out into the night. He was pleased with the way the ceremony had gone. Billy had been shocked as hell, to say the least, but he'd pressed through the initiation. Especially when he'd learned it was either that or he was going to be killed on the table.

God, the expression on Billy's face when he'd seen the Omega had been priceless. Nobody expected evil to look like that, and you could almost be fooled. Well, at least until the Omega's gaze fell upon you. Then you got a taste of your own death.

A little sip with the promise of a whole six-pack.

When it was over, Mr. X had carried Billy to the house, and Riddle was resting in the guest room. Kind of. He was throwing up right now, and that would last for the next couple of hours, while the Omega's blood subjugated what had been pumping in Billy's veins for his eighteen years of life. Riddle also had a chest wound. The raw gash ran from his throat down to his sternum, the skin having been soldered shut by the Omega's fingertip. That was going to hurt like hell, at least until the morning. By nightfall tomorrow, however, he'd be strong enough to go out.

Mr. X got in the Hummer and headed south. He'd told one of the prime squadrons to cover the downtown area, and he wanted to watch them in action. He hated to admit it, but perhaps Mr. O had a point about motivation. Besides, he needed to see how the group functioned in a battle situation. With Mr. M's demise, he was toying with letting Riddle fill out the ranks, eventually, but he wanted a sense of the squadron's current dynamics before he made any decisions.

Billy also needed to be assessed. Having trained him in the martial arts, Mr. X was confident in Riddle's fighting skills. He just wasn't sure how the guy would react to his first kill. Mr. X suspected it would be with excitement, but you never knew. He certainly hoped Riddle would make him proud.

Mr. X smiled, amending himself.

He hoped Mr. R would make him proud.

Havers was getting antsy. The night-dwelling humans presented no threat to him, but he couldn't stomach their vices. In the back of the alley, two were necking, or perhaps going even further, and one was smoking crack. Between the grunting and the sickening smell, Havers was dying to get home.

"Well, aren't you the fancy one."

Havers shrank back. The human female in front of him was dressed for sex, a narrow spandex strip covering her breasts, her skirt so high it barely covered her crotch.

A walking advertisement for penile implantation. His skin crawled.

"You looking for a date?" she asked, running a hand over her stomach, and then through her greasy short hair.

"No, thank you." He walked backward, going deeper into the alley. "Thank you very much. No."

"And a gentleman, too."

Good lord, she was going to touch him.

He put his hands up. Kept moving away. The farther he got down the alley, the louder the music became, as if he were getting close to a back door.

"Please leave me," he said as some god-awful, obscenity-laden song flared.

Suddenly, the woman paled and took off as if she were running from a crime scene.

"What the hell are you doing here?" The male voice behind him was a dark, nasty one.

Havers turned around slowly. His heart started to pound. "Zsadist."

FORTY-SEVEN

Wrath had no interest in whoever was pounding on the door of his chamber. He had his arm wrapped around his *shellan*'s waist and his head tucked into her neck. He was going nowhere unless someone was half-dead.

"Damn it." He shot out of bed, grabbed his sunglasses, and stalked naked across the room.

"Wrath, don't hurt them," Beth said with amusement. "If they're bothering you tonight, they probably have a good reason."

He took a deep breath before throwing open the door. "You'd better be bleeding—" He frowned. "Tohr."

"We have a problem, my lord."

Wrath cursed and nodded, but didn't invite the brother in. Beth was naked in that bed.

He pointed across the hall. "Wait there."

Wrath threw on some boxers, kissed Beth, and locked his chamber. Then he went into Darius's room.

"What's up, brother?" He wasn't happy about the interruption, or that some type of shit had wings and was airborne. But it was good that Tohr had come. Maybe things were thawing between them.

Tohr leaned back against D's desk. "I went to Screamer's to meet the brothers. I got there late."

"So you missed Rhage working out some chick in a dark corner? Pity."

"I saw Havers in an alley."

Wrath frowned. "What was the good doctor doing in that part of town?"

"Asking Zsadist to kill you."

Wrath quietly closed the door. "You heard this? Clearly?"

"I did. There was a lot of money on the table."

"What was Z's response?"

"He said he'd do it for free. I left and came here immediately in case he moved on you right away. You know how he works. He's not going to take his time about it."

"Yeah, he's efficient. It's one of his strengths."

"And we've only got a half hour until daybreak. Not enough to do anything offensively tonight unless he shows up here in the next ten minutes."

Wrath looked at the floor, putting his hands on his hips. By vampire law, Z was now under a death sentence for threatening the king's life.

"He'll have to be put down for this." And if the brotherhood didn't take care of the job, the Scribe Virgin would.

Man, Phury. The brother was not going to take this well.

"This is gonna kill Phury," Tohr murmured.

"I know."

And then Wrath thought of Marissa. Havers was also dead for all intents and purposes, and the loss of him was going to rip her apart.

He shook his head, dreading that he was going to have to kill someone she loved so much after everything she'd been through already as his *shellan*.

"The brotherhood needs to be told," he said, finally. "I will call them."

Tohr pushed off the edge of the desk. "Listen, do you want Beth to come stay with me and Wellsie until this is finished? She might be safer at our house."

Wrath glanced up. "Thanks, Tohr. I would. I'll send her over as soon as the sun sets tonight."

Tohrment nodded and walked to the door.

"Tohr?"

The brother looked over his shoulder. "Yeah?"

"Before I mated Beth, I was sorry for what I said to you. About you and Wellsie and how devoted you are to her. Now . . . I, ah, I understand firsthand. Beth is everything to me. More important even than the brotherhood." Wrath cleared his throat, unable to go on.

Tohr came forward and put his hand out. "You are forgiven, my lord."

Wrath grabbed the outstretched palm and yanked his brother into his arms. They clapped each other on the back hard.

"And Tohr? I want you to know something, but you've got keep it from the brothers for now. After Darius's death is avenged, I'm stepping aside."

Tohr frowned. "Excuse me?"

"I'm not fighting anymore."

"What the hell? Like you're taking up knitting or something?" Tohr pushed a hand through his short hair. "How are we going to—"

"I want you to lead the brothers."

Tohr's mouth fell open. "What?"

"There has to be a total reconfiguration of the brotherhood. I want them centralized and run like a military unit, no more of this fighting-alone crap. And we need to recruit. I want soldiers. I want whole battalions of soldiers and training facilities, the best of everything." Wrath eyed him steadily. "You're the only one who can do the job. You're the most levelheaded and stable of them."

Tohr shook his head. "I can't . . . Christ, I can't do that. I'm sorry—"

"I'm not asking you. I'm telling you. And when I announce it at my first forum, it's law."

Tohr let out his breath in a low hiss. "My lord?"

"Yeah, well. I've been a rotten king. Actually, I haven't

done the job at all. But that's going to change now. Everything's going to change. We're going to build us a civilization, my brother. Or rather, rebuild one."

Tohr's eyes glistened, and he looked away, casually rubbing under them with his thumbs. As if there were nothing much going on, just a little irritation. He cleared his throat. "You're ascending to the throne."

"Yeah."

Tohr dropped to the floor on one knee. Bowed his head.

"Thank God," he said hoarsely. "Our race is whole again. You're going to lead us."

Wrath felt sick. This was exactly what he didn't want. He simply couldn't bear the potential for tragedy inherent in his being responsible for so many. Didn't Tohr know he wasn't good enough? Wasn't strong enough? He'd let his parents die, had acted as a feeble weakling, not a worthy male. What had truly changed?

Only his body. Not his soul.

He wanted to walk away from his birth burden, just leave . . .

Tohr shuddered. "So long . . . We have waited so long for you to save us."

Wrath shut his eyes. The desperate relief in his brother's voice told him how badly a king was needed. How hopeless so many were. And as long as Wrath was alive, by law no one else could fulfill the role.

Tentatively, he reached out and placed his hand on Tohr's lowered head. The weight of what lay ahead of him, of them all, was too immense to comprehend.

"We're going to save the race together," he murmured. "All of us."

Hours later, Beth woke up hungry. Slipping free of Wrath's heavy arm, she put on a T-shirt and drew his robe around herself.

402

"Where are you off to, *leelan*?" Wrath's voice was deep, lazy, relaxed. She heard his shoulder crack, as it did when he stretched.

Considering the number of times he'd made love to her, she was surprised he could move at all.

"I'm just going to get something to eat."

"Call for Fritz."

"He did quite enough last night and deserves the rest. I'll be right back."

"Beth"—Wrath's voice was sharp—"it's five in the afternoon. The sun is still out."

She paused. "You said I might be able to go out during the day, though."

"It's theoretically possible—"

"So I might as well find out now."

She was at the door when Wrath flashed in front of her. His eyes were fierce.

"You don't need to know at this moment."

"It's no big deal. I'll just head up—"

"You're going nowhere," he growled, his massive body throwing off all kinds of aggression. "I forbid you to leave this room."

Beth closed her mouth slowly.

Forbid me? He forbids me?

We're going to have to nip this one right in the bud, she thought, sticking her finger in his face.

"Back off, Wrath, and wipe that word from your vocabulary when you're speaking with me. We may be married, but I'm not going to be ordered around like a child by you. Are we clear on this?"

Wrath closed his eyes. Worry bled through the harsh lines of his face.

"Hey, it's going to be fine," she said, stepping into his body. She hefted up his arms so they were around her shoulders. "I'll just duck my head out into the drawing room. If anything happens, I'll come right back down. Okay?"

He gripped her, holding her tight. "I hate that I can't be with you."

"You're not going to be able to protect me from everything."

The growl came back.

She kissed the underside of his chin and hit the stairs before he started arguing again. When she got to the top landing, she paused with her hand on the painting.

Down below, she heard the sound of a cell phone ringing. Wrath stayed in the doorway of the chamber, looking up at her.

She pushed the painting open a crack. Light pierced the darkness.

Down below, she heard him curse and shut the door.

Wrath glared at his cell phone until it went silent.

He paced. He sat on the couch. He paced some more.

And then the door opened. Beth was smiling.

"I'm good to go," she said.

He rushed over, feeling her skin. It was cool, healthy. "Did it burn at all? Did you feel hot?"

"No. The brightness hurt my eyes when I went outside—"

"You went outside?"

"Yeah. Whoa." Beth grabbed for his arm as his knees went out. "Dear God, you're pale. Here, lie down."

He did as he was told.

Holy Christ. She'd gone outside in broad daylight. His Beth had waltzed outside into the sunlight. Where he wouldn't have been able to reach her at all. At least if she'd stuck to the drawing room, he might have had a chance . . .

She could have been incinerated.

Cool hands brushed some hair out of his eye. "Wrath, I'm fine."

He looked up into her face. "I feel like I'm going to pass out."

"Which is physiologically improbable. Because you're lying down."

"Damn, *leelan*. I love you so much I'm scaring the crap out of myself." When she pressed her lips to his, he put his hand on her neck, holding her in place. "I don't think I can live without you."

"Hopefully, you won't have to. Now tell me something. What's your word for husband?"

"*Hellren*, I suppose. The short version is just *hell*."

She laughed softly. "Go figure."

His cell phone started ringing again. He bared his fangs at the damn thing.

"Answer it while I hit the kitchen," she said. "Do you want anything?"

"You."

"You already have me."

"And thank God for that."

He watched Beth leave, catching the sway of her hips and thinking that when she came back down, he wanted to take her again. He just couldn't get enough. Giving that female pleasure was the first addiction he'd ever had.

He grabbed the cell phone and didn't bother checking caller ID. *"What."*

There was a pause.

And then Zsadist's growl shot into his ear. "Aren't you full of the warm fuzzies. Mating day not going so good?"

Well, now. This was going to be interesting.

"You got something on your mind, Z?"

"I understand you called the brothers early this morning. Every one of them except me. You lost my number? Yeah, that has to be it."

"I know exactly how to reach you."

Z let out a frustrated breath. "Man, I get tired of being treated like a dog. I really do."

405

"Then don't act like one."

"Screw you."

"Yeah, you know what, Z? We've reached the end of the line, you and I."

"And what's brought this on?" Z laughed harshly. "Actually, save it. I don't care, and hey, we don't have time to shoot the shit anyway, do we? You gotta get back to your female, and I didn't call you to bitch about being out of the loop."

"So why are you on my phone?"

"You need to know something."

"From you?" Wrath drawled.

"Yeah, from me," Z hissed back. "Marissa's brother wants your head on a stick. And he was willing to pay me a couple million to do it. Later."

The phone went dead.

Wrath dropped his cell on the bed and massaged his forehead.

It would be nice to believe Z had called because he wanted to. Because maybe he'd made a commitment that he didn't want to keep. Because maybe he'd finally found his conscience after a hundred or so years of total immorality.

Except he'd waited for hours, which meant Phury had probably worn him down. Talked him into fessing up. How else could Z have known that the brothers had been spoken with?

Wrath grabbed the phone and dialed Phury's number. "Your twin just called here."

"He did?" Total relief marked the brother's voice.

"You're not going to be able to save him this time, Phury."

"I didn't tell him you knew. Wrath, you gotta believe me."

"What I believe is that you'd do anything to take care of him."

406

"Listen to me, man. You gave me a direct order to say nothing, and I obeyed. It was hard as hell for me, but I said nothing. Z came to you on his own."

"Then why did he know the others had been called?"

"My phone rang and his didn't. He was guessing."

Wrath shut his eyes. "I gotta take him out, you know that. The Scribe Virgin will demand nothing less for his treason."

"He can't help that he was approached. He told you what happened. If anyone deserves to die, it's Havers."

"And he will. But your twin accepted an offer to kill me. If he can do that once, he can do it again. And maybe next time he won't come forward after you work him over, you feel me?"

"On my honor, he called you on his own."

"Phury, man, I'd like to believe you. But you shot your own leg off to save him once. When it comes to your twin, you will do and say anything."

Phury's voice vibrated. "Don't do it, Wrath. I beg you. Z's been better lately."

"What about those dead women, brother?"

"You know it's the only way he'll feed. He has to stay alive somehow. And in spite of the rumors, he's never killed the humans he feeds from before. I don't know what happened with those two prostitutes."

Wrath cursed.

"My lord, he doesn't deserve to die for something he hasn't done. This isn't fair."

Wrath closed his eyes. Finally, he said, "Bring him with you tonight. I'll give him an opportunity to speak in front of the brotherhood."

"Thank you, my lord."

"Don't be grateful. Just because he opens his mouth, it doesn't mean he'll be saved."

Wrath turned the phone off.

He sure as hell wasn't granting the audience for

407

Zsadist's sake. It was for Phury. They needed him in the brotherhood, and Wrath had a feeling the warrior wouldn't stay unless he felt as if his twin had been dealt with properly. And even then, he might bolt anyway.

Wrath thought about Zsadist, picturing the male in his mind.

Havers had picked the right assassin. It was well-known that Z wasn't tied to anyone or anything, so the good doctor was right to assume the warrior wouldn't have a problem betraying the brotherhood. It was also clear to any observer that Z was one of the few males on the planet lethal enough to kill Wrath.

There was just one thing that was off. Z didn't care about material possessions. As a slave, he'd never had any. As a warrior, he'd never wanted any. So it was hard to believe that money would motivate him.

Then again, he was perfectly capable of killing for fun.

Wrath froze as his nose started to tingle.

Frowning, he went over to one of the vents that brought fresh air into the chamber. He drew in a great breath.

A *lesser* was on the property.

The same one who'd been in the Hummer at Billy Riddle's house.

Beth put some leftover filet mignon and a little horse-radish sauce between two slices of bread. As she bit down, she was in total heaven. Food just tasted better.

While she ate, she looked out the kitchen window at a maple tree. Its dark green leaves were totally lifeless. Summer still. There wasn't a breath of wind, as if the air itself had heat exhaustion.

No, something was moving.

A man was coming through the hedge, approaching

408

the house from the property next door. Her skin prickled in warning.

Which was ridiculous. The guy had on a gray Caldwell Gas & Electric uniform and was carrying a clipboard in one hand. He didn't look particularly threatening, what with his pale hair and his relaxed demeanor. He was big, but he moved casually, just another bored meter reader who was wishing he had a desk job because of all the heat.

The phone on the wall rang and she jumped.

She reached over and picked up, still keeping her eyes on the man. He stopped as he saw her.

"Hello?" she said into the receiver. The CG&E guy started walking again, coming up to the back door.

"Beth, get down here *now*," Wrath barked.

At that moment, the meter man looked through the kitchen door's glass panels. Their eyes met. He smiled and lifted his hand.

Chills went over her flesh.

He's not alive, she thought. She wasn't sure how she knew it; she just did.

She dropped the phone and ran.

There was a crashing noise behind her as the back door splintered, and then she heard popping sounds. Something hit her in the shoulder with a sting. And then she felt another prick of pain.

Her body began to slow.

She fell facedown onto the kitchen tile.

Wrath yelled as he felt Beth hit the floor. Bolting up the stairwell, he burst into the drawing room.

The sun hit his skin and burned like a chemical spill, forcing him back into the darkness. He flashed down to his chamber, picked up the phone, and called upstairs. It rang and rang and rang.

His breath pumped in and out of his mouth, his chest moving in a series of rough contractions.

Trapped. He was trapped. He was trapped downstairs while she was . . .

He let out a roar that was her name.

He could sense her aura dimming. She was being taken away, taken somewhere away from him.

Fury poured out of his heart, a black, deep freeze that made the mirror in the bathroom fracture in a series of cracking sounds.

Fritz picked up. "We've been broken into! Butch is—"

"Get me the cop!" Wrath screamed.

Butch came on the line a moment later. He was breathless. "I couldn't catch whoever it was—"

"Did you see Beth?"

"Isn't she with you?"

Wrath let out another roar, feeling the walls press in around him. He was utterly helpless, caged by the sunlight that washed over the earth above him.

He forced himself to breathe deeply. Only managed one breath before he went back to panting.

"Cop, I need you. I need . . . you."

FORTY-EIGHT

Mr. X floored the minivan. He couldn't believe it.

He absolutely couldn't believe it.

He had the queen. He had abducted the queen.

This was the chance of a *lesser*'s lifetime. And it had happened so smoothly, as if it was all meant to be.

When he'd approached the house, he'd merely been on a scouting mission. It had seemed far too coincidental that the address the vampire had given him last night in the alley was the same as that of the warrior he'd blown up. After all, why would the Blind King hang around the mansion of a dead warrior?

Assuming it had to be a setup, Mr. X had fully armed himself and gone to Darius's before dark. He'd wanted to survey the house's exterior, see if any of the upstairs windows were blacked out, and check the cars in the drive.

But then he'd noticed the dark-haired woman in the kitchen. With the Saturnine Ruby on her finger. The queen's ring.

Mr. X still couldn't fathom why she was able to go around in the daylight. Unless she was part human. Although what were the chances of that?

At any rate, he hadn't hesitated. Even though he hadn't planned on infiltrating the place, he'd broken down the door, surprised and grateful when the security system didn't go off. The woman had been quick on her feet, but not quick enough, and the darts had worked perfectly now that he'd calibrated the dosage correctly.

He glanced into the back.

She was out cold on the minivan's floor.

This evening was going to be intense. There was no doubt that her male would come after her. And because the Blind King's blood was surely in her veins, he'd be able to find his mate no matter where Mr. X took her.

Thank God it was still daylight and he had time to fortify his barn.

And he was tempted to call in for reinforcements. Though he was confident in his skills, he knew what the Blind King was capable of. Total destruction of the property, a complete razing of the house, the barn, and everything in them, would be the very least of it.

The problem was, if Mr. X summoned other members, he'd have to pierce the veil of his infallibility.

Besides, he did have his new recruit.

No, he would do this without a lot of hangers-on. Anything that drew breath could be killed, even that warrior. And Mr. X was willing to bet that, with the female as a bargaining chip, he had some serious leverage.

Undoubtedly, the king would trade himself for the safety of his queen.

Mr. X chuckled. Mr. R was going to have one hell of a first night.

Butch left the chamber and ran up to the guest room he and Vishous had crashed in again.

V was pacing, trapped on the second floor because there was no way to get downstairs without being hit with light. Clearly, the mansion was meant for use as a private residence, not as a battle station.

And the defect was a serious problem in this kind of emergency.

"What's happening?" V demanded.

"Your man Wrath's in one hell of a state, but he managed to tell me about the guy you met in the Hummer last night. That blond sounds like an instructor I met a couple of days ago at a local martial-arts academy. I'm heading there now."

Butch grabbed for the keys to the unmarked.

"Take this, man." Vishous threw something into the air.

Butch caught the gun with a swipe of his hand. Checked the chamber. The Beretta was fully loaded, but with nothing he'd ever seen before.

"What the hell kind of bullets are these?" They were black and transparent at the tips, gleaming like they had oil inside.

"You're not going after a human, cop. If one of those *lessers* comes at you, you shoot them in the chest, got it? Don't pussyfoot around, even if it's broad daylight. You go right for their chest."

Butch looked up. He knew he was crossing a line if he took the gun, going over to another side of the world.

"How will I know them, V?"

"They smell sweet, like baby powder, and they'll look right through you, right into your soul. They tend to have pale hair, eyes, and skin, but not always."

Butch tucked the semiautomatic into his waistband. And put his old life into the ground permanently.

Funny, the decision was an easy one.

"You clear on this, cop?" Vishous clapped him on the arm.

"Yeah."

As Butch bolted for the door, V said something in a foreign language.

"What?" Butch asked.

"Just aim straight, true?"

"I've never missed yet."

FORTY-NINE

Marissa couldn't wait to see Butch. She'd been thinking about him all day long, and it was finally time to go to him.

Except even though she was in a rush, she was going to stop on her way out and speak with Havers. She'd waited for him to come back home the night before, passing the time by helping out the nurses in the clinic and then reading in her room. Finally, she'd given up and left him a note on his bed, asking him to come find her when he got in. He hadn't stopped by, however.

And this failure of communication had gone on long enough.

She went to the door of her bedroom, surprised when it wouldn't open. She frowned. The handle wouldn't move. She tried again, jiggling the thing, then throwing her strength into the brass. It was jammed or locked.

And her bedroom walls were lined with steel, so she couldn't dematerialize.

"Hello!" she called out, banging on the door. "Hello! Havers! Someone! Would someone kindly let me out? Hello!"

She eventually gave up, a chill condensing in her chest.

As soon as she fell silent, Havers's voice drifted into her room, as if he'd been waiting on the other side the whole time.

"I'm sorry it has to be this way."

"Havers, what are you doing?" she said against the door panels.

"I have no other choice. I can't have you going to him anymore."

She made sure her words were loud and clear. "Listen to me. Wrath is the not the reason I've gone out. He's been mated to someone whom he loves, and I feel no ill will toward him. I've . . . I've met a male. Someone I like. Someone who wants me."

There was a long silence.

"Havers?" She hit the door with her fist. "Havers! Did you hear what I said? Wrath is mated, and I've forgiven him. I wasn't with him."

When her brother finally spoke, he sounded as though someone were choking him. "Why didn't you tell me?"

"You didn't give me a chance to! I've tried for the last two nights!" She banged the door again. "Now let me out. I'm supposed to meet my . . . someone at Darius's."

Havers whispered something.

"What?" she demanded. "What did you say?"

"I can't have you going there."

As the anguish in his voice snuffed out her anger, the back of her neck grew tight with alarm. "Why not?"

"It's no longer safe in that house. I . . . Dear God."

Marissa splayed her hands out flat. "Havers, what did you do?"

There was only more silence.

"Havers! Tell me what you have done!"

Beth felt something hit her face hard. A hand. Someone had slapped her.

With a groggy jerk, she opened her eyes. She was in a barn. Strapped down to a table with metal bands around her wrists and ankles.

And Billy Riddle was standing over her. "Wake up, bitch."

She struggled, straining against the cuffs. As he

watched her, his eyes lingered on her breasts and his mouth pressed into a tight line.

"Mr. R?" Another male voice. "You do recall that you're out of the rape business."

"Yeah. I know." Billy's glare got worse. "Makes me want to hurt her just thinking about it."

The blond-haired man who'd abducted her came into Beth's line of sight. He had a shotgun on each shoulder, muzzles up.

"I'll let you kill her, how's that? She can be your first."

Billy smiled. "Thanks, sensei."

The blond man turned toward the barn's double doors. They were wide open, revealing the dimming light in the sky.

"Mr. R, we need to keep focused," he said. "I want these guns loaded and lined up with boxes of ammo on that work-table. We should put out knives, too. And go get the can of gasoline from the garage as well as the butane blow torch that's next to the Hummer."

Billy slapped her one more time. And then did as he was told.

Beth's mind turned over slowly. The drugs were still in her system, making everything seem like a dream, but with every breath she took, the fog was lifting. And she was getting stronger.

Wrath's violence was so deep, so vicious that it put frost on the walls of his chamber, and his breath came out in cloud bursts. The candles flickered slowly in the dense air, throwing off light, but no measurable heat.

He'd always known he was capable of great rage. But what he would bring down on those who had taken Beth from him would be for the history books.

There was a knock on the door. "Wrath?"

It was the cop, and Wrath willed the door open. The

human seemed momentarily thrown by the temperature in the room.

"I . . . ah, I went to the Caldwell Martial Arts Academy. Guy's name is Joseph Xavier. No one's seen him today. He called in and got a replacement for his classes. They told me where he lived, and I did a drive-by. Condo on the west side of town. I broke in. It was clean. Too clean. Nothing in the fridge, nothing in the garage. No mail, no magazines. No toothpaste in the bathroom. No evidence that someone pulled out in a hurry, either. He may own it, but he doesn't live there."

Wrath was having a hard time concentrating. All he could think about was getting free of this godforsaken hole in the earth and locating Beth. Once he was outside, he'd sense her. His blood running through her veins was like a GPS chip. He'd be able to find her anywhere on the planet.

He grabbed his cell phone and dialed. As Butch made a move to go, Wrath said, "Don't leave."

The cop settled on the leather couch, eyes alert, body calm. Ready for anything.

When Tohrment's voice came through, Wrath pulled the trigger on the brotherhood. "At ten o'clock tonight, you will take the brothers and you will go to the Caldwell Martial Arts Academy. You will infiltrate and search the place, and then you will throw the security alarm. You will wait until the *lessers* arrive and then you will slaughter them and burn the building to the ground. Do you understand me? Ashes, Tohr. I want fucking ashes."

There was no hesitation. "Yes, my lord."

"Watch Zsadist. Keep him with you at all times, even if you have to chain him to your side." Wrath glanced over at Butch. "The cop will monitor the building from now until sundown. If he sees anything of significance, he will call you."

417

Butch nodded, already getting to his feet and heading to the door. "I'm on it," he said over his shoulder.

There was a pause on the cell. "My lord, do you need us to help you find—"

"I will take care of our queen."

FIFTY

For the next hour, Beth watched her two captors run around as if they were convinced Wrath was coming at any minute. Except how would he know where she was? It wasn't like the blond guy had left a ransom note. Or at least, not that she'd been aware of.

Pulling against the metal bands once more, she looked across the barn. The sun was just going down, the shadows long on the grass and the gravel drive. As Billy shut the double doors, she caught a last glance of the darkening sky and then watched as he slid home a series of thick bolts on the doors.

Wrath would absolutely look for her. She had no doubt of that. But surely it would take hours for him to find her, and she wasn't sure she had that kind of time left. Billy Riddle stared at her body with such hatred, she had to believe he would snap. Sooner rather than later.

"And now we wait," the blond man said, checking his watch. "It shouldn't be long. I want you armed. Put a gun on your belt and strap a knife on your ankle."

Billy was only too happy to gear up, and he had a lot to choose from. There were enough semiautomatics, shot guns, and sharp blades to outfit an army unit.

As he picked up a six-inch hunting knife, he turned and looked at her.

Her palms, clammy before, ran wet with sweat.

He took a step forward.

Beth frowned, looking to the right just as the other two did. What was that sound?

Some kind of rumble. Thunder? A train?

419

Whatever it was, it was getting louder.

And then she heard an odd tinkling noise, like wind chimes. She glanced across the barn. On the table where the ammunition was laid out, loose bullets were jumping around, knocking into one another.

Billy stared at his leader. "What the hell is that?"

The man took a deep breath as the temperature dropped a good twenty or thirty degrees.

"Get ready, Billy."

By now, the sound was a roar. And the barn was shaking so violently, dust from the rafters was falling, a fine snow that clouded the air.

Billy reached up to cover his head.

The barn doors splintered apart, blown open by a cold blast of fury. The whole building swayed under the force of the impact, beams and boards shifting, groaning.

Wrath filled the doorway, the air around him warping with vengeance, with menace, with the promise of death. Beth felt his eyes on her, and then a booming battle roar came out of him, so loud it hurt her ears.

From then on, Wrath reigned.

In a movement so fast her eyes couldn't track it, he went at the blond, grabbing the man and hammering him into a stall door. The blond wasn't even stunned and nailed Wrath with a hard uppercut to the jaw. The two battered and rammed and hit each other, slamming into walls, knocking out windows, breaking tables. In spite of the weapons they carried, they stuck with hand-to-hand combat, their faces harsh, their lips peeled back, their tremendous bodies doing damage and being injured by turns.

She didn't want to watch, but she couldn't turn away. Especially as Billy grabbed a knife and launched himself onto Wrath's back. With a vicious twist, Wrath peeled the guy off of him and pitched Billy into the air.

420

Riddle's body flew across the space to the other end of the barn, landing in a pile of arms and legs.

Billy struggled to his feet, dazed. Blood streamed down his face.

Wrath took tremendous kicks to the body, but he didn't slow. And he was able to hold the blond off long enough to flip open one of the metal bands that held Beth's wrists in place. She went to work on the opposite side, freeing her other hand.

"The dogs! Let loose the dogs," the blond man cried out.

Billy staggered from the barn. A moment later, two pit bulls came shooting around the corner.

They went right for Wrath's ankles, just as the blond unsheathed a knife.

Beth freed both her feet and popped off the table.

"Run!" Wrath yelled to her, ripping one dog off his leg while blocking a blow to the face.

Screw that, she thought, picking up the first thing she found. It was a ball-peen hammer.

Beth went after the blond man just as Wrath lost his balance and went down. Lifting the hammer as high as she could, she threw every ounce of strength that she had into the damn thing. And brought it down square on the back of the blond's head.

There was a crack of bone and a burst of blood.

And then one of the dogs wheeled around and bit her in the thigh.

She screamed as its teeth tore through her skin and sank into her muscles.

Wrath tossed the *lesser*'s body off him and leaped to his feet.

One of the dogs was on Beth, its mouth around her upper leg. The animal was trying to roll her on to the ground so it could go for her throat. Wrath lunged forward only to pause. If he pulled the dog free, the thing was liable to take a whole hunk of her thigh with him when it went.

Vishous's voice came to Wrath in a rush: *Two guards tortured will fight each other.*

Wrath tore the dog off his own ankle and threw it at the one that was attacking Beth. The other animal was knocked free. And the two pit bulls went after each other.

Wrath ran over as she fell. She was bleeding. "Beth—"

A shotgun went off.

Wrath heard a high whistle and felt his neck burn as though he'd been hit with a torch.

Beth screamed as he wheeled around. Billy Riddle repositioned the gun on his shoulder.

Fury made Wrath forget everything. He stalked toward the new recruit, not stopping even when the shotgun was up and pointed at his chest. Billy pulled the trigger, and Wrath moved to one side before diving forward. He took the *lesser*'s neck in his teeth and ripped it open. Then he snapped Billy's head around until it cracked loose.

Wrath turned around to go back to Beth.

But fell to his knees instead.

Confused, he looked down at himself. There was a hole the size of a melon in his abdomen.

"Wrath!" Beth limped over.

"I'm . . . hit, *leelan*."

"Oh, God." She ripped the robe from her body, stuffing it against his stomach. "Where's your phone?"

He lifted one hand feebly as he fell over on his side. "Pocket."

She grabbed the cell and dialed the house. "Butch? Butch! Help! Wrath's been shot in the belly! I—I don't know where we are—"

422

"Route 22," Wrath murmured. "Ranch house with a black Hummer in front."

Beth repeated his words, pressing the robe into his wound. "We're in the barn. Come fast! He's bleeding."

A low growl came from the left.

Wrath looked over just as Beth did. The surviving pit bull, bloodied, but still angry, was advancing.

Beth didn't hesitate. She unsheathed one of Wrath's daggers and crouched.

"Just get here, Butch. *Now*." She flipped the phone shut and dropped it. "Come on, you ugly-ass dog. Come on!"

The dog circled, and Wrath could feel himself being eyed. For some reason the animal wanted him, maybe because he was bleeding so badly. Beth moved with the pit bull, arms held wide.

Her voice throbbed. "You want some of him? You're going to have to get through me."

The dog leaped at Beth, and as if she'd been trained to kill, she got down low and plunged the knife up into the animal's chest cavity. The thing dropped like a stone.

She left the knife in place and scrambled back. She was shaking so badly, her hands were like birds as she lifted the cloth at his stomach.

"It doesn't hurt," he whispered, smelling her tears.

"Oh, Wrath." She grabbed his hand, gripping it hard. "You're in shock."

"Yeah, probably. I can't see you, where are you?"

"I'm here." She put his fingers to her face. "Can you feel me?"

Barely, but it was enough to keep him going.

"I wish you were pregnant," he said hoarsely. "I don't want you to be alone."

"Don't say that!"

"Ask Tohr and Wellsie to take you in."

"*No.*"

"Promise me."

"I will not," she said fiercely. "You're not going anywhere."

She was so wrong about that, he thought. He could feel himself slipping away.

"I love you, *leelan*."

Beth started to sob. Her strangled cries were the last sound he heard as he fought against the tide and lost.

Beth didn't look up when the cell phone started ringing.

"Wrath?" she said again. "Wrath . . ."

She put her ear to his chest. His heart was still working, but the beats were faint, and he was breathing, though slowly. She was desperate to help him, except she couldn't do CPR. Not until his vitals crashed.

"Oh, God . . ."

The phone kept ringing.

She grabbed it off the dirt floor, trying to ignore the spreading pool of blood around Wrath's body. "What!"

"Beth! It's Butch. I'm with V. He and I are going to be there soon, but he needs to talk to you."

There was a whirring noise in the background, as if a car engine was screaming.

Vishous's voice was intense. "Beth, here's what you need to do. Do you have a knife?"

She eyed the remaining dagger on Wrath's chest. "Yes."

"Get it. I want you to cut your wrist. Do it vertically down the forearm, not horizontally, otherwise you'll just hit bone. Then put it to his mouth. It's his best chance of surviving until we can get him help." There was a pause. "Put the phone down, honey, and get the knife. I'll talk you through it."

Beth reached over and extracted the blade from Wrath's holster. She didn't hesitate to slice her left wrist open. The pain made her gasp, but she didn't dwell on the burning as she put the wound to Wrath's mouth. She picked up the phone with her free hand.

"He's not drinking."

"You've already cut yourself? Good girl."

"He's not . . . he's not swallowing."

"Hopefully some's getting down the back of his throat."

"He's bleeding from there, too."

"Jesus . . . I'm driving as fast as I can."

Butch spotted the Hummer. "Over there!"

Vishous drove right across the lawn, and they leaped from the car, punch running for the barn.

Butch couldn't believe the scene inside. A couple of slaughtered dogs. Blood everywhere. One *really* dead body—Jesus, that was Billy Riddle.

And then he saw Beth.

She was wearing a long T-shirt that was covered with blood and dirt, her eyes gone mad as she knelt by Wrath's body with one wrist to his lips. When she noticed them, she hissed and brought up her knife, prepared to fight.

Vishous went forward, but Butch grabbed his arm. "Let me go first."

Slowly, Butch stepped over to her. "Beth? Beth, you know who we are."

But the closer he got to Wrath, the crazier her eyes became. She pulled her wrist away from the man's mouth, ready to defend him.

"Easy, girl. We're not going to hurt him. Beth, it's me."

She blinked. "Butch?"

"Yeah, baby. It's me and Vishous."

She dropped the knife and started to cry.

"Okay, it's okay." He tried to get her into his arms, but she dropped back down to Wrath. "No, baby. Let V look at him, okay? Come on, it'll just take a minute."

She allowed herself to be pulled back. As Butch tore off his shirt and wrapped it around her waist, he nodded to V.

Vishous dropped to Wrath's side. When he looked up from the other vampire's stomach, his lips were tight.

Beth sank down, putting her wrist back in place. "He'll be all right, won't he? We'll just move him to a doctor. To a hospital. Right? Vishous, right?" Desperation made her shrill.

And then suddenly, they weren't alone.

Marissa and a distinguished, frantic-looking man appeared out of nowhere.

The guy went to Wrath's body and lifted the wad of blood-soaked satin. "We've got to get him to my OR."

"My car's on the front lawn," V said. "I'll come back and finish things when he's safe."

The man cursed as he examined the neck wound. He looked at Beth. "Your blood's not strong enough. Marissa, get over here."

Beth was fighting back tears as she lifted her wrist from Wrath's mouth and looked up at the blond woman.

Marissa hesitated. "Are you okay with my feeding him?"

Beth offered Wrath's dagger handle first. "I don't care who he drinks from if it will save him."

Marissa cut herself easily, as if she'd done it many times before. Then she lifted Wrath's head up and pressed the wound to his mouth.

His body jolted like it had been hooked up to a car battery.

"All right, let's move him," said the man who'd taken charge. "Marissa, you keep that wrist right where it is."

Beth took Wrath's hand as the men got him up off the barn floor. They carried him as gently as they could over to Vishous's SUV, laying him out flat in the back.

Marissa and Beth got in with Wrath as Butch and Vishous took the front seat. The other man disappeared.

As the Escalade roared over the back roads, Beth stroked Wrath's arm, up and down his tattoos. The skin was cold.

"You love him so very much," Marissa murmured.

Beth looked up. "Is he drinking?"

"I don't know."

FIFTY-ONE

In the surgical suite's anteroom, Havers snapped off his latex gloves and threw them into a bio-trash container. His back ached after having spent hours leaning over Wrath, stitching up sections of the warrior's intestine and fixing the wound in his neck.

"Will he live?" Marissa asked as she came out of the OR. She was weak from all the blood she'd given. Pale, but intense.

"We'll know soon enough. I hope so."

"As do I." She walked past him, refusing to meet his eyes.

"Marissa—"

"I know you are sorry. But I am not the one to whom you should offer your regrets. You might start with Beth. If ever she is ready to hear you."

As the door slid shut with a hiss, Havers closed his eyes.

Oh, dear God, the pain in his chest. The pain of deeds that could never be undone.

Havers sagged against the wall, pulling the surgical cap off his head.

Thankfully, the Blind King had a true warrior's constitution. He was stout of body, fierce of will. Although he wouldn't have survived without Marissa's nearly pure blood.

Or, Havers suspected, the presence of his dark-haired *shellan*. Beth, as she was called, had stayed by his side throughout the operation. And even though the warrior had been unconscious, his head had stayed turned toward her. She'd spoken to him for hours, until she had only a hoarse whisper left.

And she was still in there with him now, though she was so exhausted she could barely sit up. She'd refused to let her own wounds be examined, and she wouldn't eat.

She just stayed with her *hellren*.

With a lurch, Havers went over to the deep prep sinks. He gripped the stainless-steel gunnels and stared at the drains. He felt like throwing up, but his stomach was empty.

The brothers were outside. Waiting for news from him.

And they knew what he had done.

Before Havers had gone in to operate, Tohrment had grabbed him around the throat. If Wrath died on the table, the warrior had vowed, the brothers were going to string Havers up by the feet and beat him with their bare fists until he bled out. Right in his own house.

No doubt Zsadist had told them everything.

God, if only I could go back to that alley, Havers thought. *If only I hadn't gone there at all.*

And he should have known never to approach a member of the brotherhood with such a treasonous request. Not even the soulless one.

After he'd made the offer to Zsadist, the brother had stared down at him with those terrifying black eyes, and Havers had immediately realized he'd made a mistake. Zsadist might have been full of hate, but he wasn't a traitor against his king, and he was offended that he'd been asked.

"I'll kill for free," Zsadist had growled. "But only if I were going after you. Get out of my sight before I get out my knife."

Rattled, Havers had rushed away, only to find himself

being tracked by what he'd assumed must be a *lesser*. It was the first time he'd ever been close to one of the undead, and it was a surprise that the society member was so fair of hair and skin. Still, the thing was pure evil and ready to kill. Trapped in a corner in the alley, scared out of mind, Havers had started talking, as much to get the job he wanted done as to keep himself from getting slain. The *lesser* had been skeptical at first, but Havers had always been persuasive, and the word *king*, used liberally, had gotten its attention. Information had changed hands. The *lesser* had walked off. And the die was cast.

Havers breathed deeply, bracing himself to go out into the hall.

At least he could pledge to the brothers that he'd done the best he could with the surgery.

Although that hadn't been because he'd wanted to save his own life. Such an acquittal was impossible. He was going to be put to death for what he'd done; it was just a question of when.

No, in the OR, he'd performed to the best of his ability because it was the only way he could make up for the atrocity he'd committed. And because those five heavily armed males and that fierce human man waiting outside had looked like their hearts were breaking.

But neither of those had been his truest motivator.

He'd been galvanized most by the burning pain in that dark-haired Beth's eyes. He knew well that horrified, impotent expression. He'd been wearing it himself as he'd watched his *shellan* die.

Havers washed his face and went out into the hall. The brothers and the human looked up at him.

"He has survived the surgery. Now, we have to see if he holds on." Havers went over to Tohrment. "Do you want to take me now?"

The warrior stared down at him with hard, violent eyes. "We'll keep you alive to care for him. And then he can kill you himself."

Havers nodded and heard a soft crying sound. He looked over to see Marissa clasping a hand to her mouth.

He was about to go over when the human male stepped in front of her. The man hesitated before holding out a handkerchief. She took what he offered and then walked away from them all.

Beth put her head down on the far corner of Wrath's pillow. He'd been transferred to a hospital bed from the operating table, though he was not going to be moved into a normal patient room. Havers had decided to keep him in the OR in case he needed to be operated on again on an emergency basis.

The white-walled facility was cold, but someone had put a heavy fleece on her. Evidently, they'd also wrapped a blanket around the bottom half of her body, too. She couldn't remember who had been so kind.

As she heard a clicking sound, she glanced over at the mountain of machines Wrath was hooked up to. She measured each one of them without having much idea what the readouts meant. Provided that none of the alarms were going off, she had to imagine it was okay.

The sound came again.

She looked down at Wrath. And shot to her feet.

He was trying to talk, but his mouth was so dry, his tongue was thick.

"Shhh." She gripped his hand. Put her face in his line of vision in case he opened his eyes. "I'm right here."

His fingers twitched in hers. And then he faded away again.

God, he looked like hell. Pale as the ceramic tiles on the OR's floor. Eyes sunk deep into his skull.

He had a thick bandage on his throat. His belly was wrapped in gauze and cotton pads, with drains leading out of the wound. There was an IV pumping fluids and painkillers into his arm and a catheter bag hanging off the bedside. A tangle of EKG wires were stuck on his chest, and an oxygen sensor was clipped onto his middle finger.

But he was alive. For now.

And he'd stirred to consciousness, even if it was just for a moment.

It was like that for the next two days. He would surface and sink, surface and sink, as if he had to keep checking that she was with him before he went back to the herculean job of healing his body.

Eventually, she had to sleep, so the brothers brought in a more comfortable chair, and someone gave her a pillow and a blanket. She woke up an hour later, still clutching Wrath's hand.

She ate when she was forced to, because Tohrment or Wellsie demanded that she did. And she took a shower in the anteroom. Quickly. When she got back, Wrath's legs and arms were flailing wildly and Wellsie had called for Havers.

The instant Beth took Wrath's hand, he calmed right down.

She didn't know how long the waiting would go on. But every time he came back to her, she drew a little strength.

She could wait. For an eternity, she could wait for him.

Wrath's mind came back online in a rush of activity. One minute he wasn't aware of anything; the next, his circuits started firing again. He didn't know where he was, and his eyelids were too heavy to open, so he did a quick scan of his body. Lower half felt okay, toes moved, legs were still attached. *Whoa, ouch.* His stomach felt like it had been punched with a tire iron. But his chest was solid. Neck was burning. Head was achy. Arms were good. Hands—

Beth.

He was used to feeling her palm against his. Where was she?

His eyes flipped open.

She was right beside him, sitting in a chair, her head down on the bed as if she were asleep. His first thought was that he shouldn't wake her up. She was obviously exhausted.

But he wanted to touch her. Needed to.

He tried to reach out with his free hand, but his arm felt like it weighed four hundred pounds. He struggled, willing the limb across his body, dragging it over the bedcovers inch by inch. He didn't know how long it took. Maybe hours.

But then he finally touched a lock of her hair. The silken feel of it was a miracle.

He was alive, and so was she.

Wrath started to cry.

The instant Beth felt the bed shudder, she woke up in a panic. The first thing she saw was Wrath's hand. His fingers were wrapped around a long strand of her hair.

She looked up at his face. Tears were rolling out of his eyes.

"Wrath! Oh, love." She leaned up to him, smoothed his hair back. He was totally distressed. "Are you hurting?"

He opened his mouth. Nothing came out. He started to panic, his eyes peeling open until the whites showed.

"Easy, love, take it easy. Just relax," she said. "I want you to squeeze my hand, once for yes, twice for no. Are you in pain?"

No.

She gently stroked the tears from his whiskered cheeks. "Are you sure?"

Yes.

"Do you want me to get Havers?"

No.

"Do you need anything?"

Yes.

"Food? Drink? Blood?"

No.

He began to get agitated, his pale, wild eyes imploring her.

"Shhh, it's okay." She kissed his forehead. "Just calm down. We'll figure out what you need. We've got plenty of time."

His eyes fixated on their linked hands and came back to her face. Then his gaze locked on their hands and returned again.

"Me?" she whispered. "You need me?"

He squeezed and wouldn't stop.

"Oh, Wrath . . . You have me. We're together, love."

Tears poured out of him in a mad rush, his chest quaking from the sobs, his breathing jagged and raw.

She took his face in his hands, trying to soothe him. "It's all right. I'm not going anywhere. I'm not going to leave you. I promise you. Oh, love . . ."

Eventually he relaxed a little. The tears slowed.

A croak came out of his mouth.

"What?" She leaned down.

"Wanted to . . . save you."

"You did. Wrath, you did save me."

His lips trembled. "Love. You."

She kissed him gently on the mouth. "I love you, too."

"You. Go. Sleep. Now."

And then he closed his eyes from exhaustion.

Her vision went blurry as she put her hand over her mouth and started to smile. Her beautiful warrior was back. And trying to order her around from his hospital bed.

Wrath sighed and seemed to sink into sleep.

When she was sure he was resting peacefully, she stretched, thinking the brothers would appreciate knowing that he'd woken up and been well enough to talk a little. Maybe she could find a phone and call the house.

When she peered into the hall, she couldn't believe what she saw.

Right in front of the OR's door, in a great, breathing barrier, the brothers and Butch were sprawled out on the floor. The men were fast asleep, looking as exhausted as she felt. Vishous and Butch were propped up against the wall next to each other, a little TV and two guns between them. Rhage was flat on his back, snoring softly, with dagger in hand. Tohrment had his head balanced on his knees. Phury was lying on his side, clutching a throwing star to his chest as if it soothed him.

Where was Zsadist?

"I'm over here," he said quietly.

She jumped and looked to her right. Zsadist was fully armed, gun strapped on his hip, daggers crossed over his chest, length of chain shifting in his hand. His glittering black eyes regarded her steadily.

"It's my turn to stand guard. We've been taking shifts."

"Is it so dangerous here?"

He frowned. "You don't know?"

"What?"

He shrugged and looked down the hall. One way, then the other. Scanning.

"The brotherhood protects what is ours." His eyes refocused on her. "We would never leave you or him undefended."

She sensed he was evading, but wasn't about to press. All that mattered was that she and Wrath were safe as her husband's body healed.

"Thank you," she whispered.

Zsadist looked down quickly.

How he hides from any warmth, she thought.

"What time is it?" she asked.

"Four in the afternoon. It's Thursday, by the way." Zsadist brushed a hand over his skull trim. "So, ah, how's he doing?"

"He woke up."

"I knew he'd live."

"Did you?"

His lip lifted in a snarl, as if he were going to make some kind of crack. But then he seemed to catch himself. He stared at her, his scarred face remote.

"Yeah, Beth. I really did. No shotgun's ever going to keep him from you."

And then Zsadist's eyes shifted away.

The others started to stir. A moment later, they were all on their feet, staring down at her. Butch, she noted, seemed right at home with the vampires.

"How's he feeling?" Tohr asked.

"Good enough to try to tell me what to do."

The brothers laughed in a rush. The sound was one of relief. Of pride. Of love.

"Either of you need anything?" Tohr asked.

Beth looked at their faces. Each one was expectant. As if they hoped she would give them something to do.

This really is my family, she thought.

"I think we're okay." Beth smiled. "And I'm sure he's going to want to see all of you soon."

"What about you?" Tohr asked. "How're you holding up? You want to take a break?"

She shook her head and pushed open the OR's door. "Until he can walk out of here on his own two feet, I'm not leaving that bedside."

As the door closed behind Beth, Butch heard Vishous whistle under his breath.

"That is one fine female, true?" V said.

There was a low, affirmative grumble.

"And someone you do not want to mess with," the brother continued. "Man, you should have seen her when we came into that barn. She was standing over his body, ready to take the cop and me on with her bare hands if she had to. Like Wrath was her cub, you feel me?"

"Wonder if she has a sister?" Rhage asked.

Phury laughed. "You wouldn't know what to do with yourself if you ran into a female of worth."

"This coming from you, Celibate?" But then Hollywood rubbed the stubble on his chin, as if considering the ways of the universe. "Ah, hell, Phury, you're probably right. Still, a male can dream."

"He sure can," V murmured.

Butch thought of Marissa. He kept hoping she would come down, but he hadn't seen her since she'd left the morning after the surgery. She'd looked so drawn, so distracted, but it wasn't as if she didn't have enough on her mind. Her brother's death was coming soon. Sooner still as Wrath recovered.

Butch wanted to go to her, but wasn't sure if she'd welcome his company. He just didn't know her well enough. They'd had so little time together.

437

Was he a curiosity? Some fresh blood she wanted to taste? Something more?

Butch looked down the hallway, as if he could call her into being.

God, he ached to see her. If only to know she was okay.

FIFTY-TWO

A couple of days later, Wrath struggled to sit up before the brothers came in. He didn't want them to see him flat on his back. The IV running into his arm and all the machines behind him were bad enough.

But at least the catheter had been out since yesterday. And he'd managed to shave himself and take a shower. Having his hair clean was a beautiful thing.

"What are you doing?" Beth demanded as she caught him moving around.

"Sitting up—"

"Oh, no, you don't." She grabbed the bed's remote and tilted up the head.

"Ah, hell, *leelan*, now I'm just lying down while sitting up."

"You're fine." She bent over to tuck the sheets in, and he caught sight of the curve of her breast. His body swelled. In the right place.

But the rush made him think of the scene he'd walked in on at that barn. Of her latched down to that table. He didn't care that *lessers* couldn't get it up.

He caught her hand. *"Leelan?"*

"Yes?"

"Are you sure you're all right?" They'd talked about what had happened, but still he worried.

"I told you. My thigh's healing up—"

"Not just the physical stuff," he said, wanting to kill Billy Riddle all over again.

Her face clouded for an instant. "I told you, I'll be fine. Because I refuse to have it any other way."

439

"You're so brave. So resilient. You amaze me."

She smiled at him and leaned down for a quick kiss.

He held her in place, talking against her lips. "And thank you for saving my life. Not just back in that barn. But for all the rest of my days and nights."

He kissed her a little more deeply and was happy to hear her gasp of pleasure. The sound brought his erection back to life, and he brushed his fingertips over her collarbone.

"How 'bout you hop on up here with me?"

"I don't think you're quite ready for that yet."

"Wanna bet?" He took her hand and put it under the hospital sheets.

Her throaty laugh as she gripped him gently was yet another marvel. Just like her constant presence in his room, her fierce protection of him, her love, her strength.

She was everything to him. His whole world. He'd gone from being blasé about his death to being desperate to live. For her. For them. For their future.

"What do you say we give it another day?" she said.

"An hour."

"Until you can sit up on your own."

"Deal."

Thank God he was a fast healer.

Her hand left his body. "Should I let the brothers in?"

"Yeah." He took a deep breath. "Wait. I want you to know what I'm going to say."

He tugged her down, so she sat on the edge of the bed.

"I'm leaving the brotherhood."

She closed her eyes as if she didn't want him to see how relieved she was. "Truly?"

"Yeah. I've asked Tohr to be in charge. But I'm not taking a vacation. I have to start ruling our kind, Beth. And I need you to do it with me."

Her lids flipped open.

He touched her face. "We're talking king and queen time. And I'm going to be honest with you. I have no idea what I'm doing. I've got some ideas, but I'm going to need your help."

"Anything," she said. "Anything for you."

Wrath could only stare at her in wonder.

God, she really knocked him out. Here she was, ready to take on the world with him even though he was flat on his ass in a hospital bed. Her faith in him was astounding.

"Have I told you that I love you, *leelan*?"

"About five minutes ago. But I never get tired of hearing it."

He kissed her. "Get the brothers. Tell Butch to wait in the hall. But I want you to stay while I talk to them."

She let the warriors in and then came back to his side.

The brotherhood walked up to the bed cautiously. Although he'd had a brief meeting with Tohr that morning, this was the first time he'd seen the rest of his warriors, and the first time they'd seen him. There was a lot of shallow coughing, like there were lumps being cleared out of throats. He knew what that felt like. He had a knot in his own.

"My brothers—"

At that moment, Havers came through the door. He stopped dead in his tracks.

"Ah, the good doctor," Wrath said. "Come in. We've got some unfinished business, you and I."

Havers had been in and out of the OR with regularity, but Wrath hadn't felt up to dealing with the situation until now.

"It's time," he commanded.

Havers took a deep breath and walked up to the bed. He bowed his head. "My lord."

"I understand you tried to have me killed."

To the male's credit, he didn't try to run. He didn't

prevaricate. And although his sorrow and his regret were clear, he did not argue for leniency.

"Yes, I did, my lord. I was the one who approached him." He pointed to Zsadist. "And, when it was clear your brother would not betray you, the *lesser*."

Wrath nodded, having already talked to Tohrment about what had really gone down that night. Tohr had caught only part of Z's response.

"My lord, you should know that your brother was ready to kill me just for asking him."

Wrath eyed Zsadist, who was staring at the doctor like he wanted to mount the male's head on a wall. "Yeah, I heard that didn't go over too well. Z, I owe you an apology."

The warrior shrugged. "Don't bother. They bore me."

Wrath smiled, thinking that was so like Z. Pissed off no matter the circumstance.

Havers looked around at the brothers. "Here in front of these witnesses, I accept the sentence of death."

Wrath stared hard at the doctor. And thought of all those years the male's sister had suffered. Even though Wrath had never intended for her life to be so grueling, the outcome had been his fault.

"Marissa was the reason, wasn't she?" Wrath said.

Havers nodded. "Yes, my lord."

"Then I'm not going to kill you. You did it because of the way I treated your loved one. Vengeance is something I can understand."

Havers seemed to wobble from shock. Then he dropped the chart he was holding and collapsed by the bed, grabbing Wrath's hand and putting his forehead on it. "My lord. Your mercy knows no bounds."

"Yeah, the hell it doesn't. I am giving you your life as a gift to your sister. If you ever pull a stunt like that again, I'm coming after you with a dagger. We clear?"

"Yes, my lord."

"Now leave us. You can poke and prod me later. But knock before you come in, got it?"

"Yes, my lord."

As Havers scooted out the door, Wrath kissed Beth's hand. "Just in case we're busy," he whispered to her.

A low, collective chuckle filled the room.

He glared at the brothers to shut them up and then made his pronouncement. He knew he'd shocked the hell out of his warriors when there was a long silence.

"So are you down with Tohr, or what?" he asked the group.

"Yeah," Rhage said. "I can deal."

Vishous and Phury nodded.

"Z?"

The warrior rolled his black eyes. "Come on, man. What does it matter to me? You, Tohr. Britney Spears."

Wrath laughed. "Was that a joke, Z? After all this time, have you finally found your sense of humor? Hell, you're giving me another reason to live."

Z flushed and snarled a little while the others chided him.

Wrath took a deep breath. "And my brothers, there's something else. I'm ascending to the throne. As I've told Tohr, we need to rebuild. We need to revive the race."

The brothers stared. And then one by one, they came up to the bed and swore their fealty in the old language, taking his hand, kissing the inside of his wrist. Their grave reverence shook him, moved him.

The Scribe Virgin was right, he thought. These were his people. How could he not lead them?

When the warriors were finished with their oaths, he looked at Vishous. "Did you get the jars of the two *lessers* from that barn?"

V frowned. "There was only one. The recruit that you

and I met the night of your mating. I went back and stabbed the body while you were being operated on. Got his jar from the house."

Wrath shook his head. "There were two. There were definitely two. The other one was the *lesser* who was driving that Hummer."

"You sure he went down?"

"He was on the ground with a blow to the head." Abruptly, Wrath sensed Beth's disquiet and squeezed her hand. "Enough, we'll talk about this later."

"No, it's all right—" she began.

"Later." He kissed the back of her hand and stroked it across his cheek. Holding on to her eyes with his own, he tried to reassure her, hating the world he'd brought her into.

When she smiled at him, Wrath tugged her down for a quick kiss and then looked back at the brothers.

"One more thing," he said. "You're going to move in together. I want the brotherhood in one place. At least for the next couple of years."

Tohr winced. "Man, Wellsie's going to hate that. We just finished installing her dream kitchen."

"We'll work out something for you two. Especially because there's a child on the way. But the rest of you are going to be roommates."

There were grumbles. Serious grumbles.

"Hey, it could be worse," he said. "I could make you live with me."

"Good point," Rhage said. "Man, Beth, if you ever need a break from him—"

Wrath growled.

"What I was *gonna* say," Hollywood drawled, "was that she could move in with all of us for a while. We'll always take care of her."

Wrath glanced up at Beth. God, she was so beautiful. His partner. His lover. His queen.

He smiled, unable to look away from her eyes. "Leave us, gentlemen. I want to be alone with my *shellan*."

As the brothers filed out, they were laughing with masculine appreciation. As if they knew exactly what was on his mind.

Wrath struggled on the bed, trying to force himself upright so that he bore the weight of his upper body on his hips.

Beth watched him the whole time, refusing to help.

When he was steady, he rubbed his hands together in anticipation. He could feel her skin already.

"Wrath," she said with warning as he beamed at her.

"Come on up here, *leelan*. A deal's a deal."

Even if all he could do was hold her, he just needed her in his arms.

FIFTY-THREE

José de la Cruz shook the arson investigator's hand. "Thanks. I look forward to your written report."

The man shook his head as he glanced back at the charred remains of the Caldwell Martial Arts Academy. "Never seen anything like this. You'd swear some kind of nuclear bomb went off. Frankly, I don't know what to put in the file."

José watched the man walk over to his county truck and drive off.

"You going back to the station?" Ricky asked while getting into his own squad car.

"Not right now. I gotta head across town."

Ricky waved and headed out.

Alone at the site, José took a deep breath. The smell of the fire was pungent, even four days later.

As he headed to his unmarked, he looked down at his shoes. They were pale gray from the twelve inches of soot that covered the site. The stuff was more volcano ash than anything left behind by a normal fire. And the ruins were odd, too. Usually parts of a structure survived, no matter how hot the flames. Here, nothing remained. The building had been razed to the ground.

Like the arson investigator, he'd never seen anything of the sort.

José got behind the wheel, stuck the key in the ignition, and put the car in gear. He drove eight miles to the east, into a grittier part of town. A series of unimpressive apartment buildings appeared, urban weeds that grew up from the concrete and asphalt ground.

He stopped in front of one. Put the car in park. Turned off the engine. It was a long time before he could force himself out of the car.

Steeling his nerves, he walked over to the front entrance. A couple was coming out, and they held the door open for him. After going up three flights of stairs, he headed down a ratty hall with carpeting that was flat and brown from having borne thousands of footsteps.

The door he was looking for had been repainted so many times, its sunken panels were almost flush.

He knocked, but did not expect any answer.

Picking the lock was the work of a moment. He pushed the door open.

Closing his eyes, he took a deep breath. A body left for four or five days would smell by now, even in the air-conditioning.

But there was nothing.

"Butch?" he called out.

He closed the door behind him. The couch was covered with the sports sections of the *CCJ* and the *New York Post* from the previous week. There were empty beer cans on the table. In the kitchen, there were dishes in the sink. More empties on the counter.

José went into the bedroom. All he found was a bed with messy sheets and a lot of clothes on the floor.

He paused by the bathroom door. It was closed.

His heart started pounding.

Pushing it open, he fully expected to find a body hanging from the showerhead.

But there was nothing.

Homicide Detective Butch O'Neal had disappeared. Without a trace.

FIFTY-FOUR

Darius looked around himself. The peaceful mist of the Fade had dissolved, revealing a courtyard of white marble. From a fountain in the center, water fell in a twinkling dance, catching the diffused light and sending it back out in flashes. Songbirds called sweetly, as if both welcoming him and announcing his arrival.

So this place actually exists, he thought.

"Good day, Darius, son of Marklon."

He dropped to his knees without turning around and lowered his head. "Scribe Virgin. You honor me with an audience."

She laughed softly. As she stepped in front of him, the hem of her black robes came into his view. The glow spilling out from under the silk was as bright as direct sunlight.

"Darius, how could I refuse? It is the first congregation you have ever asked for." He felt something brush his shoulder, and the hair on the back of his head tingled. "Rise, now. I would see your face."

He got to his feet, towering over the slight figure. He kept his hands clasped in front of him.

"So the Fade is not to your liking, *princeps*?" she asked. "And you want me to send you back?"

"I humbly tender such a request, if it would not offend. I have waited the required period. I would see my daughter. Just once. If it would not offend."

The Scribe Virgin laughed again. "I must say, you make a better presentation than your king. Quite a way with words that warrior has not."

448

There was a pause.

He used the time to think of his brothers.

How he missed Wrath. Missed them all.

But the one he wanted to see was Beth.

"She is mated," the Scribe Virgin said abruptly. "Your daughter, she is taken by a worthy male."

He closed his eyes, knowing not to question. Dying to hear. Hoping his Elizabeth would be happy with whatever mate she had chosen.

The Scribe Virgin seemed delighted at his silence. "Look at you, ne'er a query in sight. Such control you have. And for your etiquette, I would tell you what you pine to know. It is to Wrath. Who is ascending. Your daughter is queen."

Darius dropped his head, not wanting to reveal his emotions, not wanting her to see his tears. Perhaps she would think he was weak.

"Oh, *princeps*," the Scribe Virgin said softly. "Such joy and sadness in your breast. Tell me, the company of your sons in the Fade is not enough to feed your heart?"

"I feel as if I have left her behind."

"She is no longer alone."

"That is good."

There was a pause. "And still you wish to see her?"

He nodded.

The Scribe Virgin moved away, over to the collection of birds that sat, trilling and happy, on a white tree with white blooms.

"What do you wish for, *princeps*? Are you seeking a visitation? Something quick? In her dreams?"

"If that would not offend." He kept his words formal because she deserved the reverence. And because he hoped it would sway her.

The black robes moved and a glowing hand emerged. One of the birds, a chickadee, hopped onto her finger.

"You were killed in a dishonorable fashion," she said,

stroking the tiny bird's chest. "And after having served the race well for centuries. You were an honorable *princeps* and a fine warrior."

"That my deeds pleased you gives me great reward."

"Indeed." She whistled to the bird. The bird whistled back, as if answering. "What say you, *princeps*, if I were to offer more than you have asked for?"

Darius's heart beat faster. "I would say yes."

"Without knowing the gift? Or the sacrifice?"

"I trust in you."

"And why could you not be king?" she asked wryly, putting the bird back. She faced him. "Here is what I offer you. Life anew. An intersection with your daughter. A chance to fight once more."

"Scribe Virgin . . ." He went down to the floor again. "I accept, knowing I do not deserve such favors."

"I will not hold you to that answer. Here is what you will sacrifice. You will have no conscious memory of her. You will not be as you are now. And I require one token of faculty."

He didn't know what the last one was, but he wasn't about to ask.

"I accept."

"Are you sure? Do you not want time to consider this further?"

"Thank you, Scribe Virgin. But my choice is made."

"So be it."

She came over to him and those ghostly hands emerged from the black robe. At the same time, the veil over her face lifted of its own accord. The light was so blinding he could see nothing of her features.

As she took hold of his jaw and the back of his head, he trembled in the face of her strength. She could have crushed him on a whim.

"I give you life anew, Darius, son of Marklon. May you find what you seek in this incarnation."

She pressed her lips to his, and he felt the same shock he had when he'd died. All his molecules exploding, his body splintering into air, his soul set free and soaring.

FIFTY-FIVE

Mr. X opened his eyes and saw a bunch of hazy, vertical lines. Bars?

No, they were chair legs.

He was lying on a rough pine floor. Sprawled out on his stomach. Under a table.

He lifted his chin and his vision went blurry again. *God, my head aches like it was cracked wide open—*

Everything came back. Fighting the Blind King. Getting hit by the female with something hard. Falling down.

While the Blind King had struggled with his gunshot wounds, and the female had been focused on her mate, Mr. X had crawled away to the minivan. He'd driven even farther out of town, to the mountains at Caldwell's very edge. By some miracle, he'd found his cabin in the dark and had barely managed to get himself inside before collapsing.

God only knew how long he'd been out cold.

Small windows in the log walls let in the early dawn glow. Was it the morning after? Somehow, he didn't think it was. He felt as if he'd lost days.

Moving his arm around carefully, he reached for the back of his head. The injury was raw, but closing.

With concentration and effort, he managed to drag himself upright so he was leaning against the table. He actually felt a little better with his head elevated.

He was lucky. *Lessers* could be permanently incapacitated from serious blows or gunshots. Not dead, but ruined. Over the decades, he'd found a number of his fellow members flopping around in hidden places, rotting, unable to heal back into fighting shape, too weak to stab themselves into oblivion.

He looked at his hands. They had the dried blood of the Blind King on them and dirt from the barn's floor.

He had no regrets that he'd run from the scene. Sometimes, the best move a leader could make was to disengage from battle. When casualties were too high, and loss was virtually assured, the intelligent maneuver was to withdraw and fight another day.

Mr. X dropped his arms. He was going to need more time to recover, but he had to get hold of his men. Leadership vacuums in the Society were dangerous. Particularly for the *Fore-lesser* in charge.

The door to the cabin swung open and he looked up, wondering how he would defend himself before realizing it was too close to daylight for the intruder to be a vampire.

What filled the jambs made his black blood run cold. *The Omega.*

"I've come to help you recover," it said with a smile.

As the door shut, Mr. X's body trembled.

Help from the Omega was more terrifying than any death sentence.

EPILOGUE

"The Tomb's mansion. I'm telling you, that's where we should go," Tohr said, as he stabbed some roast beef off the silver tray Fritz held out to him. "Thanks, man."

Beth looked over at Wrath, thinking that in the month since he'd been shot, he'd fully recovered. He was healthy and strong. Formidable as always. Arrogant. Loving. Impossible and irresistible.

As he settled back in his chair at the head of the table, he reached for her hand, stroking her palm with his thumb.

She smiled at him.

They'd been living in her father's house while he recovered, working on plans for the future. And every night, the brotherhood came for dinner. Fritz was beside himself with glee from all the people coming and going.

"You know, that's a damn good idea," V said. "I could really wire that place tight. It's isolated enough on that mountain. And built of stone, so it's fireproof. If we throw some retractable metal shutters across all the windows, we could move around during the day. Which was a critical weakness in this house when . . ." He stopped. "And doesn't it have extensive underground rooms? We could use them for training."

Rhage nodded. "The place is also big enough. We could all live there without killing each other."

"That depends more on your mouth than any floor-plan," Phury said with a grin. The warrior shifted in his chair, making room for Boo on his lap.

"What do you think?" Tohr asked Wrath.

"It's not my call. As those buildings and facilities were Darius's holdings, they have now passed to Beth." Wrath looked at her. "*Leelan?* Would you consider letting the brothers use one of your houses?"

One of her houses. *Her* houses. As someone who'd never even owned an apartment, she was having a little trouble coming to terms with everything that was now hers. And it wasn't only real estate. Art. Land. Cars. Jewelry. And the money she controlled was insane.

Fortunately, V and Phury were sharing their in-depth knowledge about the stock market with her. As well as teaching her about the ins and outs of bonds. T-bills. Gold. Commodities. They were amazingly good with money.

And very, very good to her.

She looked down the table at the men. "Whatever the brotherhood needs, they can have."

There was a rumble of gratitude, and wineglasses were lifted to her in salute. Zsadist left his on the table, but nodded in her direction.

She glanced at Wrath. "Except don't you think that we should live there, too?"

"You'd want to do that?" he asked. "Most females would prefer their own place."

"It is mine, remember? Besides, these are your closest advisers, the people you trust more than any others. Why would you want to be separated from them?"

"Hold up," Rhage said. "I thought we'd agreed we wouldn't have to live with him."

Wrath shot a glare at Hollywood and then looked back at her. "You're sure about this, *leelan?*"

"There's safety in numbers, right?"

He nodded. "But more exposure, too."

"We'd be in very good company, though. There is nobody I'd rather have protecting us than these wonderful men."

"'Scuse me," Rhage interjected. "Is everyone else here in love with her?"

"Hell, yeah," V said, tipping his Red Sox hat. "Totally."

Phury nodded. "And if she lives with us, we get to keep the cat."

Wrath kissed her and looked at Tohr. "Guess we've got ourselves a home."

"And Fritz will come, too," Beth said, as the butler walked into the room. "Won't you? Please?"

The butler seemed tickled pink to be included, and he eyed the brothers with happiness. "Anywhere for you and the king, mistress. And the more to care for, the better."

"Well, we're going to have to get you some help."

V spoke up, addressing Wrath. "Listen, about the cop. What do you want to do with him?"

"Are you asking because he's a friend of yours or a threat to us?"

"Both."

"Why do I have a feeling you're going to suggest something?"

"Because I am. He should come with us."

"Any particular reason?"

"I have dreamed of him."

The table fell silent.

"Done," Wrath said. "But dreams or not, he bears watching."

V nodded. "I will accept that responsibility."

As the brothers started to make plans, Beth stared at her husband's hand in hers, feeling an absurd urge to cry.

"Leelan?" Wrath said softly. "You okay?"

She nodded, marveling that he could read her so easily.

"I'm very okay." She smiled at him. "You know something, right before I met you I was looking for an adventure."

"Were you?"

"And I got more than that. I got a past and a future. A whole . . . life. Sometimes I don't know how to handle the good fortune. I just don't know what to do with it all."

"Funny, I feel the same way." Wrath took her face in his hands and put his lips on hers. "And that's why I kiss you so often, *leelan*."

She put her arms around his wide shoulders and nuzzled his lips with her mouth.

"Oh, man," Rhage said. "Are we going to have to watch them smooch all the time?"

"You should be so lucky," V muttered.

"Yeah." Rhage sighed. "All I want is one good female. But I guess I'll settle for quantity until I find her. Life just sucks, doesn't it?"

There was a rolling swell of laughter. Someone pitched a napkin.

Fritz brought in dessert.

"Please, if you would," the butler said, "no throwing the linens. Peaches, anyone?"

Turn the page for an exclusive sneak preview
of the next thrilling instalment in the
Black Dagger Brotherhood series!

Lover Eternal

Available now from Piatkus

Rhage felt like holy hell as he weaved down the corridor. Every time the beast came out of him, his vision headed off for a little vacation, and as usual, it was taking its own sweet time in getting back to work. And his body was whacked out, too. His legs and arms were heavy, not exactly useless, but definitely subpar.

And his stomach was still off. The very idea of food made him nauseous.

But he'd had it with being stuck in his room. Twelve hours flat on his back was enough wasted time. He was going to go to the training center's gym, get on a recumbent bike, loosen himself up a little.

Rhage stopped, tensing. He couldn't see much, but he knew for sure he was not alone in the hall.

He wheeled around and pulled the figure out of a doorway, grabbing it by the throat, forcing the body into the wall. Too late, he realized it was a female and the high-pitched gasp shamed him. He immediately eased up on his grip, but he didn't let her go.

Good lord, she is a human.

What was a human doing in the brotherhood's private compound?

"Who are you?" he demanded. "What are you doing here?"

There was no answer, just quick breathing. She was utterly terrified of him, the smell of her fear like woodsmoke in his nose.

He softened his voice. "I'm not going to hurt you. But you don't belong here and I want to know your name."

461

The skin under his palm was warm, soft. The throat was slender, the blood racing through the veins running up from her heart. Her hair was a dark, rich brown, falling over her shoulders.

"My name is Mary. I'm here with a friend."

Rhage stopped breathing. His heart skipped a beat and then slowed.

"Say that again," he whispered.

"Ah, my name is Mary Luce. I'm a friend of Bella's . . ."

Rhage shivered, a balmy rush breaking out all over his skin. The musical lilt of her voice, the rhythm in her speech, the sound of her words spread through him, calmed him, comforted him.

Chained him sweetly.

He closed his eyes. "Say something else."

"What?" she asked, obviously confused.

"Talk. Talk to me. I want to hear your voice again."

She was silent, and he was about to beg her to speak, when she said, "You don't look well. Do you need a doctor?"

He found himself swaying. The words didn't matter so much, it was her tone. Low, soft, a quiet brushing in his ears. He felt as if he were being stroked on the inside of his skin.

"More," he said, twisting his palm around to the front of her neck so he could feel the vibrations in her throat better.

"Could you . . . could you please let go of me?"

"No." He put his other hand up on her collarbone so she couldn't get away from him. "Talk."

She started to struggle. "You're crowding me."

"I know. *Talk*."

"Oh, for God's sake, what do you want me to say?"

Even exasperated, her voice was beautiful.

"Anything."

"Fine. Get your hand off my throat and let me go or I'm going to knee you where it counts."

He laughed.

Then put his lower body against her, trapping her with his thighs and hips. She stiffened against him, but he got an ample feel of her. She was built lean, but he had no doubt she was a female. Her breasts hit his chest, her hips cushioned his, her stomach was soft.

"Keep talking," he said in her ear. God, she smelled good. Clean. Fresh. Like lemon.

She pushed against him and he leaned his full weight into her. Her breath came out in a rush.

"Please," he murmured.

"Since you won't let me go, I have nothing to say."

He smiled, careful to keep his mouth closed. There was no sense showing off his fangs. "So say that."

"What?"

"Nothing. Say nothing. Over and over and over again. Do it."

She bristled, the scent of fear replaced by a sharp spice, like fresh, pungent mint from a garden. She was annoyed now.

"*Fine.* Nothing. Nothing." Suddenly, she laughed and the sound shot right through to his spine, burning him. "Nothing, nothing. *No*-thing. No-*thing*. Nooooooothing. There, is that good enough for you? Will you let me go now?"

"No."

She fought against him some more, creating a delicious friction between their bodies.

And he knew the moment when her anxiety and irritation turned to something hot. He smelled her arousal, a lovely sweetening in the air. His body answered her call, his hips moving in a circle, rubbing against her.

He was hard as a diamond.

Her hands flattened on his waist and slowly slid around to his back, as if she were unsure why she was responding to him the way she was. He arched against her and felt her palms move up his spine.

Rhage growled low in his throat and dropped his head down so his ear was next to her mouth. He wanted to give her another word to say, something like *luscious* or *whisper* or *strawberry*.

Hell, *antidisestablishmentarianism* would do it.

The effect she had on him was druglike, a tantalizing combination of sexual need and profound ease. Like he was having an orgasm and falling into a peaceful sleep at the same time. It was like nothing he'd ever felt before.

A chill shot through him, sucking out the warmth in his body.

He snapped his head back as he thought about the warning Vishous had given him.

"Are you a virgin?" Rhage demanded.

"I *beg* your pardon. What kind of question is that?" She shoved hard against his body.

Anxiety tightened his hand on her collarbone. "Have you ever been taken by a male? Answer the question."

Her lovely voice turned high, frightened. "Yes. Yes, I've had . . . a lover."

Disappointment loosened his grip. But relief was right on its heels.

All things considered, he wasn't sure he needed to meet his destiny this ten minutes.

Besides, even if she wasn't his fate, this human female was extraordinary . . . something special.

Something he had to have for himself.

LOVER AWAKENED

In the shadows of the night in New York, a secret
band of brothers exists like no other – six vampire
warriors, defenders of their race. Of these, Zsadist is
the most terrifying member of the Black Dagger
Brotherhood.

A former blood slave, the vampire Zsadist still bears
the scars from a past filled with suffering and
humiliation. Renowned for his unquenchable fury
and sinister deeds, he is a savage feared by humans
and vampires alike. Anger is his only companion, and
terror is his only passion – until he rescues a beautiful
aristocrat from the evil Lessening Society.

Bella is instantly entranced by the seething power
Zsadist possesses. But even as their desire for one
another begins to overtake them both, Zsadist's thirst
for vengeance against Bella's tormentors drives him to
the brink of madness. Now, Bella must help her lover
overcome the wounds of his tortured past, and find a
future with her.

978-0-7499-3823-9

LOVER REVEALED

In Caldwell, New York, there's a deadly war raging between vampires and their slayers. Now, an ally of the Black Dagger Brotherhood will face the challenge of his life and the evil of the ages.

Butch O'Neal is a fighter by nature. A hard living, ex-homicide cop, he's the only human ever to be allowed in the inner circle of the Black Dagger Brotherhood. And he wants to go even deeper into the vampire world to engage in the turf war with the lessers. He's got nothing to lose. His heart belongs to a female vampire, an aristocratic beauty who's way out of his league. If he can't have her, then at least he can fight side by side with the Brothers.

Fate curses him with the very thing he wants. When Butch sacrifices himself to save a civilian vampire from the slayers, he falls prey to the darkest force in the war. Left for dead, found by a miracle, the Brotherhood calls on Marissa to bring him back, though even her love may not be enough to save him . . .

978-0-7499-3822-2

LOVER UNBOUND

Dr Jane Whitcomb, leader of a cardiac trauma team, is about to leave the medical centre for the night when an emergency is brought in – a man with a gunshot wound to the heart. As she examines him, however, she begins to suspect that her dangerously sexy new patient is not entirely human.

One night, while he's still in recovery, this tattooed stranger reaches out to her. He seems soothed by her presence. And she is oddly captivated by his.

She will soon learn that he is Vishous – V for short – the smartest vampire in the Black Dagger Brotherhood. But his tortured past has left him avoiding intimacy. It is against V's nature to let anyone see his vulnerable side. Except Jane. He has the oddest sense that she understands . . .

978-0-7499-3848-2

LOVER ENSHRINED

Phury, Zsadist's twin brother and a vampire in the
Black Dagger Brotherhood, makes the ultimate
sacrifice and stands in for a fellow brother to
become the chosen – one who will save the brotherhood's bloodlines.

Tormented by the love he has for his twin's mate, he
devotes his passion to the higher good of his race and
forbids himself from being distracted by a
romantic relationship.

The war with the Lessening society is graver than
ever, and the brothers need the few warriors they have
to fight. Phury is resigned never to divert himself
with love or put his brothers in jeopardy, until he
comes face to face with the only woman who can
tempt his heart and make him question his chosen
destiny . . .

978-0-7499-3903-8